SWORD
of the
WAR
GOD

ALSO BY TIM HODKINSON

The Whale Road Chronicles
Odin's Game
The Raven Banner
The Wolf Hunt
The Serpent King
The Bear's Blade
Blood Eagle

The Knight Templar Richard Savage Series
Lions of the Grail
The Waste Land

Other Titles
The Spear of Crom

TIM HODKINSON

SWORD
of the
WAR
GOD

HEAD
of ZEUS

An Aries Book

First published in the UK in 2024 by Head of Zeus,
part of Bloomsbury Publishing Plc

9 7 5 3 1 2 4 6 8

A catalogue record for this book is available from the British Library.

ISBN (HB): 9781804540602
ISBN (XTPB): 9781804540619
ISBN (E): 9781804540589

Cover design: Simon Michele

Map design by Jeff Edwards

Printed and bound in Great Britain by
CPI Group (UK) Ltd, Croydon CRO 4YY

Head of Zeus Ltd
First Floor East
5–8 Hardwick Street
London ECIR 4RG

WWW.HEADOFZEUS.COM

For the Rhinemaidens:
Trudy, Emily, Clara and Alice.

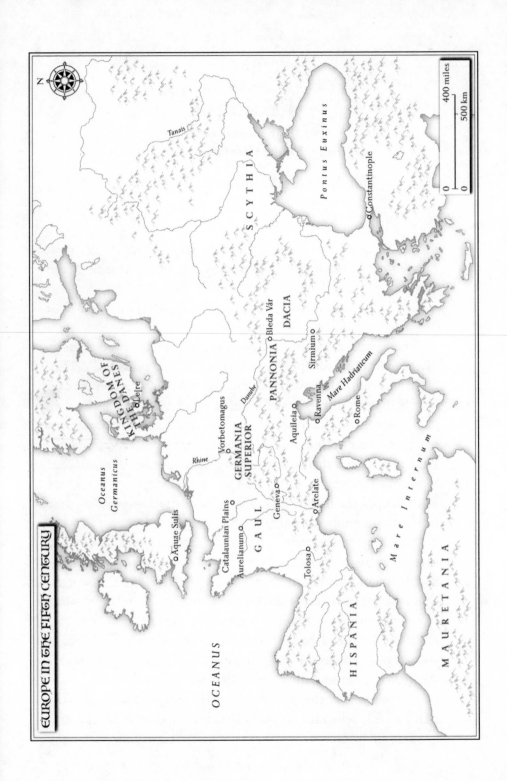

EUROPE IN THE FIFTH CENTURY

N

400 miles
500 km
0
0

Tanais

S C Y T H I A

Pontus Euxinus

o Constantinople

DACIA

o Bleda Vár

PANNONIA

Sirmium o

Mare Hadriaticum

o Ravenna

Aquileia o

o Rome

KINGDOM OF
THE DANES

o Lejre

*Oceanus
Germanicus*

Vorbetomagus
o

GERMANIA
SUPERIOR

Rhine

Danube

o Aquae Sulis

Catalaunian Plains
o

Aurelianum o

Geneva o

o Arelate

G A U L

Tolosa o

Mare Internum

M A U R E T A N I A

H I S P A N I A

O C E A N U S

Prologue

AD 422

Kingdom of Asaland, in southern Scythia

THE GABLE WALL was burning. Flames licked its stout timbers as thick grey smoke roiled up into the thatched roof above.

The king's hall was aflame. The battle was lost. The kingdom had fallen.

There was a mighty crack, then the great double doors of the hall crashed open, smashed in by the power of a Hun battering ram. Hun warriors poured in, their mail shirts and iron helmets glinting in the firelight.

Twelve Aesir warriors formed a line across the centre of the hall, their round shields locked together to form a wall. Each shield bore their sacred symbol, an angular knot of three interlinked triangles. Their angry eyes glared at the Huns from behind the iron visors of their helmets. Their spears were levelled and ready for battle.

Standing before them was their king. He was taller than everyone else in the hall. His long iron-grey hair fell around his shoulders and his beard cascaded down the glinting iron mail that covered his chest. Like his warriors, his helm was visored but only one eye – his left – glowered from behind the face guard. A bloodied bandage covered his right eye. The king's sword was sheathed at his waist, his shield was slung across his back and he stood with arms folded across his chest.

At the sight of the waiting Aesir the Huns rushing into the hall paused, reluctant to charge further despite their superior

1

numbers. For a few moments the two enemy sides regarded each other in silence, the only sound the crackling of the flames that licked the timbers above. Lumps of burning thatch began to drop down from the roof.

A Hun warlord shoved his way into the hall through the throng that clogged the broken door. He was Uldin, cousin of the Hun King and the commander of the victorious army. Despite his rank, he was dressed the same way as his men, in leather and iron. His higher status was shown by the gold rings that wrapped his arms and the necklaces that decorated his neck.

'What are you cowards doing?' Uldin harangued his men. 'They are beaten. Finish them!'

By Uldin's side was a young Hun nobleman. He had long black hair and keen eyes that watched everything with a cold, hungry gaze that at times unnerved even his closest companions.

'Is that you, Uldin?' the king of the Aesir said. 'And is that little Attila beside you? One of Mundzuk's sons? Is King Oktar too scared to come here himself and instead sends his lapdogs?'

'There are enough of us to deal with what few warriors you have left,' Uldin said, his lip curling into a sneer.

'But it seems they're too frightened to attack us,' the king of the Aesir said with a provoking smile. 'Don't you know the first rule of leadership? Don't ask anyone to do what you are not prepared to do yourself.'

Uldin gave a derisive snort. His sword in his right hand and his left thumb shoved into his belt, the Hun commander swaggered out in front of his men, approaching the line of Aesir shields.

'You think I am scared of you?' he said. 'You're finished, old man. Your pathetic little kingdom has been a thorn in my people's eye for too long. You've resisted King Charaton, then King Oktar. Now it is I, Uldin, and my warriors who have brought you at last to your knees.'

'Through the treachery of one of my nobles!' the king of the

Aesir said through gritted teeth. 'Otherwise you would have failed like all the rest.'

'Regardless of how you came to it, defeat is now your lot,' Uldin said. 'Why continue to fight? Surely you know it's hopeless. You fought well. There is no shame in doing what so many other nations have done already. Submit now to King Oktar. Become part of his realm.'

'And live like slaves for the rest of our lives? Never!'

The king of the Aesir's voice thundered around the burning hall as he swept his sword from the sheath at his waist. The slightly curved blade flashed like lightning as it reflected the flames. An audible gasp ran through the watching Huns.

They all knew the mighty reputation of that sword.

'Just hand over the sword and surrender,' Uldin said. 'Save your life and those of your men.'

'Surely you know the legend of this sword, Uldin?' the king of the Aesir said. 'If it is drawn it must taste blood.'

'So that is your answer?' Uldin said, raising his own sword. 'Very well. King Oktar will reward me with my weight in gold when I present your severed head to him.'

Uldin rushed forward, screaming a wild battle cry. Emboldened by their leader, the Huns charged after him. Uldin swept his sword at the king of the Aesir, who countered the blow with his own sword. The two blades met in a clang of metal on metal that resounded around the hall.

With astonishing speed, the Aesir king lunged forwards, driving the point for his sword into Uldin's right shoulder. It split the Hun's armour as if it were wool and plunged deep into the flesh beneath. Uldin cried out, as much in surprise as in pain. The tendons of his right arm severed, the limb went slack and Uldin's sword clattered to the ground.

The king of the Aesir pulled his sword back. Then with a mighty sweep he severed Uldin's head from his shoulders. It tumbled to the ground, his helmet making a dull clang as it hit the tiles that decorated the floor of the hall.

With a great roar the Aesir warriors charged forwards. The Huns saw the hate in their eyes and knew they had entered the strange fighting trance those warriors were famous for. Once in it they seemed to feel neither pain nor pity. It was a kind of war madness their king inspired, and each warrior somehow took on the strength of ten men and killed without mercy.

The interior of the burning hall dissolved into battle chaos as shields clattered against shields and weapons sang the bloodthirsty chant of steel on steel.

Then came a great groaning sound that drowned out even the din of battle. Attila looked up and saw that the burning roof was collapsing. He stumbled backwards, shoving fighters out of his way as the great timbers began to fall.

Now aware of the danger, the others began to run as well, though the crush of men in the hall meant it was impossible to move fast or far enough to get away. Attila found himself flung to the floor as men fell over others in their desperate attempts to escape. Someone landed on him and all went dark.

With a deafening crash and a blast of scalding hot air the roof timbers crashed to the floor, spreading burning, splintered wood and smouldering thatch in all directions.

Then relative silence descended. The ring of battle was gone and all that could be heard was the crackling of flames and the groans of the dying.

Attila shoved aside the man who lay on top of him and scrambled to his feet. The man was a Hun, but he was dead, his head smashed in by a block of falling timber. Had the other man not fallen on top of him it would have been Attila's skull that block had stoved in.

He looked around at the scene of chaos and destruction. Most of the roof had caved in. There were burning and splintered beams scattered everywhere, burying friend and foe alike. It seemed very few others had survived, and those few were in a terrible state.

Attila's eyes widened as he spotted something on the floor a few paces away. Half covered by shattered wood from the roof lay the great sword the king of the Aesir had borne. It must have been knocked from his grasp as the roof collapsed. A few paces away was the king's body, part of the beam that had felled him lying across his back.

With trembling fingers Attila reached past the burning wood and pulled the sword clear.

Holding it before him, he watched in fascination as the reflections of the flames around him danced along the blade. He felt he could sense the strange power the sword bore within it. It was like it was calling to him, and to *him* specifically, a call that spoke in silence to something that lay deep in his heart.

Attila smiled, continuing to look at the sword for long moments.

'What's that you've got there?'

A familiar voice broke his reverie. Looking around, his face fell into a scowl as he saw Bleda, his older, overbearing brother, had entered the hall through the shattered entrance.

'It's the Sword of the War God, brother,' Attila said. 'And it has chosen to fall into my hands.'

Bleda raised an eyebrow. He held out his hand.

'Well, you'd better give that to me,' he said in a demanding tone. 'It belongs to King Oktar and we must now return it. What of the king of the Aesir? Oktar will reward us greatly when we give him that one's head.'

Attila hesitated for a moment, his eyes flitting back to the beauty of the sword, then with a sigh he obeyed his elder brother and passed the sword to him. He drew his knife and turned to begin the unpleasant task of decapitating the king of the Aesir's corpse.

Attila stopped. He blinked, unable to believe what his eyes told him.

The body was gone.

Part I

Götterdämmerung

Was mich nicht umbringt, macht mich stärker
What does not kill me makes me stronger

Friedrich Nietzsche, *Götzen-Dämmerung*

CHAPTER ONE

AD 437

Vorbetomagus, City of the Burgundars, beside the river Rhine

DRUMS BEAT IN the depths of the forest. Hagan could hear their sound drifting through the night air like the distant hammer of apprehensive hearts, hearts very much like his own.

He gripped his spear, his knuckles showing white in the gloom as he listened to the thumping drums. The chief warriors of his folk – the heroes, champions and noblemen of the Burgundar tribe – were out there somewhere in the great forest that surrounded the city. Out there, away from the gaze of the uninitiated, they were performing the secret war rituals as they and their forefathers had done on the eve of battle since time immemorial.

The priests condemned such practices as apostate returns to paganism but they still happened. Hagan had lived through nine winters when his people had embraced the faith of Christ and forsaken their old gods. Six more winters had passed since but Hagan still knew the names of the old gods and sometimes, in times of worry or fear – times like now – he would whisper the name of Tiwass or Ingwass, just in case they still listened and might grant him the courage or luck he needed.

He would need both when the sun rose. When the morning came Hagan would fight in his first battle.

Tonight, he had to wait on the edge of the forest, holding his father's cloak and bag. Godegisil was now out in the woods with the other Burgundar warriors. The rituals they performed steeled their hearts for the slaughter and terror of the impending battle and would also – with luck and the blessing of the old gods – bring victory. Hagan could only wait for them to return. This was not because he was too young. Initiation as a warrior only came after a Burgundar had fought in a battle, and, more importantly, made his first kill. Even then only the bravest were chosen.

Hagan rubbed the stubble at the back of his shaved head. When he had killed a man he would be allowed to let his hair grow; long hair marked out the warriors from the priests, the farmers, and the rest of the ordinary folk and the slaves. Hagan longed for that day, when he would go into the woods alongside his father and undertake the initiation ritual. He would become a Burgundar warrior. That day would be the proudest of his life and, he hoped, his father's.

That though was a dream for the future. Hagan's wildest ambition at the moment was just to survive to see the next sun set.

Hagan adored his father. The big man was a lord of the Dagelung clan, one of the five great kindreds of the Burgundars. He was not incredibly wealthy like some of the other nobles but what he lacked in gold he made up for in skill, courage and aggression. Godegisil was the chief of the Burgundar champions. The next morning he would lead the Burgundar War Horde onto the battlefield and bring honour to him and glory to all their folk.

To Hagan, who was still growing to his full potential, his father was as big as one of the great oak trees in the forest and just as stout. Others thought Godegisil stern, war-mad, even terrifying, but Hagan and his little brother Raknar saw another side to him at home. For someone who had killed so many men, Godegisil was always kind and encouraging to his own family, and he protected them with even more ferocity than he protected the whole tribe.

Of the very few sources of pride in Hagan's life, this was the greatest. All his friends were more wealthy, more good-looking, or more talented – in swimming, feats of strength or fighting. Hagan was a good hunter and a passable fighter but that was about it. Yet the fact that it was his father who led the war horde, who bore the very honour of the tribe on his shoulders, meant Hagan could hold his head up among his peers. He knew some of his friends – friends like the son and daughter of the king – would not seek his company if his father was not such a great man.

Hagan inhaled a deep breath of the warm summer night air, smelling the sap of the trees and the scent of the green leaves that covered their branches. Life had returned to the world after winter. It was hard to think that Death also lurked in the forest, waiting to end the lives of so many in the morning.

Out there in the darkness were the enemy too: the Romans. The Burgundars had caught nine Roman scouts that morning – a very propitious number – and their severed heads now sat on top of spikes outside the gates of the Burgundar's city, Vorbetomagus.

The Romans had pitched a great camp in the forest which blazed with light. Its glow reached up through the trees into the sky as if the sun that usually set beyond the horizon had settled that night amid the forest instead. The wind carried the distant sound of voices shouting orders in their foreign tongue, as well as the sound of an army preparing for war: the hammering of rivets into armour, the scraping of blades on sharpening stones and blasts on their signalling horns.

Through it all came the relentless thump of the Burgundar drums. The Romans would hear them too and would know they meant death. As the night drew on, Hagan began to feel the cold. He huddled inside his cloak as he sat against a tree trunk. There were a few other lads around him, also waiting for fathers, uncles and brothers. Though none of them would admit it, Hagan had no doubt their silence was due to their

11

churning stomachs and fluttering hearts at the thought of the battle to come. He felt exactly the same.

The moon rose high in the sky, bathing the canopy of trees in silver light. It was so bright it cast shadows on the earth, the tree branches looking like skeletal fingers reaching out, as if Death was already trying to claim what was his.

At long last the drumming slowed, then stopped altogether. The young lads started to become restless, knowing that the older men would soon return. Sure enough, before long figures began to emerge from the shadows beneath the trees.

Had they not seen the men when they entered the forest, Hagan and the others might have been frightened by the sight of the returning warriors. Their chests were bare and their bodies were smeared with black paint. Some wore masks made from the heads of wolves or bears, others had their faces painted black, the whites of their eyes standing out in contrast. They carried spears and the blades had likewise been painted black. All wore the pelts of animals around their shoulders. Each warrior bore a large round shield painted with the emblem of whichever of the five Burgundar clans he belonged to: the bear for the Dagelungs, the wolf for the Volsungs, lightning for the Leuhtungs, the Sun Wheel for the Solungs and the eagle for the Nibelungs. Around the edges of the shields magic words were painted in runes, the ancient letters of their folk, not the Roman letters they had started to use along with their new faith in Christ. Most prevalent among them, Hagan saw, was the rune that looked like an arrow pointing up to the sky: the symbol of Tiwass, God of War. These would have to be washed off before the priests came to bless the war horde in the morning.

This was all visible in the light of the moon, whose silver beam somehow made the scene even more eerie. Just what happened during the warrior rite was a secret guarded tighter than the river oysters in the Rhine guarded their pearls. From the sweat that streaked the paint on the men's bodies and faces, though, Hagan could tell that whatever their ritual entailed, it had required exertion.

Hagan smiled, spotting his father approaching with the others. Godegisil was a head taller than most of the other warriors and as the leader of the Dagelung bear clan, he wore the pelt of a black bear around his shoulders.

The lads got to their feet, each one reuniting with the male relative he had been waiting for and handing them the cloaks or hats they had been minding for them.

Hagan held his father's cloak out. Godegisil took the bear pelt off. Sweat steamed into the night air from the big man's shoulders as he took the proffered cloak and wrapped it around himself. Hagan turned to follow the others who were returning to the city but his father laid a hand on his shoulder.

'Stay a moment, Hagan,' his father said. 'I wish to talk.'

Hagan frowned. Godegisil almost always regarded Hagan, Raknar and their mother, Gunteka, with a half-smile on his face, as if he was pleased with his family. Now his face was serious. His eyes did not twinkle. Like most fathers and their sons, they laughed, they joked, they shouted and they fought, but they never *talked*. The prospect made Hagan even more nervous than the thought of going into battle in the morning.

Godegisil gestured that Hagan should retake his previous seat with his back to the tree. As Hagan sat down again his father sat on a tree stump opposite. He did not say anything as he waited for all the others to leave. Whatever he had to say, it was only for his son to hear.

The champion looked up at the sky. Some stars were managing to make themselves seen through the glare of the moon.

'Do you remember when you were young, lad?' Godegisil said. 'We used to gaze up at the stars and I'd tell you stories about the shapes they made and what they meant.'

'I think I can make out the wagon of Tiwass,' Hagan said,

a fond smile coming to his lips. 'And there is the magic boat Wade the cunning smith sails around the sky in.'

His father brought his gaze back to earth and fixed his son with a steady glare. Hagan swallowed.

'I saw a strange thing today,' he said. 'Years ago, when I was a little younger than you, I was hunting in the forest with my father. Not this forest. One far to the north of the Rhine. We Burgundars have not always lived here at Vorbetomagus, as you know. That day I had outstripped everyone else while hunting a stag. I was always like that.'

He gave a little sardonic grunt. 'Always had to be first. Always had to be better. But I got that stag. I caught up with it in a clearing and killed it. I stabbed the big brute through the heart with my spear. I turned around and saw a great black bear had come into the clearing behind me. He was huge. Much taller than me on his hind legs and with a streak of white fur down one side of his face from some old injury. Just like me.'

He ran his forefinger down the long scar that snaked its way down his left cheek.

'Naturally I panicked,' Godegisil continued. 'I tried to pull my spear out of the stag but it wouldn't move. The blade was lodged behind his ribs.'

'So what did you do?' Hagan said, leaning forward, eager to hear how his father had got out of this dangerous situation.

'I thought to myself: *Godegisil, this is it, lad. You're dead,*' his father said. 'But the bear just looked at me. Looked me right in the eye, the way I'm looking at you now. Have you ever seen a bear's eyes, lad? They look like a man's. It's like there is a human soul in there behind all that fur, claws and teeth. Then he turned and ran off into the forest.'

Hagan frowned, disappointed at this anticlimax.

'I told my father about it,' Godegisil said. 'He said he reckoned it wasn't a natural animal at all. He thought it was my *fetch*. My spirit animal. The thing is, when we were hunting those Roman scouts this morning I rode into a clearing in the forest. There was a bear there.'

Hagan felt a shiver like icy water run down his spine.

'I swear by all I believe in that it was the same one,' his father went on. 'Same colour. Same size. Same white streak down his face. He had not changed at all. But I am twenty years older. Again he just looked at me, then ran off. You know what that means, don't you?'

Hagan swallowed again. It felt like there was something stuck in his throat. He nodded. A fetch visited the human it watched over twice: once when you were young and once more, just before you died.

'This is all nonsense,' Hagan said. 'Father Ulfius teaches us that fetches are demons of Hell,' he said. 'Like all the spirits, giants and gods of the older days. They were sent to deceive us and lead us astray.'

'That old goat Ulfius knows about being led astray alright,' his father said with an amused smile. 'The nuns in the convent lead him off the straight and narrow path almost every night. No, Hagan, it looks like my time has come. There is a battle tomorrow, and I will not survive it.'

'You will!' Hagan said. 'We've beaten the Romans before. We will beat them again.'

'We have beaten them indeed,' his father said. 'And we will beat them this time too. But men die in war and it seems that my time will come tomorrow.'

Hagan glared at his father. For the first time ever he saw not the all-powerful champion of the folk, the invincible hero, but just a man who was ageing. His eyes were sinking into his face and lines spread from their corners.

'Why are you telling me this?' Hagan said. He was unable to hold back a sob.

'Because if I am to die, Hagan,' Godegisil said, 'there is something you must know. Look at me.'

Hagan, ashamed of the tears gathering in his eyes, had

15

dropped his gaze. He looked up again and locked eyes with his father, who glared at him, the scar that ran down his left cheek livid in the moonlight.

'Hagan, I am not your father.'

Hagan gasped. His mouth dropped open.

'What?' His voice was choked.

'I've always treated you as if you were my son,' Godegisil said in a hurry. 'I've raised you as if you were. I've never thought of you in any other way. I've always tried to be a good father to you.'

'And you have been...' Hagan said. Nausea crawled like a worm around his jaw muscles. *Until now*, a bitter voice within his mind said.

'But you are not my son in the natural way,' Godegisil said. 'I was away. Fighting in the wars in the west. I left Gunteka behind. When I came back she was pregnant with you. She told me she had been forced into bed. I believed her. I still do. It was not her choice. Your mother is a good woman. You know that.'

Hagan bit his lower lip. He tasted the iron flavour of his own blood.

'It was partly my fault,' Godegisil said, shaking his head. 'I left her alone.'

'So who is my real father?' Hagan said.

'I don't know,' Godegisil said. 'Your mother never told me. She swore an oath that she would not. She said it was for my protection. You know what that means, don't you? He must be someone we know. She knew if I found out who it was I would kill him and that whoever it was is powerful, or dear to me. I wouldn't care if I died after I got revenge for her but she said she didn't want to lose me. She said perhaps one day she will tell me but until then she made me swear an oath never to ask. And I did. I do know one thing, though.'

'What is that?' Hagan asked, he felt desperation grasp at his heart.

'You know that amulet she wears?' Godegisil said.

16

'The bronze one with the strange horse and bird on it?' Hagan nodded. His mother seldom took off that piece of jewellery, yet despite its beauty she never flaunted it. In fact, she did the complete opposite. Whenever she left their home she always tucked the amulet away under her dress as if she did not want anyone to see it.

'Aye,' Godegisil said. 'She tore it away from the man who forced himself on her. He was so lost in his lust he did not realise she had it.'

'She wears it in remembrance of him?' Hagan said, shaking his head.

'No,' Godegisil said. His voice was cracked and Hagan could sense the impotent rage that boiled in the big man's chest. 'She says she wears it so she never forgets what was done to her – as if she ever could! And she says that one day she will wear it in front of everyone and bring shame down on him for what he did. That of course proves that it was someone we know.'

Hagan felt sick and dizzy. He looked down at his feet and pressed his hand to his forehead.

His father – or the man he had always thought of as his father – placed his hands on his shoulders.

'Hagan, I know this must be hard for you,' he said. 'I thought perhaps I would tell you all this some time far in the future when we have lived our lives. But I have seen my fetch for the second time now. Tomorrow night I could be on my funeral pyre and you will have to light it. You had to know now.'

Hagan looked up. His eyes sparkled with tears. He did not know what to say. All he could do was shake his head.

'We should go,' Godegisil said. 'The morning is coming and with it we will go into battle.'

CHAPTER TWO

THE ROMAN ARMY – the physical manifestation of Imperial might – marched onto the battlefield in imposing style.

They filed into position with iron discipline. Each company marched in step until they arrived at their allotted point, when they turned to the right and stopped, standing rigid in formation. Each man carried a large oval shield on his left arm, with his unit's insignia painted on the front: a black lion, a horned moon or a bull. Each soldier carried a heavy-bladed spear – a *spicula* – in his right hand. Sheathed at their sides were their *spathae*, their long swords. Their torsos were protected by leather jerkins and gleaming shirts of iron mail. They wore conical iron helmets, the officers' having long plumes of horsehair sprouting from the crown.

Their standards waved above their ranks in the warm breeze of the summer morning. Most were scarlet, with the same lion, bull or crescent moon designs on them, but at regular intervals in the Roman line standard bearers held aloft multi-coloured or striped banners in the shape of sharp-toothed creatures. The creatures' heads were on the top of standard poles, the wide mouths open to let in the warm, early summer breeze and inflate long cloth 'bodies' which twisted and flapped behind them. They looked like snakes, slithering through the air above the marching soldiers. The wind made a hissing sound as it rolled over their iron maws. These were the famous *dracones*, the dragon standards of the Roman Army.

18

The standard of the General, a golden cross on a blue background, fluttered at the centre of the line. On either side of it the legionaries lined up, dividing into their *cohorts* and *milites* units and displaying their shields to the enemy.

Once in position they stood, silent as stones. It was a display of power, designed to intimidate the opposition and show the discipline, organisation and might of Rome. Sometimes this was all was needed to send rebellious barbarians fleeing back to whatever benighted forests they had crawled from.

It did not work on the Burgundars.

If anything, the sight of the Roman banners only provoked the horde of warriors facing them to higher levels of anger and scorn. This was not the first Roman army the Burgundar War Horde had confronted.

'Look at them waving their pathetic dragons,' Godegisil shouted to those around him. 'Don't they know our folk are called the Dragon Slayers?'

He was now in his place of honour in the front rank of the Burgundar champions. Those warriors who stood beside him in the shield wall laughed or sneered.

The Burgundar War Horde was drawn up in their own fashion, a long shield wall that crossed the meadow before the city of Vorbetomagus and the deep, shadow-haunted forest that surrounded it. Vorbetomagus was the capital of their folk land. It was their home, and their formation made one thing clear: they would defend what was theirs.

The battle lines of the two armies faced each other, perpendicular to the wide, mighty river that looped through the forest and past the walls of the city.

In the front line of the Burgundars were the heroes of the folk; the mightiest of their warriors and the great lords of the kingdom. They looked magnificent. Their visored helmets gleamed in the sun. Some had the wings of great birds of prey – falcons, hawks or kites – nailed to each side. A long crest of horsehair, dyed red, tumbled from the crown of Godegisil's.

They wore coats of mail, each tiny ring polished in sand until it glittered like silver in the morning sun. Each champion's round shield was painted with the emblem of his clan – the wolf, the bear, the lightning symbol, the Sun Wheel or the eagle. Godegisil – as the leader of the Dagelung bear clan – wore his black bear pelt around his shoulders.

Behind them stood the other big, strong men in the prime of their lives. The next ranks were made up of the sons of the nobles who were new to war, as well as the older men who could still fight but whose strength and prowess were fading. Behind them were the poor folk, the levy of the free men: simple farmers, craftsmen and others who had come because of duty. Their king had called them and they had come to defend their homeland against Rome's greed and aggression. They wore what little armour they had, perhaps a leather cap or jerkin. Their weapons were rusty and old, or just the implements they used to till the soil.

Hagan was in the third rank. He grasped his spear in his right fist and his round shield in his left. Both hands were slick with sweat and he worried that would make his grip slip when he needed it most. He shuffled his feet back and forth. Like the other young Burgundars, his armour was less impressive than those fighters' in the front ranks or that worn by the older warriors beside him. He had yet to prove his worth in battle. When – if – he did and made a name for himself, perhaps then a nobleman or maybe even the king himself would take him into his service as an oathsworn warrior and give him weapons and armour. Or perhaps he would kill a man in the battle and take his weapons. It would be his first step on the path to glory.

Until then, like the rest of the younger fighters, Hagan had to make do with whatever family heirlooms they could find. A padded jerkin made of deer leather with studs of iron sewn into it protected Hagan's body, along with a spare shield of his father's. His father had also given him an old helmet he had taken from a dead Roman soldier years ago. Its cheek pieces were strapped tight under Hagan's chin. The leather padding was worn and thin, making the metal of the rim dig into his forehead a little. It stank of the years of sweat it had absorbed, most of that not his own. Hagan had decorated the helmet with the mottled feathers of a bird both in a rather vain attempt to make it look more impressive and for fear that in the press of battle someone on his own side would mistake him for a Roman. He had done his best to paint a bear on his shield as well, but it had ended up looking more like a mouse so he had filled it all in.

'We are the Dragon Slayers alright,' one of the older warriors in the third rank said from the side of his mouth. 'But where is the Dragon Slayer King?'

Several of those around him said 'Aye' or nodded their agreement.

Hearing the words of the older warrior, Hagan felt a thrill of consternation that men in their own army would voice such thoughts at a time like this. His father would not like it.

Hagan frowned. The man he called his father, he should say. His head still spun from the words Godegisil had spoken to him the night before.

'Have you something to say, Childeric?' Godegisil said over his shoulder, one bushy eyebrow raised. 'Perhaps you left your courage behind in bed this morning?'

'My courage is right where it should be, Godegisil,' the older warrior said. 'In my heart. You need have no fear of that.'

'Good,' Godegisil said. 'Though you're so far back there you probably won't need it today.'

The other big men in the front ranks guffawed.

Hagan's own heart was a maelstrom of conflicting feelings. His eyes felt raw. He had slept little the night before, both from the thought of impending war and because of what Godegisil had told him. Who was he really? And what would life be like from now on, if they both survived the day? His father – could he even call him that now? – had promised he would treat

Hagan no differently but now they both knew this secret, could that really be true?

Nor had Hagan been able to look his mother in the eye that morning as she, fretting and with tears in her eyes, had waved him off to war. He felt a stab of guilt in his heart as he thought how his reticence must have made it even worse for her.

This was Hagan's first real battle. He had been on raids of other tribes but nothing like this: thousands of men facing off against each other across a meadow to decide... what? He was not sure. Rome had invaded their territory, he knew that. And the Romans were tyrants. The Burgundars had to fight if they did not want to come under the heel of the Empire.

He felt excitement but his breathing was short and fast and he was sweating. Even though he had emptied his bowels several times already that morning he still felt as if their contents had turned to water and might flood his legs with cowardly and embarrassing shit at any moment.

Being the son of one of the king's greatest champions brought an expectation with it. All the folk would be watching him, trying to tell if he was going to follow in Godegisil's footsteps or would he be a disappointment? Could he even come close to what his father would achieve this day?

He felt his heart lurch as he thought of what he had learned the night before. The expectation was doubly unfair. Godegisil was not his real father so why should Hagan be expected to emulate him?

He tried to force his thoughts onto what the coming battle might bring. Some of the more experienced warriors had said how most battles just involve shoving the man in front of you. It was the men in the shield wall at the front who would do most of the fighting. All the same the press of those around him increased his nervousness. Hagan was more at home in the forests hunting than in this crush of warriors.

Hagan clenched his teeth, wondering if, when the moment came, he would really be able to push his spear into another man's guts. To watch, as the life bled from him and he fell to the earth at Hagan's feet. What would that feel like? Worse: what would it feel like to have a Roman's cold steel slice into his own flesh? Would he be able to cope with the pain or would he die screaming and crying, an embarrassment to all around him?

As if to provoke his misgivings further, a shrieking rose from another crowd that had gathered a little way from the opposing armies. They stood just before the stone wall that surrounded the Burgundar city. They were the women and children of the Burgundar tribe. They had gathered outside the city gates to watch their menfolk do battle. In war all of the folk had a role to play. The women and children might not fight, but they would scream encouragement from the side, reminding the men who it was they fought for.

Their presence also meant every deed each man performed – both heroic and cowardly – would be seen by the watching eyes of the whole people. Each of those deeds would be remembered in glory or damned in infamy in the songs and sagas of the Burgundars – their collective memory – for the rest of time.

Hagan swallowed hard. His mother was in that crowd. As was eight-year-old Raknar. Their eyes would be on him today. If he lost his nerve he would bring shame on the reputation of the whole family. He had to be brave no matter what his pounding heart and churning guts wanted to tell him otherwise. Even though he now knew Raknar was really his half-brother, it made no difference. The lad still looked up to him. It was his duty not to let Raknar down.

Hagan took another deep breath. A part of him hoped that the boast the man he had always called his father would come true and the Romans would never get further than the first rank of the shield wall. The press of the men of his folk around him and even the watching gaze of the women and children, despite the expectation it brought, was reassuring. All the folk were here. They would face this foe together.

Almost together. Hagan wished his three best friends, Brynhild, and Gunhild and her brother Gunderic, were there too. They had played together as children, grown up together and gone through so much, the four of them. Now here was the first battle their folk would fight of their lifetime but they were in different places. But it would always be so, he knew. Gunderic and Gunhild were the children of the king. They had other parts to play.

'So where *is* the king?' Childeric, the older warrior who had spoken before, said in a low voice.

A murmur went through the assembled warriors. Gundahar, the much feared and utterly fearless king of the Burgundars, should be here to lead them. He had defeated Roman legions before. He had forced Rome to terms and carved out a kingdom from its Empire for his wandering folk to finally be able to settle down in. Gundahar had defeated everyone he had ever fought. Yet this battle was about to start and there was no sign of him.

At that moment a gasp rose from the assembled warriors of the army.

'The Swan Maidens!' Giselher, one of the lads near Hagan said, his voice hoarse with wonder.

Men began pointing towards the river. A morning mist still hung over the Rhine. From it slid a long, narrow boat. It had no sails. Instead a row of oars undulated up and down its sides, like the wings of a dragon. On the boat were twelve young women. Each was swathed in a long cloak made of swan feathers. They raised their arms in unison and it looked like a flock of swans spreading their wings. Their long white dresses appeared to sparkle by some sort of magic in the early morning sun. As the ship slid past, their voices rose in unison as they sang an eerie, ethereal song.

'Do you think they can see me?' Giselher said.

The Lore of the Burgundars said that when the Swan Maidens came to watch a battle they would weave a special song about those warriors who performed great deeds of courage. Even if he died that day, whoever caught their eye would live forever in the memories of the Burgundar folk, his actions preserved in the songs of glory handed down from mother to child.

Everyone knew that these mystical maidens were really high-born girls of the tribe, chosen for their beauty, their virginity and devotion to the faith. Certain older women of the tribe picked them and they were taken in secret to learn the lore and the songs of the folk. It was a tradition going back to the very roots of the world, the ancient times when the Burgundar folk had lived far to the north, and the maidens bore a strange, mystical air about them. When the Burgundars went to war, the maidens slipped away, donned their robes and sailed their ship down the mighty Rhine before the army. Their appearance was like adding the strength of ten thousand warriors.

'They say the Swan Maidens reward the greatest warriors with more than just praise songs,' another of the young men near Hagan said, a lewd smirk on his face.

'Hush lad,' Childeric said, his voice filled with rebuke. 'Those are holy women. Pure and devoted to the Gods.'

He bit his lower lip.

'To God,' he then added.

Godegisil turned and used his considerable shoulders to push his way back through the massed ranks.

'I want to give my boy some last advice,' he said in a loud voice as he shoved his way to where Hagan stood, lest some thought he was trying to shirk his place at the front.

He wrapped one huge fist around Hagan's upper arm and steered him out of the pressed mass of warriors. When they were far enough away that others would not hear, Godegisil fixed Hagan with an iron-like glare. Hagan returned the look to the man he had always called his father with a mixture of devotion, respect and terror.

'I don't want the others to hear this but I am worried too. Where is the king?' Godegisil said in a low, gravelling voice.

'Where do you think he is?' Hagan said.

'I don't know,' Godegisil said. 'I saw him heading towards the river earlier. He had slaves with him. He should be back here by now. I hope this is not to do with that damned gold.'

Godegisil was now looking towards the water as the boat with the Swan Maidens disappeared back into the mist. He seemed distracted and was talking almost as if to himself. Realising this, he shook his head and locked eyes with his son again.

'If he doesn't turn up it will be like taking the heart from every one of these warriors,' he said. 'Swan Maidens or no Swan Maidens. The men will not fight. And I wouldn't blame them. The king provoked this fight after all.'

'You think he's run away?' Hagan said, his voice high with consternation. The very thought was preposterous. Gundahar feared no one. He would never forsake the people he had led for so many years.

'Of course not,' Godegisil said, his eyes flicking away from his son's once again. 'But something may have happened to him. I want you to go and find him.'

'But if I leave,' Hagan said, glancing towards the ranks he had come from.

'Just go, lad,' his father said, cutting off his protest. 'And hurry. Run to the riverbank and the forest beyond. See if you can find the king or this battle will be lost before it even starts.'

CHAPTER THREE

HAGAN DROPPED HIS shield and spear then jogged away towards the path that led to the forest. He did not dare look around lest he caught the stares of the other warriors. Despite this he could sense their eyes were on him. He knew they would be wondering why he was leaving the battle lines. No doubt they suspected Godegisil had used his position of privilege to send his son out of harm's way. All Hagan wanted to do now was find the king as fast as he could then get back to take his place in the battle line.

Once he found the king, though, he faced a dilemma. Godegisil was intimidating, but the king was terrifying. Gundahar had eyes that could bore through you like a hot poker pushed through wood. He was not a tyrant but he was a hard ruler. He was lethal to his enemies, ruthless to any rivals and stern and unforgiving to the folk he led. If Hagan found the king, what would he say to him? How could a boy ask Gundahar what he was doing without suggesting he was shirking his responsibilities? How would the king react if he even suspected Hagan was in any way suggesting cowardice?

Beyond the meadow on the banks of the Rhine where the army was lining up, Hagan entered the deep forest that surrounded the city. By the time he was on the track that led through the trees, he was sweating and uncomfortable. The padded jerkin was heavy and his old Roman helmet was too big. He had tied the straps as tight as he could but it still moved around on his crown. Several times it slid forward, half blocking his vision so he had to shove it back.

His anxiety at missing out was heightened by the mounting turmoil of the gathering armies he could hear behind him. Adding to the tramp of marching feet, the blaring of horns and the shouted orders, the cries of the watching Burgundar women and children rose like a shrill crescendo. In sharp contrast, the forest around Hagan was quiet, the heavy carpet of pine needles and brown leaves deadened all noise except the dull thumping of his own footsteps.

Here and there to his left he glimpsed snatches of sunlight on water through the tree trunks, which told him he was still travelling parallel to the river. Despite the dense thickness of the trees, as he followed the twisting, turning path he knew where he was going. He had played in these woods since he was a small boy and knew every nook and cranny of them, at least the parts of the forest nearest to the city. Beyond that – the deep, dark endless heart of the forest – was somewhere no one went. It was the haunt of outlaws, demons and elves. Most folk who wandered in there never came back.

Then he burst into a clearing and stumbled to a halt.

Hagan realised then that somewhere along the winding path he had missed a fork he should have taken. By mistake he must have gone down one of the many offshoot paths that led to the riverbank instead of along it. He cursed himself for not concentrating on the task in hand.

He had emerged onto a small bay in the riverbank. It was filled with the long, narrow boat of the Swan Maidens. This was grounded amid the reeds and the maidens were filing down a gangplank onto the riverbank. They were pulling off their swan feather cloaks and hoods, talking in excited tones about the upcoming battle. He could see from their smiles and wide eyes they shared none of Hagan's misgivings about the outcome of the conflict.

Now close to them, Hagan saw that many of them were girls

he knew from the court of the king. They were the daughters of noblemen and champions like his father.

He gasped, finding it hard to believe what his eyes told him. Even though everyone over the age of perhaps eight knew the maidens were not supernatural, their identities were a closely guarded secret. They were picked by hand by unknown women elders and trained in their songs and rituals in strict privacy. This was not a sight ordinary folk – especially menfolk – were supposed to see.

The girls saw him and stopped chattering. They looked as shocked as he was. Then the silence was broken by the irate howl of an old woman who rose from a bench on the boat.

'How dare you come here!' she cried, pointing a bony finger at Hagan. 'Where the Swan Maidens come and go is not for the eyes of mere men.'

Hagan felt a shock run through his chest as she drew a long knife from a sheath at her belt. Other women on the rowing benches also stood up. He recognised some of them too: noblewomen and cousins of the king and queen. They all now glared at him with eyes as hard as iron. Several of them drew knives as well. They all came hurrying down the gangplank onto the riverbank. There they came straight for Hagan.

He remembered the spear and shield he had left at the edge of the battlefield. He felt paralysed, indecision rooting him to the spot. Did they really mean to do him harm? Their identities and true nature was a tradition sacred to the folk but surely they would not kill to protect it? And if they tried to, could he actually fight the Swan Maidens?

'Stop.'

One of the maidens spoke. Her voice was loud and commanding. She strode in front of Hagan and held up a hand towards her fellows. The women stopped, frowns on their faces.

Hagan recognised her voice, and her identity was confirmed when she pulled off her swan feather headdress. It was Gunhild, daughter of King Gundahar. His friend.

Relief flooded his chest.

Despite the situation, he felt a rush of excitement at the sight of Gunhild's blonde hair as it tumbled around her shoulders. They had been friends since childhood, playing together with the other noble children in and around the king's great feasting hall and the woods around the city. As they grew older, Hagan found he felt a longing that went beyond the feelings for a good friend. Gunhild was beautiful. Not just pretty but captivating, the sort of beauty men killed each other over. Hagan knew he would never be one of those men. His father may have been a champion of the folk and a nobleman but the daughter of a king would marry the son of a king, not one of a landowner, no matter what his prowess in battle.

'He should not have seen us without our robes,' the old woman said, pointing her knife at Hagan. 'Now he knows who we all are.'

'This is Hagan, son of Godegisil our greatest hero,' Gunhild said. 'He will not betray our secret. Will you?'

She looked around at Hagan, one eyebrow raised.

Hagan shook his head quickly.

'Never,' he said. 'I swear on my life.'

'It might come to that,' the old woman said. 'Though his father has risked his life for the folk many times. For the sake of Godegisil I would prefer not to harm him. Can we trust him?'

'I will vouch for him,' Gunhild said. 'He will never speak of this again.'

'I will vouch for him too,' another of the Swan Maidens said. She was looking at Hagan with an amused smile on her lips. Unlike Gunhild this girl's hair was black as a crow's wing. It was his other friend, Brynhild.

Hagan looked around. Angry eyes surrounded him. The women appeared sceptical but then he saw several of them nodding. Those with knives lowered their blades.

'Very well,' the old woman said. 'But if he tells our secrets to anyone then you will share in his blame, sisters. And the punishment that it will bring with it.'

'I accept that,' Gunhild said.

'So do I,' Brynhild said.

Gunhild grabbed Hagan by the sleeve and steered him away from the cove, propelling him like a man sleepwalking away from the clearing and the maidens gathered within it.

'Thanks,' Hagan said after they had gone a little way on down the path through the trees and had lost sight of the others.

'Don't thank me,' Gunhild said. 'Just never tell anyone what or who you saw back there. If you do I get the blame as well. By rights they could have killed you. You know that? I think old Gutrune was actually going to.'

'I'll never speak of it again,' Hagan said. 'But I can't believe you're a Swan Maiden! You never said anything.'

'It's supposed to be a secret,' Gunhild said with a sigh.

'But how did you manage it?' Hagan said. His eyes were wide with excitement. 'How do you all sneak away to meet without anyone noticing? You...'

He hesitated.

'You look like an angel...' he managed to croak.

'Never mind that now,' Gunhild said. Her tone was scolding. 'What are you doing here? Why aren't you with the others on the battlefield?'

She stopped. He turned around to see her shoulders were slumped, her jaw dropped a little. There was deep concern in her expression.

'Oh, Hagan!' she said. 'You're not running away are you? You're the son of one of our mightiest heroes!'

Hagan frowned, his cheeks reddening.

'Of course I'm not,' he said. 'Why would you even think that?'

She smiled. The expression made Hagan think his heart was melting.

'You do look very grand in your war gear,' she said, a

31

wistful expression crossing her face as she pulled lightly at one of the studs of metal on the jerkin protecting Hagan's chest. 'My old friend, little Hagan. Now he's all grown up. A man in his war gear. A warrior.'

Hagan's face flushed a deeper crimson and he looked at the ground.

'Not really,' he said. 'This old gear isn't very grand. Someday I'll have better armour. You'll see. Maybe even after today, if I perform great deeds. And I will if I get the chance.'

'Well you won't do that skulking around in the forest,' she said. 'What are you up to anyway?'

'Your father is not at the battlefield,' Hagan said. 'My father is worried. He saw him heading towards the river.'

Gunhild's face fell once again.

'It's that cursed treasure, isn't it?' she said.

'Treasure?' Hagan said. 'My father mentioned gold as well. What does this mean?'

Gunhild shook her head.

'Come with me,' she said. 'I think I know where he is.'

CHAPTER FOUR

GUNHILD LED THE way along a path that led deeper into the forest. After a short time she stopped and appeared to be examining the trunks of some of the trees. She went to one in particular – a stout pine – and ran her fingers over the bark.

'It's this way,' she said, pushing aside some undergrowth that grew beside the pine tree. To Hagan's surprise he saw another path leading off into the trees that had been concealed by the bushes. Gunhild moved off down this new track. Hagan went after her, pausing for a moment to note there were cuts in the bark of the pine tree – markings made so the path could be found by those who knew where to look.

They trekked through the undergrowth for a while then Gunhild stopped once more and examined more tree trunks. They took another turn and journeyed ever deeper into the forest. This happened two more times and the track became little more than an animal path. Hagan was surprised and impressed that Gunhild was still able to follow it. He had been through the forest many times hunting but it looked like she was every bit as able as him at tracking.

After a time sounds came through the trees from up ahead: raised voices and the noise of shovels scraping rock and stones. Gunhild stopped and held up a hand. Hagan stopped beside her and was about to ask what was going on but the warning glare Gunhild sent towards him told him without words he must be silent.

She reached up and pushed aside some of the undergrowth with a careful movement. With her other hand she beckoned to Hagan to look. He peered through the leaves and saw beyond it a narrow glade. A small stream came tumbling through the forest floor at one end, emptying into a creek of the Rhine that had stretched a long finger into woods. The little glen was surrounded on both sides by thick pine forest, obscuring it from view of any unknowing passers-by.

Where the stream met the top of the creek was the rocky entrance to a small cave in the side of the glen. It was oval, about half the height of a man and stretched away into darkness. Three slaves Hagan recognised from the Royal Household – young men who tended to do a lot of the heavy lifting and agricultural work – stood on top of the arch of stones that marked the cave entrance. One had a pick and the others had shovels. They were hacking away at the stones below their feet. Some stones had already fallen down and half blocked the entrance. Another two slaves had worked long, sturdy poles into the rocks above the entrance from below and were working them up and down, loosening them from their surroundings.

Watching them was the king.

Gundahar was a big man, though not as big as Godegisil. His long mail coat gleamed as if every ring was made of silver. The thought of what it must have cost made Hagan's head spin. Across his broad back a round shield was slung by a leather strap. The shield was decorated with two gold and silver Nibelung eagles that faced each other across the iron boss. On his head was the Kin Helm, the great helmet which denoted kingship of the Burgundars. It was conical, with cheek plates fastened under the king's chin to protect the sides of his head. A long iron neck guard reached to his shoulders. A great metal boar, its back dented by several sword blows, ran across the crown of the helmet from front to back. The wings of a falcon were fixed to the left and right of the boar.

When the battle began, there would be no doubt who the king of the Burgundars was. Hagan felt a surge of pride that Gundahar was his ruler. With such a man to lead them, how could they fail to win victory?

Gundahar was watching the slaves work with a stern glare. The king's bushy, arched eyebrows always gave him a fierce look but this morning he appeared especially intense. His teeth were clenched in a tense grin of impatience.

'Hurry up, you lazy dogs!' Gundahar shouted. 'I don't have all day.'

The slaves, familiar with the anger of the king, redoubled their efforts. They kept their eyes down lest they met his fiery gaze.

What were they doing? Hagan shot a questioning glance at Gunhild but she just shook her head and looked back at the activity around the cave entrance.

As if aware – or wary – that he was being watched, the king began to sweep his gaze around the whole of the glen. Gunhild's eyes widened and she closed the gap in the undergrowth with a careful but swift movement. Grimacing, she held a finger to her lips. Hagan wondered what was going on that could make his own daughter so worried that the king might see her observing him.

For long, agonised moments they crouched in silence, unaware if the king knew of their presence or not.

Then there came shouts of relief and triumph from the slaves, followed by the loud rumble and clattering of falling rocks. Gunhild pushed aside the undergrowth once more and they peered through to see that the slaves had managed to collapse the top of the cave into the entrance, blocking it with rubble.

'Good work, men,' the king said, some of the fierceness dissipating from his face. 'Come here and I will reward you for your efforts.'

The slaves too smiled, happy or perhaps relieved that their

35

efforts had pleased the king. Those on the top of the cave entrance clambered down to join the others on the bank of the creek then they shuffled forwards to where Gundahar waited. Hagan noticed he now wore a broad smile, though it did not seem to reach his eyes which remained dark and filled with menace.

'We are pleased just to serve you, lord,' one of the slaves said. 'That is reward enough.'

'I insist,' Gundahar said.

There was a flash of sun on steel as the king ripped his sword from its sheath. His movement was so fast the first slave was still mid step as Gundahar slashed the blade backhanded across his torso. A red trench opened from the man's right hip to his left shoulder. He gasped, astonished, then the huge wound parted like two lips and the man's insides tumbled out in a horrific cascade of green, white and purple entrails.

Gundahar took the hilt of his sword in both hands and swept it around in a great arc, beheading the second slave with one blow. The man's head went tumbling backwards to the ground while his severed neck spurted blood into the air to spatter the face of the appalled slave standing behind him.

One of the remaining three slaves recovered fast from his surprise and jabbed his shovel at the king. The blade just skidded off the king's mail shirt. Gundahar drove his sword through the man's guts. The last two slaves dropped their wooden poles and threw their hands up, shock pushing them into their accustomed obedience.

'No, Lord King!' one of the men said in a terrified howl. 'Please spare us. What have we done to deserve this?'

For a moment Gundahar stood, sword raised to strike, looking down at the slaves kneeling before him. His grin was gone, replaced by what seemed to Hagan to be an expression of sadness or regret.

'No one can know where this place is,' he said. 'Only I.'

'We won't tell anyone, Lord King!' the other slave sobbed. 'Spare us, I beg you. I swear on the lives of my family.'

Gundahar shook his head. His eyes became fierce and hard once more. He slashed his blade across both their throats in one movement, opening terrible wounds that pumped their lifeblood out onto the forest floor. Both men dropped to their knees, as if in prayer, then toppled forwards onto their faces.

The king stood for a few moments, panting from his sudden effort. Then he used his boot to shove the bodies and parts of bodies one by one into the water of the creek.

Then Gundahar began to take another look around the creek and glen.

Quick as a flash, Gunhild closed the gap in the undergrowth again. Once more she and Hagan crouched in agonised silence. Shock at the sudden violence he had witnessed flowed down Hagan's spine like icy water. With it now was a new terror. He understood why Gunhild was so worried about the king knowing they were there. If Gundahar was prepared to murder the slaves to keep whatever secret this place held, would he also kill his daughter's friend? Perhaps even kill his own daughter?

Then they heard heavy footsteps loping over the forest floor; dull thumps on the thick carpet of dead pine needles. The sound was accompanied by the rattling of the metal rings that covered the king's body. Gundahar was running.

Hagan's heart felt like it was frozen in his chest. If the king was leaving then surely he was coming their way. He would find them, and then what? Kill them as well? The terrifying thought that he could be about to face his king in combat made his throat tighten. Hagan thought yet again with dismay of the shield and spear he had discarded to run into the forest. All he had now to protect himself was a long-bladed knife. That would be as useless against Gundahar's superior armour as the slave's shovel had been.

He was going to die.

Then to Hagan's relief the footsteps did not get closer but instead faded off into the distance.

When silence returned Gunhild let out a heavy sigh. Hagan, realising he had been holding his breath, did too. They rose to their feet. Gunhild parted the undergrowth and they both saw the glen and creek were now empty, apart from the grisly corpses bobbing in the shallow water of the creek. The collapsed entrance to the cave completely hid it and it now resembled a rock-strewn bank.

'Now you have seen two sights today that you should not have,' Gunhild said in a quiet voice. 'Two things you must never speak of again.'

'Where has the king gone?' Hagan said.

'To the battlefield, I hope,' Gunhild said. 'My father uses another track to get here. One known only to him. The way we came by I worked out myself.'

'How do you know about this place?' Hagan said.

'I followed my father here by his own path once before,' Gunhild said. 'He did not know I was there. I was a lot younger and knew he sneaked away into the woods every now and then on some secret task. That time he killed two slaves who had carried a chest here for him. I could not let him know I knew about this place. It would be the death of me too. So I worked out another way to get back from here, and left markers on the trail in case I had to find my way back.'

'He wouldn't hurt you, surely?' Hagan said, eyes wide. 'His own daughter?'

'Gold puts a sickness in the minds of men that takes away all pity,' Gunhild said.

'Gold?' Hagan said, excitement replacing the tension in his voice. 'Is that the treasure you spoke of? Is that what is here?'

He glanced at the collapsed entrance to the cave.

Gunhild shook her head.

'See? It's infecting you already,' she said. 'Even from a distance.'

'But what—'

Gunhild cut him off with a wave of her hand.

'There is no time now to explain,' she said. 'You must go. My father is on his way to the battlefield so your task is done. I will lead you back. We need to hurry or it will be all over before you get there.'

CHAPTER FIVE

GUNHILD TOOK HIM back through the forest to the place beyond where the Swan Maidens' boat was moored amid the reeds.

'This is where we part ways,' Gunhild said. 'You must go to the battlefield. I will join the other women.'

'I have so many questions,' Hagan said.

He felt an overwhelming urge to wrap his arms around her, pull her close to him and press his lips to hers. He was going to war. Perhaps to his death. Perhaps this was the last time he would ever see her.

As if anticipating his action, Gunhild stepped back.

'There's no time now,' she said. 'And it's a very long story. When the battle is over and we have time some night beside the fire I will explain everything. But right now you need to go.'

Hagan nodded. She was right. For all he knew the Romans were already advancing.

Then their eyes met. Hagan felt like he was frozen, locked in by her gaze.

'You look like an angel,' he said. 'With the feathers and robe, I mean.'

'Good luck,' she said. 'Make us all proud of you today. I know you will.'

She turned and hurried off through the trees.

Hagan stood for a few more moments, watching her go, then turned and ran as fast as he could back to the battlefield.

To his relief the fight had not yet started. The Burgundars still waited in their lines while across the meadow, perhaps three hundred paces away, the Romans maintained their own line.

Hagan picked up his spear and shield where he had left them and shoved his way back into the sweating, tight-packed press of men who waited for the fight.

'I thought you'd run away and left us,' one of the other lads said.

'Of course not,' Hagan said. 'My father asked me to do something.'

As if overhearing his words – which was impossible given the distance from the third to the front rank, the noise and the chatter – Hagan's father looked around. When he saw Hagan had returned he shot a questioning look in his direction.

Hagan nodded in a response he hoped gave reassurance to his father that the king was on his way.

'It must be starting soon,' one of the older warriors said. 'Here come the priests.'

A procession of holy men, clad in long robes woven with golden thread, one carrying a censer filled with holy incense, another carrying a huge, bejewelled cross began to walk along the front of the Burgundar army. The priests were chanting and moving their hands, pronouncing blessings on the warriors preparing for battle. As they reached them the warriors of each section knelt and bowed their heads to receive the consecrations.

Each man crossed themselves but Hagan noticed many of the older men around him also made the two-fingered gesture of the old gods of the people. Childeric was one of them.

'Aren't you afraid of sending your soul to Hell by doing that?' Hagan said. 'You could die today!'

'All our souls are going to Hell, lad,' the older man said. 'Hel is the name of the Queen who rules the world of the slain in the faith of our folk. The Christians just stole her name.

Tiwass has always been our God, lad. Ever since the world was young. This Jesus God is just a fashion. Like the clothes we sometimes wear made in a certain style. Or the way we cut our hair. We did not follow him before and in years to come we may not follow him any more. Tiwass will always be there, however.'

Hagan glared around, fearful someone might overhear.

'But the king says we must worship Jesus now,' he said.

'The king may not always be the king,' Childeric said in a low voice, looking around him. 'But a god will always be a god. Tiwass was the god of your father. And mine. And my father lived a long and prosperous life. And if I survive to the age he did then it'll be a long time before I worry where my soul ends up.'

'The priests say Tiwass was just the Devil in disguise,' Hagan said.

'This is your first battle, isn't it, boy?' Childeric said.

Hagan nodded.

'Well, you will find that you might need to act like the Devil himself before the day is over. If you don't you won't see the sunset. On the other hand if old Tiwass can help with that then I'm all for him.'

Another similar procession of holy men was making its way along the front ranks of the Romans. When both arrived about the centre of their lines, the Roman holy men turned towards the Burgundar and began shouting and gesturing towards them in a manner that was far from friendly.

'What are they shouting about?' Hagan said.

'They are calling us heretics, lad,' Childeric, the older warrior who stood nearby said. 'They are calling down Jehovah's curses on us and damning us all to Hell.'

'That doesn't sound very...' Hagan rummaged his mind for the right word. 'Christian of them. Don't they know we worship the same God?'

'The same God, yes,' Childeric said. 'But they have different beliefs about the *Logos*, his son. It's hard to explain. Our priests say that it is they, the Romans with their Trinity, who are the real heretics.'

Hagan frowned. Nothing the older warrior said made sense to him. It unnerved him. If no one knew who the real god was, how could they be sure what happened when death came? And death was here. He hovered in the woods, waiting to start his dreadful harvest. His expression made this clear to Childeric.

'Suffice to say, lad,' Childeric said, 'when the dead from today's battle meet in the afterlife, all ours will be with Jesus in his Heaven. Their lot will be somewhere a lot hotter and a damn sight more uncomfortable.'

The other warriors around him laughed.

Then the king arrived at last. Gundahar came galloping onto the battlefield mounted on a magnificent white horse. He rode along the Burgundar battle lines, one arm aloft, his mighty sword waving in the air. On his other shoulder was his shield, painted with the eagle of the Nibelungs, the king's clan. All his warriors cheered.

'There he is at last,' Childeric said. His chest swelled and his back straightened. 'I knew he'd come. And he's brought the young lion with him too!'

Behind the king rode a young man around the same age as Hagan. The resemblance ended there. He was tall and slender and his mail coat shimmered like the king's. His helmet was polished and bore the wings of a raven, one nailed to each side. A long, golden-hilted sword was strapped under his left arm. His shield too bore the emblem of an eagle.

Hagan knew him well: he was Gunderic, the son of the king. As with Gunhild and Brynhild, Hagan had grown up together with Gunderic, running around the Royal Household. They were friends, though in the constant state of rivalry that often passes for friendship of young men of their age.

Hagan made a face. Part of him was pleased to see his friend, but another part of him felt jealous of the magnificent war gear he wore. Hagan knew he could never compete with the king's son in wealth, influence or good looks, but still he could not help himself trying.

'He looks good in all that armour,' one of the other lads nearby said. 'But can he fight?'

'We'll see soon enough,' Childeric said with a sniff.

'Will we?' the lad said. 'When the fighting starts Gunderic won't be anywhere near the likes of us.'

The king and his son stopped in the middle of the line, near to where Hagan stood. Gundahar made his horse rear so that it thrashed its forelegs in the air and his men all cheered once more.

'By God, you all look fearsome today,' the king shouted. 'I don't know about the Romans but you terrify me!'

The Burgundars let out a storm of war cries.

'Today, men, we fight Rome,' the king said when the noise died down. 'Once that might have struck fear into the hearts of us all. But no more. We beat them before. There is nothing to be scared of from these pathetic soldiers and their womanly dragon banners. They're standing there shivering in the cold, wishing they were in the bathhouse or the theatre. They have no stomach for battle and campaign. They will run for home as soon as we charge. We've seen it before. Many of you fought with me at Noviomagus and Argantoratum. Did we not even have our own tame Emperor for a few years?'

The Burgundar warriors laughed.

'Yes, but Aetius defeated us,' Childeric said from the corner of his mouth. 'And that's the same general over there today, if I'm not mistaken.'

'What does he mean about the Emperor?' Hagan said. The other young men around him looked equally mystified.

'More than twenty-five winters ago – before any of you lot were even a notion in your fathers' loins,' Childeric said, 'our folk first crossed the mighty Rhine and moved south into the Empire.'

The young fighters around him all groaned. They had heard about the great move south so many times from the older folk.

'Back then, Rome was at war with itself,' the old warrior continued. Hagan's ears pricked up. This was new to him. 'Of course, if she hadn't been, the Great Old Whore would never have let us get halfway across the river. Gundahar there – along with the king of the Alans – supported a Roman called Jovinus in his claim to be Emperor. They forced him to allow us to set up home here within the Empire. They made him do all sorts of things, most of them humiliating. He was their lapdog and we were half his army. Jovinus only managed to hang on to the Purple for a couple of years. Then he lost his head. We stayed here, however. Did your father never tell you how we came to live in Vorbetomagus?'

Hagan frowned. He knew the Burgundars came originally from somewhere far to the north but he had never heard of this Emperor Jovinus. Perhaps he had heard the story before but he could not remember. When it came to lore, Hagan preferred the tales of the ancient heroes, with their dragons and old gods, to what happened a few winters past.

It seemed strange not to think of Vorbetomagus as the Burgundars' home. He had grown up here. The city, these forests and the mighty Rhine had surrounded him since he was born. They were his earliest memories. Yet men like his father and Childeric had spent their childhood somewhere else. Home was a different place for them. It was hard to imagine.

Gundahar went on.

'Now Rome is back. She pokes her big nose towards the Rhine where she has been humbled so many times before, right back to the days when Arminius slaughtered the legions in the forests. Today, we will make that Roman nose bleed again. This is a war they have provoked. We did not want to fight, but now we have to, we will and by the Lord God we will win! We will conquer this proud Roman Aetius and send him and his pathetic army back to Ravenna where they belong. Are you with me?'

The warriors erupted in a torrent of screamed war cries, chants and cheers. Despite what he had witnessed earlier, Hagan felt a surge of pride. The thought came to him again: with such a great man as Gundahar to lead them, how could they lose this fight?

The king kicked his heels against his horse's flanks. He moved on down the ranks to deliver his inspiration to the next section of the army. To the surprise of Hagan and those around him, Gunderic did not follow his father. Instead he swung himself out of the saddle and onto the ground. Then he slapped the horse's rear, sending it galloping on without him.

Gunderic strutted to the shield wall, the front line where the champions and heroes of the tribe stood. He grinned, acknowledging their good wishes and the pats on the shoulder and back they gave him.

'Let me through, men,' Gunderic said. 'I must take my place with the others my age.'

The men of the front rank cheered their prince. They parted shields and he shoved his way back through the ranks, looking left and right until he spotted Hagan.

'He's definitely his father's son,' Childeric said. 'He knows what it takes to get men to follow him.'

Hagan felt a rush of pride that made him grin like an idiot. All the fear and tension that had built up within him fell away.

'You have come to stand with us?' he said, hardly able to believe it.

'Of course I have,' Gunderic said as he pushed himself into position beside Hagan. 'If there is a battle I can't have my old friend Hagan taking all the glory, can I?'

He winked.

'Let's not get too cocky,' Childeric said. 'General Aetius will not be a pushover. That's still the Roman Army over there.'

'Shut your mouth, old man,' one of the young warriors said. The presence of the king's son had given him courage to speak his mind. 'I'm sick of listening to you. If you don't want

46

to fight then go home and die in your bed like the coward you are.'

'I am no coward, boy,' Childeric said, turning to glare at him. 'I killed my first man long before your mother and father ever lay down together to make you, you snivelling brat. And I'll kill more today. I'll die if I have to. It doesn't mean I don't have the right to say what I think. Burgundars are free people. We can say whatever is in our hearts. Don't mistake experience for fear.'

He tossed his long hair as the young man looked down, rubbing the shorn stubble on the back of his head.

'How do you know so much about the Roman Army anyway?' Hagan said.

'I spent ten years in it, boy,' Childeric said. Hagan noticed he braced his shoulders and straightened his back again as he spoke. 'The Romans call us barbarians but they need us to do their fighting for them. That's why I don't fear them. But we should respect them.'

Several of the young warriors gasped. Hagan felt confusion, knowing now that one of the enemy – albeit a former one – stood beside him. But was he really the enemy? He knew Burgundar warriors joined the Roman Army at times when it was not engaged in fighting them, but it was seldom spoken about. He had thought it was something everyone knew happened but never discussed.

'Grow up, lads,' another of the older warriors said, noting the looks on their faces. 'Most of us have spent some time in the Roman Army. It's a great way to see the world. And the training in warcraft is second to none.'

'And that,' Childeric said with a wink, 'is also how we know how to beat them.'

A Roman on horseback was riding along the front of their ranks like the king had done with the Burgundars. He was straight-backed and wore a metal cuirass that was moulded to the form of a muscled torso. Under it he wore a white linen tunic and breeches. On his head was a brass helmet that gleamed like gold and had a tall white horsehair crest that ran front to back across the crown. Behind him flowed a red cloak.

'There he is,' Childeric said. 'That's General Aetius. He's a Roman through and through. He's very dangerous. If we could kill him I'd say the rest of that Roman army will turn tail and run away.'

There was movement in the front ranks and Hagan saw his father walking out in front of the others. He strode forward holding his spear and shield up above his head.

'It looks like your father is going to try to do just that, Hagan,' Childeric said.

CHAPTER SIX

GODEGISIL RAISED BOTH arms high, shaking his shield and spear in the air.

'I challenge you, Aetius,' Godegisil shouted. 'Fight me man to man. We will settle this by single combat. The outcome of the battle can be sorted by just us two. No one else will have to fight or die.'

The Roman commander was quite a distance away, but it was clear that he saw and heard the challenge. Aetius stopped his horse and wheeled it around in the direction of Godegisil. Hagan saw him shake his head before turning his horse and galloping on down the Roman line.

The Burgundars jeered.

'Coward,' one of the lads near Hagan said and spat.

Then there was movement in the Roman shield wall. It parted and a tall legionary pushed his way out in front of the Roman line. He waved his heavy spear in the air and stomped forward across the meadow towards Godegisil.

'I'll wager that's an Armenian,' Childeric said. 'They're hot-headed and their discipline leaves a lot to be desired. My old centurion would have beaten him senseless with his vine stick for that. "No individual actions", he used to say.'

Hagan felt a surge of apprehension. His father was about to risk his life and his honour, right there in front of the whole army and with the rest of the Burgundar folk watching. The Armenian looked like a giant. Then again, he had seen

49

Godegisil fight many single combats and he had never lost, so Hagan's anxiety was mixed with a thrill of pride that it was his father who was brave enough to be the one to start the battle.

The sourness gripped his heart again. It was the man everyone thought was his father. It was as if the words Godegisil had spoken the night before had placed a worm in his heart that was now gnawing at the roots of everything that pleased him or gave him happiness.

The two warriors advanced towards each other, their helmets gleaming in the morning sun. Their armour rattled and clinked with every determined step. They met in the middle and both men stopped, facing each other a little way apart.

Godegisil touched his helmet with the tip of his spear then fell to a defensive crouch, shield held before him in the fist of his extended left arm and spear in his right, levelled and ready. His Roman opponent did the same, though he kept his shield closer to his chest. A great tumult arose from both armies as each side cheered on their own champion.

The Roman hurled his spear at Godegisil. A collective gasp arose from the watching Burgundars. The attack was sudden, delivered with fearsome force and at such close range there was barely an instant for their hero to react.

With surprising dexterity for a man his size, Godegisil dove to his right and rolled through a somersault, tumbling over his right shoulder. The Roman's spear shot past, just missing him as he rose back to his feet and launched his own spear, all in one fluid movement.

The Roman, surprise written all over his face, threw himself backwards at the waist and leaned to his left. Godegisil's spear flew past not much more than a hand's breadth from the man's nose.

Both armies cheered. Hagan knew this was not just a contest between champions with the honour of both sides at stakes. The skill displayed by the heroes was an impressive spectacle.

For most watching – those for whom one of the combatants was not their own father – this was superb entertainment.

Godegisil ripped his wide-bladed sword from its sheath and moved to attack. The Roman saw him coming. Realising he did not have time to draw his own sword, he plucked a dart from behind his shield and threw it at Godegisil. The Burgundar ducked behind his shield and the dart thudded into the painted linden wood.

In the momentary respite the Roman jumped backwards, creating space between him and Godegisil and pulled his sword – a Roman spatha – from its scabbard. The two warriors began to circle each other, shields raised and swords ready, each man stalking the other with careful, deliberate steps like two stags confronting each other at rutting season.

The Roman lunged. He launched himself forward, his spatha flashing in the sun. Godegisil parried with his own sword. The clang of metal on metal rang across the meadow. Godegisil smashed his shield into the Roman's and shoved with his left shoulder, sending his opponent stumbling backwards.

There followed an exchange of blows, each warrior battering the other's shield with a welter of blows that thundered across the meadow. Hagan watched, enraptured, barely able to breathe. The effort his father and the Roman were putting in must be exhausting. It would not be sustainable for long.

Godegisil stepped towards his opponent, slashing at him with an overhead swipe aimed at dividing the other's head in two. The Roman raised his shield to block the blow. As his blade hit the shield, Godegisil lashed out with his foot. His boot smashed into the Roman's knee. The man shouted what was probably a curse in his own tongue. He sidestepped away but now moved with a noticeable limp.

Despite this, the Roman resumed the attack. With a great shout he came forwards, swinging his sword in a side swipe meant to take Godegisil's head from his shoulders. The Burgundar champion ducked and the blade sliced air instead.

Godegisil shifted his boot and made as if to kick the Roman's leg again. The Roman, moving by instinct rather than forethought, dropped his shield to protect his injured knee. As soon as he did so Godegisil struck, stabbing his sword directly over the top of the Roman's shield. The blade slid over the metal rim band and into the Roman's screaming mouth. His eyes bulged as the tip of the sword went through the roof of his mouth and crunched into the skull behind. A torrent of blood washed over Godegisil's blade and down the front of the Roman's mail shirt. His legs went limp, as if the bones in them had turned to water. The big warrior crashed to the ground like a scarecrow cut from the post that supports it. He hit the ground in a clatter of armour, dropping his sword and shield on the way.

A collective groan rose from the ranks of the Roman army. At the same time another great shout came from the Burgundars; a cry both of triumph and bloodthirsty glee at the death of one of their enemies. The first of many, they hoped.

Hagan felt relief wash over him that his father had survived. As well as this he felt his chest swell with pride that his father had been the first one to spill Roman blood. It was Godegisil who had displayed such prowess and courage before both the enemy and – more important – the watching Burgundar folk.

He felt some of the darkness drain from his heart. So what if Godegisil was not his real father? As far as everyone else was concerned he was. As well as that the sight of Godegisil's deeds strengthened his own resolve. Hagan felt his previous anxiety drain from him. A fierce determination glowed in his heart that if he got the chance today, he would be just as brave as the man he called father. He would kill his enemies and protect his kin folk.

Godegisil stood in the midst of the battlefield, his bloody sword raised in the air, screaming defiance at the ranks of Romans before him.

Emboldened by the initial victory, other heroes and lords of the Burgundars began coming forward, taunting the Romans and shouting challenges for more single combats.

Goaded by the provocation, several Romans began to move forwards from their shield wall to go out to meet the Burgundars in the middle of the meadow.

With the sound of beating hooves, the Roman general, Aetius, came galloping along the front of the Roman line. Clearly agitated, he waved his drawn sword and shouted at the Romans who had broken ranks. Hagan could not hear his words due to the tumult around him but it became clear he was ordering his soldiers to get back in line. Those Romans who had come forwards – some with shrugs to show their reluctance, some scurrying like scolded children – returned behind the line of their comrades' shields to the further jeers of the Burgundar champions and the watching war horde behind them.

Those around Hagan jumped up and down with delight. The Burgundars had won the first confrontation. If this was an omen for how the battle would go then today they would win a great victory.

'This will be a great day for our folk,' Gunderic said. 'We will defeat Rome in a glorious victory. Did you see the Swan Maidens?'

Hagan nodded. He bit his lip, longing to say more, to reveal he knew one of the most closely guarded secrets of their tribe. He knew something even the prince did not. It was especially hard not to tell him about Gunhild. The three of them had been firm friends since they had been little children.

'Did you see Gunhild?' Gunderic said.

Hagan looked around. There was a mischievous smile on the bottom half of Gunderic's face, visible beneath his helmet visor.

'You know?' Hagan burst out with a frustrated gasp. Yet again the king's son had one over him. 'How?'

Gunderic just shook his head.

'She is my sister, Hagan,' he said. 'There is much you don't know about her.'

Hagan turned his attention back to the battlefield, recalling the secret path Gunhild had led him through in the forest. Did Gunderic know about this mysterious gold too?

Once all the unruly Romans had returned to their ranks Aetius wheeled his horse around and took another look at the Burgundar army. He was too far away for Hagan to make out the expression on his face but he seemed to be surveying what he no doubt regarded as a barbarian horde, perhaps reassessing their threat.

Hagan wondered if perhaps his father's deal would be enough and the Romans would pack up and leave the field there and then.

It was a futile hope.

Aetius raised a whistle to his lips and blew several short blasts on it, the sharp sounds audible above the din of voices. The Roman buccinators joined in, making ever louder blasts on their long, curved brass horns. At the sound the shouts of the Burgundars died away to silent anticipation.

'They're signalling something,' Childeric said. 'This could be the advance. Ready yourself, lads.'

Hagan took a deep breath, in through his nose and out through his mouth, trying to quieten the worms of fear which had begun to writhe in his belly again.

Then came the thunder.

CHAPTER SEVEN

HAGAN FROWNED. IT felt as though the ground had begun to tremble beneath his feet. What at first sounded like thunder continued rolling, getting ever louder by the moment. He looked at those around him but saw only similar mystification to his own on the faces of the young men around him.

'Cavalry,' Childeric said. 'Lots of it. They're going to charge us.'

An uneasy murmur went through those around Hagan. Everyone glanced around.

'Where are they coming from? I can't see them,' Gunderic said. His voice was high-pitched and Hagan was surprised. Was his old friend panicking?

If so, he could not blame him. Hagan's own heart gave a flutter at the thought of facing a charging horse. Pressing into a mass of men locked in the shoving battle of the shield wall was one thing, but standing up to the weight and power of a galloping horse with its thrashing hooves and a mounted warrior on its back was another thing altogether.

'Easy, lads,' Childeric said. 'Calm yourselves. Horses are not stupid creatures. If we hold our shield wall with spears to the fore no horse in its right mind will charge into such a sharp hedge. Cavalry are just an annoyance. Have no fear and stand fast.'

Mollified a little, Hagan and the others tightened their grips on their spear shafts, their knuckles turning white.

'You all know the orders,' Childeric shouted. 'Stand firm. Hold the shield wall. There was a time, the time when our ancestors fought the Romans, when we would have gone charging straight into them, stark naked, howling and screaming like madmen.'

Some of the older men around him nodded.

'The Romans learned that all they had to do was hold a shield wall,' Childeric said. 'Keep their discipline and hack, stab and take one step forward, in unison. Repeat. Until they were at the far side of the battlefield and we were all dead. We fought as individuals instead of an army. But we've learned too. Now we know that if we stick together and hold our shield wall, then we will win. Remember that lads: hold your position and support the men in front and beside you. Never mind what's happening on down the line. If everyone does that we will all see the sunset tonight.'

The thundering of hooves grew ever louder until it drowned out even the blaring of the Roman horns.

'It sounds like there are a lot of them,' one of the others said. Hagan could hear a slight tremor in his voice.

Then came a strange sound like a great wind or a whooshing made by a huge bird flapping its wings. Among it were whistles and odd howling.

'That way!' the youth beside Hagan shouted.

He was pointing to their right, where a line of thick forest flanked the sides of the two opposing armies. Hagan turned to look. It was as if a wall of dark smoke was rising from the tree line. As it passed the tops of the trees, the leaves and branches waved and buckled while the great noise transformed into a loud swishing like the flow of a fast-moving river.

'Arrows!' Childeric said. 'Shields up!'

Without need for thought, the warrior training he and the others had gone through so far told Hagan to drop to one knee and raise his shield above him towards the sky.

Once in position, the reality of what was happening entered

his mind. He could scarcely believe so many arrows could fly at once. He waited for long moments, crouched in the shade, teeth clenched, listening as the whooshing of the falling arrows got ever closer.

Then came a thunderous rapping, as if a madman were using his shield and the others around him to batter out a crazy tattoo. Hagan's shield bucked and rattled. His eyes widened as the iron head of an arrow burst through the back of it, sending wooden splinters flying.

A new fear gripped Hagan's heart. What was the cavalry up to while the Burgundars crouched under their shields, unable to see what was going on? Were they advancing all the while, about to wade into the Burgundars' ranks while their shield wall was down?

The manic drumming on their shields eased as the last of the arrows rained down. Hagan rose to his feet and looked around. There seemed to be arrow shafts everywhere: sticking out of the ground like newly sprouted twigs, embedded in the faces of the Burgundar warriors' shields and, for those not fast enough to get under cover, in their torn flesh.

A young warrior near Hagan writhed in agony. He had been careless, leaving his left leg outside the protective circle of his shield. Now an arrow transfixed his ankle, skewering it to the ground. There were multiple others injured too. One warrior had been struck right through the neck and he lay still and unmoving, his face a ghastly shade of white, his eyes staring at something an impossible distance away in the sky.

The old folk of the tribe said there were three mighty, uncanny women who governed the fates of all people. They sewed a tapestry that told the story of everything in the known world. Each man's life was represented by a thread. It were these women who decided the length of that life and who it interacted with by where in the tapestry they embroidered it. When they cut the thread, that life was done. It was their power that directed everything. All was deliberate and deliberated.

Bishop Ulfius said this was all heathen nonsense. Looking around, Hagan could not but help agree with Ulfius. There was nothing planned about this carnage. He felt a thrill of horror at the sheer randomness with which the arrows had distributed death and injury among the Burgundar horde. If the Three Mighty Women were responsible here their beneficence was haphazard and arbitrary.

Hagan looked to where Godegisil was, isolated and alone away from the rest of the Burgundar army. He and the rest of the champions who had left the shield wall, experienced as they were, had been swift to raise their shields and were now emerging, unscathed, from beneath them. With relief Hagan saw Godegisil stand up, sweep the arrows from his shield with a contemptuous swipe of his bloody sword and scream his defiance towards the Romans who stood a little way off, watching.

The corner of his eye caught movement and Hagan turned back towards the forest line that ran along the flank of both shield walls. A great rushing noise – the combined thudding of horse hooves and the screaming of war cries, burst from the darkness beneath the trees.

A moment later horsemen exploded from the dark undergrowth. They were clad in scale mail. They wore very tall, fur-rimmed helmets. They did not bear the expected lances of the Roman cavalry, instead each rider bore a bow. Their hair was a uniform black and their eyes appeared longer and more narrow than those of most men Hagan had ever seen. Their faces were twisted into screaming masks of hatred.

'Huns!' Childeric shouted. 'Fucking Huns!'

For the first time that day the older warrior seemed excited. His eyes were wide and his voice raised in pitch.

Horns started blasting frantic signals among the Burgundar ranks.

'Turn and face them,' someone nearby relayed the meaning of the horn blasts. 'Right wheel. Put a shield wall in front of them.'

'Right wheel!' Gunderic shouted.

Hagan scowled. There was no need to repeat the order. Gunderic just wanted to look like he was the one in charge.

The horsemen swarmed onto the battlefield in what looked like an endless stream from the tree line. There were hundreds, perhaps thousands of them. Hagan's section of the Burgundar army began to turn around to face them. Men crashed into each other in the panic. One of the young warriors stumbled and a whole line of them fell over each other.

The discipline, training and experience of most of the war horde held. Despite the desperately short time they had to complete the manoeuvre, the Burgundars still managed to rotate half their front rank through a quarter circle to confront the oncoming cavalry.

Hagan and the others now found themselves facing charging horsemen. They were still three ranks back but he still felt a cold chill at the sight of the onrushing beasts and their terrifying riders.

The front rank of the Burgundars locked their shields together and lowered their spears. Almost as one they tensed every fibre of muscle in their bodies in anticipation of the coming attack. The ground thrummed beneath Hagan's feet from the beating hooves.

'Brace!' one of the older warriors nearby shouted.

The second and third ranks of men moved one leg back and put their shoulders to the backs of the men before them.

The horsemen were perhaps thirty paces away.

Hagan tensed his thighs, braced his shoulders and clamped his teeth together, every nerve strained to the point of snapping, as he waited for the inevitable impact.

Twenty paces away and charging straight towards the Burgundar shield wall in one long line, the Hun horsemen were close enough that Hagan swore he could smell the horses' breath. Despite what Childeric had said, it looked like these Huns were indeed about to charge directly into the

Burgundar shield wall. They were fifteen paces away. Then ten. Then...

Nothing.

Hagan looked up. He saw a blur of movement. Instead of one long line the riders had somehow swerved just before hitting the shield wall and now they rode in every direction, a swirling mass of horses and men. They all raised their bows, arrows notched. How they were steering their mounts Hagan had no idea.

'Down, you fools!' Childeric shouted from Hagan's right.

Hagan's eyes widened as he realised what was happening. He dropped into a crouch, getting behind the shelter of his shield even as the horsemen unleashed another torrent of arrows, this time from mere paces away. Again his shield rattled and bucked from many almost simultaneous strikes. He heard cries and screams of pain from those around him.

As soon as the arrow storm ceased, Hagan surged to his feet again, along with those around him. Except not all of them rose. This time the Hun arrows, fired at such short range and so unexpectedly, had taken a much heavier toll.

Hagan felt dismay claw at his courage as he saw how many warriors around him now clasped at arrows that impaled their flesh. Others lay silent and unmoving in the mud, their bodies riddled by arrow shafts. To his further terror, he saw that there were now gaps in the front ranks of the shield wall.

He shouted but the sound that came out was incoherent yelling. Others were crying warnings too and men were already rushing to fill the spaces.

With astonishing speed and horsemanship, the swirling mass of riders before them somehow formed into two columns that made straight for the gaps in the Burgundar shields. Just before the riders made it into them, the Burgundars in the front rank slammed their shields together to close the holes.

Hagan blew his cheeks out with relief. If the horsemen had

managed to get among the Burgundars it would be the end for the warriors on foot.

Somehow the horsemen pounding towards the shields managed to swerve away from the bristling line of spear points levelled at them. Their skill was incredible. It was as if the horses and men were one, and the whole horde could all read each other's thoughts.

'How do they do that?' one of the other youngsters said. 'How can they stay mounted, steer their horses and shoot all at the same time?'

'They're Huns, lad,' Childeric said. 'They are born in the saddle.'

Hagan had heard of the Huns. They were a people who had burst onto the Roman Empire from the east. Their depredations of the peoples from their far homeland all the way into Scythia had caused untold thousands to flee their path, causing an endless churn of nations within the world. They killed everything in their way and anything they did not understand they destroyed. He had heard his father and others talk of the Huns with hushed respect. With a chill of fear he realised this was who their opponents were to be that day.

'Hold firm, boys,' one of the warriors in the front rank shouted over his shoulder. 'They can't get at us if we keep our formation.'

Horns sounded from the forest the Huns had first emerged from. Hagan looked and saw there were a group of six mounted men, their horses stationary, watching the proceedings. Gold and silver glinted from their bridles and the manes of their horses. Hagan judged these could only be the Hun commanders. Two of them bore great horns. At the sound of their signal the charging horsemen all whipped around again, almost as one. They began to ride along the Burgundar shield wall.

As they passed, the Burgundars hurled throwing axes, spears and darts at them. Several of the horsemen were brought down to cheers from the Burgundar warriors. The horsemen swung around the corner created in the Burgundar shield wall when half of it turned to face the new danger from the forest at their side.

'Where are they off to now?' Childeric said.

Hagan felt some relief as the Huns went charging past his part and down the rest of the shield wall. Perhaps they were withdrawing?

As they charged, the Huns raised their bows and sent another volley whooping into the air. Hagan and those around him flinched then stopped, realising this arrow storm was not coming in their direction.

'What are they shooting at now?' one of the young lads near Hagan said.

The answer came in a rising wail of first fear, then agony. It was much higher-pitched than the cries that had come from the warriors hit by arrows previously and Hagan felt a thrill of horror as he realised where it came from.

'The women and children!' he shouted. 'They're attacking the women and children!'

CHAPTER EIGHT

HAGAN LOOKED TO his left and saw many in the crowd of watching women and children had fallen. Their prone bodies, dressed in their finest clothes for the occasion of the battle, were now splattered red with blood. The thundering of hooves mixed with the high-pitched squeals of frightened and wounded children and the horrified and agonised screams of the women with them.

The Hun cavalry rode into the gap between the two opposing armies. The Burgundar champions – Hagan's father among them – who had advanced into that space between the armies were still there, exposed and away from their own lines by the sudden attack.

'Run! Get back to our lines,' Childeric shouted. The men of the shield wall started shouting similar encouragement.

'If the Huns catch them in the open like that then I don't care what their prowess is,' Childeric said in a lower voice, 'they'll be mown down like hay at the harvest.'

The champions stood between the Huns and the women and children, however. A heavy feeling wrapped around Hagan's heart. He knew they would not run. What sort of heroes would they be if they bolted for safety, leaving their women and children at the mercy of the charging Huns?

He was right. They did not run. Instead they turned to face the approaching horsemen.

The Huns unleashed a volley of arrows. Hagan saw his

father and the other champions drop behind their shields. He heard the clattering of arrows hitting Burgundar shields. Those around Hagan groaned in dismay as some of the champions were cut down by the hail of arrows. For men who had fought many single combats in their own and the tribe's honour, it was an ignoble end.

Godegisil stood up from behind the cover of his shield. He sheathed his sword then pulled his *francisca* from his belt. He held the short-handled, arc-headed throwing axe above his head, arm cocked, as the horsemen pounded towards him. The other heroes did the same. The francisca was a weapon all Burgundar warriors practised with from nearly as soon as they could walk. It was their weapon of choice, and many enemy tribes had learned the hard way to respect the wicked blade that could cause death and injury even when thrown from thirty paces away.

Hagan heard his father scream a defiant war cry, audible even above the thundering of hooves. The Burgundar champions all hurled their axes at once. The franciscas tumbled through the air, their wicked-sharp blades flashing in the sunlight as they spun end over end through the air. Each axe found its target, hitting horsemen or their mounts. A whole row of riders went down in a tangle of thrashing hooves and injured or dead men.

Hagan yelled in triumph but his cry died in his throat. There were many more riders coming behind. To the shock of all watching, they galloped over the broken bodies of their fallen comrades and charged on. They swirled around the Burgundar champions like a black river bursting its banks and flooding around the stout trunks of trees in the forest.

Godegisil drew his sword once more and readied himself, bouncing from left foot to right foot as another horseman bore down on him. The rider loosed his bow. With amazing speed, Godegisil blocked it with his shield, stepped close to the horse and struck with his sword. The blade separated the horseman's leg at the knee. Screaming, the Hun toppled off his saddle leaving an arc of blood in the air behind him. When he hit the ground the impact sent his helmet flying from his head and Hagan saw that the man's skull was nearly as tall as his helmet. It looked strange, elongated, as if he had worn the helmet since birth and somehow his head had taken on its conical shape.

In a moment there were two more horsemen in the rider's place. Acting in tandem, one shot his bow from the left and the other from the right. Godegisil again managed to block the arrow from the left but it was impossible to protect himself from both. The second rider's arrow smashed through the rings of his mail shirt and bore into the flesh of his right shoulder.

The Burgundar champion looked angry rather than in pain. He slashed the arrow shaft with his sword then swiped his blade across the back of the man who had shot him as he rode past, opening up a deep red wound that sent his enemy toppling from his saddle.

Even as he did so, another oncoming rider shot an arrow into Godegisil's exposed left side. This time Godegisil was hurt. He doubled over.

A fourth rider came forward, bearing what looked like a long noose at the end of a rope in his hand. He spun it around his head as he rode. Then he cast it. The noose floated through the air and fell over Godegisil's shoulders. The Hun rode past him, pulling the noose tight to pin the Burgundar's arms to his sides.

Godegisil, now unable to raise his arms, braced his feet, dipped and drove himself away from the horseman, using all the power of his massive thigh muscles to power forwards. The Hun, holding tight to the other end of the rope, was pulled from his horse and crashed onto the ground.

The tension released, Godegisil tried to use the blade of his sword to cut through the noose that constricted his arms. A look of frustration crossed his face. The blade, sharp as it was, seemed to have no effect on the rope.

Hagan looked on in horrified fascination. He shouted out, starting to push forward into the men in front of him, desperate to help his father. To his surprise he felt a hand on his shoulder, holding him back. He turned, a questioning look on his face.

'No,' Childeric said. It was he who had grabbed Hagan. He glared straight into the youth's eyes. 'We must stand firm. Or we will all be lost.'

Hagan felt tears sting his eyes. He knew Childeric was right, but he also felt he couldn't just stand by while the man he still thought of as his father was in such peril.

He looked around again. Godegisil was upright and trying to free himself but three more arrow shafts now impaled him: two in his chest and one in his back.

'How is he still standing?' Gunderic said, his mouth open in amazement.

The big Burgundar champion staggered in a circle. He tried to swipe his sword at the riders who swarmed around him but could not raise it past his waist due to his constricted arms. The arrows that skewered his flesh also pinned Godegisil's fur pelt cloak to his body. He looked like a bear wounded by hunters and dogged by a pack of hounds. As Hagan watched, four more Huns loosed their bows and hit their mark. His body now riddled with arrows, Godegisil arched his back; his mouth, visible under his helmet visor, was set in an agonised grimace. His clenched teeth were coated with blood, yet he did not cry out.

Another Hun rode at Godegisil. From paces away he loosed his bow. The arrow streaked straight through the left eye hole of the Burgundar's helmet visor. Its head burst through the back of the helmet with a spray of blood.

Godegisil dropped both his sword and shield and fell flat on his back.

66

Hagan looked on aghast. A nauseous sensation writhed in his guts at the realisation he had just watched the death of the man he had always called father and done nothing to prevent it.

'If you'd gone to help him you'd be as dead as the rest of them are,' Childeric said, pointing to the corpses of the other champions that now littered the meadow. The pride of the Burgundar folk, their mightiest champions and bravest warriors, were dead, riddled with arrows, bound by nooses or crushed under the hooves of the charging Huns. Hagan felt a chill. If their best were dead already, how would the rest of them fare?

He glanced across the battlefield and saw the Romans had still not moved. Their general, Aetius, was on his horse before them again. He seemed to be agitated as ever. He was shouting and waving his sword.

The heroes had at least disrupted the Huns' charge at the women and children. In the short time it had taken to deal with them, though, the Huns had changed from a charging line to a swirling mass, shooting arrows at the Burgundar champions from all around. In the brief respite, someone among the women and children had had enough sense to get them moving towards the relative safety of the city walls. Women trailed the larger children by the hands while others scooped up the younger ones and carried them on their shoulders. The crowd was now running en masse towards the ancient stone gatehouse that marked the main entrance to Vorbetomagus.

The Huns pounded after them.

Hagan could see the women and children would not make it to the gates before the Huns reached them. The riders were already drawing their bows again.

It was too much for many in the Burgundar shield wall. All discipline disappeared, and many left formation and began running after the Huns, desperate to do something to save their families while they still could. In moments the whole unified block of the army confronting the Romans turned into a disarrayed, charging mob. The remaining Burgundar war leaders screamed at the men around them to hold firm but to no avail. The Burgundar horns sounded unheeded calls to regroup into a shield wall.

The Hun leaders watching from the forest edge sent out another signal from their own horns. At this sound from their rear, the Hun cavalry divided into two groups. The leading horsemen kept on pounding after the women and children running for the city gates. Most of the rest of the Huns skidded to a halt, swung their horses around and began charging back towards the pursuing Burgundars.

Hagan saw now that the attack on the women and children had been a ruse; a ruthless tactic to make the Burgundians break their shield wall. Like their heroes and champions before them, the rest of the warriors were now at the mercy of the horsemen, and mercy was not a quality that could be seen on the faces of their foes.

The horsemen powered into the Burgundian horde, launching arrows and spears as they went. As the riders swirled around them, warriors spun around, desperate to not leave their backs exposed to a foe now both before them and among them. Each turned to face a different enemy that threatened him individually, only to leave his back exposed to the others coming from a different direction.

The Huns galloped back and forth among them, loosing arrows from their saddles left and right, killing men from mere paces away. Other Burgundars went down under the thrashing hooves. Many Huns cast the same sort of nooses they had trapped Godegisil with over the heads of Burgundars, either choking them or pinning their arms to make it easier for their fellow Huns to kill them.

Hagan just stared, frozen at the sight. His consternation and fear turned to utter terror as he realised that their war

68

horde – the pride of the Burgundars – had been shattered and now Death rode among them.

He felt a hard shove on his right shoulder.

'Wake up, lad,' Childeric was shouting. 'Form up or we're all dead men.'

CHAPTER NINE

HAGAN LOOKED AROUND and saw Childeric had pulled three others around him into a square formation. Gunderic, the king's son, faced one way, shield and spear pointing outwards. At his back was one of the other older warriors, facing in the opposite direction. Childeric was between them, protecting their flanks, and now Hagan stepped back to join them he closed the square on its fourth side.

It was a formation Hagan and the others had practised many times. He and Childeric now protected each other's back while Gunderic and the other warrior protected each other in the same way. No matter which direction an enemy came from, one of the Burgundars would be facing them.

Glancing around, Hagan saw some others had also formed these smaller defensive formations. Those few who were still standing, fighting off the horsemen who swirled around them. The others were not so lucky. The Huns cut them down one by one. As each man tried to fight off a horseman another would cut him down from the back or the side.

Hagan saw horsemen were pouring into the half-closed gate of the city too, chasing the women and children who had gone that way. Smoke was already beginning to rise from behind the city walls.

From the edge of the forest, the gold- and silver-clad Hun leaders rode forward onto the meadow, coming closer to the maelstrom of fighting. Now and again Huns would ride at

Hagan's group but between them they always managed to fend the enemy off, and protect each other from arrows shot at their backs. Several times the Huns riding forward swerved away, unable to get close enough to cause harm and unable to attack from behind.

The horsemen began galloping around them, leaving them alone. Why would they attack men who could defend themselves when there were so many other easier victims all around?

'What are the Romans doing?' Gunderic shouted. He was glaring across the battlefield where the Roman shield wall still remained, unmoved. 'Why don't they attack?'

'Why should they, lad?' Childeric said. 'Their new allies are doing all the work for them. Why should they put themselves in harm's way?'

Hagan felt he was in some sort of daze. The turf of the meadow had been churned to mud by the thrashing hooves of the Huns' mounts. The air was filled with a deafening cacophony of men and horses screaming, steel clashing on steel and the thudding of hooves. Arrow-riddled corpses and severed body parts lay all around. His people were being slaughtered around him. His entire world was being put to the sword.

Suddenly a new line of horsemen entered the battlefield. There were ten of them, rising in a line. Their mail coats still shimmered but were splattered with blood. They rode into the Huns, striking down several with heavy sword blows.

'It's the king!' Childeric shouted.

Hagan felt his heart leap at the sight of Gundahar, astride his white horse, wielding the great sword of the Burgundars. Perhaps he could rally the horde! Perhaps victory could still be snatched from this awful carnage.

Gundahar and his remaining oathsworn champions cut a bloody swathe through the Hun cavalry. Mounted themselves, they stood a better chance than the Burgundar foot warriors.

71

Before long they were near to where Hagan and the others stood.

'Father!' Gunderic screamed at the top of his lungs. 'It's me, Gunderic. Let me fight with you!'

Gundahar heard him and turned his head. Hagan felt a lurch of panic. If Gunderic left their formation it would leave one of their flanks exposed to attack. With some relief he saw the king shake his head.

'We must surrender, son,' he shouted back. 'We cannot win this battle. Remember what I taught you. Where is that Roman, Aetius?'

'There, lord,' Childeric said, pointing with his spear to where the Roman general still sat on his horse, just in front of his own line of shields.

Gundahar spurred his own horse towards Aetius. Seeing him, the general turned his mount to face him.

Hagan saw that the Hun leaders were now pointing at the king. Their signal horns sounded. Many riders broke away from the main mass of battle and began pounding towards Gundahar. At another blast of the horns they unleashed a volley of arrows. The storm of shafts streaked across the battlefield and into Gundahar and his horse. Struck countless times, both man and steed stumbled and fell headlong into the mud. The horse rolled over and Hagan thought he could hear the crunching of the king's bones as the great beast's body passed over him.

For a few moments the watching Burgundars stared in disbelief. Then Gunderic let out a groan. Hagan thought briefly that this was another experience they had shared to go with all the others from growing up: they had both watched the deaths of the men they called father that day.

Aetius, meanwhile, kicked his heels, sending his horse rushing towards the leaders of the Huns. Hagan could not understand why but Aetius looked apoplectic with rage. When he reached the Hun leaders he screamed something at them while waving his arms. His protestations were met with impassive looks from the Huns, however. Aetius then wheeled his horse and began to ride back to his own line.

'What do we do now?' Hagan said over his shoulder to the others.

'You heard my father,' Gunderic said. 'We must surrender.'

'You saw what happened when he tried,' Childeric said. 'The Huns will cut us down. Stand firm, lads, or they'll cut us down like the rest.'

Most of the isolated Burgundar warriors had now either been killed or fled to the trees. The Huns then began to concentrate on the small formations like the one Hagan stood in. Three Huns would charge at a formation, shooting arrows, then while the Burgundars ducked for cover a fourth Hun would ride in and cast his noose. It might fall over one of the Burgundar's shoulders, head, snag a hand or even his shield. The Hun then whirled his horse and galloped away, trailing the unfortunate Burgundar out of position, or ripping his shield away. Once the formation was broken more Huns rode in to finish off the rest.

Hagan watched as another Burgundar, a noose caught around his left foot, was dragged out of a nearby formation and trailed off behind a Hun rider, yelling and trying to cut the noose as he went, to no avail.

'Why can't they cut those nooses?' he said, aware that rising panic was making his voice rise in pitch also. 'My father couldn't cut the one that held him either.'

'They're made of animal hide,' Childeric said. 'It's too tough for a single blade to slice easily.'

One by one, with relentless, methodical ruthlessness, the little defensive formations were assaulted in this manner and destroyed. It was only a matter of time before the Huns got round to Hagan and the others.

'We should move towards the trees,' Childeric said. 'If we stick together and guard each other's backs we should make it.'

'No! We must surrender to the Romans,' Gunderic said. 'That was what my father was trying to do.'

Then he was running, breaking away from their little formation and towards the Roman shields.

'No, you fool!' Childeric yelled. 'You'll leave us open to attack.'

It was pointless. Gunderic ran on. Now he was waving his hands above his head.

'Pax! Pax!' he shouted. 'I am Gunderic, son of King Gundahar.'

Aetius spotted him and began to ride across the meadow towards him.

'All is lost, lads,' Childeric said. 'We can't hold position with just three of us. The army is destroyed. Run for it. It's every man for himself now. Try to get to safety if you can.'

'But—' Hagan began to protest but as he glanced over his shoulder he saw that the other two men in his formation had already broken away and were running as hard as they could for the trees beside the river.

When he looked forward again he saw a Hun already galloping towards him. He had his bow drawn and was lining up Hagan for a shot.

Hagan planted his spear butt in the earth then drew his throwing axe, just as he had seen his father do. He hurled it at the oncoming horseman. The rider ducked and the axe missed, but it was enough to put the Hun off releasing his arrow. As he straightened up again Hagan grabbed his spear and launched it at him. Intent on raising his bow to shoot, the Hun moved into the path of the oncoming spear. The blade struck him in the chest. With a yelp of both surprise and pain, the Hun toppled backwards out of his saddle.

Hagan felt a thrill rush through his heart. He had brought down his first warrior in battle. Momentarily forgetting the dire situation he was in, he glanced around to see if anyone else had witnessed it. All he saw however were countless swirling riders and the carnage that had once been the Burgundar army. He also now had only a knife to defend himself and that would not be much good against horsemen.

Nearby was a fallen warrior of his tribe, his chest transfixed by four arrows. His francisca still in his belt. He had never had a chance to even draw it. Hagan grabbed it then loped off for the trees as Childeric and the other man had done.

Glancing over his shoulder he saw two horsemen pull off from their formation and begin to pound after him. One was trying to aim his bow while the other was swinging a noose. Hagan tried to run faster but his shield was heavy and an encumbrance. The thought of being without the protection it gave was frightening but he realised if he continued to carry it he would never make the trees.

Hagan dropped his shield and sprinted as hard as he could for the forest. In a few moments he made it to the relative cover of the forest edge. As he entered the dense undergrowth he looked around and saw the Huns following him turn their horses around, reluctant to follow him into the dangerous tangle of trunks, branches and brambles where their horses would cease to be an advantage and an ambush could lurk behind every bush.

Hagan kept going. The trees around him were full of other men fleeing for their lives like he was. Soon he was on the narrow path he had taken earlier to try to find the king. He charged along it, batting away branches that got in his way or thorns that tugged at his jerkin.

Now the immediate threat to his life was lifted, Hagan's thoughts turned to the rest of his family. They had been among the other women and children watching the battle. Were they too now dead like his father? Was he now alone in the world?

He thought of his mother's kind face and the urgent, glowing almost worship his little brother had looked at him with that morning when he had stood in his war gear before them. Tears filled his eyes and he could not stop them streaming down his face. He had to find them. His father was gone now so it was up to him to protect them.

He knew there was a way back to the town walls through the forest. A little further along there was a fork and the right-hand path would take him to outside the city walls.

Hagan stopped. Looking around he realised he had made the same mistake as before. Instead of fleeing along the riverbank he had ended up in the same clearing around the small bay again. If the Huns were chasing him into the forest he was now cut off from the city but such concerns were no longer a problem for him.

For a moment his heart leapt at the thought that Gunhild – a friendly face – was perhaps still there. Perhaps at least they two might be able to get away.

Then he looked around and his blood turned to ice. The Swan Maidens' boat was still grounded in the reeds, but the little clearing was now a scene of horror.

CHAPTER TEN

HAGAN HAD ONCE seen the aftermath of when a fox had raided a chicken house. The sight that greeted his eyes now was very like that. There were white feathers and blood everywhere. Two of the girls lay on their backs, dead. Their throats had been opened, leaving wounds like obscene second mouths beneath their chins. Their dresses were ripped away and their groins were a mess of blood and gore.

The headless corpse of the old woman, Gutrune, lay half in and half out of the water. Two laughing Hun warriors were throwing some sort of ball to each other. One had just thrown it as Hagan arrived. The second Hun, realising he was not going to catch it, volleyed it with his boot instead. It spun end over end through the air then landed with a sickening crunch not far from Hagan. He looked down and saw it was Gutrune's head. Her mouth was open, as if she were screaming in denunciation of the disrespect her remains were enduring.

Another Swan Maiden screamed and writhed on the ground nearby. A Hun lay on top of her, his breeches pulled down to his knees, his naked buttocks heaving up and down. Was the girl Gunhild?

The two Huns who had been playing with the old woman's severed head froze when they saw him. Their hands dropped to their sword hilts. Then one of them smiled and patted his helmet then pointed at Hagan. He babbled something in his own tongue that Hagan did not understand, but among it he heard the word Romani. Due to the old Roman helmet he wore, the man must have thought him one of General Aetius's soldiers. He turned away again.

This was an advantage not to be wasted. Hagan sprinted towards the struggling pair on the ground. As he ran he raised the curve-bladed axe. The other two Huns started in surprise. They both reached for their sheathed swords again but Hagan had already reached his target. He planted his left foot between the prone Hun's shoulder blades and brought the axe down on the back of his head. It sliced through the metal of his helmet and Hagan heard a crunch as it went into the man's skull beneath.

The Hun stiffened, his back arched and his arms flew out sideways. Hagan yanked his axe back. It came away with a nauseating tearing sound and the Hun's helmet came with it. It dropped from the axe blade and as it did, Hagan blinked, unsure if he could believe what he was seeing. The man's helmet was tall but he had assumed it was filled with padding. Now he saw that like the Hun he had seen earlier fall from his horse, this one's head was distorted, and not just from the blow of Hagan's axe. It looked as if someone had grabbed the Hun's skull and stretched it so his forehead was unnaturally long. His skull, now with a red trench opened in it by Hagan's axe, rose up to a tall point. It was like nothing Hagan had ever seen before. Was this Hun actually an elf or some other supernatural creature?

He caught movement from the corner of his eye. With some effort he tore his gaze away from the strange sight, for the dead Hun's two companions were now coming for him.

Twisting at the waist, Hagan hurled his axe at the first one. It tumbled end over end once and embedded itself with a soft thunk right in the centre of the running man's chest. He cried out and fell backwards.

That left only one Hun, but this one brandished a short

sword with a curved blade while all Hagan had was the short knife, his *seax* – still sheathed at his belt.

The Hun realised he had the advantage. He slowed down, an unpleasant grin spreading across his face. He swiped the sword through the air, making Hagan jump backwards, away from the dead Hun with the strange head. Hagan pulled his seax free of its sheath but he knew it was useless. The reach the sword gave the Hun made his short blade almost of no consequence.

The Hun chuckled. He feinted, jumping forwards as if to stab at Hagan. Hagan jumped away again. The Hun laughed outright. He feinted again, once more making Hagan jump to avoid being stabbed. The bastard was enjoying himself.

'Just get on with it!' Hagan shouted. 'Attack. Get it over with.'

The Hun shook his head. Hagan thought this was not because his request was being denied but because the attacker did not understand his tongue.

The Hun's grin disappeared as the girl his companion had been raping shoved aside the rapist's corpse and rose from the ground like an avenging wraith. It was not Gunhild.

It was Brynhild.

Her nose was broken and bleeding, her left eye was blackened and almost closed. Her magnificent flowing robes, once white, were now blood-splashed tatters and Hagan could see more than one stab wound in her torso. Despite this, she grabbed her assailant's fallen sword and stumbled forward to attack.

Sword grasped in both hands, she lunged at the remaining Hun. Looking more annoyed than worried, the Hun swept her blade aside with his own, then lashed out with his boot, sending the slight girl flying backwards onto the ground once more.

It was all the distraction Hagan needed. He leapt forward, getting as close to the Hun as he could. Now they were so close the Hun's advantage of having a long-reaching weapon became the opposite. He was still turning his head back to the renewed threat from Hagan as the Burgundar lad drove his blade into his neck.

A gush of warm blood erupted around Hagan's knife hand. It tumbled down the Hun's chest to splatter the rings of his armour. He stumbled backwards, a look of surprise and panic now on his face and his free hand went to the wound at his throat. Hagan was surprised to see how much blood was streaming from him and surmised he must have cut one of the large veins in the man's throat.

The Hun swiped his sword at the air, as if in a vain attempt to keep Hagan and the girl away. Then he took another faltering step backwards. The look he regarded Hagan with was now one of disbelief, as if he could not believe this mere boy had been the death of him. Then his legs buckled and he dropped to his knees.

Hagan could not tear his eyes away as the Hun held his gaze. He felt a strange mixture of horror and fascination as he realised he was watching a man die, and that he had been the cause of that death. He had already killed the other two but this, with its shared final moments, was somehow both more personal and more appalling.

The Hun tried to say something but all that came from his mouth was a gush of blood. Then something seemed to leave his eyes and he pitched over, dead.

Hagan stared at his body, aghast for a few moments. He was sweating heavily and very out of breath.

'Hagan.'

The sound of his name broke the brief reverie. Brynhild had spoken in little more than a gasp. She still lay on the ground. Her hands made weak movements, as if she were trying to pull her torn robes together to preserve what little remained of her destroyed modesty.

Hagan staggered over to where she lay and crouched beside her. To his astonishment she was smiling.

'You saved me,' she said, through blood coated teeth. 'My hero.'

'You saved me too,' Hagan said. His mind was a whirl of confusion. He could tell she must be in agony. Should he hold her hand? Throw his arms around her? That was unseemly. She was the daughter of a nobleman and almost naked. 'If you hadn't jumped on that last one—'

Brynhild just shook her head.

'You are so handsome. You know I always kept a little hope in my heart that one day you and I would marry?' A tear ran from her left eye. 'You would become the chief champion of our folk, just like your father. We would have many fine sons and beautiful daughters. We would live in a hall of our own.'

Hagan's mouth dropped open. He had known Brynhild for years but had absolutely no idea she had ever harboured such thoughts towards him. The idea that any of the girls his age – let alone a Swan Maiden – would look at him in that way was beyond belief to him. Especially his old friend Brynhild. She spent most of her time riding horses and everyone always thought little interested her beyond the king's stables.

He wanted to say something but could not think of any words.

'Now that will never be,' Brynhild said.

'Don't say that,' Hagan said, his tongue finally loosened. 'I will get you to a safe place. Your wounds will be treated—'

She shook her head, then her face creased in a grimace of pain.

'I have not long left,' she said, her voice now little more than a whisper. 'You must escape. Our folk must live on. Some

81

of the other Swan Maidens got away. You must find them and help them.'

Hagan looked up. Hope entered his heart again for the first time since the Hun cavalry had charged from the forest.

'Did Gunhild escape?' he said.

The look that crossed Brynhild's face suggested Hagan had just dealt her a blow every bit as deadly as the Huns who had stabbed her.

'Of course, Gunhild,' she said. 'You always liked her best, didn't you? Same as the other boys. She was always the most beautiful one. Well yes, she did. Ostara is with her. At least the last time I saw them... I hope she got away.'

Guilt replaced the brief moment of hope that had filled Hagan's heart.

'Find her, Hagan,' Brynhild said, another tear rolling from her eye. 'Get them all to safety. Guard the customs of our folk. That is what Gutrune taught us: our songs and our customs are the soul of the folk. While they survive in one person's memory our people will never die.'

Brynhild's teeth clenched with intense pain. She screwed her eyes shut, reached up and grasped Hagan's hand. Hers felt cold but her grip was tremendous. Then it went slack. With a gasp, Brynhild's body went limp and she fell back onto the grass.

Hagan stood up. It was hard to believe what was happening. His entire world was falling apart around him. Brynhild knew, like he did, that their very existence as a people was on the verge of being extinguished. He had to find what was left and save it. But what could he, one lad in his first battle, do against the might of Rome and the horse-riding devils it had unleashed upon the Burgundars? The king was dead. Their fighting horde had been destroyed, and if it had not already, the city would soon fall. All he had left now was whatever remained of his family.

He had to find them. Retrieving the francisca and grabbing

one of the Hun's fallen swords, he ran off back through the forest towards the path that led to the walls of the city. A little later he reached the edge of the trees once again, arriving not far from the stone gate that guarded the way into Vorbetomagus.

CHAPTER ELEVEN

THE FIRST THING Hagan noticed was the change in the level of noise. In the short time he had been in the forest the battle – what there had ever been of it – had ended. The meadow was now littered with the corpses of Burgundar warriors. They lay alone or in heaps, each body skewered by two, three, sometimes multiple arrows. Huns rode around at a lazy pace, picking off at will the few survivors who ran this way and that across the battlefield.

Not all the bodies were warriors. There was a swathe of corpses of women and children lying near the walls of the city, the casualties of the hail of arrows the Huns had shot to incense the Burgundars into breaking their shield wall. The bodies continued here and there right up to the gate, marking the trail of where the panicking crowd of watching families had fled towards the safety of the city walls.

His mother and brother would be inside Vorbetomagus somewhere. If he was to find them he had to go in. Yet with mounting dread he saw black columns of smoke were already roiling into the sky from behind the city walls. Buildings were burning.

The gate of the city was not closed. Hun horsemen clattered in and out of it and Hagan wondered how he might get in. Then there came a break in the incessant coming and going. Hagan slipped out from the cover of the trees and ran towards the gate. He only got halfway when something on the ground caught his eye.

He recognised the brown-yellow cloak because he had worn it many times when he was a boy. He had always hated it. The colour was like mud and the wool coarse and made the skin on his neck itch. When he had grown too big for it, it had been the turn of his little brother, Raknar, to wear the dreadful thing.

Hagan swallowed. The cloak was wrapped around the body of a small boy of about Raknar's age who lay face down in the dirt. Three Hun arrow shafts went through the garment and into the back of the child. Blood had seeped into the wool of the cloak, but not that much.

Hagan dropped to a crouch beside the body. He pushed it half over so he could see the face. It was Raknar. His eyes were wide and stared, unblinking, though mud stuck to them, his visage twisted in testament to the agony and terror that had filled his final moments of life.

Choking a cry, Hagan looked around, already knowing what further horror would lie not far away. A few paces from his brother's corpse was the body of a woman. She too lay face down, if that could be said for one who had no face. The woman's head was little more than a horrible pulp of bones, hair, blood and brains. The hoofprint of a Hun horse was visible on what remained of the back of her skull. Hagan recognised her dress and her cloak, however. There was no doubt it was his mother.

They had not made it even as far as the city gates. The Huns had cut them down as they ran for safety.

Through the fog of horror Hagan noticed something. Around his mother's neck were the links of a necklace. Godegisil's words from the night before resurfaced in his memory and without thinking Hagan crouched down and lifted it, tugging it free of the bloody mess. As he did so he noticed that his mother's blood was still warm. Perhaps if he had got here a little sooner he could have saved her.

Or died with them, the voice inside his head told him.

He stood up again, looking at the amulet that dangled from the end of the necklace. It was gold and had a strange horse inscribed on it. Above the horse flew a bird. His mother had snatched it from the man who had raped her and at the same time given life to him. Now it was the only link he had to either of them.

For a moment Hagan felt totally empty. Then a rime-cold anger filled the depths of his guts. He looked around, no longer caring if the Huns spotted him. He wanted them to see him, he wanted them to attack. There was nothing left for him now. Nothing to fight for. Nothing to protect. He would try to kill as many of these hateful bastards as he could before they took his life as well.

A discarded spear lay nearby. Hagan grabbed it and ran through the gatehouse and on into the city beyond. The scene that greeted him was even more horrific than the battlefield outside.

CHAPTER TWELVE

BISHOP ULFIUS HAD often preached in the great church in the middle of Vorbetomagus about Armageddon and the last days, when Satan's legions would lay waste to the world. The scene that greeted Hagan inside the walls of the city reminded him of the horrors that Ulfius had warned them to expect on that final day.

Vorbetomagus had been built many years ago by the Romans, long before his people had settled there. It had lasted and grown over many centuries. Now within a morning it was being destroyed. Buildings blazed, sending black smoke into the sky or drifting through the streets to sting tears from the eyes. Market stalls and carts were overturned and smashed. There were dead bodies everywhere – men, women and children, either shot by arrows or hacked to pieces. The drains, rivulets that ran along the sides of the stone-paved streets, were red with blood.

Those already dead were the lucky ones. Without shame, Huns were raping women and girls on the paving stones of the streets. Other survivors ran this way and that, desperate to flee the relentless horsemen who rode up and down the streets, shooting without mercy or riding down running Burgundars, crushing them to pulp under the hooves of their steeds. Many of the Huns laughed with clear delight at the carnage they created. Their horses and armour were spattered with the blood of their victims. The noise of it all rose into the air, a cacophony of screams of terror and howls of agony.

At first Hagan just stared, his heart paralysed by despair and his mind frozen by horror. Then he saw there was something going on at the far end of the street. The main street that came through the gate led to a large space, the public market square outside the hall of the king and the great church and Roman basilica where the Council of Wise Men met. Through the smoke and the running people, he could make out a crowd of warriors gathered together. There were not many of them, but even at this distance he could see from their helmets and shields that they were Burgundars. If there were warriors left, then Hagan's place was to be with them. He had to get to the square.

There was little point running straight down the main street. The Huns would kill him before he got far. Instead, he ducked into a narrow gap that ran between two buildings and hurried along it until he reached the back. There was a narrow alley that ran along behind the buildings that fronted onto the main street, parallel to it. It was not obvious to anyone who had not grown up in the city, and the Huns had not yet discovered these back streets.

Smoke drifted into the alley but it was quieter than the main street. Hagan ran along it, passing several small groups of Burgundars – women, children, old men and merchants – who were cowering there, hiding from the massacre that was taking place a few bare paces away.

The sight gave him hope. Perhaps not all of his folk were being slaughtered. Perhaps there were many more hiding like these people or fled into the forests who could keep their tribe alive. They looked at him as he passed with wide, terrified eyes and faces smeared with soot from the fires. He nodded to them, hoping that the sight of a Burgundar warrior still alive and in battle gear would perhaps give them as much encouragement as they had given him.

The back alley ended in a wall. On the other side of it Hagan could hear the clatter of hooves on the paving stones and heard the defiant shouts of war cries and screams of the dying.

He paused for a moment. If he stayed here in the back alley it was relatively safe. Perhaps he should hide there, wait for the storm to pass and then sneak out of the city after darkness fell?

Sneak out like a rat, a voice within his heart said. It sounded like his father's. Another of Godegisil's sayings surfaced in his mind:

Will you run today, just to die another day?

Hagan took a deep breath. Like his father and the other Burgundar champions facing the Hun cavalry and certain death, he would not run.

But Godegisil was not your father, the dark, cynical voice within his heart that had tested his courage all day, reminded him.

'It is of no consequence,' Hagan spoke aloud, even though he was talking to himself. 'He was a brave man. I shall try to follow his lead.'

Another alley led off at a right-angle to one he was in, towards the bottom of the main street. Hagan jogged along it, approaching the chaos and slaughter. He emerged at the edge of the square, heat from a nearby burning building making his eyes water while the tremendous noise once again battered his ears.

The Burgundar warriors in the square stood in a larger version of the square formation Childeric had pulled him into earlier. There were perhaps thirty of them, standing shoulder to shoulder. Most had shields which they linked together to form a wall, their spears poking out between and over them. The shields were battered and peppered with arrows. Some of the warriors were wounded.

The Huns in the square rode back and forth, shooting the occasional arrow, the Burgundar spears proving a sharp deterrent to any horsemen who thought of riding too close.

In the midst of the beleaguered Burgundar group Hagan spotted a familiar face. Childeric was there, shouting defiance at the enemy and shaking his spear at everyone who rode past.

Hagan had to cross about thirty paces of open square to get to the others, a space that was roamed by Huns on horseback. He would have to run as fast as he could if he was to make it.

He remembered the Roman helmet he wore and how it had briefly fooled the Huns by the riverside. Perhaps this ruse would work again. Hagan reached up and pulled the bird wings off the helmet so as to make it as Roman-looking as possible. He also unlatched the strap beneath his chin to make it easy to remove. Then he began to jog forward.

He crossed ten paces before the Huns had even noticed him, intent as they were on the group of Burgundar warriors in the middle of the square. Then one of the horsemen spotted him. He swung his horse around and levelled his bow.

'Pax! Pax! Amica!' Hagan shouted. He knew some of the Roman tongue and hoped the Huns knew so little of it they would mistake him for a Roman.

It was enough to make the Hun pause at least. He lowered his bow and turned his horse away. Then a frown creased his face and he turned back, once more raising his bow at Hagan.

Hagan threw the francisca. It smashed through the Hun's bow and hit him in the face, knocking him backwards off his horse. As his body struck the ground Hagan rushed past it towards the Burgundar shield wall.

Seeing the Hun fall from his horse, the Burgundars also turned their attention to the warrior now running at them. Hagan ripped the Roman helmet off his head lest his own fellows mistake him for the enemy too.

'Hagan! Get over here, lad!' Childeric cried out.

Hagan sprinted the last few steps. The Burgundars opened their shield wall and he dashed through, collapsing onto the paving stones of the square as the shields clapped together behind him again.

'You made it, lad,' Childeric said, grinning, as Hagan lay, panting on the ground. 'Good to see you again. You came looking for your family?'

Hagan nodded. 'They're dead.'

Even though the words came from his own mouth it still seemed unreal, as if this were all a bad dream and his father would wake him soon to join the other young lads for morning weapons training.

'Same for all of us,' Childeric said. 'Our loved ones are either dead or they've got away. I pray to the Lord Tiwass that my own family have escaped. We've lost today, boys, but we can still give these Hun bastards a pain in the arse. We can do something we'll be remembered for!'

'It looks like you've made it just in time for the finish,' another of the warriors said as Hagan clambered to his feet.

The sound of many horses' hooves clattering on paving stones filled the air. Gasping for breath, Hagan struggled to his feet with a helping hand from Childeric. They saw the square around them was filling with more and more Huns.

'We must be the last ones holding out,' Childeric said. 'They've brought all their friends to finish us off.'

Hagan realised the only weapon he had left was the short knife at his belt.

'So be it,' he said through gritted teeth as he drew the blade.

Before long the edges of the square were all thronged with horsemen. They blocked all the streets leading away from the square as well. It looked like there were hundreds of them. With impressive discipline they filed in then stood their horses, watching the beleaguered group of Burgundars they now surrounded with their narrow eyes, their faces impassive.

'We're stuck here,' a Burgundar said. 'There's no way out now.'

'What are they waiting for?' Hagan said.

As if in response, two more horsemen came riding into the square. Hagan saw the bridles and strappings of their horses were adorned with gold and silver bracteates, flat, thin medals that showed their wealth. They wore much the same armour as the others but around their throats were thick gold necklaces, and rings of similar precious metals bedecked their forearms.

'We are honoured with a visit from their leaders,' Hagan said, his voice heavy with sarcasm.

A hush fell on the square as the Hun leaders rode into it. In moments the only sound was the hoofbeats of the two men's horses, the crackle of flames from blazing buildings and the distant screams of those being murdered in other parts of the city.

Just beyond throwing distance of the Burgundars, the two men stopped and dismounted. Both of them were stocky; short in stature with broad chests. They had flat noses and black beards and both walked with an arrogant swagger that came from the confidence of power. They surveyed the square with small, dark eyes that took everything in. Strange as their countenances were to Hagan, there was a resemblance between the two men that suggested they were related, possibly brothers. They looked to be in the prime of their lives. One was a little older and bigger than the other.

Then they took off their helmets. Hagan saw both had the same strange, elongated heads he had seen before. He wondered yet again if these men were not from another world.

'Are they demons?' The strange quiet made him speak in a hushed tone himself.

'No, lad,' Childeric said. 'They are all too human.'

'Why are their heads like that?'

'Some say it is because a Hun wears a helmet from the day he is born,' Childeric said. 'But the women look that way too. I've been told that the rich Huns bind their babies' heads with planks and bandages so they grow that way. It's a sign of superior status. These two must be important.'

With his thumbs hooked in his belt, the taller of the Hun leaders cocked his head towards the Burgundar shield wall. He barked something in his own tongue. It sounded harsh and growling. The rest of the Huns all laughed. As their laughter died away he shouted another order. This time the Huns all raised and drew their bows, aiming them at Childeric, Hagan and the others in the middle of the square.

The Hun leader raised his arm in the air. It was clear that when he dropped it they would all shoot at once.

Hagan looked around. There were hundreds of them. Even behind their meagre shield wall the arrow storm that would come their way would be impossible to stop. If any of the Burgundars managed to survive that, the Huns were bound to just unleash more and more until they were all dead.

This was the end.

'Let's show them how Burgundars can die, lads,' Childeric said.

Hagan marvelled at the strength of the older man's voice. There was no quiver, nor a crack, nothing to show he had any fear for the certain death they were facing.

'Let this, the last stand of the Burgundars, echo in eternity,' Childeric said. 'Folk will tell their children and their children's children how we few stood against so many. We did not surrender. We fought on to the end.'

Hagan's heart swelled at the words and he felt a strange calm settle over him. Then he looked at the ranks of Huns levelling their arrows in his direction and realised they were the only ones to witness what was about to happen. There would be no one of their own people to tell their story.

Childeric's words were empty. No one would ever hear if they faced death without fear or if they wet themselves and cried for mercy. None of it mattered.

The sound of more horses approaching, accompanied by

the sound of a Roman *buccina* blaring broke the silence. The Hun leader, his arm still raised in the air, frowned and looked around.

Eight riders on white horses charged down the main street. They were Romans. One of them bore the great curved brass trumpet that they could hear over everything else. Another bore one of the long, flowing dragon standards. In the lead was General Aetius. Behind him, to Hagan's surprise, rode his old friend Gunderic, son of the Burgundar king.

Riding at a frantic pace, Aetius just managed to stop before running into the two Hun leaders, his steed's hooves skidding to a stop across the paving slabs mere paces from where they stood.

The Roman general's face was a deep crimson. When he opened his mouth it became clear this was not just from the exertion of riding down the street. A tirade of shouted words tumbled from him, accompanied by much finger-pointing. Hagan could not understand the words the general spoke but it was clear he was very angry with the Hun leaders.

The older Hun leader lowered his arm in a slow, deliberate manner, ensuring that his men did not interpret the gesture as the signal to shoot. They lowered their bows.

'What's he saying?' Hagan said to Childeric, assuming someone who had spent ten years in the Roman Army would have a command of their tongue. Hagan himself knew little beyond what they had to recite in church.

'I don't know, lad,' the older warrior said. 'He's speaking in their tongue – the language of the Huns. Whatever he's saying though, he's not happy about something, that's for sure.'

The elder of the two Hun leaders responded with something and his younger brother – if that was what he was – smirked. This seemed to send Aetius almost apoplectic with rage.

The Roman swung out of his saddle and stomped over to the Huns. He began yelling at them again, this time in Latin. This time the Huns just shook their heads and looked disappointed.

'Ah!' Childeric said. 'It seems our Hun friends here are mercenaries in the pay of the Romans. They have been a bit overzealous. Aetius is shouting that they were paid to defeat our warriors, not kill everyone and destroy everything.'

Hagan looked at the devastation around him and his jaw dropped open slightly.

A look of annoyance crossed the face of the older Hun leader. He raised his hand in the air again. The Huns raised their bows once more.

Shouting and holding his own hands up, the Roman ran out in front of the raised bows, putting himself between them and the Burgundars in the square. If the Huns shot their bows, they would hit him as well.

The Huns hesitated, looking to their leader as to what they should do.

Aetius turned to the Burgundars and shouted something.

'He wants us to raise our right hands,' Childeric said. The others all looked at each other, puzzled.

'Do it, lads!' Gunderic called from across the square. 'It's the only way to save yourselves. For my sake – do this.'

With a shrug, Hagan set his knife down and raised his right hand. The other Burgundars did the same.

Aetius said something else.

'He wants us to repeat what he says,' Childeric said, translating for his fellow Burgundars.

The general began pronouncing strings of words in a very deliberate manner. Whenever he paused he nodded to the Burgundars and they did their best to repeat what he had said. After several of these he nodded and dropped his hand.

'What just happened?' Hagan said. 'What did we all just say?'

Everything had taken such a strange turn he wondered if this really was a dream, or if perhaps those three mighty, uncanny women who governed the fates of all people might be perhaps drunk.

'The Huns can't shoot us now,' Childeric said.

'Why not?' Hagan said.

'Because we're now on the same side, lad,' Childeric said. 'We just swore the *sacramentum militare*, the Oath of Allegiance to the Emperor. We've all just joined the Roman Army.'

Part II

Ubi Sunt

Hwær cwom merge? Hwær cwom mago? Hwær cwom
maþþumgyfa?
Hwær cwom symbla gesetu? Hwær sindon seledreamas?
...Hu seo þrag gewat,
genap under nihthelm, swa heo no wære.

Where is the horse gone? Where the rider? Where the giver
of treasure?
Where are the seats at the feast? Where are the revels in the
hall?
...How that time has passed away,
grown dark under cover of night, as if it had never been.

The Wanderer (tenth-century Old English poem)

CHAPTER THIRTEEN

AD 443 – Six Years Later

Kingdom of the Danes

A SLATE GREY SEA washed over the shale and pebbles on the beach. Many warriors were gathered there, their heavy woollen cloaks wrapped around their shoulders, helmets and mail *brynjas* polished to gleaming, every shield painted new and bright in the dimming light of the short winter day. Flakes of snow fluttered and twisted on the breeze, catching in the unbound hair of the group of women in dark robes who cried ostentatious laments. Their show of grief was impressive, which was only to be expected. Not only was this the funeral of a king, but they were professional mourners, paid to be sad.

The cold was driven away by waves of heat that undulated from the great fire blazing on the shore. King Half of the Danes was dead, and the flames of his funeral pyre lit the evening and sent a column of smoke spiralling into the sky above. Twelve more women, dressed in long, dark blue robes that sparkled and glittered as little seashells and pieces of glass, sewn into the material, caught the firelight, danced around the bale fire. They bore long metal wands in the shape of spinning distaffs, symbols of their status as *hellrūnes*, witches who guarded the mysteries of the passage from the world of the living to the world of the dead. These women carried out all the rites associated with the funeral.

The chief of the hellrūnes, an old woman with a hooked nose and hollow cheeks, stood staring into the fire as if watching something deep in its heart, some sort of fiery vision that was invisible to the other mortals who gathered around the pyre. She wore dark robes like the others but instead of a distaff she gripped a long knife in one bony-knuckled fist. Fresh blood dripped from the blade.

The woman's presence sent a chill down Gunhild's spine. She called her the 'Angel of Death' – though not to the woman's face. Not that the old witch would understand what an angel was. These Danes she had come to live among since the extermination of the Burgundars were still very much heathens.

There were more bodies on the fire than just the king's. Two slave girls burned there as well. The king had died over a week before but the girls had been alive until the fire was lit. Gunhild found it hard to believe the girls had actually volunteered for their grisly deaths. Was the life of a slave really so bad that they preferred to offer their throats to the knife of the old hellrūne and end it all? Or was their faith so strong they really believed the tale they had been told, that they would go to the world of the dead and serve the king in his luxurious new home?

Gunhild felt her lip curl. They would continue to serve the king just as they had done in life. She had been his wife, yet Half had spent most of his time in the beds of others like those girls. She had watched earlier as they danced, pranced and giggled, their minds befuddled by strong drink and strange herbs the hellrūne had given them to eat, before the old witch slit their throats and their bodies were cast onto the fire. Then she had killed Half's hunting dogs and they too went into the flames. Now all the bodies were shrivelling away, their hair gone, their flesh melted, their bones baking to ash in the heat.

Gunhild looked at the burning skeletons and wondered why she did not feel anything. She was still a young woman but was she so inured to horror, had she seen so much death in her short life, that it no longer moved her?

Beyond the shore, watching from a distance, were the ordinary folk. The mood of the crowd was sombre and pensive compared to the open hysteria of the wailing women. The passing of a king was always an uncertain time. A good king brought peace and good fortune to the people. When he died no one knew what lay ahead. Would his successor be strong enough to hold back the enemies of the Danes? Would he be a benevolent ruler or a tyrant?

Gunhild knew how they felt. She may not have been on the pyre, but now Half was dead what was her status? She had come here as a stranger, a wanderer with no land, no gold, nothing to offer except her beauty, which, she had to acknowledge, was greater than most women's. King Half had not been able to see past it, anyway. He had dismissed her lack of dowry and married her for her looks and the title she still had claim to: heir to the kingdom of the Burgundars.

That title was worth nothing, though. Most of the tribe were dead. Those few warriors who had survived the battle which left Vorbetomagus a smoking ruin had been marched off, conscripted into the Roman Army. They would be sent into battle against the Empire's enemies until they were all dead too.

Still, after too much mead Half had often talked of taking an army and claiming that realm that was now rightfully his through marriage. It never came to anything. He was usually just trying to please her so he could get her into bed.

Six winters had passed since Gunhild had escaped the massacre of her people at Vorbetomagus. As the Huns were shattering the Burgundars' shield wall on the battlefield, another contingent had attacked the city from the opposite direction. Some of these men had burst in upon the Swan Maidens as they were finishing changing in their glade beside the river. The Huns had caught some of them but many of the girls had escaped. It was thanks to old Gutrune, who had come between the Huns and her girls, her knife ready, her eyes as determined and cold as the old Angel of Death here. She had managed to stall the Huns long enough for Gunhild and some of the others to flee into the forest.

There they scattered, running in every direction off through the trees. Gunhild had never seen any of the others again, apart from one: Signy, the daughter of one of the other noble families of the Burgundar. They had stuck together. Seeing the burning city, the shattered army and the Huns killing at will they had fled deeper into the forest, heading north and not stopping until they were well away from Vorbetomagus.

Signy had a sister who had been married into a noble family of the Alemanni tribe, as part of a peace agreement with the Burgundars. Gunhild and Signy had first sought refuge with her. It was while staying there that the news had come of the annihilation of the Burgundars and that the Huns were hunting down remaining survivors. It was not safe to remain where they were, so they moved further north. Signy's sister had in turn a sister-in-law who was married to the king of the Suebi, and Gunhild and Signy had gone there next.

There was no going back. Vorbetomagus was gone and with it the Burgundar kingdom. The news came also that the Romans were resettling Franks there, new allies they hoped would prove more faithful to the Empire than the Burgundars. There was nothing to return to. Their home was gone. Their people were dead except for a few scattered survivors like them.

So began Gunhild's long journey north. They made use of a network of noblewomen spread across the royal houses of Gaul and Germania by marriage alliances. While their accommodation was comfortable – the halls of kings or the villas of noblemen – they were always guests, outsiders who were tolerated for a time in sympathy. They learned to recognise the signs of when that sympathy ran out. There were guests and then there were parasites, and two young women with no husbands, no wealth and no prospects, escapees from the Romans, quickly became regarded as the latter. When that time came Gunhild and Signy knew it was time to move on.

While in northern Gaul, Signy had accepted a marriage proposal from a young nobleman. His position was well beneath her former status, but Signy had had enough of running. Gunhild had moved on, alone.

She was not short of proposals herself, but she was proud. The one treasure she still possessed was her beauty. Minor noblemen, even some lesser kings, offered to make her their consort, but she knew enough of the world to know that position held no security. Gunhild had seen enough of her father's women tossed aside as soon as their looks started to fade.

Her route seemed to take her northwards and netherwards, like the journey the old folk believed the dead took to Hell, the kingdom they all went to after life. The further she got from Vorbetomagus the worse the weather got, the more uncomfortable the houses were, and the scarcer the wine and other comforts available within the Empire became.

Eventually, at a feast in Frisia, King Half had seen her. Half already had two other wives – noblewomen of good, wealthy clans – but they were growing old and crabbit, he said. They had given him sons to carry on his dynasty and daughters who could be married off to seal peace deals and expand his influence. He had done his duty, so what was the problem if he took a third wife who was young and beautiful, even if she was destitute?

For a time Gunhild had been a queen. Now King Half was dead, killed on a foolish raid upon the Franks he was warned not to go on, and once more she was nothing. A queen without a country. A stranger among the Danes.

The king's other two wives were already looking at Gunhild with more than their usual venom. Now Half was no longer there to defend her, their previous forced toleration of Gunhild could be abandoned. Both of them had strong, ruthless sons who would soon be trying to kill each other over who would inherit the Kin Helm, the helmet that symbolised kingship of their people. If she didn't move fast, Gunhild had no doubt she would be one of the corpses they left behind on their climb to power.

She turned away from the roaring fire and began to make her way up the pebbles of the beach. Not far away a figure was standing at the top of the shale. He had not been there the last time she looked. He was tall and slender and his long blond hair blew in the wind. He had a long cloak wrapped around his shoulders that was threadbare in places. His torso was wrapped in mail, but it was dull and there were holes in it. He had a sword sheathed under his left arm and a battered old Roman Army shield over his shoulder. The round face of his shield was gouged and chipped but a black eagle was marked on it in fresh paint.

Gunderic?

Gunhild stopped dead at the sight of him, doubting the evidence of her own eyes. Was this a ghost come to haunt her? A *draugr* risen from the grave to torment the living?

For the first time in years she spoke in her own accent. 'Is it really you?' she said breathlessly.

'It is,' the newcomer said, his face breaking out into a grin. 'Good to see you again, sister.'

Then she was scrambling up the last of the beach and threw her arms around him.

'It looks like I got here just in time,' Gunderic said. 'Some of these folk in the pagan north still expect a king's wife to go on his pyre with him.'

'Thankfully the Danes are not among them,' Gunhild said. She stepped back, looking him up and down, as if trying to ascertain if he was really there or not.

'I thought you were dead!'

'Likewise,' Gunderic said, still grinning. 'And when I found out you weren't, you were damned hard to find.'

'You must have been taken into the Roman Army, then?' Gunhild said. 'Like the others who survived. How could you fight for the bastards who destroyed our people and our kingdom?'

Gunderic sighed; his eyes drifted off towards the churning waves beyond the shore.

'What choice did I have, sister?' he said. 'It was that or execution. And with me would have been executed all the other surviving men of our folk.'

'Are there many others?' The tremor in her voice betrayed her desperation that the answer would be yes.

'There were enough,' Gunderic said. 'But it was not the Romans who were responsible for the slaughter at Vorbetomagus. It was the Huns. Their commanders had something to prove. It was revenge for our father's great raid on them. He killed their king and took his sword. They wanted back what he took from them.'

Gunhild's jaw dropped open a little. She had heard the tales about their father's attack on the Huns, carried out with a small warband of trusted men. It had been kept very secret beforehand – only warriors from two of the Burgundar clans had been involved, the Nibelungs and the Volsungs – to make sure they took the Huns by surprise. Even the Swan Maidens knew nothing of it. They had attacked the Huns in the night and sent them running. It was a great victory and afterwards celebrated with much feasting. The bards had composed at least two songs and one poem about it.

It was not just glory and the sword of the Hun King that Gundahar had won that night. The Huns had a huge hoard of gold and silver, booty plundered from across Scythia and Germania, and he had taken the lot.

'They always said that gold was cursed,' Gunhild said, shaking her head. 'I know that many of those who had accompanied our father on that raid later died suddenly but I always thought it coincidence. But now you say it has brought calamity to our people.'

Then she scowled. 'Are you trying to blame *our father* for

the massacre?' she said, her eyes blazing. 'How could you even *think* such a thing?'

'Of course not. But it wasn't completely the Romans' fault either. In my time in the Army I met officers who were there on that day,' Gunderic said, his grin now gone. 'I even got to know General Aetius, the commander. All of them were shocked at what the Huns did. They overstepped the mark and the killing got out of hand.'

'Don't make excuses for them,' his sister said, sneering. 'Has your time in their army turned you into a Roman? They paid the Huns to fight for them. They were all one horde. Don't make excuses for the bastards! Rome's bloody hand was behind it. It is Rome, not our father who is guilty.'

'Do you think it was easy for me?' her brother said. 'It wasn't. It was tough! Not just the hardship of army life, but knowing that every day I would put on the uniform of those who destroyed my home and slaughtered my people!'

'That must have been hard, I grant you,' she said, her tone softening. She laid a hand on her brother's forearm. 'Still, at least you weren't alone, like I was. You were with the other Burgundar men forced to fight for them. Are any with you now?'

'If only that were true,' Gunderic said. 'As a king's son they put me in a cavalry regiment. I was there with all the other rich boys. But I did well. I saved a Roman consul's son in battle. I was discharged from the Army with honours.'

'They let you go?' Gunhild said, a puzzled frown on her face.

'It's not a prison,' Gunderic said, a bemused look on his face. 'But granted, they do have their hands full at the moment. They need every man they can get. Which in a way has led me to come here to find you. I have great news. General Aetius became *Magister Militum* of the Roman Army – the highest-ranking soldier there is. He knows the legions cannot hold down every rebellious tribe in the Empire, even with the help

106

of the Huns. So the Romans are making treaties with friendly tribes. They allow them to live within the borders of the Empire as long as they vow to fight off barbarians from outside intent on attacking Rome.'

'So they still use *barbarians* to do their fighting against other barbarians?' Gunhild said, arching one eyebrow. 'Except now they don't have the expense of supplying uniforms or weapons.'

'Grow up, sister,' Gunderic said, his voice becoming harsh. 'Rome may not be the great Empire she once was, but she is still the greatest power in the world. Do you want to be with her or against her? You've seen what the price of defying her is.'

'Wait,' Gunhild said, realisation dawning on her mind. 'Are you saying that this Aetius has offered you one of these treaties?'

'A *foedus*? Yes,' her brother said. 'Gunhild, not all our folk were wiped out at Vorbetomagus. They were scattered to the four corners of the earth, yes, but enough have survived that if gathered together we could start all over again. The kingdom of the Burgundars can rise again. We will be free once more! And I will be king, just as I was born to be.'

'What?' Gunhild shook her head, scarcely able to believe what she was hearing.

Her brother's eyes widened with excitement.

'Aetius has granted me a new kingdom,' he said. 'Geneva in the province of Maxima Sequanorum, and the lands around the great lake there.'

Gunhild's mouth dropped open completely. Until moments before she had believed she was the last of her people, doomed to wander the earth alone until she died, taking with her from the earth the tales and songs of her folk, erasing all remnants of the Burgundars from the memory of the world. Now not only was her brother standing before her but he was saying there were others of their tribe too, and they even had a new homeland. For a moment her vision swam and she thought she might faint.

'There are folk from nearly all the Burgundar clans scattered across Europa and beyond,' Gunderic continued. 'When they hear we have a new homeland they will come to it. Our people can live again. We, the Nibelungs, will be strong again!'

'This Aetius has promised you will be king?' Gunhild said.

'Naturally,' Gunderic said, his chest swelling. 'The Nibelung clan has led the Burgundars for a hundred winters and more. We will carry that tradition on.'

Gunhild felt her heart beat faster. Her life as a landless, friendless wanderer was over. She would be the sister of the Burgundar king, one of the ruling Nibelungs once more. The prospect was intoxicating. Was this a dream? It all seemed too good to be true...

'And what was his price?' Gunhild said. 'A Roman would not offer a kingdom to a barbarian just because he saved some Roman's son!'

'Well... there is the matter of the Alemanni,' Gunderic said. 'They are growing in power, and the understanding is that we will keep them in check.'

Gunhild knew her brother well. She could see he was sheepish, looking at the ground instead of her.

'What else?' she said, narrowing her eyes.

'The thing is,' Gunderic said, his cheeks turning red, 'the Huns told Aetius about the treasure. They didn't find it at Vorbetomagus. The Lord knows they tore the city apart trying to find it.'

Gunhild recalled the last time she had seen her father at the cave by the Rhine. She bit her lip. With that amount of gold, anything could become possible. Just knowing where it was granted power.

'When General Aetius confronted the Hun leaders about the destruction they had caused they told him about it,' her brother said. 'When we met last year the Magister Militum asked me if I might know where it was hidden.'

Gunhild took a sharp intake of breath.

'And did you know?' she said.

'I did,' Gunderic said. 'Our father confided in me that it was concealed in a cave near the river.'

Anger flared in Gunhild's heart. She had found out by coincidence. Gunderic, the boy, the son and heir, had been brought into their father's confidence. It made no difference that she was the elder of them, and the firstborn too.

'So you bought this new kingdom with our father's gold?' she said through clenched teeth. 'It wasn't really about saving a Roman's life, or the need for keeping the Roman border safe? It was all just a grubby little deal over *gold*.'

'In part, yes,' Gunderic said. He spoke in a low voice and glanced around, as if fearful some of the Danes might overhear. 'Not just the gold but the sword as well. Apparently it is very important to the Huns. Look, it was just between me and the general, alright? And now you. It is not to be mentioned beyond us. Understand?'

'You never could keep your mouth shut,' Gunhild said with a derisive snort. 'Especially when it mattered most.'

'Look, Gunhild,' her brother said. Now there was anger in his voice too. 'Listen before you pour any more of your scorn on me. Firstly: what does it matter? We have a new kingdom granted to us. Our folk can live again. What is that compared to all the gold in the world?'

'What of vengeance, Gunderic?' Gunhild said. 'This Roman dog and his Hun allies killed our father, destroyed our homeland and massacred our people. And now you say you've given him our treasure – *our birthright* – as well? We should be pulling out his eyes after nailing him to a cross, Gunderic. Not kissing his arse.'

Her brother did not respond.

'And you ask what does it matter?' Gunhild was incredulous. 'Look at you. Your cloak is threadbare. Your breeches are patched. Your mail is full of holes. What sort of king are you going to make? How many warriors will follow a lord who cannot give them gold? How will we build a kingdom with no wealth?'

To her surprise, Gunderic was now smiling again.

'I'm not as dull-witted as your think, sister,' he said. 'I can scheme as well as Father. Or you, for that matter.'

He glanced around again, making sure there was no one close enough to overhear them.

'What if I told you there may still be a way to get the treasure back?' he said.

'Then I'd say we should do anything we can to make that happen,' his sister said.

'Anything?' Gunderic said, arching his right eyebrow.

Gunhild nodded.

He looked down at his feet again. Then he looked up again and met her gaze.

'That's good,' he said. 'Because I may need you to get married.'

CHAPTER FOURTEEN

GUNHILD'S JOURNEY SOUTH was considerably faster than her trek north years before. It still took weeks, however. Gunderic had come in a ship with a contingent of twenty warriors, Burgundars he had rescued from their twenty-five-year-long commissions in the Roman Army, on the premise that he needed them to fight off the Alemanni who threatened the new Burgundar lands and hence Rome.

Half's family had not tried to stop Gunhild leaving. Indeed, they appeared more than happy to see her go. So she sailed south, away from the land of the Danes and through the narrow sea between Britannia and Gaul. The sea was rough and the weather foul. They were cold, wet and miserable and spent their time either huddling for shelter from the incessant rain or throwing up over the sides. There was little time for talk, especially not whatever strategy Gunderic had in mind for regaining the treasure hoard from the Romans. Gunhild did try to broach the subject twice, but on both occasions Gunderic had glanced towards nearby warriors and touched his forefinger to his lips, making it obvious that whatever his plans were, they were not for sharing.

Sometimes they were able to put into a port where they stayed in a comfortable tavern, ate good food and drank decent wine. Other stretches of shore, Gunderic avoided. The people in Armorica, he told Gunhild, were in revolt against Rome, and without her legions to enforce law pirates now ranged the coast. The further south they sailed the better the weather became and the less the sea rolled and heaved.

Gunhild was delighted to see Gunderic's warriors had painted their Roman shields with the emblems of their Burgundar clans. There were wolves, lightning symbols and sun wheels. Gunderic had painted an eagle on his. There were no bears.

'Are there no Dagelungs?' Gunhild said one day, as she and her brother ate their meagre suppers of boiled, salted fish.

Gunderic shook his head.

'There were enough of them taken into the army after Vorbetomagus to form a cohort,' her brother said. 'But last I heard they went with Aetius to fight the Visigoths. It did not go well. I've never come across a Dagelung since.'

For a moment there was silence. Both contemplated those who were missing from their little circle of friends.

'It seems strange for us two to be back together but not Hagan,' Gunhild said. 'It was always the three of us together.'

'And Brynhild,' her brother said. 'Did she escape, do you think? She was a Swan Maiden like you, wasn't she?'

Gunhild shot a reproachful glance at him. He was not meant to know such things. Then she sighed. What did it matter now?

'I don't think she did, no,' she said, sudden tears stinging her eyes. 'Sorry.'

'Oh,' was all her brother said, turning his eyes towards the deck.

They sailed through two terrifying storms. Lightning split the sky, the waves rose like mountains, howling wind threatened to tear the sails from the mast and rain lashed the deck. It was all the more frightening to think that to the west lay nothing but endless ocean. If they were driven off course they could be lost forever.

The storms passed though and they rounded the coast of Hispania and sailed through the Pillars of Hercules into the Great Middle Sea. From then on the journey became close to pleasant. They bought excellent food in ports and enjoyed pleasant nights on land away from the constant rolling of the ship's deck.

Even here though, as they sailed towards the very heart of the Roman Empire, there were parts of the coast that had to be avoided. Gunderic might have been no real friend of Rome but his ship was Roman and, despite their painted shields, his and his warriors' war gear was from the Roman Army. Gunderic had no desire to be the victim of mistaken identity by another of Rome's foes. To the north the Visigoths had formed their own kingdom in Hispania and Southern Gaul in defiance of Rome. To the south lay Africa and another kingdom the Vandals had driven the Romans from. Everywhere, it seemed, Rome's power was on the wane. The thought made Gunhild question the sagacity of Gunderic's strategy.

'Are you sure this treaty is wise, Gunderic?' she said one evening. They sat at a table set up for them near the prow. For once, they were as alone as they could be on the ship. The others were all eating under a canopy further down the deck. They had bought amphorae of excellent Gaulish wine in the last port they had stopped at and fresh fish for a change from the salted. Gunderic poured them both a goblet of ruby red wine then sat back, a half-smile on his lips.

'Rome is still the greatest power in the world,' he said. 'It's better to be with them than against them. Though if Aetius ever finds out about what happened to the treasure then he'll make what happened at Vorbetomagus look like a child's birthday party.'

'What do you mean?' Gunhild said, frowning.

Gunderic leaned on his elbows on the table. He looked at his sister with eyes that were steady but they were set in a head that wavered a little.

'How many goblets of wine have you had?' Gunhild said.

'Not enough,' Gunderic said. 'That's one thing the Romans do so damned well – make wine.'

Gunhild realised that her brother was quite drunk. He had been sitting alone for some time, and must have already downed several goblets of the intoxicating drink.

Gunhild sensed that her chance to delve into the subject of her proposed marriage had finally arrived. So far on the journey Gunderic had insisted on total secrecy.

The sound of raucous singing came from the other end of the deck where the rest of the warriors were.

'It's good to hear the old songs,' Gunderic said. 'The chants of our people. They tell the tales of who we are. Where we came from. The Lore of the Burgundars. Soon we will be home, sister.'

He smiled and raised his goblet in a toast.

'Home, Gunderic?' Gunhild said. 'What is home any more? We grew up in Vorbetomagus. The Rhine was where we swam as children. This journey we are on will end... where? A new land?'

'Our home is wherever our folk are,' Gunderic said. 'It's not about land. If we are with our own folk, who cares where we are?'

'You've seen this new land?' Gunhild said.

'I have,' Gunderic said. His eyes lit up. 'It is beautiful. There are meadows, rich and fertile. There is barley, grapes, there are even salt mines. The mountains are high but they rise all around my kingdom. They protect it like a ring of teeth.'

'And what of my husband-to-be?' Gunhild said, 'Why do you want me to marry this man I've never met? Can you at least tell me his name?'

Gunderic glanced around to see no one was close enough to hear. Then he took a swig of wine. He pursed his lips and met Gunhild's gaze.

'It's Sigurd Volsung,' he said.

'You're joking!' Gunhild said, her eyes widening. She blew out her cheeks as she recalled the blond-haired boy, the son of one of their father's noblemen. 'What age is he? Ten?'

'Perhaps last time you saw him, yes,' Gunderic said, smirking. 'He's all grown up now.'

He grunted. 'That's an understatement, actually,' he went on, pouring himself another goblet of wine, 'He's huge. A giant among men. Tall, broad-shouldered, strong as an ox. After the fall of Vorbetomagus he spent some time in hiding, working for a blacksmith, which may account for the power of his arms. He's not too strong when it comes to wits though. He will be my champion like Hagan's father was for our father.'

'I remember Sigurd's father,' Gunhild said. 'He was a mighty hero of our people too. Like Godegisil. But he was a nobleman, Gunderic. I am the daughter of a *king*.'

'His father died with the other heroes of our folk at Vorbetomagus,' Gunderic said. His mood became suddenly intense and he leaned across the table. 'We must build a new warrior horde, sister. With new traditions to go with what is left of the old ones. It won't be easy but we will do it. We have to or our folk will be lost again. In this world, those not strong enough to protect themselves are the first to fall. It happened to us before. It *won't* happen again. When I am king, I won't let it.'

He spat the words through clenched teeth, eyes blazing.

'And I have a role to play in that?' Gunhild said. 'Is that why you want me to marry Sigurd?'

'No,' her brother said. 'And it's not my idea, by the way. It's his.'

'His?' Gunhild said. 'Does he even know who I am?'

'He remembers the beautiful princess from long ago, before the Burgundar kingdom fell for the first time,' Gunderic said. 'And there is something else. I hesitate to tell you this, sister, as it will swell your already large head. Tales of the fall of the Burgundars at Vorbetomagus have spread all over the Empire since then. You won't be aware of it but one has sprung up that says you are the most beautiful woman in the world: the lost princess of the Burgundars and her uncannily fair looks has become a tale told around the hearths of tribes across Gaul, Germanica and beyond. Sigurd has heard these legends.'

Gunhild could not help a little smile. Her good looks were the only treasure she possessed now and she was well aware of their value.

'So without actually seeing me this Sigurd Volsung says he wants to marry me?' she said. 'Because of a legend? He must be as dull-witted as you say.'

'It is enough that everyone else *thinks* you are the most beautiful woman in the world for him to want to marry you,' Gunderic said, refilling his goblet. 'He is... like that, I'm afraid.'

Gunhild rolled her eyes. She knew exactly the type of man Sigurd was likely to be.

'What a charming match you have made for me, brother,' she said. 'I hope whatever the price was, it was worth it.'

'Oh it is,' Gunderic said, the smile returning to his lips. He glanced around again, as if to check if any of the others had moved closer. 'I can assure you of that.'

'There's no one to hear us but the wind and the seabirds,' Gunhild said. 'So you can tell me everything.'

She levelled her gaze with Gunderic's.

'And let me assure you, brother,' she said in a cold, hard voice. 'Unless you tell me everything, including what *I* will get out of these arrangements, and I can see *why* you expect me to enter a match that is beneath me, there will be no marriage.'

His lip curled a little.

'You think you have a choice in any of this?' he said. 'A landless woman with no wealth? What could you do to stop it?'

Gunhild reached across the table and grasped her brother's forearm. Her long nails dug into his flesh like the talons of an eagle grabbing a rabbit.

'There are many paths open to me,' she said. 'Don't fool

yourself that there isn't. I could poison this Sigurd Volsung's drink. I could poison yours.'

Gunderic looked down at his wine.

'I could run away in the night,' she went on, 'and if you found me I could end my own life and then you would have nothing: no sister to marry off to get whatever it is you're getting. In fact, I could do that right now. I could jump off this ship—'

'No!' her brother cried out. She could see the look of panic on his face and knew her words had had the desired effect. Her heart leapt. She was not completely powerless after all. Whatever her brother's scheme was, she was key to it.

She could use this to her own advantage.

'Then tell me everything,' Gunhild said, with a murderous smile. 'Why am I to marry this boy?'

Gunderic sighed and took a hefty swig of wine. He met her gaze once more. His blue eyes were steady now and showed no sign of their former intoxication. It was as if the seriousness of whatever was in his mind had chased away the fumes of the wine.

'No,' he said in a firm voice. 'I cannot.'

'I meant what I said, Gunderic,' Gunhild said.

'I have no doubt about that,' Gunderic said. 'But you will just have to trust me on this. It's not just for my sake but for yours also. And for the sake of what few remain of our folk. If General Aetius, or any Roman for that matter, finds out why I need you to marry Sigurd Volsung, they will kill every last one of us. There will be Burgundars nailed to crosses every step along the Via Helvetica from Geneva to Ravenna. You and I will be on the first two.'

Gunhild let go of his hand. She could see he was serious.

'When we are safe within the boundaries of our own kingdom,' Gunderic said, 'our new kingdom, away from prying eyes and ears of any Romans, then I shall tell you everything. I promise. Until then we must not talk of it.'

'I see,' Gunhild said with a curt nod. 'Very well. It had better be good.'

'Oh, it will be,' her brother said, the grin returning to his face. 'Trust me on that.'

CHAPTER FIFTEEN

THE SEA VOYAGE finally ended at Arelate on the southern coast of Gaul. The ship sailed up a wide canal to a fortified harbour packed with ships from all over the known world, from Greek and Egyptian trading ships to several huge *naves longae*, warships of the Roman navy. They had not been in port long before a delegation of Roman officials arrived. They were looking for Gunderic.

The welcoming committee were civil servants and senior military personnel sent by the Magister Militum to ensure the king of the Empire's newest *foederati* made it safely to his new kingdom. If Gunderic had been tight-lipped on Gunhild's marriage plans and the treasure of their father on the voyage, he was silent as a stone now they were surrounded by representatives of the Roman state.

Indeed, Gunderic appeared more Roman than the Romans themselves, grumbling about politics and the crumbling state of the Empire with the civil servants and swapping old war stories from his time with the Army with the soldiers. They stayed one night in the thriving port and Gunderic even insisted they attend the *venationes* and beast fights at the amphitheatre.

'There was a time when we could have seen gladiators fight here, but not *these* days,' he complained as they sipped wine and ate dainties. He sounded like some old senator, dismayed at the steep decline in Roman *virtus* the current age had brought.

The next day they set off north on the Via Agrippa, the

main road that would take them towards the province of Maxima Sequanorum, where the new lands of the Burgundars lay. Letters provided by the officials allowed the Burgundars to use Imperial horses they collected from a *stabula* on the edge of the city. A military escort in the form of two *turma* units of cavalry accompanied them along the long, straight road.

The passports they had been supplied with allowed them to stay in *mansiones*. This network of hostelries run by the state allowed those travelling on Imperial business to change horses or rest for the night. They were comfortable enough, though functional rather than luxurious, but compared to the rat-infested hall of King Half with its leaking thatch, each *mansio* was like a palace to Gunhild.

The commander of the cavalry was gruff with his own men but polite to Gunderic and Gunhild. The Roman and Burgundar contingents of warriors maintained a respectful distance from one another, even in the evenings, but it was never left in any doubt that it was the Romans who were in charge.

Gunhild believed her brother about the seriousness of the consequences if the Romans found out whatever it was he was up to, so she did not mention it on the journey. They were never alone so there was little chance to press the matter anyway.

It took six days to reach Lugdunum, the capitol of Maxima Sequanorum, then they turned east on the Via Vienne Aust, the Roman road that led to Geneva.

Craggy mountains, their summits covered in snow, rose to the north as they travelled on. A mighty, wide river wound its way back and forth beside the road. It rained every day and the horses' hooves sometimes skidded on the paving stones of the road. The countryside looked fertile but the further they travelled, the more deserted it appeared to be. The farmsteads they passed became further and further apart. Eventually, all the settlements they rode past were abandoned and falling into ruin.

'Where are the people?' Gunhild said as they rode along. 'I presume someone lived here before General Aetius was so generous as to give it to us.'

'The Allobroges tribe lived here since the days of Julius Caesar,' Gunderic said. 'But the Alemanni draw ever closer from the north-east. They raid into these lands and life on the borders has become too dangerous for ordinary folk. Most have moved away.'

'Driving out the Alemanni will be your first job, Lord King,' Lucius, the cavalry commander said. He used a respectful title but his tone of voice left no doubt that he was conveying the expectations that rested on the Empire's new allies. 'It won't be easy. The Alemanni are tough bastards. But that's what the Magister Militum put you here for: to stop the Alemanni from bothering the good citizens of the Empire.'

'And it leaves plenty of room for our folk to move into,' Gunderic said to Gunhild.

As they moved further into the territory, signs of that movement began to appear. The occasional abandoned farmsteads and settlements began to show signs of repair and new habitation. They were ringed by newly dug defensive ditches and palisade fences, their freshly sharpened tops still white. Smoke drifted from within into the clear blue sky. Fields around them showed signs of cultivation. There were flocks of sheep and herds of cows. Gunhild's heart quickened when she saw wolves, lightning, sun wheels and even black eagles painted on the gates of the palisades. They were crude but unmistakable: the emblems of the clans of the Burgundars.

The road led towards a very large settlement at the point where the wide river ran into an enormous lake, quite easily the largest Gunhild had ever seen. If it were not for the outlines of ragged mountains visible on the far shores she would have sworn they were riding towards the sea. The town had a wall of stone which the Romans must have been involved with building. There was also a great wooden bridge stretching across the river's mouth. It joined the main town to some sort of offshoot of it on the lake shore across the river. There was a large harbour in the lake filled with boats. Their masts made a little forest beside the water.

'That's Geneva,' Gunderic said, pointing to the city on the lake shore. 'It will be our new home.'

News of their arrival spread and as they got closer to the city people began to come out to line the roads. They waved and cheered as the company rode by. Gunhild did not recognise any specific faces, but they looked and felt familiar: the way they wore their hair, their clothes, and above all the tongue they shouted greetings in. They were Burgundars.

Gunhild felt tears sting her eyes and found it hard to swallow. The feeling of relief was overwhelming. She really was back among the people she thought were gone forever.

The expectation on the faces of the people also made her remember she was not just back among her own folk. She was part of the royal clan of the Burgundars, the daughter of their last king and the sister of their new one. She was a rare surviving link to their past and it was now her role to help lead them into whatever future awaited them in this new land.

There was also a physical difference in the crowds of the people lining the road and singing old familiar songs, compared to the old days in Vorbetomagus. There were a lot of young people. Gunhild felt she was older than most of them. There were a few old men and women, but very few men in their prime. It seemed most of the folk who had survived the massacre at Vorbetomagus were the ones small enough to hide, fast enough to run away, or too old to have gone anywhere near the battle. Or perhaps the rest of their surviving men were still in the Roman Army. The warriors who had accompanied them from the land of the Danes made up a small contingent. Gunhild felt a pang of worry. Would they be able to protect their new borders without a horde of fighting men?

At the gates of the city the crowds were more packed. A delegation of official-looking people stood in the middle of the road, waiting for the arrival of the royal siblings. One wore a toga, notable as it was starting to go out of fashion, even for those in public life. He was middle-aged and balding with a large belly. Beside him was a man in the robes and headgear of a Christian bishop.

They reined the horses to a halt and dismounted. Their cavalry escort remained on horseback, each trooper eyeing the crowd for any hint of trouble.

'Welcome to your kingdom, Lord King,' the churchman said in Latin, dipping his head to Gunderic. 'I am Publius Salonius and I am happy to say that the Holy Father, the Pope, has appointed me as bishop of this region.'

'Has he?' Gunderic said. 'How good of him. I wasn't aware of requesting any ecclesiastical assistance just yet. I have barely sat down myself on my new throne.'

'The Holy Father was most anxious that this new kingdom is founded in the right way, at least from a Christian sense,' Bishop Salonius said, with a condescending smile. 'He is aware of the Burgundar people's previous errors of faith and their adherence to the Arian heresy. He is most keen that this rebirth of the Burgundar kingdom will from its very inception be within the bosom of the True Faith, that is, the Church of Rome. It is my joyous task to set up the Church in this land where it has been so far abandoned.'

'Of course, of course,' Gunderic said. 'And I share his ambitions. I was in the Army, of course, and we were taught the True Religion there. Let me know whatever you need.'

'Well, Lord King,' the bishop said with an apologetic smile, 'unfortunately these undertakings are expensive. The Church will need financial support if she is to grow here. Substantial financial support.'

'Gaius Marcus Flavius, Lord King,' the balding man in the toga said. 'While Bishop Salonius represents spiritual matters I am here on state matters. I will provide you with the necessary guidance that will ensure you can set up the necessary civil apparatus to run an efficient Roman client kingdom.'

'The Empire has been very generous to me,' Gunderic said, smiling. 'Now let us go to our new home.'

As the procession entered the city, the sense of dereliction there was palpable. There were many stone Roman buildings, but there were holes in their walls and roofs and many of them looked empty. The paved road petered out mere steps within the walls, its stones robbed for other purposes and replaced by wooden planks.

At the same time there were many signs of repairs. There had been rudimentary fixes to some of the crumbling walls. Thatch filled the holes in shingled roofs and the street was lined with crowds of people.

Gunhild felt excitement coursing through her. The faces of the people they passed recognisable as Burgundars, like those they had passed outside. They cheered and waved as the royal siblings passed. Gunhild noted again the looks of expectation in the eyes of those in the crowd.

In the centre of the city they came to a large hall. It was long and narrow, with great double doors at one end, but like the rest of the city it had seen better days. One of the doors was askew. It looked like it had fallen on its hinges and was now jammed half open. Birds flew in and out of the disintegrating roof, for there were many holes in the rotting thatch.

'This was the grand hall of the king of the Allobroges,' Gunderic said as they approached the entrance. 'The people who lived here before. But it was abandoned with the rest of the city when the Alemanni moved within striking distance of Geneva.'

'And does that not mean that we are now in striking distance?' Gunhild said.

'The Allobroges were conquered by Rome four centuries ago,' Gunderic said, making a face. 'They became *civilised*

– soft. They were too reliant on Rome's army and not on the strength of their own sword arms for protection. When the Army was stretched too far, fighting crises in the rest of the Empire and unable to protect the Allobroges, they had no choice but to move somewhere safer. We Burgundars are not like that. We are strong enough to look after ourselves. That's why General Aetius has granted us their land.'

Gunhild looked around. There were many crowding around them, certainly enough to make the Roman cavalry nervous, but their numbers were still meagre enough, especially when it came to men of fighting age.

'What if the Alemanni raid again?' Gunhild said. 'Do we have enough warriors to defend ourselves? What if *they* decide they want this land instead of us.'

'They are not strong enough yet,' her brother said. 'Otherwise they would already be here. They will come, eventually, and when they do we will be ready for them. We *must* be ready for them.'

'You better be,' the Roman cavalry commander said with a guffaw. 'It's what you're here for.'

He, the civil servant and the bishop all laughed. Gunhild caught the glowering look her brother shot in the Romans' direction. The position and purpose of the Burgundars was clear. Gunderic might be a king of his people, but when it came to the Roman Empire, such a barbarian chieftain was still lower in the pecking order than a Roman bishop and even a civil servant.

'And so we are now a buffer between the barbarians and the road to Rome,' Gunhild said.

The smile faded from the face of Flavius, replaced by an unmistakable look of contempt. He cocked his head back so he looked down his nose at her.

'Roman women know their place in society,' he said. 'Their opinion, especially on political matters, is of no consequence.'

'Come now,' Gunderic said, forcing a smile to his face.

'Let's not fall out so soon. My sister was always a girl of strong opinions. Don't let her irritate you. Shall we go in?'

Gunhild glared at her brother, her cheeks flushing. At the sight of it the Romans smiled again. Gunderic led the way into the hall, entering through the jammed open door. The cavalry troopers formed a line across the entrance, stopping the crowds from following.

The inside of the hall was gloomy. Deep shadows masked the corners of the long central room. The floor was tessellated but many tiles were missing, leaving gaps in the mosaic pictures of heroes, gods and twisting vegetation. There were two large fire pits filled with the mouldering ash of long-dead blazes. A long table stretched across the length of the hall, disappearing into the darkness at the end. There were wooden platters and overturned goblets on it, draped in heavy blankets of cobwebs. The occasional chair and bench sat shoved back from the table as if long ago feasters had finished their meal, left in a hurry and never returned.

The air was heavy with the stench of mould and rancid grease. Dust motes circled in the shafts of sunlight that came through the holes in the roof above. As well as the birds that flew through those holes, there also came a scratching and rustling from the thatch that made Gunhild's skin crawl; it was the unmistakable sound of rats. At some time in the past a seed had also come through one of the holes in the thatch and taken root in the dirt floor. Now a young tree reached up, poking its branches towards the light.

'This is quite the royal palace,' Gunhild said.

'One day, sister,' Gunderic said, ignoring her sarcasm, 'this will be the most magnificent of feasting halls. Kings will come from all over the world. Mighty warriors will hear of its fame and beauty and come here to pledge allegiance to my warband.'

He spread his arms wide and looked all around, his expression suggesting he was imagining the place far differently to what lay at present before his eyes.

'So this is Gunhild, the most beautiful woman in the world?'

A new voice swam from out of the gloom at the far end of the hall, making all in their party turn around. He spoke in the Burgundar tongue though with a northern accent. Gunhild peered hard and saw for the first time that a man sat at the far end of the long table. He was reclining in a grand wooden chair so large and ornately carved that it must once have belonged to the king of the Allobroges. He had both feet on the table, crossed at the ankles, and his hands clasped behind his head.

He unclasped his hands, swung his legs off the table and stood up. Gunhild's eyes widened. Flavius the civil servant frowned. The cavalry commander stiffened his back and the bishop drew a sharp intake of breath.

The man now standing at the end of the table was a giant.

CHAPTER SIXTEEN

THE MAN WALKED forward, approaching along the side of the table. Even at a distance it was easy to see he was a head and shoulders taller than anyone else there. Those shoulders were broad, his arms like the thick branches of a tree, knotted and bulging with muscle and sinew.

As he walked into a shaft of sunlight that pierced the gloom from a hole in the roof, they could see that his hair was red-gold. It was thick and long, hanging around his shoulders in curling locks. He had a short, trimmed beard the same colour as his hair and a pair of the most piercing grey eyes Gunhild had ever seen. He was young – younger than Gunhild or Gunderic, perhaps nineteen winters or so old.

This must be the man I am to marry, Gunhild thought, as twin sensations of relief and approval surged in her heart. He was much more than the callow minor nobleman she had been expecting.

He was dressed for war. Though he wore no helmet, he bore a huge sword in a jewelled scabbard under his left arm. He wore curious armour. Unlike the countless interlinked metal rings that made up most warriors' mail shirts, this man wore a long leather tunic. On top of this, countless small rectangular iron plates were threaded in rows covering his whole body to halfway down his arms and thighs. Each metal scale had been polished and shone like a mirror. Even in the gloom of the hall they reflected points of light in every direction. He had the look of a giant metal reptile, a dragon walking on its hind legs. Each step of his heavy boots was accompanied by the rattling and clinking of his metal scales.

'Allow me to introduce Lord Sigurd of the Volsung clan,' Gunderic said. He was grinning in a way that reminded Gunhild of their father when he showed off his greatest deerhounds to noblemen.

'You really are as beautiful as the legends say you are,' the big man said, staring at Gunhild with his strangely compelling eyes.

'That's Byzantine armour, isn't it?' The cavalry commander spoke in Latin. 'You don't see much of that here in the Western Empire. Where were you in the Army?'

Sigurd slid his gaze towards the Roman, then looked back at Gunhild.

'My lady, with you by my side we will be the most famous couple in the world,' he said in Burgundar.

The cavalry officer frowned, unhappy to be ignored.

Gunhild opened her mouth but no words came out. She did not know what to say. The big man's gaze seemed to captivate her. She felt her heart begin to race. Sigurd's size and heavily muscled body at once frightened and excited her.

'That's quite a sword, too,' Flavius said, his eyes narrowing. His question appeared to be a pointed one.

Sigurd looked away from Gunhild and smiled. He patted the sheath of the great sword.

'This old thing?' he said, now speaking in the Roman tongue. 'It's just something I found lying around.'

'Did you now,' Flavius said. 'Just *where* did you find it?'

'There will be time to talk of these things later,' Gunderic said. 'Right now we have more important business to attend to: the marriage of my sister.'

'What?' Gunhild said. 'Now?'

'Why not?' Gunderic said. 'There is not a moment to lose. We have much work to do.'

'But I have just met this man,' Gunhild said.

'And you have already agreed to the marriage,' Gunderic said. He looked her straight in the eye. Gunhild knew he was trying to tell her that there was more to this. She could tell he was silently pleading with her to just go along with it.

'It is my great pleasure to officiate at your marriage today, my lady,' the bishop said, stepping towards her. He had a sickly smile on his face. 'This will be my first service to the royal family.'

With stunning dexterity for one his size and in armour, Sigurd Volsung skipped over the table and took Gunhild by the arm.

'My lady?' he said, cocking his other arm towards the broken doors at the end of the hall.

It became clear to Gunhild that she was the only one there for whom the events unfolding around her were a surprise. A little dumbfounded, she let herself be led down the hall floor.

The little company left the hall once more. Outside, the waiting crowds cheered to see them again. At the sight of Sigurd and Gunhild now arm in arm they cheered even louder. It was clear Sigurd Volsung was no stranger to them.

Gunhild was led across the square outside the great hall to a church. Like any other Roman church it was built in the style of a basilica: tall, and oblong in shape, with large double doors at the entrance. It was as dilapidated as the other buildings, but a new iron cross was fixed to the wall above the doors. Inside, the dust and cobwebs had been swept away by a company of slaves who scurried away when Gunhild and the others entered.

At that point Sigurd let go of Gunhild's arm and strode ahead to the altar. Gunderic stepped over and linked arms with his sister.

'I know it should have been our father who brings you to be married,' he said with a forced smile. 'But I will have that honour today.'

He grasped the wrist of the arm he had linked with hers. His grip was tight, as if he was worried she might flee.

The bishop went ahead to the altar, turned and glared at Gunhild, a stern expression on his face. The cavalry commander and the civil servant both looked on with similar, haughty looks.

It was clear that this marriage was about to go ahead, no matter what Gunhild herself wanted. Panic rose in her heart. This was all happening too fast. She may have reluctantly consented to this marriage at her brother's entreaties but now it felt like Gunderic and these Romans were rushing her into this alliance. Were they frightened she might change her mind?

The thought of that calmed her a little. If they were worried she might back out of the marriage then it must be very important to them. Perhaps she was not so powerless after all.

Gunhild looked around her. The church was now filling with other Burgundars, these better dressed than the people in the fields and streets. There were no Roman togas, but their tunics and breeches were of fine wool, denoting both wealth and higher social status. They had emblems embroidered into the left shoulders of the cloaks they wore: wolves, bears, lightning symbols and sun wheels. Among them she finally saw faces she recognised: these were the survivors of the noble clans of the Burgundars.

The sight sent her into a turmoil of emotions. Despite her unease at the rush to marry her off, her heart soared again at this proof she was once more among her own people. They looked at her with the same adoring, expectant looks as the ordinary folk in the street had.

Gunhild took a deep breath. It was clear this marriage meant much to them. If anything, she would go through with this for them.

As she was led towards the altar, Gunhild wondered if she would suddenly wake up and find it was all a dream, and that she was still lying in Half's bed in the land of the Danes.

Instead, as her brother let go of her arm and she joined Sigurd standing before the altar, the others lined up behind them, and the bishop held up his right hand as he began to intone words in the tongue of Rome. All but Gunhild bowed their heads. The wedding was underway.

Gunhild glanced at the big man with the strange eyes who stood beside her. The latent power in his massive body was frightening. What sort of a man was this Sigurd, really? He bore himself with a confidence that was alluring. He was good-looking and the reception the crowd had given him showed he was popular. That boded well.

As the bishop continued to chant the words of the ceremony Sigurd glanced at her. His face broke out into a grin and he looked like the cat who had got the cream. Gunhild realised he also put great store in this marriage. Clearly, having the woman believed to be the most beautiful in the world as his bride was important to his own standing. By marrying him Gunhild was enhancing this man's reputation like a jewelled pommel on a sword hilt.

She smiled. This powerful young man was still frightening, but if she could tame him to her will, perhaps she could use that for her own advantage. Her beauty had always been her most effective weapon against the power held by men.

The bishop completed the mass, raising a chalice of wine and blessing the host. He chanted on in the Roman tongue then at a significant point said something to Sigurd. The big man screwed up his face in annoyed incomprehension.

'The ring,' Gunderic prompted from behind the couple at the altar.

Realisation dawned on Sigurd's face and he reached into a leather pouch tied at his waist. He withdrew a ring, lifted Gunhild's hand and slid it onto her finger. It was a little too big, which meant it slipped on with ease.

Gunhild gasped. The ring was gold – pure gold – almost as thick as her little finger. The weight of it was heavy on her hand. It was worth a fortune... A smile dawning on her face, she looked up and saw Sigurd – now her husband – beaming down at her.

The bishop pronounced they were now husband and wife. Sigurd cupped the back of Gunhild's head in one hand and crushed his lips against hers. A murmur of approval went round the church. On Gunhild's part there was just surprise. Sigurd's lips were pursed but passionless. This was a gesture that cemented an agreement, like the handshake she had seen horse dealers make after sealing a sale.

Someone must have signalled to the crowds outside as the sound of louder cheering could be heard. Amid a tide of applause, smiles and good wishes, Sigurd took Gunhild's hand and led her back down the aisle.

Gunderic skipped ahead of them and led the way out of the doors, presenting the newlywed couple to the crowds waiting outside.

'And now, we will feast!' he announced.

CHAPTER SEVENTEEN

THEY WENT BACK to the hall and the remaining big door was flung open. The big long table had been cleared of the remains of the long-abandoned feast and slaves had lit the long fire pits in the floor and placed torches in brackets in the walls. As the people flooded in, the royal party sat down at the top of the table. Gunderic took the high seat where Sigurd had previously sat.

People began flocking into the hall carrying platters of food they must have cooked in their houses. These they laid on the table. For a royal wedding, it was a rather meagre banquet, but there was plenty of it. It looked like the meat was the bounty of hunting in the nearby fields and woods: there was no beef or lamb but lots of venison and fowl. This was confirmed when a young aristocratic-looking man in an expensive wool cloak, a large hunting horn slung over his shoulder by a leather strap, approached Gunderic where he sat.

'You've done well, Heiric,' he said. 'We will not starve with you as the Hunt Master of the new royal house.'

The young man took off the horn and handed it to Gunderic.

'As the Hunt Master of our people,' he said, bowing his head. 'I wish to present this to you, my lord.'

Gunderic took the horn and placed it under the table.

Along with the game there was plenty of fish from the enormous lake nearby, as well as bread and vegetables. Peasant food, Gunhild thought to herself. There was plenty of fine wine, however. The rich red beverage made from the abundant local grapes was in seemingly endless supply.

Gunhild tried her best to talk to her new husband, to try to find out something about him, but there was always someone else at the table wanting to poke their nose into the conversation. She did at last snatch a few moments between just the two of them.

'I remember you as a boy,' she said. 'You were gangly but not as strong as you are now.'

She ran her forefinger along Sigurd's meaty left forearm that rested on the tabletop. He smiled at her, catching her gaze with his strangely alluring eyes.

'Did you get all these muscles working with the blacksmith?' she said.

Sigurd's smile disappeared, replaced by a scowl. He snatched his arm away.

'I'm no longer the slave of a blacksmith.'

As the evening wore into night, the Burgundars began to sing the songs of their folk; ancient chants, lively choruses and arcane dirges that spoke of heroes and villains, half-forgotten gods, glorious victories and direful betrayals: the lore that made up the story of the Burgundar people.

'Barbarians can certainly sing,' Flavius said.

The others around him nodded.

'There is little intellectual content to it,' Bishop Salonius argued. 'The words are all vulgar, battles and murders. But the tune and timbre somehow plucks at the heartstrings of the listener...'

'Any more of that wine, Gunderic?' Lucius asked. His face was growing flushed and his eyes watery. 'It's damn fine stuff.'

Gunderic signalled to a slave hovering nearby with a large jug. The man hurried forward to fill the Roman's cup.

'I'm glad you like it,' Gunderic said. 'It's from my new realm. I sent some out to your men as well.'

'They better damn well not drink it,' the cavalry commander

said. 'They're supposed to be on duty. Any man who touches it I'll have flogged. I trust my decurion, though. Marcus will make sure none of them touch a drop until off duty.'

Most of the cavalry troopers had been ordered to post a guard outside the hall in case anything untoward happened. The lucky elite – the officers – had joined the rest of the feasters at the long table. Its benches groaned under the weight of perhaps two hundred people. Lively conversation and laughter filled the air.

'You've really fallen on your feet here, Gunderic,' Flavius said. 'Good wine. Plentiful fertile land. No natives to wrestle for it. Not yet, anyway. Aetius must think much of you to have granted you all this.'

'Or he has a great fear of the Alemanni,' Gunhild said.

The Romans glanced at her, scowls of irritation on their faces.

'Of course, at any grand feast in Rome women would not sit at the top of the table with the men,' the bishop said to Gunderic. 'We have much to teach you about how to run a civilised court if you are to be a good foederati. Rome has been good to you, and she expects a return on her investments.'

'It's not the Alemanni Aetius is scared of,' Flavius said. The effects of the wine were becoming evident in his eyes, which appeared glassy and rolled a little. Gunhild had heard the Romans only drank wine watered down, unlike the 'barbarians' who preferred the taste undiluted. 'It's the Huns.'

'The *Huns*?' Gunderic said. 'Aren't they your allies?'

'*Our* allies, you mean,' Lucius said, casting reproachful looks both at Gunderic and Flavius.

'The Alemanni lands are beyond those mountains, and beyond them, across the Danube, are the Hun lands,' Flavius slurred, ignoring the disapproval of Lucius. Politics was clearly his favourite subject. 'If the Huns turn on us in the west – as they already have done in the east – and they link up with the Alemanni, which they've done in the past, then with our armies busy in Gaul fighting the Bacaudae and the Visigoths, there is nothing to stop them pouring straight through into the heart of the Empire at Ravenna. It will be the end of Rome as we know it.'

'Well, there is something here now to stop them...' Bishop Salonius said with a nasty smile.

'Us,' Gunderic said. His voice was cold.

There was a heavy silence for a moment.

'Don't worry about that,' Lucius said, breaking the mood. 'Bleda is king of the Huns in the West. He is our friend. He'll keep his hot-headed little brother in check. If it was Attila we had to deal with I'd be worried. But Bleda can be relied on.'

'And Attila can't?' Gunderic said.

Lucius grunted.

'The only thing you can rely on Attila for is treachery,' he said. 'A stab in the back. The man is the Devil incarnate. Cruel, vicious, greedy. Utterly ruthless. The only thing that frightens him is his brother Bleda, who like I said is on our side, thanks be to God.'

'Be assured,' the bishop said with a condescending smile as he laid his right hand on Gunderic's left hand, that rested on the table top, 'Bleda is a friend of Rome. I have it on good authority that he is even interested in joining the true Church. God works in mysterious ways. He will keep us all safe from the swords of devils like Attila.'

An expression crossed the cavalry commander's face, as if he remembered something through the fog of wine fumes.

'That reminds me,' he said, turning to Sigurd. 'That sword of yours, lad. It's very impressive. Reminds me of a Hun sword in some ways. Where did you get it?'

'I told you before,' Sigurd said, speaking through clenched teeth. 'I found it.'

'It has a Hunnish curve to it,' Lucius said. 'Let me have a look at it.'

Sigurd just looked at him.

'I said, let me take a look at it,' the cavalry officer said once more, his words now bearing a hint of menace. 'Gunderic, tell your dog here that when a Roman officer asks for something he should give it to him. Otherwise the Roman won't be so polite next time.'

Sigurd and Lucius locked eyes for a moment. Then Sigurd looked at Gunderic. Gunhild saw her brother respond with a nod.

'Good,' Lucius said, holding out his hand across the table.

'You look with your eyes,' Sigurd said, sliding off the baldric that held his sword under his left arm. He held his sheathed sword level over the table, one hand on the hilt, one hand on the bottom of the scabbard.

The animosity between the two men hung in the air like the build-up to a thunderstorm. It began to spread through the hall as conversation died and all eyes turned to look at the big man with the sword and the Roman confronting him across the table.

'Unsheath it,' Lucius said. His smile gone again. 'I want to take a better look at the blade.'

'And why would you want to do that?' Sigurd said.

'As I said, it has a Hunnish curve,' Lucius said. 'I wish to see if there is any writing incised on the blade.'

'Is that important?' Sigurd said.

'It might be,' Lucius said. 'Just do what I say.'

He and Flavius exchanged a glance that had some sort of meaning, though Gunhild, watching on, could not fathom what it was. Around them a hush had descended on the whole of the table.

'As you wish,' Sigurd said, drawing the blade from its scabbard. Torchlight danced across the polished surface of the steel, which was rippled like a still pond that had frozen to ice just after a stone had been dropped in it. There were indeed words incised down the middle of the blade. They were in strange lettering that Gunhild did not recognise.

'My word!' the bishop said. 'I've never seen such a beautiful sword. What do the letters say?'

'They bear the name of the sword and tell of the curse placed upon it,' Sigurd said. He rotated the blade in one hand so it stood upright.

'The sword has a name?' Flavius said. He licked his lips as if excited by what the answer might be.

'It is the Sword of the War God,' Sigurd said, regarding the blade with a faraway look, as if fascinated by the scintillations of light that danced across its mirrored surface.

Lucius and Flavius exchanged another glance. This time there was no mistaking what it meant. It was a look of triumph.

Lucius stood up. All signs of befuddlement from the wine were gone.

'Hand the sword over,' he said. 'General Aetius asked me to be on the lookout for a certain sword while here and this is it. It looks like the general's suspicions about the Burgundars are correct.'

'Suspicions?' Gunderic said, rising to his feet himself. 'What are these *suspicions*?'

'You know full well, Gunderic,' Lucius said. 'Your kingship is the gift of Rome and she can take it away as easily as she granted it. Now tell your big lout of a warrior here to hand over that sword or you'll be back cleaning out Roman cavalry stables before you know what's hit you.'

'Unfortunately I did not get the chance to explain, my Roman friend,' Sigurd said. 'There is a legend associated with this sword, which was why I was reluctant to draw it. Long ago dwarfs and elves cursed the blade, so that whenever it is drawn, it must taste blood.'

'What do I care of barbarian legends?' Lucius shouted. 'Hand over that sword!'

He thrust his hand forward again.

In one swift movement so fast it caught everyone by surprise, Sigurd grasped the sword hilt in both hands and raised it. He brought the blade down, severing the Roman's lower arm in a diagonal cut from the inside of his wrist to the outside of his elbow. Lucius's hand and a triangle of his lower right arm dropped with a meaty thump onto the table.

The Roman screamed, as much from astonishment as agony. His eyes bulged as he grabbed his ruined right arm with his left fist.

'Oh no,' Flavius groaned from his seat.

Sigurd pulled the sword back then plunged it into the cavalry officer's guts. Its point exploded from Lucius's back as he doubled over around the blade. The Roman gave a gasp of agony as Sigurd wrenched the sword out of the Roman's body, splattering the table and the diners around him in a shower of bright red blood. All was still silent, though a woman seated nearby let out a startled 'Oh!'

'Please, don't!' Flavius pleaded. He held both hands up and lowered his head, as if unable to meet the stern gaze of Sigurd's light-coloured eyes. 'I don't deserve this—'

Sigurd's blade flashed through the air again, this time in a mighty sideways swipe that took Flavius's head from his shoulders. As it made its deadly sweep it also severed both of the civil servant's upheld hands.

Gunderic grabbed the great hunting horn from under the table and rose to his feet. He raised the horn to his lips and blew a great blast that thundered through the hall.

The hall erupted into shouts, screams and cries of pain. Gunhild looked around and saw the cavalry officers on their feet, some with their tunics splashed with blood. They were struggling with Burgundars who had fallen upon them at the sound of the horn. The torchlight flashed on knife blades.

CHAPTER EIGHTEEN

'YOU PLANNED ALL this?' Gunhild said to Gunderic.
                'I couldn't tell you,' her brother said. 'In case the
Romans found out. We had to take them by surprise.'

The door of the hall burst open. A Roman cavalry trooper
came stumbling in. He was clutching a stab wound in his chest
that had pierced his mail shirt. Blood pulsed down his side.

'Treachery!' he shouted. 'Commander, we're under attack.'

His eyes roved around the room, taking in his dying commander who was now curled on the floor, his lifeblood spilling
from his punctured stomach and severed arm, the decapitated
Flavius, and the other cavalry officers who were struggling for
their lives with the very people who until moments before they
had been exchanging pleasantries with over dinner.

'To me, your Holiness!' the trooper shouted to the bishop.

Sigurd whirled around, bringing his sword to bear on the
priest. But Salonius was already gone, scrabbling under the
table. He rolled to his feet on the other side then started off in
a staggering run towards the doors at the far end of the hall.

Gunderic drew his own sword. He and Sigurd stalked down
the table to where the remaining cavalry officers were fighting
with the Burgundars. In moments the Romans lay sprawled on
the floor, blood spilling from slit throats or sword wounds in
their backs or bellies.

The bishop had made it to the doors and out into the
darkness outside, flanked by the wounded cavalry trooper.

'After them!' Gunderic shouted and the folk in the hall all charged towards the door. Gunhild joined the throng through the entrance and out into the night. Outside in the city other Burgundars were flocking down the streets bearing torches and weapons. The ordinary folk carried pitchforks, spades and other farm implements, or old weapons: spears or rusty swords. Gunhild saw alongside them companies of young men in war gear, the warriors whose earlier absence had concerned her. They were poorly equipped – some had ill-fitting helmets, some had rusty mail shirts that still bore the holes where blades had killed their previous owners – but all their weapons were polished and serviceable, and the looks in their eyes showed they were deadly serious about the work they had come to do.

There was another bloody fight underway. The square was littered with more corpses, both Roman soldiers and the attacking Burgundars who had surprised them. Steam rose from the pools of blood into the chilled night air. The cavalry troopers, armed but on foot, had lost several men, killed or wounded. Yet many more Burgundars lay dead and the Romans had managed to fight off the initial assault.

They were now forming a line on one side of the square before the church that so recently had been the scene of Gunhild's marriage. The streets in either direction, but most importantly towards the gate in the city walls, were blocked by throngs of hostile local people. The Romans' only hope was to find a defensive position where they could hold the Burgundars off.

'Attack them!' Gunderic shouted. 'Don't let them form up.'

Gunhild thought she heard a note of panic in her brother's voice.

With the enthusiasm and fire of youth, the mass of young Burgundar warriors rushed across the square at the Romans. The troopers were outnumbered but they managed to form their line in time, just before the mass of their enemies crashed into them.

The Burgundars screamed battle cries and there was a great crashing of metal on metal but the Romans were silent. They countered the wild blows of their assailants with measured thrusts. The young Burgundars threw themselves on the Roman line in a frenzy of aggression, but the troopers went about the work of killing them with methodical movements, each stab, strike or block practised thousands of times on the parade ground. Each man protected himself and, if the man to his right had a chance to strike, he protected his back as that trooper lunged forward to stab his opponent.

Soon the bodies were piling up but none of them were Roman. Before long the initial vigour of the Burgundar attack dissipated. Their energy and rage spent, the young men withdrew, dragging their wounded back to safety on the other side of the square. They were sweating heavily and panted for breath, exhausted by the frenzy of blows they had unleashed.

The Romans, on the other hand, looked like they could keep on fighting all night. They had lost men in the initial surprise attack, but there were still fifty-one left from the two turmae of sixty-four. The efficient organisation and training of the Roman Army took over. They did not even need their officers. Each man knew exactly what he was supposed to do without being told.

Gunderic cursed.

'Your rebellion will be over before its even begun if we don't deal with them,' Gunhild said.

'*My* rebellion?' he said, turning to glare at her. 'You're involved in this just as much as I am, sister. Do you think Rome will distinguish between any of us when it comes to crucifixion?'

'We could let them go,' Gunhild said. 'We've precious few warriors as it is. Why lose more if there is no need?'

'Because if the bishop escapes,' Gunderic said, 'he'll be back here with half the Roman Army before you know it. We will lose everything before we even start.'

'I thought the army was too busy in the west?' Gunhild said, a note of panic entering her voice.

'Most of it, yes,' Gunderic said. 'But we're still very weak. Like you said – we've few enough warriors right now. We can train men to fight but until we grow our strength the Romans could overwhelm us with a few cavalry regiments from the interior army that guards Ravenna. We need time, which we won't have if Rome is alerted to our plans now.'

The Burgundars, after a brief respite, made another assault on the Roman formation. This time Sigurd ran in with them. The big man hacked and slashed but even he could not make a difference, and indeed would have been wounded himself if not for his amazing Byzantine scale armour, which sword blades seemed to slip over rather than pierce. After this second fruitless attack the Burgundars once more retreated across the square, this time accompanied by the jeers of the Roman cavalrymen.

'It's no use,' Sigurd said, panting. 'Our men are just boys. They're no match for trained soldiers. If I had a couple of hardened warriors with me I could perhaps do something but with this lot I can't even dent their line. We need something to draw them out of formation.'

Fear flashed across Gunhild's face. If the Romans began to move they might fight their way through the crowd and get to the city gates.

'The bishop must not escape,' she said.

All three of them stared, teeth clamped in frustrated anger, at the line of cavalry troopers across the square.

The sound of hooves clattering on paving stones reached their ears. Gunhild turned towards the noise and saw that a band of riders were pushing their way through the people who thronged the street that led to the gates.

'Who is that?' she said.

'If it's Roman reinforcements we're finished,' Gunderic

said. He brandished his sword. 'Well, so be it. I will go down fighting.'

'Those aren't Romans,' Sigurd said.

Once through the crowd the riders thundered into the square. There were about thirty of them. They wore mail shirts and helmets. Their leader had the wings of a raven, one on each side, nailed to his helmet. Some bore spears and others swords. Each one had a black cloak that swirled behind them in the night air like the wings of bats.

They formed a long column and galloped across the square towards the Romans, screaming war cries that sent a shiver through the bones of everyone watching. At the sound of their screeches Gunhild realised with a jolt that not only were these newcomers not Roman, they were not men.

Who were these women? The old folk had told tales of Great Uncanny Women who made appearances at times of great portent. Were these female warriors such a thing? She shook her head. She had been a Swan Maiden and knew such things most likely did not exist, or at least often involved trickery and collective self-delusion.

The Romans stood steadfast in formation as the women on horseback galloped towards them, knowing that if they stood firm the beasts would not charge straight onto the sharp ends of their swords, no matter how much their riders goaded them.

Just before they did, however, the lead rider turned her horse to the right. The others followed her and they rode along the Roman line instead of straight at it. Some hurled franciscas down on the foot soldiers, others spears. Men cried out as they were struck and went down. Holes appeared in the previously uniform Roman line.

The women whirled their horses around and rode back down the damaged Roman line, this time striking the troopers below them with their swords or thrusting down at them with spears. With the advantage of height they inflicted yet more damage. Within moments the Romans broke ranks and began to flee for the church.

Without mercy, the fearsome women on horseback cut down more of them as they ran. Cheering, the Burgundars rushed forward again and killed the stragglers.

The remainder of the Roman troopers closed around the bishop. With no way out, they backed away towards the church. Sigurd ran towards them, seemingly heedless of any threat to his own life.

Two of the troopers came forward to meet him. One slashed at the big man with his long-bladed cavalry spatha. The sword merely slid across the surface of Sigurd's unusual armour, leaving nothing behind but the horrible scraping sound of metal on metal. The second trooper stabbed at Sigurd but could not pierce the armour either. Sigurd responded, stabbing the first man through the throat then swinging his sword in a sideways swipe that severed the left leg of the second trooper halfway down his thigh. He collapsed to the ground screaming and soon bled to death.

The troopers had bought enough time for their comrades to make it to the church, however. They entered and slammed the door. What was now a mob of Burgundars swarmed after them, rushing across the square and surrounding the church. Gunhild, Gunderic and Sigurd strode among them. The leader of the women on horseback rode over to them.

'My lady, I do not know who you are or why you choose to help us tonight,' Gunderic said to their leader. 'But you have my thanks.'

The woman on the black horse with the raven wings nailed to her visored helmet laughed. Gunhild noticed with a chill that decapitated human heads hung by strands of what was left of their hair from the woman's saddle and horse trappings. Most were little more than skulls, but one was fresh enough that dull eyes still peered from under its drooping lids.

'Am I changed so much, Gunderic, that you do not recognise me?' the horsewoman said. To their surprise she spoke in the Burgundar tongue, and with the same accent as them.

The woman undid the leather strap beneath her chin and pulled off her helmet. A torrent of black hair tumbled around her shoulders.

'Brynhild!' Gunhild cried out. 'I heard you died at Vorbetomagus!'

'Part of me did,' Brynhild said, her smile fading. 'Like many of our sister Swan Maidens. But I survived. So did Ostara, the Mistress of the Maidens, who nursed me back to health. We found the rest of the surviving Swan Maidens – except for you, Gunhild – you had disappeared – and we wandered far. We kept the Order going. Ostara made sure we did not forget the lore of our people. Eventually we found a refuge high in the mountains, far from Rome, the Huns, and all men and their wars and violence. We welcome women from all tribes, if they are fleeing from the oppression of men.'

Gunderic exchanged glances with Sigurd, who smirked.

'That sounds like paradise,' he said. 'For a rapist. I take it no king knows of this kingdom of women?'

Brynhild's lip curled.

'Several have found us,' she said. 'And now they are dead. We don't just chant old songs and weave necklaces of edelweiss. We have learned the craft of war. As you have seen tonight.'

She flicked her head towards the dead Romans lying in the street, then tapped the freshest of the heads that hung from her saddle with her toe.

'We are no longer the white Swan Maidens who watch who lives and who dies in battle and sing the praises of the bravest,' she said. 'Now it is *we* who choose who dies and we make it happen. We are the *Valkyrjur*, the Choosers of the Slain.'

'I'm so glad to see you are alive!' Gunhild said. 'If only Hagan were here, our old group of friends would be complete.'

Some of the fierceness dissipated from Brynhild's face.

'Hagan is alive,' she said. 'Or at least he was when the battle ended at Vorbetomagus. I saw him.'

'So there's a chance we could all be together again!' Gunhild clasped her hands and jumped up and down.

'Have you come to join us in our new kingdom?' Gunderic said. 'You would be most welcome. We need cavalry.'

Brynhild shook her head.

'We have our own lands to guard,' she said. 'The Alemanni get ever closer. And the Huns behind them. However, we came here tonight as escort for another king who most certainly is coming here to join you.'

'Where is this king?' Gunderic said, looking around.

'He and his close companions are several miles behind us on the road,' Brynhild said. 'We rode ahead to see if everything was safe for him to approach the city. Lucky for you we did, Gunderic.'

She smiled and winked at the new king of the Burgundars, who blushed.

'Now our work is done here,' Brynhild said. 'And you have work to finish.'

She pointed her bloodied spear at the closed door of the church.

'I think you can probably handle a priest and a handful of Romans without our help? Later tonight the wise king will arrive here. He has been with us some time and taught us many new and deadly arts of war. You will do well to give them hospitality. You will benefit much from an alliance with him.'

'Stay,' Gunhild urged her. 'Let us talk, find out what each of us have been doing these years. We can be together again like in the days of our childhood.'

'Those days are gone,' Brynhild said, shaking her head. 'And we must go too. I do not like to leave our realm unguarded for too long. But now I know you are here, perhaps we will see more of you in the future. For now: farewell.'

She kicked her heels against her horse's flanks and rode off back towards the city gates. The other black-clad women followed her.

For a moment Gunderic, Gunhild and Sigurd watched them go, then they turned back towards the church.

Gunhild saw that the previous joyous expressions of the crowd were gone, replaced by anger and hatred. Shouts of 'Get those Roman bastards!', 'Slaughter them!' and 'Vengeance for Vorbetomagus!' echoed around the mob. It was as if Gunderic's horn blast had unleashed a tide of boiling resentment that had been dammed up since the fall of their former homeland.

Sigurd, bloody sword still drawn, threw his considerable shoulder against the door of the church. It bucked and rattled on its hinges but it did not open.

'They've barred it,' the big man said, standing aside and nodding to some of the Burgundar warriors nearby. The young men charged forwards, smashing their shoulders against the church doors. The doors rattled but still held.

Then others brought benches from the feasting hall and the Burgundars began to use them as rams to batter the church doors. After three coordinated assaults the sharp sound of wood cracking came from inside, audible even above the baying cries of the mob in the square.

The Burgundar warriors slammed their shoulders into the door again. With a snap of splintering wood the church door sprang open, sending the warriors sprawling inside. Gunhild just had time to see the faces of the cavalry troopers, white with dread, before her view was blocked by the mass of bodies swarming into the entrance.

'Let me through!' Gunderic shouted, fighting to get to the front through the throng of his own people. Sigurd went before him, his great mass shoving people out of the way. Gunhild slipped in behind her brother and was swept along with the excited, bloodthirsty crowd as it gushed into the breached doorway.

Gunhild heard a frightened voice shouting 'Pax! Pax!' in Latin, then there were cries of anguish, rage and pain followed by a very sudden hush.

Sigurd, Gunderic and Gunhild struggled through the shattered doorway and to the front of the crowd beyond. The last of the cavalry troopers were now dead on the floor, overrun by the overwhelming numbers of the Burgundars. The bishop had retreated to the altar. He stood there, face aghast, arms held out before him as if to protect himself, even though the nearest potential attacker was the entire length of the aisle away. The scene was lit by the burning torches carried by the Burgundars, which somehow made it all the more lurid.

The Burgundars filed into the end of the church, forming a semi-circle inside the doorway. Gunhild felt a thrill of trepidation at the sight of the hacked corpses of the troopers. What had they done? In this sudden bloodletting they had killed Roman soldiers and a senior Roman official. The Empire would not stand for that. There would be retribution. The same thought appeared to be spreading through the crowds as they all stopped, not daring to advance any further into the church. Their noise and fury abated to a trepidation-filled muttering.

The bishop noticed the change and straightened up. He dropped his left arm and pointed at Gunderic with his right.

'Sacrilege!' Bishop Salonius said in a thunderous voice. 'You have spilled blood in this holy place. You have defiled the house of the Lord with your treachery. God will punish you.'

He cast his gaze around the crowd at the far end of the aisle. Gunhild saw that his terror was gone. He now had the air of a priest filled with righteous fury and haranguing his sinful flock.

'God will punish all of you!' Salonius shouted. 'Unless you turn on this treacherous maggot who calls himself your king. Rome will not stand for this. She will send her legions to crush you once again. You and your families will be slaughtered.

Your souls will burn in Hell. Your only hope is to show you do not support him. I am a bishop of the Church. Heed my words! Turn on him and put that vile traitor Gunderic to death. Do this or you will all perish under the vengeance of Rome.'

No one moved. Gunderic looked around and saw a warrior standing nearby armed with a spear. He snatched it from his grasp.

The bishop's mask of confidence dropped and his former terror returned.

'Don't!' he cried. 'I am a—'

Gunderic hurled the spear. It shot down the aisle and hit the bishop in the centre of his torso with a wet thump. The spearhead burst through his back and he staggered backwards, a red stain spreading rapidly around the shaft that protruded from his chest. The bishop collided with the altar and toppled back onto it. He let out one, rasping breath then lay still. His blood pooled across the flat stone top of the altar then began to dribble down the front, running down the cross that was painted on the stone.

'You're just another Roman bastard,' Gunderic said.

As his words echoed around the lofty roof of the church a shocked silence descended.

Gunderic strode down the aisle. The only sound was the click of his boots on the flagstones. He wrenched the spear from the dead bishop's body and held it aloft.

'Rome and her cursed Hun allies took much from the Burgundar folk,' he said. 'Tonight, we have begun to take it back. We have a new land and on it we will live as free folk, not lapdogs of the Romans. We have only ourselves to rely on and that is how it should be. Yes, we are surrounded by enemies but we will withstand them because what happened to our people will never happen again. We cannot, we *will* not allow it to.'

The young warriors at the other end of the aisle nodded and muttered a few 'Ayes'. Gunhild saw they were still a little half-hearted however.

'Fear not Rome's legions,' Gunderic continued. 'They are busy fighting for survival in Gaul. When – *if* – they turn on us we will be ready to stand against whatever is left of them. Rome is finished as a power. Now it is the time for free people like us to take what they can. To forge their own kingdoms. It will be a hard struggle, but tonight we took the first step. We have made it clear to Rome where we stand. We Burgundars have the heart and the spirit to make this land strong and now, we also have the wealth! I promise every warrior who fights for me new weapons, new mail and gold!'

The Burgundars cheered. This time they were more enthusiastic.

'Now come: let us go back to the hall and finish our feast, for now we really have got something to celebrate,' Gunderic said. 'This is our first day of real freedom.'

The crowd filed outside once more. The dead Burgundars were carried away on wagons for their corpses to be tended to and prepared for a decent burial. The dead Romans were dumped in a heap for burning, all except the body of the bishop, which was left lying on top of the altar. It seemed everyone was too reluctant even to approach the dead holy man.

Back in the hall the feast resumed, though it was a much more subdued affair than before. Gunhild could feel the trepidation in the air. She, Gunderic, and her new husband sat at the top of the table. Gunderic laid the spear, still wet with the bishop's blood, on the table before them and downed a goblet of wine. Sigurd did not say anything, he just laid a hand on top of Gunhild's and beamed at those around them as if enormously pleased with himself.

Gunderic drank several more cups of wine. There was a strange, fixed grin on his face, more of a look of desperation than happiness. After he poured his next cup Gunhild took her hand away from Sigurd's and laid it on her brother's wrist, stopping him from raising his wine cup to his lips.

'Well, brother,' she said. 'I am now married as you

requested. And we have murdered our Roman benefactors in what appears very much like a pre-arranged ambush. You owe me an explanation. I want to know everything.'

Gunderic nodded.

'Very well, sister,' he said.

CHAPTER NINETEEN

GUNHILD RELEASED GUNDERIC'S hand and he took a swig of his wine. Then he clicked his fingers to those seated nearby and gestured that they should all go away. When only Sigurd, Gunhild and Gunderic remained at the table he leaned forwards.

'It seems,' Gunderic said in a low voice that suggested he did not want anyone overhearing, 'that the Magister Militum, General Aetius, is perhaps not the upstanding Roman Patrician he would have everyone to think he is.'

'A corrupt Roman politician?' Gunhild said, shaking her head. 'What a surprise.'

'He was a good general,' Gunderic said. 'He really was. Like others though I suppose a time comes when one has to look to their own future. It was Aetius who asked about the treasure our father won from the Huns. I did not just offer the knowledge up to him. When Aetius was seventeen Rome sent him as a hostage to the king of the Huns. He spent many years living among them and still keeps in contact with people there. He had heard of the raid our father carried out on the Huns. How their King Oktar was killed and how they lost a vast hoard of gold and treasure. It was a great disgrace for them. So I made the arrangement with Aetius. He got us our treaty and we were granted our new land. In exchange I told him our father's hiding place for the treasure.'

'And the Romans have it now,' Gunhild said.

'No. That's just it,' Gunderic said with a chuckle. 'I should have known Aetius was up to something when he told me not to mention the gold to anyone. Anyway: as far as I was concerned it was gone and I—'

He stopped and glanced at her.

'*We*, would have to build up everything from scratch,' he went on. 'What did it matter? I had a new kingdom to lead my people to. I felt like that man God sent to lead the Israelites out of Egypt. What was his name again?'

Gunhild frowned, trying to remember. She had become a Christian with the rest of the Burgundars on the orders of her father when she was twelve. Within six winters the Burgundar kingdom had fallen and for most of the time since she had been living among the heathens in the north. Her knowledge of the religion was a little rusty.

'Moses!' Gunderic found the name himself. 'Just like Moses, God must have been on my side. Aetius must have decided to keep the treasure all to himself, or at least keep it as secret as possible. The legions did not march back to Vorbetomagus. Instead there was a small Roman delegation on its way to meet the Huns north of the Rhine. They were from the Eastern Empire: important officials accompanied by elite cavalry, but nevertheless only a few units.'

'What were Eastern Romans doing in Germania?' Gunhild said. 'It's a long way from Constantinople.'

'They were trying to negotiate with the Huns. In the Western Empire, Aetius may have had the Huns on his side,' Gunderic said, 'but they've crossed the Danube and cut a bloody swathe through the lands of the Eastern Empire. You heard Lucius earlier: the Huns always have two kings.'

'Two?' Gunhild said. She could not imagine her father sharing the kingship with anyone. 'Does that work?'

'It stops one man becoming too powerful, they believe,' Gunderic said. 'Apparently they had a sole ruler once and the fellow started thinking he was a god. He caused all sorts of problems. The idea is that with two kings, each one can keep the other in check.'

'What if there is a disagreement between them?' Gunhild said, looking sideways at her brother. 'Such things happen. Especially between siblings.'

'Then they kill each other,' Gunderic said with a grin. 'They used to have a holy sword, sacred to their War God, which passed between them year about. The Huns thought it granted ultimate power. Whichever king bore it made the final decisions.'

Gunhild glanced at the now sheathed sword at her new husband's side. The cavalry commander had commented on its Hunnish curve. Her mind raced ahead of her brother's words as everything fell into place like the *tessella* tiles that made the pictures on the floor below.

'After Oktar's death, Ruga did indeed rule alone,' Gunderic said. 'But when he died they reinstated the dual kingship. Ruga's nephews, Bleda and Attila, took over. Bleda works with the Romans in the West but Attila has been running riot in the East.'

'And these Eastern Romans were trying to stop that?' Gunhild said.

'The classic Roman tactic: divide and conquer,' Gunderic said, tapping a forefinger on the table. 'Aetius's Eastern counterpart, Flavius Ardabur Aspar, was on a mission to meet Bleda to see if he might be persuaded to oust his less friendly brother Attila. Our friend Aetius made them take a detour through Vorbetomagus on the way. They dug up our father's treasure where I told Aetius he could find it.'

Gunderic moved his gaze away from his sister. She could sense his shame at what he had done.

'So the Romans did take it all,' she said. She felt tears in her eyes but did not let them fall. She had begun to hope that the vast hoard of wealth somehow might still be there, for her to take her share of and with it a chance for her to win her own freedom. She almost envied Brynhild, with a realm of her own in the mountains. Though it must be poor, she thought. There was no wealth to be had up there and squeezing a living from the land would be hard work.

'They did,' Gunderic said, his face lighting up again. 'But not for long. They went further north-east to meet the Huns, who were raiding along the Rhine at the time. While they were waiting at the prescribed meeting place they were ambushed. The cavalry escort and soldiers were wiped out. When Bleda and the Huns arrived, all that was left was the looted caravan and a few survivors either too badly wounded or incapable of running away.'

'Who did this?' Gunhild said in a breathless voice.

'I did,' Sigurd said, beaming from ear to ear. 'After our folk were decimated at Vorbetomagus, my mother sent me for safety to her uncle who was a nobleman in Santen. The Eastern Romans crossed our lands without permission. We had a right to extract tribute from them.'

'I thought you were brought up by a blacksmith?' Gunhild said.

'For a little time, that is true,' Sigurd said, his smile fading a little. 'When I first arrived in Santen my uncle was frightened of what the Romans might do if they found he was harbouring one of the Burgundar nobles, so he sent me to work for his smith. That was an act of cowardice he lived to regret.'

'How so?' Gunhild said.

'The blacksmith was no ordinary servant,' Sigurd said. 'He was called Regin and he was in fact a disgraced old warrior of my uncle's. He had been maimed and made to work in my uncle's smithy as punishment for some misdeed. Naturally Regin harboured a grudge. He taught me how to fight. How to plot and scheme. When the time came we killed my uncle and I became Lord of Santen.'

'Sigurd and his warband ambushed the Romans before they met the Huns,' Gunderic said. 'They never knew what hit them. As far as Aetius is concerned, the treasure was lost in a random attack by unknown but very lucky Germans, many miles north of here.'

'We have much to thank you for,' Gunhild said, smiling at her new husband and looking at him with new eyes. 'You have regained the treasure hoard of our father.'

'The treasure hoard of the Burgundar folk,' Sigurd said, leaning forward. 'And I do not need your thanks. The only reward I asked for was the hand of the most beautiful woman in the world in marriage. And my share, obviously.'

'We have the wealth we need to start building a new kingdom,' Gunderic said. He looked around him, a faraway expression on his face. 'I will renovate this hall. We will cut down that tree and repair the roof. The floors will be re-laid. We will have tapestries woven that tell the lore of our folk. This hall will become famous throughout the world as the home of heroes.'

'You might have to keep the tree,' Gunhild said with a smile. 'I suspect it is now all that is holding the roof up.'

'I will keep it then,' Gunderic said, the faraway look still in his eyes. 'It is a symbol of the new roots we have put down here, and the mighty trunk that will grow from them.'

'But Aetius must suspect something,' Gunhild said. 'You heard Lucius. He and Flavius were told to be on the lookout for that sword.'

'Aye,' Gunderic said, taking another drink of wine then biting his lower lip. 'I wonder how he came to that conclusion?'

'You said yourself he's not stupid,' Gunhild said. 'But when will I see this hoard of treasure? I am entitled to my share, after all. It belonged to my father too.'

A strange expression crossed Gunderic's face. Gunhild was not sure if it was rage or suspicion. Then it was gone.

'All in good time, sister,' Gunderic said. 'It is well hidden not far from Geneva, just like our father hid it near Vorbetomagus.

You will have your share, but no one else ever will. *Ever.* It will only be the three of us, understand?'

There was an urgency in his voice and a sparkle in his eyes that reminded Gunhild a little of their father when the gold sickness had struck him. She nodded.

'You made a very bold move tonight,' Gunhild said. 'We killed Roman soldiers and important officials. We killed a man of God in his church. I hope it was worth it.'

Gunderic set down his wine cup and lifted the bloody spear, regarding it with a thoughtful look for a few moments.

'You know,' he said, 'from ancient times to the times of our fathers, our people always made a sacrifice at the most important times in the destiny of the people. They killed beasts. At really important times they killed men. This, tonight, was our sacrifice. This was the blood sacrifice that will usher in the new dawn of the Burgundar kingdom.'

For a few moments no one spoke. Then Gunhild said, 'If this was a sacrifice, who were we honouring?'

At that moment there came a loud knock on the door of the hall.

CHAPTER TWENTY

THE KNOCKING WAS loud. It resounded above the subdued conversation of the hall, killing off what little conviviality there still was. When it stopped a total hush descended.

The few Burgundars who remained in the hall all exchanged glances, some curious, some fearful. It was late in the night and whoever was calling would have walked past the pile of Roman corpses outside. If it was a stranger, there would be no hiding what the Burgundars had just done.

Men set down their food and grasped their weapons again. Gunderic, already holding the spear, stood up. Sigurd alone seemed unperturbed. He lounged back in his seat and poured himself another goblet of wine.

Gunderic nodded to those nearest the doors. They hauled them open with a great creaking of hinges. For a moment it looked like there was only darkness outside, then a man walked out of it and entered the hall. He was tall and dressed in an old mottled cloak that may once have been dark blue. Years of weather had faded it to grey. On his head was a wide-brimmed hat. It was partly slouched to one side.

He was not a young man; his very long hair and beard, combed very smooth and very straight, were both as grey as unpolished chainmail. Despite his age he stood firmly upright. There was no sign of the bowed shoulders or ale-filled paunch that came to most men in the later part of their middle years.

In one hand he carried a spear but he used it like a long

walking staff. It was most probably this that he had used to rap so loudly on the door. Over his shoulder was slung a leather satchel that bulged, showing there was something round inside it. His breeches were tightly cross-gartered around his legs with leather straps and to everyone's surprise, he was barefoot.

As he got closer Gunhild saw that beneath where the man's hat slouched to the right, his eye was covered by a patch of black material. His left eye, even in the gloom of the hall, was such a dazzling blue it almost seemed to glitter.

Beside the stranger was a young woman. She was perhaps eighteen, blonde-haired and of a beauty that rivalled even Gunhild's. She wore a tight-fitting blue dress that made most of the men in the room stare. A large black cat sat on her shoulder.

The pair advanced up the hall between the fire pits. All eyes in the room watched them. When they got to the middle they stopped.

'I am looking for the ruler of this new kingdom of the Burgundars,' the one-eyed man said. He spoke in the Burgundar tongue, but with an accent that suggested he was perhaps of another Germanic tribe from somewhere to the east.

'That is I,' Gunderic said. 'I am Gunderic, son of Gundahar. Who are you, stranger? And why have you come here to my hall?'

The stranger raised his staff in one hand.

'Hail, Gunderic, new king of the once-mighty Burgundars,' he said. There was a slight smile on his lips. 'I knew your father. You look like him. Not as tall, though. Many call me Gest.'

'*Guest?*' Gunderic said. 'If that is so, you are an uninvited one.'

'But no less welcome for it, I would hope,' the stranger said. 'It is not the only name I am known by. This is the Lady Freya. She is daughter to my chief councillor, Forsetti, who waits outside with the rest of my folk. We have come far and we are weary. I beg you for your generosity and some of the famed hospitality of the Burgundars. We have travelled through the snow-covered mountains. We need the warmth of your fire to dry out and bring heat into our chilled bones. We need water to drink and, perhaps, a little refreshment?'

'We are not the Burgundars of the past,' Gunderic said. 'We have suffered much and lost a great deal since my father's day. Forgive me if we seem a little inhospitable, but it has been a momentous evening for us.'

'So I see,' Gest said. 'There is a pile of dead Romans stacked in the street outside. The sight gladdens my heart. The only sight that would make me happier would be a pile of dead Huns beside them.'

Murmurs of assent and relief, ran around the Burgundars in the hall.

'You speak of things close to our own hearts, stranger,' Gunderic said. 'But how do we know you are not some Roman spy, or scout from the Alemanni, sent here to try to judge the strength of the new rulers of this land?'

'You don't,' the man said. He looked around the room with his haunting eye, a supercilious smile on his lips. 'But I don't need to spy to tell you are weak. Your warriors look like they got their war gear from robbing graves. They are mere beardless boys and there are barely enough of them to defend this hall, never mind your whole realm, should the Alemanni decide to invade. As for you, Gunderic, you are a king in threadbare britches and a patched old Roman Army cloak. You have not the wealth to build a kingdom. Look at the state of your hall! It is barely standing. It even has a tree growing through it.'

The watching folk in the hall gasped. Several of the warriors started to their feet, hands falling to the hilts of their sheathed weapons.

'Watch your tongue, dog,' Gunderic said through gritted teeth. 'You are talking to a king. You would do well to remember that or I will have you tortured in the very fires you ask to warm yourself by.'

'And you do likewise,' the stranger replied in a thunderous tone that took everyone by surprise. 'I too am of royal blood. I was the High One of the kingdom east of the river Tanais. Gest is not the only name I have been known by. I am also called Wodnas. I am known as the Traveller, the Warrior and the Helmet-wearer. I am the Third, the Hel-Blinder. Battle-Glad I am called. Death-Worker, Hider, One-Eye, Fire-Eye, Lore-Master, Masked One, the Deceitful. I am the Fury that flows in the blood of warriors and I have come here to your kingdom, to the new hall of the Burgundars, with knowledge you would do well to listen to.'

The hush descended once more on the people inside the hall. This time it was one of reverence. The girl beside the one-eyed stranger smiled. The cat on her left shoulder stood up, arched its back, and curled past the back of her head to perch on her other shoulder.

Gunhild swallowed a mouthful of wine. She had heard legends of this man while among the Danes. He was a great and powerful king who ruled over a rich, fertile land to the east, just before the great mountain range beyond which no one lived. It was said he was very learned in the arts of war and so wise in the secret crafts some thought him a wizard. He was very rich and could make men follow him into battle without fear. He was so wise some thought he could tell the future.

'Your reputation is well known, King Wodnas,' Gunhild said. She knew this was the name he was most widely known by. 'But I always thought you were just a legend.'

'A legend?' The old man chuckled, casting his one-eyed gaze in her direction. 'At my age it is a little worrying to be referred to as a myth. Some old lore that folk whisper around the fire on a winter's night. But I see the legends of your beauty are true, lady. You must be Gunhild.'

'You spoke of important knowledge, Wodnas, Gest, or whatever it is you call yourself,' Gunderic said. 'What is that?'

163

'You think the Romans have placed you here to stave off the Alemanni,' Wodnas said. 'But they are not the ones you should fear. The Huns are gathering like a storm in the East. They have made an alliance with the Alemanni and other eastern tribes. Bleda still restrains them but sooner or later Attila will throw off the yoke of his older brother and he will come rushing over the Western Empire in a tide dimmed with blood.'

'We care nothing about what happens to Rome,' Gunderic said.

'To do that they will have to come through here,' Wodnas said. 'And through you.'

Gunhild bit her lower lip.

'The Romans told us that,' Gunderic said. 'Besides, what is that to you?'

'The Huns overran my kingdom,' Wodnas said. 'For many years we kept them at bay. We fought them hard. We fought them well. We killed a great many of them, but they are like the waves of the mighty ocean that surrounds the world. No matter how many we killed still more came. They fear the wrath of their king if they fail more than they fear death. Their numbers are overwhelming. We are not a multitudinous folk like them. We are smaller in number even than the Burgundars. We could not stand against the Hun hordes. We could have stayed and fought to the last man, but what good would that have done? We would all be dead and the Huns would still have taken our land.'

'You would have died with honour,' Sigurd said. 'Your legend would live forever.'

Wodnas turned his one eye on the big man.

'A lame man can ride,' he said. 'A handless man can still drive cattle. The deaf can still fight. And win. What use is a corpse to anyone?'

Sigurd made a face.

'The remnants of our folk gathered what we could carry and we left our homeland,' Wodnas said. 'We became landless

164

wanderers. We are now scattered to the four winds. My son led some of the Aesir west. My daughter, Gerth, took others north. I wandered north, south and west.'

'We Burgundars know what that is like,' Gunderic said.

'Aye, you do,' Wodnas said. 'Which is why we have come here. We travelled through many lands. I was with the Gepids and with Wends and with Gevlegs. With the Angles I was, and with Suebi and with Aenenes. With the Saxons I was, and with Sycgs. With the Hrons I was and with Danes, Thuringians, Gloms and Rugians.'

'He speaks in such a strange way,' Gunhild said in a quiet voice to her new husband. 'It's like he's speaking poetry.'

'It sounds like nonsense to me,' Sigurd said with a grunt.

'When I heard the Burgundars had a new land,' Wodnas continued, 'I thought: here is a people we have much in common with. The Burgundars and my people, the Aesir, both have reason to hate the Huns. So we have come here across the mountains to offer you an alliance.'

'It seems this alliance would be a little one-sided, King Wodnas,' Gunderic said. 'You will get to share our land, but what would we get in return?'

'I did not see this land overflowing with Burgundar farms and homesteads,' Wodnas said. 'That lack of numbers tells a tale all by itself. You will not have the numbers to resist an invasion unless you learn different laws of war. How to harass the enemy and disappear into the forest. How to eat away at his strength and his resolve until he leaves or is weak enough to fight in pitched battle. I can teach your warriors the secrets of war. We resisted the Huns for more than fifteen winters. You cannot do that with a band of beardless boys like you have now. I will make your warband hardened, trained killers, just like I did for Brynhild and her people. You saw how effective they were tonight. With my guidance you will kill the Alemanni with ease. And when the Huns finally come, you will be ready for them.'

'If the Huns do come,' Sigurd said, 'how do we know you won't just run away again like you did from your own homeland?'

'There is nowhere left to go,' Wodnas said with a shrug. 'South is Rome. West are the Visigoths. North, more Huns now. This land is surrounded by mountains that are like Earth's own walls, too high and snow-capped for Hun horses to cross with ease. Here we have a chance of fighting them off. If we prepare well. I want revenge! The world will not be at peace until the Huns are beaten, destroyed and no longer able to wage their wars.'

For a few moments there was silence, then the old man spoke again.

'And there is another reason for us to form an alliance,' he said. 'Kinship. Our forefathers on both sides were Goths. The Goths, like the Vandals, the Geats and the Burgundars, are all descendants of Ingvy, son of Mannus, son of Tiwass, the Great God.'

Gunderic sat for a moment, looking into his cup of wine.

'What do you think?' Gunhild asked him in a whisper.

'He's right,' Gunderic said quietly. 'We could do well from this alliance. But what if he is trying to steal our treasure?'

Gunhild frowned.

'How would he even know about it?' she said in a hiss. 'I didn't know the truth until tonight. You must know of this man. He was the greatest war leader in the east. For him to teach us his crafts would make us strong. We are lucky to have this opportunity. I think this makes sense.'

Gunderic nodded.

'We are Christians, Wodnas,' he said in a loud voice. 'And you are not. But aside from that I believe we can come to an agreement. I accept your proposal.'

'You will not regret this decision, King Gunderic,' Wodnas said.

'Brynhild told us you stayed with her,' Gunhild said. 'Where is her home now? We were close friends once. Please tell me how I can find her again.'

'She is indeed a remarkable woman,' Wodnas said. 'Though what she went through at Vorbetomagus has left her with wounds that still torment her. Not in the body, but here.'

He tapped his fist against his heart.

'Hatred and anger are what stirs her now. When we first wandered into the mountains and unwittingly crossed into her small realm,' he said with a chuckle, 'we were lucky to keep our heads on our shoulders. They do not welcome strangers. Brynhild knew her former folk had settled here but she said you were part of her past now. The darkness around her heart made her say that. We stayed with her for some time. I taught her horsewomen cavalry tactics. They are now truly fearsome. When the time came for us to move on, however, Brynhild could not resist coming along to see the new homeland of her folk. She will be a useful ally to you someday.'

'I hope so,' Gunhild said. 'This has been a momentous night. A few weeks ago I thought I was the last of our folk. Now I am surrounded by other Burgundars in a new realm of our own. I am reunited with you, Gunderic, and tonight we both met Brynhild. If Hagan were here too it would be just like the days long past...'

'Indeed,' Gunderic said. 'I sometimes wonder what his fate was. But he was part of our past. Now we have much work to do. Let us get started. We have a nation to build.'

CHAPTER TWENTY-ONE

AD 445 – Two Years Later

Kingdom of the Huns

THE GREY WATERS of the mighty river Danube curled their way through the plain like an enormous, meandering snake. The land around it was thick with trees, though at one particular loop in the river was a large settlement. It had been built by the Scythians, improved by the Romans, then destroyed by the Huns, who were now in the process of rebuilding it. Half-burned stone houses were being repaired while others too ravaged to fix were pulled down so their stones could be reused for new dwellings. The great circular wall that surrounded the city was licked by scorch marks and broken in several places. There were many round tents set up both inside and outside its circuit. Outside the wall too was penned a vast herd of horses, the steeds of the Hun warriors. Smoke rose from many campfires, and mixed with clouds of steam rising from the hot springs that burst from the land there.

Even though it was early morning the city was a hive of activity, which made an interesting view for the two men who sat on horseback on a nearby hilltop. From their vantage point they were far enough above the city that the army of slaves and the Huns driving them in the rebuilding work looked like insects swarming over a fortress a child might make in the sand or mud.

'What do you think, brother?' the older of the two men said. 'This will be my capital, my stronghold and my legacy. The world will know of the wonders and the strength of *Bleda Vár*.'

His other man, Attila, grunted. It was so like his arrogant elder brother to call this place *Bleda's Fortress* after himself.

Attila turned to look at Bleda. Both men were kings of their people yet were dressed in the leather and fur any other Hun wore when hunting. Their higher social status was only denoted by their elongated skulls, deformed in the first six months of their lives by having wooden boards strapped tight to the front and backs of their heads with stout bandaging. There were those who said this practice was cruel, others that it somehow twisted the hearts of the Hun rulers so they felt no pity or showed no mercy. To the Huns themselves however it was a symbol of the right to power and of superior character.

Both men were superb riders, even by Hun standards. That crisp day they had been part of a hunting party but had now outstripped their companions on the trail of a herd of wild boar. Riding up the wooded hillside above the city, they had come into this clearing and the view that opened before them had been enough to make Bleda rein his horse to a stop. Seeing this, Attila had done the same.

The path through the thick woods passed a long tongue of rock that protruded above a sharp drop to the mighty river that wound its way past the bottom of the hill some distance below. The height of the clearing provided a breathtaking view over the bustling city that glowed below in the radiant light of the morning sun, as well as the woods and plains beyond it.

'I have no doubt you will fill your fortress with wonders, brother,' Attila said. 'Wonders like that little monster who follows you around like a lapdog.'

Bleda chuckled, looking around the clearing.

'Where is that rascal?' he said. 'Well, if he isn't with us I don't blame him. Keeping up with a hunt is hard for someone with little legs like his. You really don't like him, do you?'

Attila shook his head, a grimace spreading across his face.

'No,' he said. 'I don't know how you stand to be around

such a deformed creature. The very sight of him makes my skin crawl.'

'The dwarf makes me laugh,' Bleda said. 'And he has provided me much entertainment over the years. But what of *Attila Vár*, brother? I have my land now but where will you rule? Where will you build your fortress?'

Attila pursed his lips.

'Not to the east, that is for sure,' he said.

Both men were silent for a moment. Their thoughts drifted back to a few years before, when the Hun army, fresh with bravado from humiliating the Eastern Romans, tried to do the same to the Sassanid Empire. That time it had been the Sassanids who provided the humiliation.

'It is time we finished off Rome, brother,' Attila said. 'It is a hollow edifice, rotten from the inside. It's riddled with decadence and corruption. All it will take are a few heavy blows and the whole thing will come crashing to the ground. Then I shall make my fortress. Emperor Valentinian's palace in Ravenna shall be Attila Vár. His sister shall be my wife.'

Bleda grunted. Then he sighed and swung his leg over his saddle and dismounted.

'Let us walk for a moment, brother,' he said.

Attila did the same, though with reluctance. He walked with the wide-legged, rolling gait of a man who spent most of his days on horseback. Both brothers had long, wiry black hair and now they were in their middle years their beards were speckled with grey. Bleda was not only the older but the taller of the two. He slid his arm around Attila's shoulders. As he did so, his brother twitched.

Bleda ignored Attila's clear dislike of the gesture and steered him towards the gap in the trees where the best view of the city below was.

'Look at this, Attila,' he said. 'You may think I am bragging, but look at this rebuilding work. It is all made possible by the wealth that comes from the Romans. The Eastern Empire now pays us seven hundred Roman pounds of gold a year. It is a vast sum, something Oktar, our uncle Ruga and our father could only have dreamed of. The Romans ransom the soldiers we take prisoner at eight *solidi* a man. Their markets are open to our merchants. They pay us all this so that we leave them alone. You are right, the Empire may be finished as a military force. But it is still rich. All we have to do is threaten war and they keep on paying us. Year after year. If we destroy the Empire then who will be paying us? Do you really want to cut off that river of gold?'

'If we invade and destroy them then we can take it all,' Attila said. 'Rather than just what they deign to pay us.'

'Not every act is a personal insult to you, Attila,' Bleda said, his patronising smile making his younger brother clench his teeth. 'We are not beggars they throw the odd coin to. The Romans struggle to pay us what they do. Their remaining provinces groan under the burden of the taxes laid on them to pay us. Some have revolted in protest. And the Romans still keep paying us because they fear us more than those rebellions.'

'You cannot trust the Romans,' Attila said. 'Eastern or Western. They are snakes with centuries of practice of deceit and statecraft behind them. The dogs will turn on us.'

'As a king, Attila, you must learn to think more like a merchant,' Bleda said. 'Yes, the Romans will eventually betray us. That is not a slight aimed specifically at us. It is just life. We must prepare for that day, and in the meantime extract as much wealth from them as we can.'

'And all the while they build the walls of Constantinople and Ravenna ever higher,' Attila said, his voice raised in pitch. 'Can't you see it is time they are buying with their tribute? And when they have bought enough their defences will be too strong for us to overcome! Then they will cease to pay and sit behind their walls, baring their arses at us and laughing. The Western Roman Empire is still on its knees from the defeat the Goths imposed on them in the time of our father. Rome is abandoned. The Emperor cowers in the swamps of Ravenna. They are ripe for the taking. The time to attack is now.'

Bleda withdrew his arm and walked a little apart from his brother.

'You always were rash, Attila,' he said, shaking his head. 'Here we are like the farmer whose cow gives him a plentiful supply of milk every year. He is rich in cheese, milk and butter. That could continue for another ten years with no effort from the farmer. But you would kill that cow so you could feast on meat for a day.'

'Better to feast on meat than drink milk like a peasant,' Attila said. His dark eyes blazed.

'I see we will not agree on this matter,' Bleda said, turning to face his brother again. He now stood before the cliff with his back to the city.

'No,' Attila said. 'We will not.'

'Which is why our forefathers in their wisdom made the tradition that there should be two kings,' Bleda said. 'With one the Over King. That is me. Therefore as Over King I make the final decision. We will not go to war with Rome in the west. Not until the time is right.'

For long moments the brothers glared at each other across the clearing. Then the sound of hooves and the thrashing of undergrowth announced that another rider was approaching. A third Hun noble from the hunting party burst into the clearing. Seeing the two kings on foot he reined his horse to a halt.

'Lords, is everything alright?' he said. He was much younger than the brother kings and sweating from the exertion of trying to keep up with them.

'Everything is fine, Ediko,' Bleda said. 'I just stopped to show my brother the magnificent view of what will be Bleda Vár. Excellent riding, by the way. Well done for almost keeping up with us.'

'Thank you, lord!' the young man said, beaming with pride.

'How is that new son of yours?' Bleda said, now smiling

172

himself. He added for the edification of his brother, 'Ediko here has a lovely new wife who has blessed him with a fine baby boy.'

'He is doing well, lord,' Ediko said. 'Getting bigger by the day.'

'It must be your first child? Or perhaps your first wife?' Attila said, his lip curling into a sneer. 'I've lost count of how many I have of both. Sometimes I think *one* is too many. The only one that counts is the one that will carry on your line. You can choose your friends, lad, but it is not the same with your relatives.'

'Lords, I believe we have lost track of the boar, I'm sorry to say,' Ediko said. 'I left the hounds at the bottom of the hill with the rest of the hunting party. They've lost the scent.'

'A fine day's sport,' Attila said with a snort. 'Brother, you said these forests held the best hunting in the world yet all we've bagged so far are a few deer. Are we to go home with so little today? Our feast tonight will indeed be a meagre one.'

Bleda stomped back to his horse and snatched his bow from where it was holstered at his saddle.

'There is plenty of game,' he said. 'The day is young and we can still take fowl. Let's see if you can still shoot, brother. This clifftop clearing is a great vantage point for bird hunting.'

He walked back over to the cliff edge above the river. Attila retrieved his own bow and did the same. Ediko dismounted and joined them, standing a respectful couple of paces behind the brother kings.

They stood, waiting in silence, until a long-billed woodcock swooped out of the trees a little further down the steep slope before them. Bleda was the first to draw and aim. He let fly his arrow and the bird dropped like a stone, bouncing off the cliff face and into the undergrowth at the base.

'The dogs can retrieve it, when they finally get here,' Bleda said.

'Behind us,' Ediko said.

Both men turned to see another bird come out of the trees, this time above them. Attila loosed an arrow but it missed, his shaft rattling off through the tree canopy. Bleda took a moment more time then shot it as it passed overhead. The bird, transfixed by the arrow, dropped to the ground, bounced on the soft earth and came to a halt at the very edge of the cliff.

'As always, you were too rash, brother,' Bleda said, walking over to retrieve the woodcock. 'If you had taken another moment you would have hit it.'

'Enough of this small talk, Bleda,' Attila said. 'You speak of acting like a merchant. I have not come here with my army just to visit my relatives. You say you are Over King and that is true, but the role is supposed to be shared between us. You for five years, then I for five. Your time is long past yet you still bear the Sword of the War God and its powers. It is now my time. It is time for you to pass over the sacred sword to me.'

Bleda slung his bow over his shoulder and bent to pick up the dead bird. He straightened up and looked his brother in the eye.

'It is true, yes, that the Over Kingship is to be shared between us,' he said. 'But there are rules, laid down by our ancestors and the priests of the Gods. The Over King bears final responsibility for decisions and for that reason he must have good judgement. For that reason it was I who was chosen to be Over King first. I was recognised as having the best judgement. One special responsibility the Over King bears – perhaps the most important of all – is to judge when his fellow king is truly wise enough to take over the role. Your words this morning on attacking Rome show you still have not achieved the necessary wisdom. I cannot hand the role over to you.'

'Cannot, or *will* not?' Attila said through clenched teeth. 'It is the Sword of the War God that grants power, not the judgement of a man grown fat and cowardly from the wealth and wine sent to him by Romans! Hand it over, Bleda.'

His brother gave a wan smile.

'You always were too superstitious, little brother,' he said. 'I do not even possess the Sword. It disappeared years ago.'

'*What?*' Attila's face twisted in disbelief.

'I never possessed it. Oktar lost the sword when he let himself be surprised by the Burgundars,' Bleda said. 'Then the Romans took it. Then they lost it. Who knows where it is now.'

'We have *lost* the great Sword of the War God?' Attila said, his tone uncomprehending. He stared over the vista below. 'How can that be?'

'We have not always owned the Sword,' Bleda said. 'Wodnas took it from us during our wars with his people in Asaland.'

'And while he bore it, Wodnas never failed to defeat us,' Attila said. 'It was only when he lost it that we were able to drive him and his people out. Does that not tell you something?'

'Wodnas is not of our people,' Bleda said. 'Who is to say his War God is even the same as our War God? Does that not tell *you* something?'

Attila glared at his brother, his mouth open a little.

'Look, Attila: I never possessed the Sword,' Bleda said. His tone was patronising. 'Yet I have ruled as Over King since the death of our uncle Ruga. What does *that* tell you? The Sword was just a sword, Attila. There was no magic in it. Naturally, we do not tell the common people that the sword is gone. That must remain a secret or perhaps many of them would cease to follow us.'

'So you admit it has power?' Attila said.

'Its power is the belief men have in it,' Bleda said.

'And yet my oh-so-wise brother has just blabbered this secret before one of those common folk?' Attila said.

Both men glanced at Ediko. The young nobleman swallowed hard.

'Ediko can be trusted,' Bleda said.

Attila's face screwed up in a mixture of incomprehension and rage. He ground his teeth. Seeing this, Bleda sighed and turned away from him to look at the city in the plain below.

'Your emotions prove you are not yet fit to become Over King,' he said over his shoulder. 'If you become Over King you will lead our people into an unnecessary war against Rome and any other tribes who stand in your way. We will have broken our treaty and the Eastern Roman Empire will stop sending tribute. Our people will lose out on all that wealth.'

He gestured toward the city. Then he turned around to face his brother again. Attila now stood, bow drawn, his arrow aimed right at Bleda's chest.

Bleda's eyes widened. He dropped the dead bird and went for his own bow at his shoulder. Attila shot him before Bleda had even touched his own bowstring. He bore a powerful Hun bow made of wood and animal bone and at such close range it sent its missile ploughing straight through his brother's ribs, unhindered by the leather jerkin he wore. It splintered bone and shredded his flesh. The serrated hunting arrowhead, designed for killing large game quickly, lacerated veins and ripped through Bleda's heart before exploding out through his back in a cloud of crimson spray. It carried on into the air above the precipice behind him. There, its awesome power finally spent, the arrow began a rapid descent into the trees below.

Bleda bent double from the impact. He gasped. He looked up, glaring wide-eyed at Attila. He opened his mouth to say something but all that came out was a gush of blood.

Attila walked over to him, lifted his right leg, and kicked his brother. Bleda stumbled a few steps backwards, then his right foot stepped onto thin air beyond the cliff edge. He spun and in a moment he was gone, tumbling down the precipice. His body thumped twice off the stones with sickening cracks that left two large red smears on the rock face. Then his corpse disappeared into the undergrowth below, like the bird he had shot earlier.

For a few moments Attila stood, looking at the empty space where his brother had stood moments before. Then he turned

176

around. Ediko stood a little way away. He gaped and his face was gaunt with shock.

'It seems my brother has met with an unfortunate hunting accident,' Attila said. 'When the others arrive you will tell them that he ran in front of your bow while you aimed at a stag and you accidentally shot him.'

'But, lord,' Ediko said, his bottom lip trembling. 'The Over King is dead. Accident or not, I will lose my own head for such a deed.'

Attila raised his right forefinger and pointed to the city below.

'We are too far away to see it,' he said, 'but right now my warriors are rising up down there. It has all been arranged. They are slaughtering my brother's trusted advisors, his bodyguards and his most loyal followers. If you like, I could make sure that this new son of yours you are so proud of and that pretty young wife are included among the slain?'

Ediko swallowed hard and shook his head.

'Please don't, Lord King,' he managed to gasp.

'You are a clever man,' Attila said. 'I think we understand each other.'

He looked at the city.

'Now *I* am Over King of the Huns,' Attila said. 'And there is no one to stop me. Bleda had grown fat and lazy. He traded comfort for glory. Now he can no longer hold back my plans. I will conquer. I will bring death and war until the world trembles at my name. The cry "the Huns are coming" will make nations quake. I will reclaim the Sword and slaughter those who took it. I will take all that is mine by right. All I need is a sign from above and I will set the world ablaze.'

PART III

THE GATHERING STORM

Nú er fyri geirrum grár upp kominn
vefr verþjóðar er þær vinur fylla
rauðum vepti Randvés bana.

The web of man grey as armour
Is now being woven; the Valkyries
Will cross it with a crimson weft.

Darraðarljóð (thirteenth-century Old Norse poem)

CHAPTER TWENTY-TWO

AD 451 – Six Years later

Ravenna, Capital of the Western Roman Empire

JUSTA GRATA HONORIA yawned and stretched, pushing the crumpled bedsheets away from her naked body. The sunlight of an early spring morning streamed into her bedroom from one of the tall windows. As the sun rose higher in the sky, the angle at which it entered changed and the beams made their way across the room until now, when they beat down onto her face. This meant that it was still morning, but only just.

The sunbeams probed her closed eyelids. Honoria opened them then immediately squeezed them shut again as the sunshine stirred the wine fumes lingering in her head to create stabs of pain that shot through her temples. Further sleep was impossible.

Not for the first time she made a silent resolution to have the bed moved.

She looked around. A wine jug lay on its side on a table beside the bed, the last of its contents dried to deep purple on the white stone tiles that covered the top. Another jug stood empty beside it. A couple of silver goblets were on the floor. The tabletop and the bedsheets were strewn with crumbs, the bones of chicken and a few squashed grapes.

Honoria sat up, letting the sheets fall away from her naked breasts, unconcerned that a young man lay in the bed beside her. He too was naked. He was perhaps nineteen or twenty, she could not remember. Handsome, short, and with a neatly trimmed beard and fashionable haircut. His sculpted and shaved muscular body told of regular visits to the gymnasium rather than hard toil in the fields.

Honoria allowed herself a smile of self-congratulation. She was at least ten years older than him. In Roman society, to be a woman of standing still unmarried at thirty-one made her practically an ancient spinster, to remain forever unwed. Even though she had not lost her looks, unlike many of her contemporaries, it was still an accomplishment that she could seduce a good-looking young man.

And slept on he did, even though the sunlight that had woken her also glared right into his face. This did not surprise Honoria. She doubted much got through that thick forehead of his. Marcus was not the brightest man of his age in Ravenna. He was very dull company. She had to drink herself silly to get down to his level and create some sort of rapport.

Then again, she thought, as a stab of bitterness turned her smile to a sneer, it may not just have been her looks and seductive wiles that had enticed this fellow into her bed. He was rich, son of one of the *honestiores* class. He was on the brink of a career in politics or the Army and looking for the fastest way to climb the steps of the *Cursus Honorum*. Even a man with his limited intelligence would know that sleeping with the sister of the Emperor of Rome could open all sorts of doors for a young, ambitious fellow like him.

While she enjoyed – indeed made the most of – the relative freedom that came from remaining unmarried, it was not from choice. Honoria had had many eligible suitors in her younger days. They had all disappeared when her brother had decreed that none of his sisters were to be married. It took levels of paranoia close to, and indeed sometimes slipping into, madness to survive at the top levels of Roman society, where everyone was your rival and the person you thought your best friend very probably had a knife for your back hidden in his toga. Marriage to a sister of the Emperor could provide legitimacy for a usurper's claim to the Purple, so Valentinian, ever wary of possible rebellion, had forbidden it.

Honoria could have understood that – just about – but her brother had gone further and insisted she and her half-sisters also remain celibate. That had proved too much. She had had several affairs since her brother's decree. With the others, she had done it more to spite her brother than to satisfy any urges of her own, but as the number of men willing to risk the danger of disobeying the Emperor just to be in her bed diminished, it was getting harder. She had begun to wonder, with a certain degree of dread, what the future held for her. Was she to become a dried-up old woman, clinging desperately to anyone from who she could secure shelter?

As if in answer to her thoughts, a loud crash came from downstairs, followed by the sound of angry voices and the frightened screams of the servants. Honoria stood up, wrapping herself in the bedsheets. The sound of running footsteps was already coming up the stairs.

'Marcus!' She turned, bent and shook the sleeping young man. 'Marcus, wake up. You have to get out of here!'

Marcus awoke, his usual confused expression even more bewildered now.

'What is it?' he just had time to say before the sound of fists hammering on Honoria's bedroom door began.

Honoria's stomach lurched. She had no idea who was outside, but it could not be good. She had either been betrayed, or her brother was being overthrown and his usurper was rounding up the rest of the Imperial family. Either could well mean her death.

'The door is locked,' she said. 'I will stall them. Get your clothes and climb out of the window.'

'Yes.' His sallow skin had turned pale.

He had only managed to sit up when the door was smashed open in a crash of splintering wood. Four soldiers rushed in.

They wore the black cloaks with black and red insignia of the Emperor's personal bodyguards from the *Palitini* field army.

Honoria saw the smirks on their faces as they rushed across the room, swords drawn, and hauled Marcus out of the bed. He started to resist but one of the soldiers dealt him a blow with his sword hilt, smashing the young man's nose and spraying blood and snot over the white bedsheets.

Two more soldiers came into the room, kicking the splintered remains of the door off their hinges on their way through. Honoria faced them, clasping the bedsheets more tightly to her chest.

'How dare you break in here?' she shouted, doing her best to channel her mounting dread into righteous anger. 'I am the sister of the Emperor!'

The continued smirks of the soldiers told her this threat bore no weight to these men.

'If only that were not true, Honoria.'

A new voice came from the doorway. A man of around thirty entered the room. He had the same wide eyes as Honoria. His black hair was cut short and curled along his forehead. He wore a metal cuirass, burnished to gleam like gold over his bright white tunic.

It was her brother: Placidus Valentinian, Caesar Augustus and ruler of the Roman Empire in the West.

For a few moments there was silence in the room as the Emperor stood, hands on hips, surveying what lay before him. Despite the anger that boiled within her, Honoria's fear deepened. She could see her brother was pale with anger. His mouth was clamped shut and the muscles of his jaw stood out.

'So the rumours are correct,' he said at length. His voice was like flint.

'What do you want us to do with him, *Imperator*?' one of the soldiers holding Marcus said. Honoria saw the tendons of his sword arm ripple.

Valentinian made a gesture with his head. The soldiers dragged the naked young man across the room to him.

'On your knees, dog,' one of them said as they forced Marcus into a kneeling position.

Marcus hung his head. It was clear he had no illusions about how much trouble he was in.

'Who are you, boy?' Valentinian said in a harsh bark. 'Speak while you still have a tongue in your head.'

'I am Marcus Antonius Falco, Caesar,' the naked young man said.

Valentinian nodded.

'You come from a noble family, boy. One with a long history of service to Rome,' he said. 'But tell me something. What makes you think you are noble enough to sleep with the sister of the Emperor?'

His voice rose until it was a strangled shout. The young man flinched.

'It was not my fault!' Marcus said. His voice cracked into sobs. 'She seduced me, lord! I think she must have used a love potion or other magic. I did not know my own mind.'

'You despicable little shit!' Honoria said. 'You knew exactly what you were doing. And you had no problem accepting that comfortable commission in the Army I secured for you.'

'Silence, Honoria,' Valentinian said. 'Both of you are to blame. Both have disobeyed my explicit command.'

'Please, lord, don't kill me,' Marcus was openly crying now. For the first time he looked up at the Emperor. Tears mingled with the blood from his shattered nose. Drool dripped from his lower lip. 'I am sorry for what I did. I did not mean to disobey you!'

'Pull yourself together,' the Emperor said, his face a mask of contempt. 'You may be from a good family but that doesn't mean you are worth killing. Take him away.'

Two of the soldiers hauled and shoved the broken Marcus

out of the doorway. The clatter of them dragging him down the stairs followed.

'What will you do with him?' Honoria said, fear making her own voice crack a little.

'Do you think I want the world knowing that my sister is a whore?' Valentinian said. 'He must be got rid of.'

'You said he was not worth killing,' Honoria said.

'By me, yes. That would make me look petty. Or worse: a tyrant. You said you had acquired a commission for him in the Army? Good. That means I will find him a suitable posting as far away from here as possible. Somewhere where no gossiping tongues from Ravenna can reach him. Somewhere very far away and very dangerous. An outpost fort in Mauretania, perhaps. One at risk of being overrun by barbarian savages and with not enough men to defend it properly...'

'And me?' Honoria said. 'Am I to be banished too?'

'Banished?' Valentinian was indignant. 'You should be beheaded for treason. You disobeyed my direct command!'

'An unjust command, Valentinian,' Honoria said. She could feel her own tears now running down her cheeks. 'How could you expect me to obey it?'

'Is it unjust that I should ask my sister to not make a whore of herself?' The Emperor's voice was rising to a squeak again. 'What's worse is that you thought you could get away with it. Did you not think I would have spies within your household?'

'You trust me so little?' Honoria's fear was turning to anger once again.

'Grow up, sister,' Valentinian said. 'An Emperor must always be vigilant. It is through those closest to him treachery will gain its foothold. And was I not right to have you watched?'

'Who betrayed me?' Honoria said, thinking about the members of her household, wondering which one had been watching her all along, reporting her every move to her brother.

Valentinian shook his head.

'So I am to be killed?' Honoria said.

'No,' her brother said, though he spoke through clenched teeth as if muttering the word was a strain to him. 'I've discussed it with Mother. You're to be married. That should stave off any scandal that might arise from your behaviour.'

Honoria's head whirled with relief, but also rage that her mother and her brother had taken it upon themselves to decide her fate.

'Who am I to be married to?' she said.

'Flavius Bassus Herculanus.'

Honoria let out a wail of despair. She slumped down onto the bed.

'Bassus Herculanus! The senator? He's twice my age!'

'He's very well respected,' her brother said.

'He's boring!' Honoria said. 'He's practically senile!'

'Once you are married to a decent man like him,' Valentinian said, folding his arms, 'it will stop tongues wagging. Who would suspect the wife of such an upstanding member of the Senate to be up to no good?'

'And what happened to your fear that traitors could use my marriage to usurp you?' Honoria said.

'Bassus is a good, reliable man,' her brother said with a shrug. 'He has neither the brains nor the ambition for betrayal. And at his age I can't see you having any children.'

He smirked.

'In fact, I can't see him doing much at all in that area,' he said. 'So get used to the idea. Mother says it is the best way to proceed.'

'You always do what Mother tells you to,' Honoria said, her voice bitter. 'She just wants everyone miserable like her.'

'Mother is not miserable,' Valentinian said. 'She is the most powerful woman in the Empire. She lacks no comforts.'

'She has not been happy since the end of her first marriage,' Honoria said. 'You know that! It's her bitterness that she can never regain that happiness which drives her to make all our lives a misery.'

'What do you mean?' Valentinian said. 'Our parents were happy together.'

'No they weren't, Valentinian,' Honoria said. 'Don't you remember the constant shouting? The awkward silences? Our mother only ever loved her first husband and she's yearned for those days ever since. Now she can't bear to see me happy and must condemn me to a marriage every bit as miserable as her second one was.'

'How can you spout such nonsense!' said the Emperor. 'Our mother was abducted by a barbarian. She was forced into marriage with him. You think she was happy? God saved her – *saved Rome* – by making the fruit of that union die before he was three.'

'Leaving no one in your way to the Purple,' Honoria said. 'Mother speaks of her days among the barbarians with nothing but fondness.'

'If you believe that you are like a foolish little girl,' Valentinian said. 'Mooning over dreams of the rugged barbarian king who will come and take you away from the family that knows best for you. Our mother was raped! Held hostage by the Visigoths. She was young and did not know her own mind, so when King Adolf told her she should marry him what else could she do?'

'She was happy! I know she was,' Honoria cried.

Her brother tutted and shook his head.

'You're marrying Bassus Herculanus and that's all there is to it.' Turning to the soldiers, he added, 'We're going. Leave enough men to guard the house, in case my sister gets any notions of running away.'

They began filing out of the room again. Two of the soldiers made no attempt to hide their blatant stares as they tried to take in as much of Honoria's naked flesh as they could.

'You should have killed me,' Honoria screamed after them. 'At least beheading would have been quick. Instead you condemn me to years of slow death!'

She threw herself onto the bed, great sobs wracking her

188

body. Utter despair filled her heart. Death really was preferable. Marriage to Bassus would be worse than being in prison. It *was* a form of prison. As the wife of a senator she would be virtually imprisoned within his house: by the invisible walls polite society put up, with their expectations for how a noble family should behave. Her future was a dark one. Year after year, slowly losing her mind to boredom in the stuffy, judgemental household of that old man.

After a time her sobs lessened and she sat up, suddenly aware that someone was watching her. She looked around and saw that Julia, the old servant woman who looked after her bedchamber, was standing in the ruined doorway, an expression of sadness and pity on her face.

Honoria's heart softened and she smiled through her tears. Julia was her oldest and most faithful servant and knew more about her than anyone in the world.

'Oh, Julia,' Honoria said with a sad smile. 'What's to become of us?'

'You should not have said such things about your mother, mistress,' the old woman said. 'It's true, perhaps that she was happy when she was with Adolf of the Visigoths but she is Roman through and through. She only wants the best for you. It was she who talked your brother out of having you executed when he found out you disobeyed him.'

'She did?' Honoria said. 'How do you—'

She stopped, eyes narrowing. How could the old woman know that? Surely Julia, her oldest and most trusted companion, could not be the spy her brother had mentioned?

Then again, she was perfect for the task...

'Leave me,' Honoria said, her voice cold.

The old servant hesitated, then disappeared from the doorway.

Honoria got up and crossed to her dressing table, which stood on the other side of the bedroom. She knew that if she wanted to escape the living death of marriage to Bassus she had to get away from Ravenna and the Roman Empire entirely. While she remained, there were too many prying eyes and her brother was all-powerful.

With new resolve in her heart Honoria took off one of her rings. She took a piece of parchment from a drawer in the table and began to write on it.

If her mother had found happiness with a barbarian king then why could not she? All she needed to do was find someone trustworthy who could deliver this letter for her...

CHAPTER TWENTY-THREE

City of Sirmium, Former Roman Province of Pannonia
Now in the Kingdom of the Huns

THE SUN WAS setting behind the walls of the city, walls which had seen better days. They had been battered down by Hun siege engines in several places and their stones were blackened where fire had licked them. The city inside was intact, however. The citizens had seen sense the moment their walls were breached and surrendered rather than make a glorious last stand that would have resulted in the deaths of everyone and the utter annihilation of the city and all its glories.

Sirmium was a former home of several Roman emperors and its glories were many: Imperial palaces, a horse-racing arena, a mint, a theatre, public baths, temples and luxurious villas all graced the city but also had contributed to making it such a prime target for Attila. If the palace at Sirmium was great enough for an Emperor of Rome, then Attila, still sole ruler of the Huns, wanted to see just how grand that was, so he could measure his own possessions to see if he was yet an equal.

The city fathers of Sirmium had paid the price for closing the gates on the advancing Huns. They had been beheaded in the forum before the palace, but Attila had spared most of the city. What was the point of capturing one of the jewels of the Eastern Empire to then just smash it to pieces?

The new ruler of Sirmium stood with his thumbs hooked in his belt, looking down with interest at a large wooden cross that lay on the grass just outside the gates of the city. Attila's most trusted warriors stood in a semi-circle around their king while several of the city's most prominent surviving citizens were also gathered there. They looked nervous, though nowhere near as much as the man who was on his knees before the king.

This man was a sorry sight. He had been stripped naked, and his exposed flesh displayed the cuts and abrasions from the sustained beating he had endured. Both his eyes were blackened, his left so swollen he could no longer see out of it. His nose was smashed to a pulp and several of his teeth lay in a bloody pool of saliva not far away. His grand clothes that had been ripped from his back lay in a heap of rags nearby.

'Lord Attila, I am so very, very sorry,' he said. He spoke in the tongue of the Huns but with the accent of a Gaul.

'I'm sure you are, Constantius,' Attila said, moving his attention to the kneeling man. 'At least you have stopped offending us by denying your theft.'

'It was not theft, lord,' Constantius said, his voice turning to a whine. 'I thought the gold was legitimate booty. Everyone else was taking what they wanted. Why should I not?'

'My warriors fought for this city, Constantius,' Attila said. 'They deserve to take their spoils of war. And when they do they first lay all of it at my feet before they dare take an ounce for themselves. You are my secretary. You write letters in Latin for me. Your scribing tool has not spilled much blood and I do not recall you laying any of what you took before me in tribute. Besides, if you thought you had a right to this holy man's gold, then why did you go to the trouble of misleading him?'

Constantius hung his head. One of the Sirmium notaries, an older man with a very long grey beard in the robes of a Christian bishop, nodded enthusiastically.

'If you had beheaded him and taken his gold perhaps I would have more respect for you,' Attila said. 'Ediko, have you found what happened to the holy man's gold?'

Ediko had done well for himself under Attila. He had been quick to prove his cleverness, loyalty and trustworthiness to ensure the king recognised how useful he was. In the last six years Ediko had risen to be one of his king's most trusted advisors, unlike many others who had paid for their mistakes with their heads.

'The secretary sold it to a Roman merchant,' he said. 'He left for Rome just before the city fell.'

Attila grunted.

'So, Constantius,' he said. 'I sent you to negotiate this city's surrender. The chief holy man gives you the treasure of his church, believing that it could be used as surety for the release of hostages we had taken. Instead you sold it to a Roman and kept the proceeds. You offered none of it to me. You saw a chance to make yourself rich and you took it.'

'Will I get the treasure back, Lord King?' the bishop said in a tremulous voice as he wrung his hands before him.

'I very much doubt it,' Attila said. 'But you will get justice. I want my own people and the people of Sirmium – who are now part of our kingdom – to know I will not tolerate corruption. I should have known when Aetius sent you to me as a secretary that you would be trouble. I'll be surprised if we don't find out that you've been spying on me all these years as well.'

'No, lord!' Constantius cried. 'I've learned my lesson. Please spare me... If you kill me, who will read or write in Latin for you?'

'That—' Attila began to say then stopped.

The sound of approaching hoofbeats made them all turn around. A Hunnish messenger rider, his horse lathered with sweat, approached. He reined his horse to a halt and swung himself out of the saddle then hurried over to where Attila stood. There he dropped to one knee and bowed his head.

'Mighty king,' the messenger said, without looking up. 'I have a letter for you. It was in the hands of a Roman messenger who was intercepted on his way here. The message is for you, personally.'

Attila raised his eyebrows. The messenger dug into his

leather satchel and withdrew a folded piece of parchment which he held up. Attila took it, picking it up gingerly as if it might burst into fire at any moment. He unfolded it and a large gold ring dropped out. Attila caught it, held it up and examined it, then he looked at the parchment and frowned.

'Did you know this was coming, Constantius?' he said.

'No, lord,' his kneeling, bleeding former secretary said. 'I know nothing of this.'

'This is written in Latin,' Attila said, proffering the parchment. 'I may be able to speak the Roman tongue but their scratchings on parchment is still a mystery to me. It seems you still have a use to me, Constantius. Read this.'

With trembling, scraped and bloody hands Constantius took the parchment and began to read.

'Lord King,' he said at length. His voice was cracked and not just from fear and the beating he had taken. 'This is a letter from Justa Grata Honoria, the sister of the Western Roman Emperor. She says she is in great distress. She is a prisoner who is being forced into an unhappy marriage and throws herself at the mercy of the mighty Attila, praying he will come for her and rescue her from her plight. In return she will give you half of everything that is hers.'

The bishop let out a gasp.

Attila held up the heavy gold ring and pursed his lips.

'Well now, this is a first,' he said. 'I have three wives already, but this is the first time a woman has proposed to me.'

'Proposed?' the bishop said. 'I don't think—'

The sharp look Attila threw in his direction silenced him before he could finish.

'And if this Justa Grata Honoria is the sister of Emperor Valentinian,' Attila said. 'Then her dowry would be considerable. Half of everything that is hers must be...'

He grinned like a wolf.

'About half of the Western Roman Empire,' he continued. 'This is perfect, absolutely perfect.'

'So you see, you still have a use for me after all, Lord Attila,' Constantius said with a pleading smile that revealed his broken and missing teeth. 'Can you forgive me? You will need someone to write the response to this letter for you.'

Attila looked at him for a moment. Then he looked at the bishop.

'You can read and write Latin, holy man. Right?'

The bishop nodded.

'Good. You will do it for me then,' Attila said. 'You can no longer be trusted, Constantius, and my new secretary, this old holy man, needs to see justice done. Crucify him.'

Constantius began to curse, then scream in terror as Attila's bodyguards closed in around him. They forced him down onto the wooden cross then held his legs together, turned his feet sideways, and held a large iron nail against the side of the upper heel.

'Please, don't,' the Gaul pleaded.

Then one of the Hun warriors struck the nail head with a hammer. There was a resounding ring of metal on metal, a horrific crunch of grinding bone, and Constantius let out a wild shriek of agony. The nail was driven through both heel bones, pinning his feet to the wood beneath. The warriors then moved on to his arms, spearing them across the cross-piece and hammering a nail through the wrist of first the left, then his right arm. Bright red copper-smelling blood gushed from all three wounds. Constantius was now screaming at the top of his lungs.

The warriors heaved the cross upright, sliding the base into a hole that had been dug for it in the ground. They filled the hole in with dirt, then stepped back sharply as a stream of urine cascaded down from above. Constantius continued to scream and writhe around in pain. He slumped down and forwards, only to increase the pain on his transfixed wrists. To try to relieve that he pushed himself up from his pinned feet, but that transferred his weight to his skewered ankles. Screaming at the pain that invoked he slumped forward, beginning the whole terrible cycle of torment once again.

Attila watched for a time, his face impassive.

'How long will it take for him to die?' he said to Ediko.

His advisor shrugged.

'Sometimes it can take days, Mighty One.'

Attila frowned in a way that suggested he could not listen to his former secretary's screams for that long. More because the sound irritated rather than horrified him.

'These Romans must be an exceptionally cruel bunch to have invented such a torture,' he said.

Attila turned and began to walk away, gesturing to Ediko that he should follow.

'Tell me, Ediko,' he said when the two of them were far enough away from the tortured screams of Constantius to hear each other talk, and at the same time not be overheard by the others. 'Did I do the right thing? Will the people think *me* cruel for this deed?'

'The people love you like a father, Mighty King,' Ediko said. 'And a good father disciplines his children. It is his right. It is expected.'

'But do they believe *I* have the right to rule alone?' Attila said. 'What do your spies tell you? Do people still talk of Bleda?'

Ediko hesitated before replying. Attila spotted it straight away.

'They do, don't they?' he said.

'Yes, lord,' Ediko said with a sigh. 'There is sometimes talk of whether you rule by the blessings of the Gods or through your own hand.'

To Ediko's surprise and relief, Attila gave a little chuckle.

'Some would say they are the same thing,' he said.

'If only you had the Sword of the War God, Mighty One,' Ediko said. 'Then no one would question whether you should rule or not.'

196

Attila held up the gold ring.

'That is now within my grasp, Ediko,' he said. 'This letter is most excellent. We have been ready for war for some time but now we have the excuse. We have the cause. We can attack them with purpose. And what more noble cause could there be than rescuing a virgin who is in distress?'

'From what I have heard, Mighty One,' Ediko said, 'the Emperor's sister is far from a virgin.'

They both turned around and watched the unfortunate Constantius squirm, flail and cry on the cross for a little while longer.

'I had not seen someone crucified before,' Ediko said. 'I didn't think there would be so much blood.'

The sun was almost set now and the entire scene was bathed in deep red light.

'This is just the start of the bloodletting,' Attila said, his eyes pointing at the crucified man but seeming like they were looking at something a thousand miles beyond him. 'There will be much more blood, destruction and suffering. But if it has to be, then let it be now.'

CHAPTER TWENTY-FOUR

Aquae Sulis, Former Roman Province of Britannia

HAGAN SIGHED AND sat back against the warm tiles. Steam rose around him. He let the heat seep into his body, relaxing his tired muscles and chasing away the aches that troubled him more and more recently.

All in all, this was one of his most enjoyable days he had spent at work in a very long time.

Hagan really enjoyed the baths. In his time in the Army and after leaving Roman service he had visited many of them throughout the Western Empire. This one in Aquae Sulis was a modest affair compared to some but no less comfortable for that. The one downside was that the heated water came from natural hot springs beneath the earth. It probably meant the place was cheaper to run but the downside was that the water itself had a strange, egg-like odour. The local Britons believed the water was heated by the breath of a goddess, Sulis, who lived beneath the earth. If that was indeed the case, Hagan thought, then the goddess must have rather bad breath.

On the plus side, most bathhouses just had three main rooms: the *tepidarium* with its pleasant heated floors to relax the muscles and open the pores, the *caldarium* with its hot water bath, body oil and scrapers to clear the skin, and the *frigidarium*, the large pool of freezing cold water that finished the bathing ritual. This one also had a *sudatorium*, a vaulted room whose walls were lined with pipes that funnelled hot air and heated the room beyond anything experienced in the hot water of the caldarium, while steam was introduced via vents in the walls to increase the temperature further.

It was there that Hagan sat, back to the wall, trying to remember he was supposed to be working. His companions, two burly Saxons with their blond hair shaved front-to-crown but long at the back and tied into plaited ponytails, lounged on the stone step beside him, enjoying the heat as much as he was. The sudatorium was a circular room with a floor of white marble surrounded by four terraced steps of darker stone. The step Hagan and the Saxon sat on was the topmost of the four. As it was the highest in the room it was also the hottest part, but it also gave them a vantage point from where they could watch over the Britons they were employed to guard.

Hagan looked at the men below. There were seven of them: four kings, two warlords and one bishop. They represented the most powerful men in Britannia, or at least what was left of it. In his short time there Hagan had learned that since Rome, beset with her own internal problems, had pulled her legions out of this province at the edge of the world, it had shattered into a hundred petty realms, each one ruled by a dictator who thought he was going to be the next emperor. In the interval they had fought each other, either through open war or treacherous murder, expanding their power or being exterminated, until only the most powerful, the most ruthless or the most deceitful remained.

To Hagan's surprise and amusement, most of these Britons still thought themselves Roman, even while the last vestiges of the Empire disintegrated around them. They had their hair cut like Romans, wore Roman clothes and went to the baths, while all around them the Pax Romana turned to banditry and chaos, social structures collapsed and power – and therefore the fate of the ordinary folk – moved into the hands of those who either had the wealth or the strength to grasp it. Such realms as this were Hell on Earth for the people forced to live in them, but the perfect place for a man with a strong sword arm to sell and enough knowledge of military tactics to make him useful in any warband.

Hagan was one such man. He rolled his left shoulder, the one which bore a raised white scar that looked like a star. It was this now long-healed injury that had ended his career in the Army before his standard twenty years was even half complete. It still troubled him, especially in the dank, cold weather of Britannia, but the heat of the bathhouse always washed that away and he felt young again. He took a deep breath through his nose, smelling the herb-scented air. Sweat dripped from his brow, his nose and covered his whole body in a sheen, which was appropriate, as the name of the sudatorium meant 'sweating room' in the tongue of the Romans.

Hagan fingered his mother's amulet, which he still wore round his neck. The dainty chain his mother wore it from had been far too short for the knotted muscles of his thick neck and it now dangled from a leather thong. At that moment it was the only thing he wore. Like everyone else in the baths he was naked. This was why the place had been chosen for this meeting of the powerful Britons: no one could sneak a weapon in.

'These Britons,' Horsa, one of the Saxons beside Hagan said with a shake of his head. 'No wonder they need us to fight for them. If they don't even trust each other how will they ever come together to fight their common foes?'

He spoke in his own tongue, but the words were similar enough that he and Hagan could understand each other, unlike the Latin-speaking Britons to whom their speech was just barbarian gibberish.

Hagan grunted his assent. The Britons had gathered here to discuss what to do about the biggest threat to their island since Rome invaded yet they still could not come together in trust.

The thought suddenly occurred to him that perhaps these

half-Romanised Britons were not that different from himself. He hated Rome but loved the baths it had created. The heated water, the comfort and the cleanliness encapsulated in many ways what Roman civilisation stood for, yet also it was Rome's contempt and jealousy of other people's freedom and her grasping, paranoid greed that had destroyed Hagan's kindred and folk.

Still, over the years he had learned through a series of bitter lessons to have a grudging respect for what was called the 'civilisation' Rome had created. Hagan sometimes thought of the rough, cold days of his childhood, when everything seemed damp and louse-ridden and they had not known such wonders as this sudatorium existed. There was an old derelict bathhouse in Vorbetomagus but it had long fallen into disrepair as no one knew how it worked.

The Burgundars had thought Vorbetomagus was the height of civilisation and their folk the greatest in the world. Looking back now, having seen a lot of that world and the wonders of the Roman Empire, Hagan knew his folk had not built that city, it was the Romans who had. The Burgundars had crossed the Rhine from the northern forests beyond the Empire and taken Vorbetomagus. The Romans who had lived there had fled, taking the knowledge of civilisation with them. He and all his people, for all their pride, gold and boasting, had just been another horde of barbarians, living amid the Roman ruins like flies on the corpse of a lion.

Hagan cast a wary glance at their potential opposition, the bodyguards of the rival British kings, who sat on the top step on the opposite side of the room. He and the Saxons were in the employ of King Vortigern, one of the Britons engaged in the discussions on the floor of the room below. Vortigern was perhaps twenty-five, handsome, though a little short, Hagan thought, and with a neatly trimmed beard and fashionable haircut. His naked body was shaved of all hair in the Roman fashion and his sculpted physique told of regular visits to the gymnasium rather than hard toil in the regular battle drill of a warrior. Like a lot of the southern Britons he had become so used to the protection of Roman soldiers that now he paid Saxon foederati and other mercenaries to fight his battles rather than relying on the strength of his own arms.

The two Britons who sat across from Hagan were the bodyguards of Emrys Ambrosius Aurellianus, a northern warlord they called 'Arthur the Bear'. The northern Britons were a different lot to the those who lived in realms like Vortigern's. Perhaps it was because they were beset by constant attacks from invaders, but the northerners seemed a hardier, more self-reliant breed. Hagan had seen Emrys in a Roman toga but Cei and Bedwyr, his two most trusted warriors who watched his back, had long hair and moustaches in the manner of free Gauls. They were heavily muscled, their noses flat from being broken and their bodies scarred from war wounds. Hagan knew them and their reputation for violence was notorious. If anything did go wrong in this meeting, Hagan and his Saxon companions would have to deal with these two and that would not be easy. Especially without weapons.

Hagan's gaze flicked to the man who sat one step down from Cei and Bedwyr. This thin man in his middle years unsettled the Burgundar more than the burly warriors who sat above him. The Bear's advisor, the man they called the Myrddin – whatever that meant – had a strange aura about him. He had entered wrapped in a long dark cloak that was now folded beside him and his head was shaved. He had a sharp-featured face and watched the discussion below with intelligent grey eyes, his brow furrowed in concentration.

After the years Hagan had spent in the Roman Army he could understand the Roman tongue, unlike his Saxon companions. That was the ulterior motive for Arminius, the commander of the band of mercenaries Hagan now belonged to: picking him to guard Vortigern during this meeting, so he could also spy on proceedings.

'The situation is intolerable,' Constantine, King of Ceredigion, said. 'The Picts cross the Great Northern Wall now it is undefended and ravage the north at will. The Scotti attack us from across the sea in their *curraghs*. They raid along the west coast, kill at will, burn our churches and take treasure and slaves. The barbarians drive us to the sea, the sea drives us to the barbarians. No one is safe. Even Calpurnius, a patrician and the senator of Bonaven, has had his villa set ablaze and his own son taken into slavery in Ireland. We must do something or Britannia will fall to these barbarians.'

Baths, senators, taxes and speaking the Roman tongue, Hagan mused. *The Roman army may have left but these men carry on like they were still part of the Empire.*

Looking around, Hagan saw that the Myrddin was looking up at him, now with narrowed, suspicious eyes. Did the man know he could understand Latin? Hagan looked away again, staring up at the ceiling and trying his best to look bored and disinterested.

'If Vortigern would perhaps donate some of his horde of foreign hirelings,' Emrys said, 'then we could carry the fight to the Picts and the Scotti. We would have enough warriors to drive them back to their own lands and teach them the price of attacking Britannia.'

King Vortigern smiled but the expression held no mirth.

'We all know why you would want me to move my warriors out of my realm, Emrys,' he said. 'It would leave me vulnerable. What would it benefit me if the Picts are driven north of the Wall yet I lose my own throne? No: we must make an appeal to Rome.'

'You would invite the legions back to our land?!' Emrys said, his voice touched with anger. 'Just when we've made ourselves free?'

'What sort of freedom has it proved to be?' Vortigern said. 'The freedom to be attacked at will by barbarians? To be beset in our own homes, within our own borders? I'd rather be bound by Roman Laws if it also meant Roman Peace.'

'And what of Roman taxes?' Conan Aurelian, the other northern British warlord, said.

'If it means the return of Law and order then so be it,' Bishop Cadoc said. He was the oldest of all those there. His ribs stood out on his scrawny naked body, which was hairless from age rather than fashionable shaving. 'Did Jesus not teach us that we should "Render unto Caesar that which is Caesar's"?'

'I cannot spare men to fight these barbarians either,' Cuneglas, the King of Gwynedd said. 'I agree with Vortigern. We should ask Rome for help.'

'It's the most practical option,' Maelgwyn, the last of the kings, said. He was a dark man with a bald crown who was examining his fingers as if bored with the discussion going on around him. 'Let's be honest. None of us trust each other enough to send our own warbands north to deal with these barbarians. Besides, if Rome can send her sons to do the dying for us then why should we sacrifice our own?'

The other kings and the bishop nodded.

'So we are agreed, then?' the bishop said. 'We will write to General Aetius and appeal for Roman military help?'

'All those in favour?' Vortigern, standing up.

The four kings and the bishop raised their hands straight away. The two warlords did not, but seeing themselves outvoted, reluctantly raised their hands as well. The Myrddin scowled and shook his head.

'Good,' Vortigern said. 'Let us not delay. Draft the letter straight away and it can be sent by the morning.'

At that everyone stood up and began moving for the door. The two sets of bodyguards made their way down from the top benches. As they passed by, Cei and Bedwyr cast supercilious smiles at the Saxons and Hagan that suggested the words *maybe next time, foreigners.* Then the whole company filed out of the sweating room.

A visit to the baths had a strict order – the tepidarium, the sudatorium, the caldarium, then finally a plunge into the cold waters of the frigidarium. From the rapid exit of the noble Britons from the sweating room and the stony lack of conviviality between them Hagan could tell the journey through the other parts of the ritual to the changing rooms would be short and unfriendly.

As they padded their way down the gloomy corridor towards the frigidarium they passed a series of small rooms available for hire when men wanted to conduct some private business for whatever reason. Hagan saw one of the bathhouse slaves approaching from the opposite end of the corridor. The slave bore a tray with grapes and other tasty morsels, a brass wine jug and two goblets on it, refreshments no doubt to be delivered to one of the private rooms.

In his time in the Roman Army Hagan had been trained to notice things. He had been part of an *exploratores* unit, scouts who went ahead of the legions into enemy territory, looking out for any natural obstacles, ambushes or traps. In such situations a change of the light or a swinging branch could be just a bird taking off, or it could be a warrior waiting behind a tree to slit your throat.

There was something about the way the slave carried the tray that was not quite right, Hagan realised. He was a young man who bounced on the balls of his feet as he walked. He was too fit, too well-fed and too upright for a slave. The tray seemed oddly balanced on his right hand as well.

Then the man dropped the tray. The hand beneath had a knife in it.

'Death to tyrants!' the man shouted. He lunged at Vortigern.

Hagan acted without thinking. He lashed out with his leg, kicking sideways. His foot caught the attacker on his right hip as he was stretching forward, knife raised to strike. It was enough to make the man stumble and his knife sliced air instead of Vortigern's flesh. The king flinched away, a look of horror on his face.

The assailant stumbled sideways then regained his balance. He gnashed his teeth in frustration, then brandished the knife again.

'Do something!' Hagan shouted at his fellow bodyguards. Both of the big Saxons were standing back. The fact that they were naked somehow made them all the more cautious.

Hagan dipped and grabbed the fallen tray as the young man came forward to attack again. Hagan put himself in front of Vortigern. The assailant stabbed at Hagan's chest. He just had time to pull the tray in front of him. The point of the blade hit the metal tray then made a nauseating squeaking, scraping sound as it skidded over the surface.

Hagan kicked the attacker again, this time in the groin. The man let out a gasp and doubled over. Hagan also cried out in pain. Naked as he was, he wore no shoes and the kick had sent pain shooting through his toes. Thankfully Horsa had finally recovered his wits. The big Saxon picked up the metal wine jug from where it had fallen and smashed it across the side of the attacker's head. The man went stumbling sideways once more. Hagan flipped the tray around and thumped the attacker over the head with it. There was a clang but the man remained upright. Then Aella, the other Saxon guard, smashed his fist into the side of the young man's jaw. The attacker's eyes rolled up into his head, his knees buckled and he collapsed to the ground.

'Treachery!' Vortigern howled.

Cei and Bedwyr grabbed the Bear and hustled him away down the corridor. The other British leaders likewise hurried away, everyone keen to get clear as fast as possible in case other murderers were about to strike. The strange man they called the Myrddin went after them, but not before he had shot a glance at the would-be killer. That glance bore enough disappointment that Hagan would have been prepared to wager silver on who had sponsored this attack.

'Bind him,' Vortigern shouted, pointing at the prone assailant. 'I want to know who paid him to try to kill me. Torture him. Do whatever you need to but I want to know their names.'

Horsa sat on the unconscious assailant while Aella went to find something to tie him up with.

'Well done, Saxon,' Vortigern said, looking at Hagan. Then his expression changed to one of suspicion. 'You acted fast. How did you know he was going to attack me?'

'He didn't look like a slave,' Hagan said. 'He bore himself with too much confidence. He's too fit. He must have bribed one of the slaves to give him his tray.'

'Bathhouse slaves are notoriously corrupt,' Vortigern said. He tutted and shook his head. 'It's typical of the terrible state we are in that decent people can't carry on their affairs in the bathhouse without fear of being robbed or murdered.'

Vortigern regarded Hagan with an expression of interest. 'You did good work today, Saxon,' the king said. 'You are quick-witted, and you've shown you are capable in a fight. I might have a very special mission for you. How would you like to go to the Centre of the World?'

At that moment Hagan caught sight of Arminius, the leader of the mercenaries he was employed by. He was running towards them, anxious to find out what the commotion was about.

'What's going on?' Arminius said.

Hagan had known Arminius since their days in the Roman Army; indeed at one time Arminius had been his commanding officer. He was much older than Hagan and though still straight-backed, retirement and the prosperity brought by his business meant his belly was expanding.

The others explained what had happened.

'It was good work by your man here,' Vortigern said. 'I want him to go to Ravenna with the bishop.'

'He's the man I was telling you about, Lord Vortigern,' Arminius said. 'I was going to send him anyway.'

A look of realisation crossed Vortigern's face that Hagan did not like the look of.

Arminius cocked his head towards Hagan and rolled his eyes in the direction of one of the doors to the private rooms. Hagan hung back, letting the others escort Vortigern out, then followed his commander into the room.

Once inside, Arminius closed the door carefully so as not to draw attention with the sound, then turned to Hagan.

'So they really are going to do it?' he said.

'Yes,' Hagan said. He proceeded to give his commander a summary of what he had overheard.

When he had finished, a broad smile spread across the lips of Arminius.

'This is excellent,' he said. 'And their appeal will go to General Aetius?'

'Yes,' Hagan said, clenching his teeth. 'It seems that old butcher still lives.'

'That's no way to talk about our old commander, lad,' Arminius said, with an admonishing smile.

'That bastard was responsible for the deaths of my family, my friends and the old of my folk,' Hagan said. 'Every day I served under him made those wounds deeper.'

'Well I hope you can get over that,' Arminius said, with a twinkle in his eye that Hagan did not like. 'Because you'll be going along with that letter to meet General Aetius.'

Hagan took a step back, fists clenched.

'There is no way—' he began to say, then he saw the knife in Arminius's hand.

The door opened and three of Arminius's Saxons filed in. They barred the exit, arms folded before their chests.

'I'm sorry, old friend,' Arminius said. 'But the general has specifically asked for some Burgundars. And he has offered good gold and silver if I can find him any.'

'You are a mercenary bastard, Arminius,' Hagan said with a sigh.

'I thought you'd have realised this by now,' Arminius said, a bemused smile on his lips. 'I'm *the* mercenary bastard.'

CHAPTER TWENTY-FIVE

Ravenna, Capital City of the Western Roman Empire

THE JOURNEY FROM the very edge of the world, Britannia, to its new centre, Ravenna, took Hagan several weeks, during which time winter turned to early spring. It was a huge distance, but under normal circumstances it should not have taken that long. Imperial messengers, galloping on the network of roads that spanned the Empire and were dotted with mansiones that allowed them to change horses every ten miles, could cover the distance in eight or nine days.

The Empire, however, had lumbered into a new crisis. The Huns, Hagan had learned, had crossed the Danube and torn a bloody swathe through Germania and northern Gaul. The roads between northern Gaul and Italia were not safe. Therefore they had sailed most of the way on board a ship of the Imperial Navy.

Hagan found it ironic that the Huns, the murderous Roman lapdogs who had slaughtered his people, had now turned on their masters just at the time he was on his way to visit the general responsible for unleashing them.

Hagan's former comrades – Arminius and his Saxon mercenaries – had kept a close watch on him the whole time. On the ship he had been reasonably free to walk around; there was nowhere for him to run away to, after all. But on land, and especially now in the crowded streets of the Roman capital, they huddled close around him. He was not bound or treated like a common prisoner or slave – they had enough respect for him as a warrior who had fought beside them not to allow that – however there was always a guiding hand on his arm, and the Saxons' hands never strayed far from the hilts of the seax knives they wore at their belts. The message was clear: if he tried to run, the knives would come out.

Whatever General Aetius was paying them to deliver a live Burgundar, it must be worth it. Why he wanted one was another question but no one seemed to know the answer to that.

Arminius, like Hagan, had once been a Roman soldier. Unlike Hagan, however, as the son of a Cherusci king, Arminius had been an officer. On retiring from the Army the German had used what he had learned fighting for Rome to set up his own private army, hiring out warriors to barbarian kings and warlords who needed trained men to augment their own.

In the chaotic world left by the ever-shrinking Roman Empire, there was a lot of work for men like the ones Arminius supplied, and he was not the only ex-Roman soldier plying this trade. As it turned out, they also had not totally cut ties with their former paymasters either. Rome herself often had need of mercenaries to augment her legions so it was good business sense to stay in touch through the network of old soldiers that spanned the known world.

It was through this that Aetius had sent his request for any surviving Burgundars with military experience to be sent to him, where they could be exchanged for a hefty sum in gold and silver. For what purpose he did not say. Suspecting the Britons they were working for were on the verge of sending an appeal for help to the Roman Magister Militum, Arminius had seen a way to kill two birds with one stone and get paid twice for the same journey: once for guarding Vortigern's emissaries on their dangerous trip to Ravenna and again for delivering a Burgundar to Aetius while they were there.

'You Burgundars are like the rarest of spices,' Arminius had told Hagan on the voyage. 'Very scarce and hard to find.'

'Thanks to Aetius,' Hagan had replied.

Arminius had told Hagan that Aetius meant him no harm, but Hagan suspected he was only saying this to keep him quiet on the voyage. He suspected that perhaps Aetius had sent out this plea for surviving Burgundars so he could finish the job he started at Vorbetomagus all those years ago and make sure every last one was annihilated.

Two could play that game. If he got within striking distance of the general, Hagan could get revenge for the death of his folk. Though, as he knew from bitter experience, such chances were very rare indeed. He had been close to Aetius a number of times during his army years and knew the man was always surrounded by bodyguards.

At Ravenna they disembarked at its bustling port. The emissaries of the Britons, which included Bishop Cadoc, huddled together while Arminius sought the correct officials who could ensure they got access to the general. After some time he returned, now accompanied by several civil servants in togas and a cohort of soldiers, *comitatenses* of the interior field army. After that they set off into the city, their legs still unsteady from the long time spent at sea.

They pushed their way through the crowded streets. It was past midday and the stone-paved streets of the city were thronged with people. Ravenna was one of the largest cities in the world now. It had already been a major port before the Imperial Court had moved there from Rome forty years before, and that re-centring of power had accelerated the growth of the city tenfold.

The soldiers went in front and behind, making room for the timid Britons and their mercenary bodyguards. Hagan was surrounded by Arminius's Saxons, just in case he decided to try to make a run for it at this very last leg of the trip.

It was cold and rain began to spit from the sky, as benefitted a day in very early spring, though nowhere near the snow and biting cold that had accompanied this time of year in Hagan's homeland.

As he pulled the hood of his cloak up, Hagan thought how far he had come since the days of his childhood. Fifteen winters had passed since he had survived the annihilation of his kindred at Vorbetomagus. In that time Hagan had wandered far and seen many things. On that fateful day he and the other remnants of the Burgundar horde, like his old friend Gunderic, had been marched away from Vorbetomagus and pressed into service in the Roman Army, leaving behind the burned-out ruins of what had once been their homeland.

Gunderic, being the son of a king, had been inducted into an elite cavalry unit. As he watched Gunderic ride away, never to see him again, Hagan had thought how another familiar part of his life was leaving him.

The rest of the Burgundars with Hagan had been drilled in Roman tactics and supplied with weapons and armour. They began intensive training in the Roman tongue, then they were incorporated as a cohort of foot soldiers – *pedes* – in a legion which was mostly recruited from German tribes.

Their commander, Flavius Maximus, was a Roman of the old kind. His discipline was harsh but, Hagan had to concede, he was always fair to his men. It was clear where you stood with Maximus: any man who followed orders and did not shirk his duty was welcome in the commander's unit and always got his fair share of the loot after battle. Anyone who didn't, did not last long.

The Burgundars, Hagan had soon learned, were not the only thorn in Rome's side. The Empire was under constant attack from tribes outside its borders and rebellions from within. General Aetius's next task had been to put down a rebellion of the Bacaudae of Armorica in north-west Gaul.

In the fighting that followed, the Burgundar cohort suffered more casualties and it was not long before it was unsustainable as a cohesive unit. They were disbanded and scattered across the other legions to make up for those other units' losses and Hagan saw the final remnants of his home and his people dispersed.

Hagan knew that standing in a shield wall waiting to die was not the best use of his talents and was eager to find something more suitable. The Army was good at making the best use of its men's skills – for its own benefit of course. Flavius Maximus recognised Hagan's hunting skills and thought they would be best employed in the exploratores, the scouts who went ahead of the legions to prepare the way.

In those years Hagan found that the 'Roman' army was in fact mostly made up of the people the Romans called barbarians. He found himself fighting alongside men from all over the known world, many of them conscripts like himself. They defeated the Bacaudae then had to march to the other side of the Western Empire to face down invading Gepids and Alans. So it went on, year after year, marching north, south, east and west, to Germania, Hispania and Gaul, defending an Empire he had no love for against invaders or putting down rebels.

Discipline was harsh, the conditions miserable, and pay days came few and far between. Often the tribes Hagan found himself fighting against shared more in common with him than the men who fought by his side did.

The hardest thing he had had to deal with was fighting alongside Huns. General Aetius, he had learned, had been brought up as a hostage in the court of the Hun King, and it seemed he had now come to depend on them for their cavalry. The Huns' effectiveness was frightening and, when let loose to do as they pleased, they were utterly ruthless. It was understandable, but for Hagan unpalatable after what he had seen at Vorbetomagus.

The Visigoths, the Western Goths, were their most persistent foes. Every time Roman forces defeated this people Hagan somehow knew they would find themselves fighting them again soon. It had been the Visigoths who had sacked Rome itself in his father's youth. It had been that calamitous defeat that had pushed the Emperor to move his court from Rome to the easier defended Ravenna. That defeat had shocked the Romans to their very souls and the memory of it continued to haunt them. It was the Goths they worried about most and, as if to taunt them, the Goths just kept on coming back.

It was a Gothic spear that had ruined the rusted iron rings of his cheap Army-issued mail shirt and led to Hagan being discharged. The wound was deep and took a long time to heal. The legion had to move on, so Hagan was handed his diploma and left behind to recover by himself.

Then began the loneliest part of his life. Miserable as army life had been, he had now lost the comradeship and routine that was such an integral part of it. He was alone. The years of army life had left him without a wife and while he was still a young man, he was older than most other men when they got married. Not many women would want a husband who was much older than them, especially one with neither land or money.

When Hagan's shoulder did recover he was faced with the dilemma of what he would do for the rest of his life. All he knew how to do was fight and hunt, but he had no people to fight for, no homeland to defend, no lord to give him bread or gold in exchange for the use of his sword arm. He was nothing. A homeless wanderer.

Yet he had found out that the world was a bloody, violent place and there was always plenty of work for a trained warrior. He had sold his skills to the highest bidder, becoming a warrior in many warbands that ranged across the edges of the Empire and beyond. Sometimes he fought for tribes who were foederati, sometimes for enemies of Rome. He had raided with Hermeric, King of the Suebi, along the coast of the Franks, fought with King Bisinus of the Thuringians, and spent some time in the wars beyond Germania the Greater.

He was never completely trusted however, never fully accepted into any of the warbands he fought with. The best positions always went to others whose blood was shared with the king or lord who led the warband. They could be trusted, unlike the sellswords who might stab their leader in the back on the promise of gold. After victories the conquered lands were given to members of the leaders' own people, the mercenaries were only ever granted coins.

There was no one Hagan could reminisce with. No one who remembered the kingdom of the Burgundars in its days of glory. While other tribes spoke mostly the same tongue as him, however heavily accented, no one knew the poetry of his people, their sagas or their customs. There was no one who he could sing the old songs with.

Eventually he had by chance run into an old Saxon comrade from the Army in a tavern in Germania. The man had told Hagan about Arminius, who was now retired from the Army and looking for good reliable men for his new venture. The Britons were recruiting sellswords to defend them from raids by the Scots and Picts and Arminius, using the logistics skills he had gained in the Roman Army, was organising squads of men from among the Saxons for that purpose. The prospect of being among fellow former soldiers, even men he didn't know, was too much for Hagan to resist. He had set off north.

Now, as he made his way along the crowded pavement in Ravenna, he mused on how he had travelled around the edges of the known world, and now here he was at the very centre of it. The Empire may not have been what it once was, but Rome, even if you considered it an empire divided nowadays, was still the single greatest power in the world.

Hagan had been in cities before but he could not remember one like this. Arminius had mentioned on the voyage that perhaps fifty thousand people lived in Ravenna. That number was unimaginable to him – it was probably more than the entire Burgundar people had numbered at the time of their

216

annihilation. Now, amid the thronging masses of the crowded city he could well believe it. It was this – the sheer size and scale of the Rome Empire – that made her so enduring and invincible. Individual tribes like his could never hope to stand against such might.

Yet even here, in the very heart of the Empire, there were signs of decay. The packed streets were busy with carts, wagons and other vehicles but the shit of the oxen and horses that drew them had not been lifted in weeks and their wheels ploughed ruts through mounds of it. He passed shops, taverns, three-storey high tenements and brothels, all busy, but many walls were scratched with graffiti or daubed with political slogans. Many of the public fountains and water troughs they passed by were dry and clogged with rubbish. Gangs of young men hung around at every crossroads, looking for the chance to cause mischief or rob unsuspecting passers-by. At the sight of the cohort of soldiers marching Hagan and the others along, they slunk away into nearby alleys.

The further they walked the more the city changed. The tightly packed buildings of the city centre gave way to large villas set back from the road in their own grounds. Eventually they arrived at a particularly large one. Here the company turned off the main road and approached the front door. This could only be the house of Aetius. Hagan felt the Saxons around him crowding closer, just in case he thought of running.

Two soldiers stood guard at the entrance. At the sight of the officials accompanying Hagan and the others, they nodded and stood aside to let them enter the main building.

They walked into the chill of the atrium of the house which had a tiled floor, a high roof and a pool to catch rainwater that came in through a skylight. To the right of the door General Aetius's old military cuirass and helmet were arranged on a stand, as if his ghost stood guard over the entrance. They were scarred with the signs of many battles. Hagan had seen the general wearing them in anger and conceded that despite his hatred for the man, Aetius had never shirked the responsibility of being at the sharp end of war, unlike a lot of leaders.

The walls on either side of the room were lined with plaster faces. Hagan knew this was a ghoulish tradition of the Romans, who made casts of their relatives' visages when they died. The line of death masks that now stared blank-eyed from the walls were the general's forefathers, generations of men who had fought for the Senate and people of Rome.

A male slave met them and ushered them up a set of stairs to a grand set of double doors. He knocked on the door then poked his head in to announce the group's arrival.

A gruff command to enter came from inside.

The slave turned around, an apologetic expression on his face.

'The general wishes to see Lord Arminius and the Burgundar first,' he said. 'If the rest of you could wait outside?'

The delegation of Britons, the bishop especially, looked most indignant but said nothing.

The slave pushed the door open then stood aside so Hagan and Arminius could enter the room beyond.

There, reclining on a couch, was General Flavius Aetius, the Magister Militum, one of the most powerful men in the Roman Empire and the single person in the world Hagan hated most.

CHAPTER TWENTY-SIX

Aᴇᴛɪᴜs, ᴜɴʟɪᴋᴇ ᴍᴏsᴛ men in their later middle age, had not gained a paunch through good wine and fine food. His corded muscles spoke of constant exercise and his brown eyes sparkled bright with vitality. In other ways he did look his age: his white hair was cropped close to hide how sparse it was, and his hawk-like nose stood out from sunken cheeks that suggested missing teeth beneath.

Hagan felt his lip curl. He longed to scratch the flesh of his forearm. He had spent a lot of time in the presence of killers but being in the same room as this butcher made his skin crawl. For a moment he felt light-headed. His gaze flicked around the room for anything that he could use as a weapon; something to stab Aetius through his scrawny chest or batter his skull in with. He knew, however, that even if he managed to do that he would not leave the villa alive: two bodyguards in full military armour stood beside Aetius's couch. Even if they did not kill him he doubted they would let him escape.

Hagan wondered what age the Magister Militum must be now. Well over fifty winters, that was for sure. Anyone who survived that long in the upper ranks of Roman society must be very shrewd indeed. Shrewd and dangerous.

Arminius snapped to attention and gave the Roman salute.

For an instant Hagan wondered if this was not just an instinctive reaction born from many years drilling in the

Roman Army. Could Arminius still in fact be in the pay of Rome? He knew of such *milites arcani*, secret soldiers who gathered information for the Empire and worked to further its aims. He never thought Arminius could be one, however. Then again, the line between arcani, mercenaries and spies was often a very vague one. Either way, Hagan felt no desire to salute the general himself.

Arminius relaxed then laid a large hand on Hagan's shoulder.

'I'm sure this man needs no introduction, Hagan,' the mercenary commander said. 'We both served under him for many years in Gaul, Armorica, Hispania, all over.'

'Oh, I know who he is,' Hagan said. 'Though I never came this close to him with so few guards in all my years of service. He is the Magister Militum, the highest-ranking officer in the Roman Army. And he is the man who annihilated my folk and our kingdom at the battle of Vorbetomagus.'

He heard Arminius take a sharp breath at this display of disrespect. Aetius however raised an eyebrow and made a wry smile. He rose from his couch and stood before Hagan. Hagan found it a little amusing to see how much shorter this greatest of Romans was than he. Aetius tilted his head back so he still looked down his nose at the barbarian, which made him look faintly ridiculous.

'So you really are a Burgundar,' the Magister Militum said. He had the same nasal upper-class Roman accent that Hagan remembered. 'Quite a rare creature to find, these days.'

'Thanks to you,' Hagan said.

Aetius held up a forefinger.

'That is a truer statement than you think,' he said. 'If it were not for me intervening to stop them, I doubt the Huns would have left any of you alive.'

'That's not how I remember things,' Hagan said, clenching his fists.

'Easy, lad,' Arminius said. 'Remember this is the Magister

Militum. He could have us both publicly flogged or sold to the Circus as slaves.'

'Don't worry, Arminius,' Aetius said. He fixed Hagan with a glare of his dark eyes. 'This man's anger is understandable. If it means anything to you, I also regard what happened at Vorbetomagus as an abomination. The Huns got out of hand. They overstepped the mark and exceeded the orders they were given. They were also obsessed with settling some score with you Burgundars. You killed one of their kings. Oktar, was it? And you stole something... a magic sword?'

Hagan frowned. Then he recalled tales of a raid the Burgundars had made on a Hun encampment near the Rhine when Hagan was a child. It was around the time they had also taken the faith of the Christians. King Gundahar had attacked the Huns in the night and killed many of them. The king had said that this victory was proof the new God favoured them and there would be no turning back to the old heathen idols. The Burgundars had become very rich then as well, which was taken as further proof of God's approval.

'They acted as they would have in any barbarian war,' Aetius continued. 'They did not know the expectations or morals expected of a civilised army.'

Hagan's jaw dropped open a little. Was this true or a trick?

'They were in the employ of Rome,' he said.

'Of course they were,' the magister said. 'What age are you now?'

'I believe I have lived through twenty-nine winters,' Hagan said. 'What's that got to do with anything.'

'Twenty-nine? So you must have been fifteen when we attacked Vorbetomagus, yes?'

Hagan nodded.

'Well, when I was fifteen I achieved the role of tribune. It's a minor status on the Cursus Honorum but important enough that I could be used as a hostage. Within a few years I was sent to the court of King Uldin of the Huns, Oktar's predecessor.

It was a dark time then. Rome was on her knees because of the damned Goths. The last thing she needed was the Huns attacking her as well. So I was sent there as guarantee of a peace agreement, an assurance that we would not attack them and they would not attack us. I'm sure life wasn't easy for you after Vorbetomagus, but can you imagine what it was like for me when I was that age? Living every day treated like an honoured guest, but knowing that if the winds of politics changed direction you would be killed – and believe me, the Huns are very creative when it comes to killing people in the most cruel and painful manner.'

'You expect me to feel sorry for you?' Hagan said. His upper lip curled again.

'No,' Aetius said. 'I don't care what you feel about me. I am merely trying to give you some context, some background so you can get a better understanding of things. I am not one of those Romans who think all barbarians are stupid. I know different. I have lived among barbarians and they are perhaps ignorant, but not stupid. It was when I lived with the Huns that I saw what an effective fighting force they were. Huns are born in the saddle. They can ride and shoot a bow as soon as they can walk. They move faster than the wind and cover vast distances. It only made sense that we Romans should employ that strength against our own enemies rather than have it deployed against us. When I returned to Ravenna I urged the Senate and the Emperor to use the Huns as mercenaries and I was right. With their help we've driven back the Goths, put down any number of rebellions and driven back a whole horde of barbarians desperate to get inside the Empire and plunder our wealth.'

'You sound like you admire them,' Hagan said.

'I *respect* them,' Aetius clasped his hands behind his back. 'I do not underestimate them. As any good general should of his foes. I know what they are capable of. You saw that yourself at Vorbetomagus. We were only there to bring you into line, not annihilate the whole nation. Once defeated you were to have been offered foederati status and become a client state of Rome. We need soldiers for the Army and you would have provided a buffer against other barbarians who wanted to cross the Rhine. The Huns, however, decided instead that they would try to kill every man, woman and child. They managed to slaughter perhaps twenty thousand of you. It was shocking. If I hadn't managed to stop them there would not be a single Burgundar left alive today. Including you.'

'Am I supposed to be grateful?' Hagan said. His eyes narrowed. 'And now your great allies have turned against you.'

Aetius sighed. He looked at the floor, then with his hands still clasped behind his back, paced four paces to the right, then returned to stand before Hagan. He looked up, cocking his head backwards once again. Hagan felt as though the dark eyes were boring into his own, trying to assess him, trying to probe into his very soul.

'Yes,' the magister said after a moment. 'Not long after Vorbetomagus, King Ruga of the Huns died. His nephews, Bleda and Attila, took power. It is the Hun tradition that they have two rulers, usually brothers. Uldin ruled alongside Charaton. Ruga ruled alongside Oktar until Oktar was killed by your tribe. Joint power was not enough for Attila, though. He murdered his brother and now rules the Huns alone. He is an arrogant bastard. And treacherous to boot. I knew him as a child. He was always the same.'

The Magister Militum shook his head, his irritation clear. He clicked his fingers at a lurking slave bearing a tray with a wine jug and goblets, who hurried over. Aetius filled a goblet and passed it to Hagan.

'A drink,' he said, pouring one for himself and one for Arminius as well.

Aetius took a swig from his goblet as if trying to dispel a bad taste in his mouth.

'Three years ago Attila made a proclamation forbidding

any Huns from entering service with the Roman Army,' Aetius said. His voice was filled with bitterness and Hagan could understand why. The Romans had come to rely on the Huns for support. This must have been quite a blow.

'Despite this provocation, we were still friendly towards them,' Aetius continued. 'Attila crucified his personal secretary because of a scandal and I even sent him a replacement. A good man. A Gaul. Do you know what Attila sent me in return? A deformed midget!'

Aetius ground his teeth and Hagan thought how often the fates of nations so often depended on personal spats between two powerful men.

'Now Attila has unleashed his armies against Rome,' the Magister said when he had regained control of his emotions. 'He has brought the Eastern Empire to its knees and now rides west. He sweeps everyone in his path aside. No one can stop him. Now he threatens Ravenna itself.'

Hagan could not help a little smirk creep onto his lips.

'This doesn't surprise me. There is a saying among my folk,' he said, 'that a wolf can sometimes look like a dog but you should never trust him. It seems this Attila was playing a very long game. First he got you to depend on his support, then he turned on you when you needed it most.'

'Ah! the simple wisdom of the barbarian,' Aetius said. 'If only it was down to just the ambitious greed of one man. Unfortunately the Emperor's slut of a sister, dismayed at the prospect of having to keep her legs shut, also sent Attila her ring along with a plea that he come and rescue her.'

Hagan could not help but burst out laughing.

'Yes, you may well laugh,' Aetius said. 'She has made Rome the laughing stock of the world. The whole reason for first the Emperor demanding the Lady Honoria remains celibate, then marrying her to a safe, reliable member of the Senate, was so no man could exploit marriage to her to set themselves up as a rival to the Emperor. Attila, of course, seized his opportunity. He insists her letter is a proposal of marriage.'

'I see the problem, at least for you anyway,' Hagan said. 'Attila actually has just cause for his war. If he marries the Lady Honoria he has a legitimate claim to be Emperor. That's quite a dowry she has brought him.'

'It's a mess. An embarrassment. This cannot be news to you?' Aetius said, narrowing his eyes. 'The scandal went through the Empire like a wildfire. The war that has resulted from it has killed thousands already.'

'Since leaving the Army I've been travelling beyond the boundaries of the Empire,' Hagan said. 'I heard rumours of great wars going on and peoples being displaced, but war is always with us. I paid no attention to them.'

'Yes, you were in Britannia,' Aetius said. 'Working for Arminius here.'

Hagan nodded.

'How are they doing up there since the legions withdrew?'

'Not well,' Hagan said. 'The Britons are making the same mistake you've made: employing foreign mercenaries to fight their wars for them. It's only a matter of time before the Saxons take advantage of their paymasters' weakness just like the Huns have done to you.'

Aetius pursed his lips as if considering whether or not to ignore Hagan's blatant provocation.

'We're here guarding a delegation from Britannia requesting Roman military help,' Arminius said. 'They are who is waiting outside, Lord Aetius.'

'Well, they can wait until we finish our business,' the general said. 'I'm afraid I've disappointing news for them anyway: they'll have to look to their own defences. We have our own problems to deal with. Come: look at this.'

Aetius went to a nearby table on which a scroll of parchment was unrolled. Hagan could see that it had pictures drawn on it.

'You are familiar with maps?' Aetius said.

Hagan nodded. 'We were given route maps in the army for finding our way on marches.'

'This is a little more sophisticated than those,' Aetius said. 'It was drawn using the best of Greek craft and knowledge. It shows the world. Now you see this?'

He pointed to a shape drawn on the map that looked not unlike a human leg.

'That is Italia,' Aetius continued. 'Rome is here near the bottom and Ravenna is near the top here. It is surrounded on three sides by the great sea we Romans call the *Mare Nostrum*. So if you want to invade, and you are not going to come by water, you must advance from the north. And Huns use horses, not ships. Now look here.'

He placed a finger further up the map, to the right and above Ravenna.

'This is the land of the Huns. It lies to the north and east of us here,' he said. 'Between the Danube and Don rivers. I said Attila has attacked the Roman Empire, but here is where he went.'

The Roman planted his forefinger to the left of where it had been.

'They crossed the Rhine and sacked Divodurum, then the cities of Remorum and then Tungrorum,' he said, moving his finger in an arc across the north of the map. 'The loss of life has been terrible. He spares no one. Women, children, monks, nuns, bishops or priests. At the rate he's creating martyrs the Lord will soon need to start building extra mansions in Heaven to house them all. People are starting to say the end of the world is coming.'

Hagan looked at the curved outline Aetius had drawn across the top of the map and frowned. Despite his dislike of Aetius he found himself intrigued.

'If he wanted to attack Rome surely he should have gone straight south-west,' Hagan said, rubbing his chin which was beginning to sprout a fashionable Roman beard. 'He seems to be going by a very roundabout route.'

Aetius snapped his fingers and pointed at Hagan.

'Lucky for us,' he said, his dark eyes flashing. 'The direct route is mountainous and very hard to take horses through. But our luck will not last. When he is done sacking Germania and Gaul and has taken everything he can in loot and plunder, he will come for Ravenna. Do you know what lies here?'

Aetius planted his forefinger at a spot directly between Ravenna and the north, directly on the path Attila would have to take to attack Ravenna.

Hagan shook his head.

'The kingdom of the Burgundars,' Aetius said.

Hagan frowned. He felt his previous ire beginning to return.

'Is this some sort of joke?' he said. 'There is no kingdom of the Burgundars any more. You made sure of that!'

'I forget you have been away for some time,' Aetius said, clasping his hands behind his back. 'You clearly are not aware then that while the slaughter at Vorbetomagus was indeed great, not all the Burgundars died that day. They were scattered to the four winds, the forests and mountains, but some survived. Gunderic, the son of your king, did great service to us in the Roman cavalry. He saved a consul's son in action and won a medal. He was discharged from the Army with honours and requested what was left of his people be given a homeland. Given what had passed, it was the least I could do, so I granted the Burgundars a foederati treaty and resettled them in the province of Maxima Sequanorum, beside the great lake at the foot of the *Alpes*.'

Aetius was now standing straight-backed, chest puffed out, one hand clasped over his heart. It looked to Hagan like he was making a speech to the Senate. It added to the sense of unreality that gripped Hagan's mind. For years he had thought there was nothing left of his kindred, that he was the last of his kind, or at least one of an ever-dwindling few dispersed across the face of the world. Now Aetius was telling him that not only had some of his people survived, they even had a new homeland, all under the leadership of his childhood friend Gunderic. For the first time in years, he felt hope spring into his heart.

Then he remembered Gunderic running away from their shield formation on that last day at Vorbetomagus, leaving them all exposed to attack so he could surrender and save himself. Hagan had witnessed it. Would the new king want reminding of that? There was something else as well...

'Why are you telling me this? What do you want?'

Aetius's face fell into a frown again.

'Unfortunately it seems Gunderic is as reliable as his father,' the Magister said. 'Brave? Undeniably. But rash and fickle too. Before Attila made his move the Burgundars closed their borders. All Roman officials were expelled. They stopped paying Imperial taxes. They don't send the levies for the Army they are obliged to. They expelled their bishops and priests.'

Hagan frowned. That was indeed strange. He recalled the Roman and Burgundar priests hurling abuse at each other before the battle at Vorbetomagus.

'Perhaps my folk have finally decided to reject the Arian heresy,' he said. In his time in the Army all public religious ceremonies were that of the Roman Church – the Faith of the Emperor. There had been no exceptions. The private religion of most of the Germanic tribes, who by and large followed the Arian version of the faith, was tolerated, though frowned upon, provided it remained private. 'Don't you have spies in this Burgundar country you speak of? I can't believe it's really closed to you.'

'We had spies, but they disappeared,' Aetius said. 'We sent a new one recently and he vanished like the others.'

'What about merchants, travellers?' Hagan said. 'No place can be completely cut off.'

'Indeed,' Aetius said. 'We get news through sources like

that, but whoever comes in and out of the land is closely watched. One thing we have heard is that somehow the court of King Gunderic is fabulously wealthy. The Burgundars have purchased the best of weapons and armour. That makes no sense. Their kingdom was destroyed. Vorbetomagus was plundered by the Huns. They took just about everything that wasn't nailed down.

'We always were a hard-working people,' Hagan said. 'I'd say we've built our wealth back to what it was.'

Aetius shook his head.

'The new land is in the midst of the mountains,' he said. 'There is no source of wealth from crops or trade. There are no mines apart from salt mines and they are too high in the mountains to be able to profit from their exploitation. They've not been to war so it isn't booty either. No – wherever this sudden wealth came from, I doubt it was from hard work and industry.'

'So why don't you send the legions in to bring these rebellious Burgundars back in line?' Hagan said with a sneer. 'Isn't that what you normally do?'

'Normally, yes,' Aetius said, seeming to take Hagan's sarcasm at face value. 'And it may come to that if we are forced to. But we have bigger problems to worry about right now. I can't divert soldiers from the north unless we are sure we absolutely have to. We need every soldier for the coming fight against Attila. But make no mistake, your Burgundar friends are about to become very important in that fight. They may have cut themselves off from the world but the world is about to come crashing back in on them.'

'What do you mean?' Hagan said.

'Attila will soon finish Gaul and turn south, heading for Ravenna,' Aetius said. 'I plan to take the army north and meet him in battle. I think we have enough troops but it will be a very close-run thing. He now has most of our damned cavalry, for a start.'

'What's this to do with me?' Hagan said. His flat tone betrayed that he already knew the answer.

'You are a Burgundar. You are one of them,' Aetius said. 'You can travel there. You know them. You will be welcomed back as one of their own. I want you to ask them to join us in the coming battle. Help us stop Attila.'

Hagan looked at Aetius, open-mouthed. Then at Arminius, then back to the Magister Militum.

'First you tell me that my folk, who you and your allies tried to destroy, not only still exist but are thriving,' Hagan said. 'Then you want me to ask them to fight *for you?*'

Aetius turned down the corners of his mouth, folded his arms and nodded.

'Yes,' he said. 'We need them to. Rome cannot do this alone. We need every ally we can get if we are to beat Attila. So far I've had pledges of support from the Alans, Saxons, Armoricans and Franks, and even the God-damned Visigoths! They all can see what a threat Attila is. Your people can join this alliance. On the other hand, if they get in the way of it then we will have to remove them.'

'I'm sorry, but you've got the wrong person,' Hagan said. 'I won't do it.'

'You'll be paid,' Aetius said.

'Really?' Hagan said. 'How much? Thirty pieces of silver, perhaps?'

'What do you want?' Aetius said. 'Every man has his price. Name it.'

'Not me,' Hagan said. Now it was his turn to fold his arms.

Aetius and Arminius exchanged looks. The magister's face darkened.

'You told me this was a good man, Arminius,' he said. 'A reliable one.'

Arminius held up his palms in a placative gesture.

'He was a good soldier,' he said. 'You asked me to find Burgundars and I found one.'

Aetius glared at Arminius for another moment, then he turned to Hagan. He looked at him for a long moment.

'Very well,' he said. 'Leave us, Arminius. You will be paid for your service. Leave us, all the rest of you except Hagan. And send in the dwarf.'

CHAPTER TWENTY-SEVEN

Arminius and the magister's bodyguards filed obediently out of the room. For a moment Hagan wondered if this could be his chance to kill Aetius. Then the sight of the person who entered the room next surprised him so much he forgot all such notions.

Hagan had heard of dwarfs in folk tales and old legends. They were supernatural creatures who lived in caves beneath mountains and were so skilled at making things their workmanship sometimes appeared like magic.

Sitting near the fire on cold winter nights, listening to stories told by the elders, Hagan had pictured them as child-sized men with long beards and nimble fingers. He had certainly never seen one with his own eyes and doubted they existed.

The man who was ushered into the room next made his eyebrows rise. He was very short, perhaps half the height of Hagan, but his body was not in proportion. It seemed as though his head and torso were average-size but his legs and arms were like those of a child. His face was flat and he had almost no nose, except for two nostril holes in the centre of his face. He had a hump at his right shoulder that made him hunch over. His legs were bowed outwards and his feet looked twisted in his sandals, so he walked into the room with a rolling gait similar to that of an old sailor Hagan had once met. His skin was dark. He wore Roman dress that had been cut to fit him. What age he was Hagan had no idea.

'Let me introduce Zerco,' Aetius said. 'A man who has experienced more in his lifetime than many will not achieve even if they were to live five times over.'

'I see my appearance disgusts you,' the short man said. He spoke Latin with an accent strange to Hagan and a pronounced lisp.

'I am sorry,' Hagan said, realising his shock had transferred into the expression on his face. 'I have never met anyone so... unusual as you.'

'It is no matter to me,' Zerco said. 'One such as I needs to learn at a very young age to ignore the harsh looks, cruel jokes, hatred and laughter of his fellow men. If he does not then he will be destined to lead a very miserable existence indeed.'

'Zerco here was once the jester of the magister militum of Constantinople, my counterpart in the Eastern Empire,' Aetius said. 'Though the man is a damned heretic. An Arian.'

He looked sideways at Hagan.

'You're not one, are you?' he said. 'You Germani all seem infected by that heresy. I'd have hoped the Army would bash that nonsense out of you.'

Hagan did not respond to the question. In truth he did not know what he was any more. Why the different ways men worshipped the same God mattered so much to some people was lost on him. He also found it hard to believe God cared a damn about the world he had created. Where was he the day the pagan Huns had slaughtered his Christian people? In the Army he had met men with many gods and none, and he had found that what really mattered was not a man's faith but whether he could rely on them in a tight situation or not.

'There's another reason why I don't just send an Imperial messenger to the Burgundars straight away, demanding they join my army,' Aetius said. 'And why I'd like someone who can get away with it to make some enquiries for me in their kingdom. There is the matter of the treasure.'

'Treasure?' Hagan said.

233

'Some years after the unfortunate incident at Vorbetomagus involving your people,' Aetius said, 'Zerco here was travelling near the city with his master, Flavius Ardabur Aspar.'

'Didn't you say he was Magister Militum in the Eastern Empire?' Hagan said. 'What was he doing there?'

'Aspar was instrumental in bringing the current Western Emperor, Valentinian, to power,' Aetius said, 'So the Emperor trusts him. Before Aspar pursued his career in the East he was involved with negotiations with the Huns and we needed him for a similar task on the Rhine. He was delivering their payments to where they were camped near Vorbetomagus, accompanied by a cohort of dragon cavalry. The camp was attacked in the night.'

Hagan recalled the type of horsemen called dragons from his time in the Army. They wore impressive heavy armour and flew long standards that streamed behind their horses like dragons flying through the air. They were elite warriors, well-trained and fearsome fighters, so whoever had managed to best them must have been either very lucky or very dangerous.

'Who by?' Hagan said.

'We don't know,' Aetius said. 'They were taken by surprise in the night by unknown warriors. The entire cavalry cohort was wiped out. Aspar escaped, but Zerco here was left behind. The raiders took the payment meant for the Huns. It was substantial. The Huns, deprived of their payment, decided to loot what they could from the surrounding countryside, including Zerco.'

'I was their slave for five years,' Zerco said. His eyes looked empty and Hagan surmised that time had not been an easy one for him.

'I mentioned the new kingdom of the Burgundars has suddenly become very rich,' Aetius said. 'It's my suspicion that they have the treasure taken near Vorbetomagus.'

'How?' Hagan said. 'The remaining Burgundars were scattered far from Vorbetomagus.'

'I…' Aetius began to speak then hesitated. He looked away from Hagan.

'I have my reasons,' he finished. 'The nearest kingdom to where Aspar was ambushed is Santen,' Aetius said. 'We may not be able to get spies into the new realm of the Burgundars but we do have them in Santen. A young lord from the city went to the new kingdom of the Burgundars shortly after it was established, when we still had some influence over the place. He was seeking the hand of the king's sister in marriage.'

'The king's sister?' Hagan said. His heart began to beat faster. '*Gunhild*? She's still alive?'

'I think that's her name, yes,' Aetius said. 'She is reckoned quite a beauty. As barbarians go.'

Hagan looked at the floor, hoping that the Romans around him did not notice how his cheeks were flushing. Gunhild was still alive. A strange, long-forgotten ache that had been frozen for many years, scarred over and forgotten, reawakened in his heart.

'Who is this prince?' he said.

'He's quite a man, by all accounts,' the Magister said with a sly smile. Hagan knew he had not been successful in hiding his feelings and Aetius now saw he did have a price after all. 'Hercules reborn, so they say. He and this Burgundar princess must be the perfect pair. Shortly after their marriage the new kingdom began to flourish and became wealthy. Is this a coincidence, do you think?'

'It doesn't sound like one,' Hagan said. 'So, say I take up your offer. What's in it for me?'

'You will be reinstated in the Army,' Aetius said. 'You will be one of the milites arcani. A secret soldier, but you'll be a *duplicarius* with double standard pay.'

'Double standard army pay?' Hagan said. 'I get three times that working for Arminius. What else?'

He still had no intention of spying on his people but now he knew some of them still lived, he felt a longing in his heart to be among them that was almost painful. Pretending to take up Aetius's offer would be a way to get away from his lonely life as a paid soldier for Arminius, while also being the fastest way to get to his folk land. He had to be convincing though, and not seem too keen.

'This new kingdom of my people is like a fledgling bird,' he said. 'I'm not sure I like the idea of dragging them into a war that could destroy them for a second time. Do they even have an army?'

'They may not have much choice in the matter,' Aetius said. 'I've already outlined one of the reasons but now Arminius is out of the room I can tell you that it's not just the hand of the Emperor's sister that has spurred Attila on. Among the treasure taken from the Huns was a particular war sword. Attila wants it back more than all the silver and gold put together.'

'What's so special about this sword?' Hagan said.

'It's sacred to the Huns,' Aetius said. 'It used to belong to some king of the Eastern Goths who the Huns could never manage to defeat. When they finally did, they won his sword and saw it as a sign from their War God of his favour. I saw it once when I was in Uldin's court. It's nothing special.'

'But Attila believes in this magic sword?' Hagan said.

'Attila is a masterful war leader,' Aetius said. 'But if he has one fault it's his superstition. When men put faith in something it can become more than the metal it is made from. The Huns think the sword confers the blessing of Mars, or whatever they call him, on their kings. Attila killed his brother to become sole ruler, so he is desperate to get the sword back. He thinks it will legitimise his claim to be king. If this lord of Santen took the treasure then he also took the sword.'

'My folk should know of this,' Hagan said with a sigh.

'They really should,' Aetius said. 'Perhaps you should look at it this way. If Attila defeats me then he will sweep south to claim his bride and finish off what remains of Rome. The only thing that will stand between him and Ravenna will be the new kingdom of the Burgundars. Do you think that small, fledgling realm will be able to stand against the might of a horde that has just defeated Rome? On the other hand... if your people won't join us, then do you think it would be prudent for me to leave at my flanks a realm that could potentially join Attila?'

'I can't see my folk joining the Huns,' Hagan said. 'Not after what they did to us in the past. We have no love of Rome but we hate the Huns more.'

'Sometimes an enemy can become a friend, if faced with a bigger mutual threat,' Aetius said. 'And it is more prudent, if they decide not to join us, that I have the legions wipe out the Burgundars on our march north to meet Attila.'

'You want me to deliver an order to my people,' Hagan said, his face turning pale as he realised what little choice anyone had in this matter. 'Their choice is to fight against Attila with Rome or to fight both Attila and Rome.'

'And I think you know how that will turn out,' Aetius said. 'But if you need any more of an incentive, I did not bring you into my confidence just to tell stories of the treasure. Once in the land of the Burgundars you can move around freely and without suspicion. You can find the treasure. And if you do, then you will be entitled to a cut of it, like the rest of us. It's worth all the wealth of a kingdom. There were three wagonloads of gold, silver and precious gems.'

'How big a cut?'

'Enough that you won't need to worry about working for the rest of your life,' Aetius said.

'Where would I go?' Hagan said. 'If I help you take the wealth of my own folk I won't be welcome among them again.'

'Who cares if you're rich?' Aetius said, spreading his arms as if to say he certainly did not. 'If you want to go back to those Godforsaken places outside the Empire then you'll have enough gold to buy a whole kingdom of your own. Or you could buy a villa here in Ravenna. Let's just say there will definitely be enough to keep a Burgundar princess in the manner in which she is accustomed.'

Aetius was tilting his chin back again. He winked. It took all of Hagan's willpower to stop himself from punching the Roman in the face.

Hagan sighed. He thought for a moment.

'Alright,' he said. 'I'll do it.'

'Excellent!' Aetius said, grinning. 'Zerco here will go with you.'

'What!' Hagan looked at the dwarf with uncertainty.

'Zerco saw the man who led the attack,' Aetius said. 'He can identify if the prince from Santen is the same man. Then you will know the treasure the Burgundars have really belongs to us.'

'He was a giant,' the short man said.

'Everyone to you is a giant,' Aetius said, a smirk on his lips.

Zerco scowled.

'Even to you he would have been big,' he said. Then he cocked a thumb at Hagan. 'Even to *him*.'

'Alright. We're agreed then,' Aetius said. 'We can bring Arminius back in. One more thing.'

He laid a hand on Hagan's arm and fixed him with his dark eyes.

'Arminius is getting a flat fee for his part in this,' he said. 'He knows nothing of the treasure. Let's keep it that way. Understand? Just keep your mouth shut about the gold. Think about it: the more people it has to be divided between, the smaller everyone's cut.'

Hagan nodded.

'This calls for another drink,' Aetius said, snapping his finger to the slave with the wine jug. He was grinning now. Hagan was not sure if it was from happiness or relief.

'There is no time to waste. Attila is on the rampage. Every day counts. It will take me some time to gather my army, so you have perhaps a month or so, Burgundar, to convince your

238

people to join my alliance. But mark my words well: if your people decide they are on the side of Attila then I will not hesitate to strike first. I must take them off the game board. This time our legions will finish the job that was started at Vorbetomagus.'

PART IV

HOME?

Ek svá vinnk, at þær villar fara
sinna heimhama, sinna heimhuga.

Such spells I weave that they wander home
Out of skins and wits bewildered.

From *Hávamál*, the wisdom of Odin

CHAPTER TWENTY-EIGHT

A LL ROADS MAY have led to Rome, but since the Imperial Court was moved to the marsh-flanked Ravenna, the fastest way to move across country from there was by boat.

After the formalities of Hagan swearing the sacramentum militare oath for the second time in his life to rejoin the Roman Army, he had little time to gather belongings for the journey before he and Zerco were led by bodyguards of General Aetius to the port where they boarded a ship of the Roman navy. There was no longer a need for Hagan to be guarded: Arminius had got his reward for bringing him to Ravenna. Now Hagan had sworn the oath of allegiance, if he did not carry out the will of General Aetius he would be a deserter and bring down on himself all the dire punishments associated with that. Besides all that, Aetius was sure Hagan was now committed to the task.

The boat was a small coastal vessel that mainly ferried supplies up and down the coast of Italia. As when he'd first sailed into Ravenna not that long ago, Hagan was stunned by the beauty of the sea they sailed over. It was still early spring, but the water was bright and clear and such an intense azure colour that it dazzled the eyes and enticed him, siren-like, to dive in. The knowledge that it was likely to be freezing cold stopped him.

They sailed north-east, crossing the *Mare Hadriaticum*, passing beaches with white sand and many towns and fishing villages. It looked like a pleasant area to spend time and Hagan hoped he could return there one summer. He was sure he could find some sort of work and perhaps spend his evenings lounging on the sandy beaches and enjoying the local wines.

Observing Hagan looking wistfully at the coast, Zerco reached up and nudged his elbow.

'If we find that treasure,' the short man said in his lisping voice, 'maybe you'll be able to buy a nice villa here, eh?'

'The only reward I seek from this journey is to be reunited with my kindred,' Hagan said.

Zerco grunted.

'So you say,' he said. 'But the general told me you refused to have anything to do with this trip until he mentioned the gold. That and the king's sister. You can protest all you want, my idealistic friend, but you're just like everyone else. At the mention of wealth or a nice pair of tits you become a slave, just the same as me.'

Hagan gave him a sharp look.

'I am not a slave,' he said. 'I am a free-born Burgundar and warrior of my tribe. And I am also now a *milite arcanum*. I'm a Roman soldier.'

'Warriors and soldiers are just the slaves of their generals and kings,' Zerco said. 'Their lives belong to men like Aetius who do what they want with them and throw them away when they need to.'

Hagan frowned and walked away. Zerco somehow made him feel uncomfortable. At first he had felt bad that perhaps he was reacting to the man's deformed appearance. Now he realised that it was Zerco's character that irritated him. Perhaps it was the hard life the short man had no doubt endured, but there was something rotten within him, like his spirit was as twisted and dark as his unfortunate body.

When the ship arrived at Aquileia, Hagan and Zerco disembarked. They wandered through the large, beautiful city, Hagan marvelling at the architecture. With its wide squares, life-like sculptures and elegant fountains, fine cathedral, big houses and busy port, it was easy to see why several emperors had maintained palaces there.

Much as he would have liked to, Hagan knew that they could not dally there. Every day that passed meant one day less Aetius would be prepared to wait for his answer. Besides that, Hagan was eager to once more be among his own folk... though if they found out he was there at the behest of Rome how would they react? He could well find himself swinging from a noose thrown over the nearest tree.

Using letters of authority from Aetius, Hagan and Zerco procured horses from an official Imperial stable. They set off along the main road that led away from Aquileia, the Via Posthumia. This road went directly west across the north of Italia, through Tarvisium, on to Vicentia and then on to Verona. Every major part of the journey was ticked off at regular intervals by milestones, the road markers that ultimately led all the way back to the Golden Milestone that stood at the heart of Rome.

Hagan mused that it was these milestones and roads that were the ultimate markers of Roman civilisation. They ran right to the limits of the Empire and then stopped. Beyond was barbarian territory. Where the borders of Rome had previously extended further, the roads were still there but falling into disrepair. Every Roman knew that when the roads ran out, you had reached the edge of the Empire.

Hagan was surprised that, despite his very short legs, Zerco was able to ride a horse well. The little man explained that four years living among the Huns had taught him everything that could be known about how to ride.

Imperial messengers could cover up to two hundred miles a day, but Hagan and Zerco could not ride as fast as them. Nonetheless the documents supplied by Aetius allowed them to make use of the same network of official hostelries where they could change horses or rest for the night, so Hagan still expected they could cover the four hundred or so Roman miles of their journey in days rather than weeks.

Hagan found himself thinking that had there not been uncertainty and perhaps serious danger waiting for them ahead, and the time Aetius was prepared to wait slipping away, the journey would have been most pleasant. The weather was mostly rainy, but on these cold, grey days he was getting the chance to see some of the greatest cities in the world, all at the expense of the Imperial purse.

At night, if they were in a city, they stayed in mid-range stabula, which provided accommodation and stables for the horses. They drank good wine and ate decent food. Hagan was able to visit the bathhouses, something Zerco declined on the basis that he did not want people staring at his unusual body. Hagan appreciated wine but Zerco always drank too much. He was also always trying to bribe or coerce female slaves to sleep with him or do other unpleasant favours for him. If nightfall found them still on the road and outside a town they stayed free of charge in one of the rather comfortable mansiones.

At Verona they changed roads to the Via Claudia Augusta which they followed as far as Comum, ticking off the milestones as they went. This city sat beside a huge lake, beyond which they got their first sight of the Alpes, the great mountains that rose like a line of jagged teeth against the horizon. That was where they were heading. As they joined the Via Helvetica, the main road that would take them most of the way to their destination, they also began to see more and more evidence that all was not well in the Empire.

There were many Imperial messengers on the roads. Several times Hagan and Zerco arrived at a mansio to find all the fresh horses had been taken. The talk around the dinner tables at these hostelries in the evenings was all about calamities in the north. The Huns, it seemed, were still rampaging across Gaul, destroying everything in their path. Anyone who tried to stop them was slaughtered. Cities had begun to surrender without a fight, preferring to submit to humiliation and looting than the certain annihilation resistance to Attila inevitably brought. It was only a matter of time before he turned south to attack Ravenna. Lots of soldiers were also in transit, whether returning from cancelled leave in Italia or on their way to new postings. Everyone was heading north towards the gathering storm.

Hagan could see the Romans were genuinely worried. They wondered aloud in tones filled with dread about what would happen if the Imperial capital fell to barbarians for the second time in a century. Could the Empire even survive such humiliation?

As they travelled north towards the mountains it got colder. Hagan began to look with growing consternation at the ragged peaks that seemed to get taller and taller the closer they rode. Winter was not long gone and the snow reached well down their rugged sides. He began to wonder if they would be able to get their horses up such steep inclines, and even if they did, they would need to find heavier clothes if they did not want to freeze to death.

'Perhaps we should think of going around the mountains by the coastal route,' Hagan said aloud as they trotted towards the ever-higher looming crags.

'That will add weeks to our journey,' Zerco said. 'Why wouldn't we take the direct route?'

Hagan sighed. The slower route would eat even more into the allotted time Aetius had given him, but that was irrelevant if he and Zerco were both dead. He gestured towards the snow-sheathed mountains.

'Look at that,' he said. 'At this time of year, crossing terrain like that could be suicidal.'

'You're scared?' Zerco said with a scoff that made the hairs on Hagan's neck bristle. 'I've been this way before. Several times. Besides, the Roman Empire doesn't grind to a halt because of a bit of snow. You were in the Army. I'm surprised you don't have more faith in Imperial logistics.'

A little further along the road Hagan found out what Zerco meant. At the very foot of the mountains there was a Roman fort and a small town. There they also found a mansio where not only could they change their horses for rugged little mountain ponies but also obtained the thick fur clothing, dried rations and other necessary equipment for their journey through the mountains, all provided by the *mansionarius*, the officer in charge.

'It will be hard going, no doubt about it,' the mansionarius said. 'But you will make it alright if you stick to the road.'

He explained to Hagan's surprise that the Roman road continued up into the mountains until it reached a narrow pass that was the only possible route through to the other side without going over the top of the towering peaks. At that time of year, attempting any other way across was simply impossible. Hagan still wondered if they were biting off more than they could chew.

'Get an early start,' the mansionarius said. 'Leave no later than first light. If you think you aren't going to make it then it's a tradition that you say a prayer to old Jove. He'll get you to the top.'

Hagan was surprised to hear a Christian Roman advising invocation of the pagan Jupiter, but nevertheless they took his advice, setting off in the crisp, cold morning just after the sun had peeked over the horizon.

It was a hard climb. Roman roads were renowned for being straight, covering the shortest distance between two points. As they climbed higher this road began to twist and turn in a series of extreme bends that allowed travellers to traverse the mountainside at a more achievable incline than if they had attempted to go straight up. Hagan was glad of the road as the surrounding terrain became rocky – then they turned a corner and all was coated in snow. They stopped to rest the horses and changed into the heavy fur clothes they had been given then set off again, climbing ever higher on the twisting road. All around disappeared under a white blanket, though the sun still shone and they could make out the path the road took, even if its surface was buried deep beneath the snow.

Just over a mile further on Hagan had to dismount. His horse was plodding through knee-deep snow already and with his weight on its back it was sinking further. Zerco made no such impression and remained mounted.

Hagan began to wade through the deep snow himself, leading his horse by the reins. Despite the snow and the freezing air that turned his panting breath to clouds of steam, he was soon sweating as much as he did in a sudatorium.

Several times Hagan looked up and thought they had reached the summit, only for another twist in the road to reveal there was still more to go. When they stopped and looked back the way they had come, the view was astonishing. Hagan found himself able to see for miles, with the rolling foothills then flat plains stretching off into the misty distance. There were tiny specks – people and cattle – that could just be made out moving on the road far below.

'This must be what God sees when he looks down from Heaven,' he said, his voice breathless both from the effort of the climb and in awe at the spectacle before him.

'Probably,' Zerco said. 'And he probably knows as much about – or cares as much – as we do for those people down there.'

The early spring day wore on and the sun began to dip towards the horizon, lengthening the shadows the mountains cast across the landscape. Ominous blue-grey clouds were gathering on the horizon and Hagan began to fear that night would fall, leaving them out in the open to face the freezing temperature that would come with the darkness.

'Now is when we offer a prayer to Jupiter,' Zerco said, as if sensing Hagan's concern.

There was a smile on the little man's lips which reminded Hagan that Zerco had said he'd travelled this route before. Perhaps he knew something Hagan did not?

When they rounded the next bend Hagan found it hard to believe his eyes. The road made a final short, steep climb then levelled onto the top of the pass. Mountains towered on either side, but what surprised Hagan was the sight of a church, its walls banked up with drifting snow, a forlorn cross on its roof struggling to peek above the gathering drifts. A short distance from it, almost completely buried in snow to the roof on one side, was a mansio. Outside it, on a stretch of road cleared of snow, was the inevitable Roman milestone.

To Hagan's further surprise, the buildings were not empty. The mansio was staffed. A welcome fire blazed in the hearth and there was a mansionarius, staff and slaves who leapt to their feet when Hagan and Zerco stumbled through the door, wiping snow from their clothes. The stables were even full of fresh horses for their onward journey.

Before long Hagan and Zerco had been given their rooms, got changed into dry clothes and were sitting beside the roaring fire, where they joined the ruddy-faced priest from the church next door. He was an older man with a ring of grey hair around a bald crown and Hagan judged that the twinkle in his eyes was more to do with the goblet of wine he nursed in both hands rather than any sense of jollity. From the familiar way he interacted with the slaves and others in the mansio it was clear he spent most of his time here rather than in his church. This was understandable. In this remote, lonely place there was probably not much of a congregation to tend to beyond the odd thankful traveller.

'The church was originally built as a temple to Jupiter,' the priest said. 'On reaching the pass safely travellers used to give thanks to the god. It's dedicated to the One True God now but the rascals still sometimes call on old Jove. I still find little trinkets, votive tablets and such left by travellers in honour of Jupiter. It's sad to think some of those folk die as they continue their journey and such actions will have damned their soul.'

'Old customs live for a long time,' Hagan said, glancing at Zerco. 'Even when people forget what their original purpose was.'

Due to the time of year they were the only travellers that night, but Hagan was surprised to learn that another party had stayed the previous night, going in the opposite direction.

'Imperial business takes no heed of the season,' the priest said. 'It doesn't stop just because it snows. Likewise, do you think Attila cares about the weather?'

So even in this remote place, Hagan mused, *they have heard Attila is on the march.*

When they told the priest where they were going, he blew out his cheeks and called over the mansionarius.

'More wine, Father?' the man said, already raising a terracotta jug in anticipation.

'Well, as you are here with it, and I wouldn't want to waste your journey, I don't mind if I do,' the priest said, holding up his goblet. 'But what I really wanted to say was that these two poor fools are headed for Geneva. Got any advice for them?'

The mansionarius raised his eyebrows.

'Go armed,' he said. He looked at Zerco then at Hagan. 'Is it just the two of you?'

Hagan nodded.

'I've seen your papers. I know you're travelling on Imperial business,' the mansionarius said. 'But with no escort? I don't want to worry you, friend, but the last Imperial party that passed through here on the way to Geneva never came back. You know the place is home of the Burgundars now, don't you?'

Hagan nodded.

'They're a vicious, savage tribe,' the mansionarius said. 'The very epitome of the word "barbarian". Let me warn you my friend: they don't like strangers.'

251

'Can you blame them?' Hagan said. 'Didn't the Romans almost wipe them out fifteen years ago?'

He had decided to keep a tight lip about his own origins. Romans tended to become more careful about what they said when they found themselves in the company of those they regarded as not Roman.

'I don't know about that,' the mansionarius said. 'But since settling around Geneva they've cut themselves off from the rest of the world. They don't allow anyone in. Don't like people knowing their business. They're rich, I can tell you that. They send out merchants to buy all sorts of expensive goods: weapons, armour, wine, high-end pottery.'

'What's so bad about that?' Hagan said, unable to help himself from defending his own folk. He recalled that Aetius had told him something similar. This really did puzzle him. His people – as far as he could remember – had always been outgoing, sociable and willing to learn more about the world.

'That's one thing,' the mansionarius said. 'But you'll see for yourself on your way to Geneva how they put off travellers coming in. And no one can live within ten miles of their borders without fear of being attacked. Even at that limit only the desperate make their homes.'

'And they're pagans,' the priest said. 'A demon from the east has come to possess their hearts and now they follow him on a dance to the gates of Hell. You'd better watch yourselves if you don't want to end up a sacrifice to some infernal devil. Especially you, my little friend.'

'What do you mean by that?' Zerco said.

'Barbarians and other backward people,' the priest said, 'are especially unkind to anyone who looks a little... different shall we say?'

Hagan's knuckles whitened around the stem of his own wine goblet.

'The Burgundars are not heathens,' he said. 'They accepted Christ as their god over twenty years ago.'

The mansionarius regarded Hagan with a new look in his eyes, as if he were now noticing the other's tall stature and blond hair for the first time.

'Perhaps, my friend,' he said to Hagan, 'you may fit in there more than I or the holy father here would. But as you are on the business of the Emperor I just want to warn you. They do not welcome Romans there. It's a very dangerous place. Get whatever it is you have to do there done and get out again as quickly as you can.'

Hagan nodded, doing his best to quell the anger at the insults to his people. There was little point in stirring up trouble here in this remote place, especially when he depended on these people's hospitality for the night.

Food arrived: great steaming bowls of stew and fresh bread. The mansionarius brought more wine and soon they were eating and chatting about other matters: the war in the north, how it had affected the price of wine, and the scandal around the dispute between the Emperor and his sister. They all warmed to each other's company and Hagan felt it was good to relax and enjoy the pleasure of fellowship for a while, especially after spending so much time with only the sarcastic and bitter Zerco for company.

All the same, when Hagan finally made his way to his room and bed, it was hard not to fend off a vague feeling of foreboding for what may lie ahead in the days to come.

CHAPTER TWENTY-NINE

NEXT MORNING THEY resumed their journey. After a hearty breakfast, Hagan and Zerco chose new horses from the mansio stables and set off over the pass. Mountains towered on either side of the narrow valley. The snow was deep and while once again Zerco could mount and ride, Hagan found himself wading through deep snow that at times came up almost to his waist. At least the ground was flat – the mansionarius had told them they would be crossing a frozen lake – but the effect of the sun glinting off the snow was dazzling. At length Hagan's head hurt and his eyes felt as though they were burning. After exhausting, slow progress the ground began to slope downwards as they followed a snow-filled river valley on its frozen path from the high lake to the plains below.

They spent most of the day descending the valley, which was as much hard work as the climb up to the pass had been. Every step was a struggle to stop from slipping and falling out of control down the slope below.

At length the snow began to peter out and they found themselves once more on the paving stones of the Roman road. As the sun passed its highest point they reached the bottom of the valley, finding themselves in a wide, flat plain that ran between the mountains they had descended from and another range just like them.

From here they headed west. The Roman road still carved through the landscape but it was not long before they began to see signs that the Pax Romana had broken down in this area. Burned-out farmsteads and villas sat beside the road. The blackened ruins were choked with weeds which showed whatever had happened to them had occurred several years before. Apart from these there were no signs of human habitation. The fields lay uncultivated. There were no cows, sheep or chickens. Even the road was webbed by grass and dotted with potholes. The entire countryside had an eerie, empty feeling.

Despite this, Hagan could not suppress an itching feeling in the back of his neck. It was a sense he had honed as a Roman scout when working deep in enemy territory and he knew not to ignore it when it whispered to his mind that they were being watched. Where from he had no idea. The countryside was flat and featureless between the mountains. There was little undergrowth or ditches to conceal anyone.

Eventually they saw a line of blue against the mountains far ahead. Hagan knew that their route took them to a large lake. The sight of the water up ahead at least assured him they were still going in the right direction.

'What's that?' Zerco said. He had a hand over his brow to shade his eyes as he peered ahead.

Hagan looked and saw up ahead there was some sort of wooden arch built over the road. A tall pillar rose on either side of the road, to about three times the height of a man. A crossbeam went over the road and from it dangled nine long objects, each one connected to the beam above by a rope. They swayed slowly back and forth in the gentle wind.

As well as the strange arch, a line of posts led away from it to the left and right. They marched away from the road across the flat fields of the valley floor as far as the eye could see, placed at intervals every bit as regular as the Roman milestones they had passed along the Via Helvetica. The posts were narrow and tall, like spears planted in the ground, and each one appeared to be topped by a ball which looked black, brown or white in the distance. Occasionally there would be something much longer and bulky dangling from the pole. These were distant and it was not possible to make out more than that they were attached at one end, judging by the way they swayed in the wind around the pole.

'It's like a fence,' Zerco said. 'Except the palisades are too far apart to keep anything in or out. Same with that arch over the road ahead. I'd say that was a gateway except it has no gates. What use is that?'

Hagan squinted at the strange constructions, trying to make out more details and puzzling over what their meaning could be. Something tapped at his mind, a memory he could not quite fathom. This was somehow familiar to him, but he could not place why or how.

'Some sort of decoration, perhaps?' he said.

Then he saw there were crows perched on the arch and on many of the round knobs on the top of the poles. As they rode closer he made out more details. He saw the weathered scraps of skin that barely covered the white bones beneath. The hollow eye sockets, their contents picked clean by the ravens. The matted clumps of hair and the air-dried lips that had shrunken back, revealing lines of teeth beneath, a strange half-smile that seemed to mock the approaching travellers or suggested an endless, jocular dream disturbed the eternal sleep of the dead.

'They aren't decorations,' he said, his voice becoming grim. 'They're human heads.'

Zerco winced.

'And that isn't a gate,' Hagan went on. 'It's a gallows.'

Zerco started as he realised the gently swinging objects above the road were dead bodies. The nooses that had ended their lives still bit into what was left of the tattered, rotting flesh of their necks. The crows had taken their eyes too. What was left of their desiccated cheeks had drawn back so they grinned, as if they were haunted by the same dream as the severed heads, except they found it even more amusing.

'This must be the border of the Burgundar lands,' Zerco said. 'They certainly have an impressive choice of boundary markers.'

'It's a ghost fence,' Hagan said, his voice harsh and gravelling.

'What?' Zerco twisted in the saddle to look at him.

'It's an ancient custom of my people,' Hagan said. 'Traitors, enemies and wrongdoers are brought to the border for execution, then their heads or corpses are placed here. Their spirits will defend our land, warning those thinking of invading us. I've only heard of it talked of in legends and old stories though.'

'Well, it looks like someone has decided to revive some old customs,' Zerco said.

'I think I will put my war gear on,' Hagan said, swinging off his horse. 'There is something strange here. It's best to be prepared for anything.'

'Good thinking,' Zerco said, also dismounting.

'You have war gear?' Hagan said, a sceptical expression on his face.

Zerco unbuckled a leather satchel that was thrown over his horse's back and drew out a shirt of mail that he pulled over his head. To Hagan's further surprise the shirt appeared to fit, meaning it must have been made for the little man. Then he pulled out a bronze breastplate, cast into the likeness of a muscled torso. Zerco strapped this on over his own chest which was about as far from the Adonis-like body modelled in metal as it was possible to get.

'I was the personal jester of Bleda, Attila's brother,' Zerco said, seeing Hagan's curious look. 'I went everywhere with him, even on campaign. He commissioned this special armour for me.'

'It certainly fits you,' Hagan said, looking at how well the armour covered the little man's body. 'But does it work? Will it stop a blade or is it just for show?'

'Oh yes, it will stop a blade,' Zerco said. 'I'd say it's more effective than that rubbish you're putting on. The man who made that worked in a *fabrica*. He had hundreds to make, as cheaply as possible. Who knows what was added to the metal to make it stretch to as many pieces as possible? Mine was made by a master craftsman who knew that if his work did not please the king of the Huns then his reward would be a nasty death.'

'You said you were Bleda's jester, not Attila's,' Hagan said. 'I thought Attila was king of the Huns?'

'He is now,' Zerco said. 'But the Huns should have two kings, usually brothers or cousins. It has always been that way. It is supposed to stop one man becoming too powerful. Bleda and Attila were joint rulers. Then Attila killed Bleda.'

'What's this Attila like?' Hagan said, wondering if he had seen the man before among the Hun leaders who had been at Vorbetomagus.

Zerco thought for a moment.

'He's like the very Devil himself,' the little man said after the pause. 'I don't just mean that he is cruel, wicked-natured and will cause the deaths of a thousand men without losing a wink of sleep over it. He is all that. But he is also proud. You can see it in the way he walks, the way he looks at everyone around him. He knows he is in charge. And, like Satan, he is overthrowing the order set by God. Not just in the Christian world. He could not share power with his brother so he killed him. He rebelled against the customs of his own people.'

'You hate him for killing Bleda?' Hagan said. 'Because Bleda looked after you?'

Zerco cast a look in Hagan's direction that suggested he had just said the most stupid of words.

'I *hate* all of them,' Zerco said. 'I cared little when Bleda was killed. I said I was Bleda's jester but that really just means they all laughed at me. I entertained them after dinner just by dancing and singing. I was doing my best but they just found it hilarious. I was more like Bleda's pet. He dressed me up in clothes like his own, like a doll or a statue. This armour was part of that. He found it most amusing to have a little version of himself. All the others did too.'

Hagan sighed. Despite his dislike of the man, he was starting to understand what had twisted Zerco's soul as much as cruel fate had twisted his body and feet.

'Life must have been hard for you,' he said.

Zerco grunted.

'You have no idea,' he said. 'But perhaps you understand why I want the treasure? When you are a very rich man no one cares that you are half the height of everyone else.'

He clenched his teeth.

'When I can pay for bodyguards – ruthless bastards who will do anything I say, Huns, probably,' he said, 'no one will laugh at me again. When I am swimming in gold no woman will scorn my advances.'

They finished arming and remounted. Hagan checked his sword, now slung in a scabbard under his left shoulder, slid easily in and out.

'Did Bleda make you weapons as well?' he said.

The dwarf laughed.

'This, my friend,' pointing a thumb to the mail that now covered his torso, 'is just to keep me alive while I run away. If we get into any problems you will be doing all the fighting.'

They set off once more, heading into the new land of the Burgundars, towards the invisible fence of spirits and under the swinging corpses that dangled from the gallows over the road. Hagan hoped it was not an omen.

CHAPTER THIRTY

THEY DID NOT get far.

As they passed under the gallows that marked the boundary of the territory, Hagan caught a glimpse of movement from the corner of his eye.

He turned his horse towards the right-hand side of the road where he had spotted the movement, ripping his Roman spatha from its sheath as he turned.

There was a man standing beside the road looking at them. Hagan blinked. He was sure the man had not been there moments before. It was like he had just appeared from nowhere.

The man was tall, thin and wore a long grey cloak that came down to his ankles. The woollen jerkin and breeches he wore beneath were plain but of good quality. He was past middle-aged, with very long grey hair and beard combed and braided. He stood upright as a statue. He had a wide-brimmed hat on, and one of his eyes – the right one – was covered by an eye patch of black material. The other one was a dazzling blue. Over his shoulder was slung a leather satchel that bulged in the middle.

He stared at Hagan with such Intensity that for a moment Hagan felt as if he were paralysed. He felt like the old man was glaring deep into his heart, probing for whatever secrets lay there.

With some effort Hagan looked away, noticing then that what he had thought was a walking staff, because of the way the old man held it, butt planted on the ground, was actually a spear.

There was something strange about the old man's presence that unnerved Hagan. Was this a ghost, one of the earth-bound spirits set to guard the border of this new land of the Burgundars?

Of course not, he chided himself, noticing for the first time the drainage ditch that ran beside the road and the scrub bushes that covered the ground around it. The old man's sudden appearance was down to concealment, not magic, the sort of skills he had learned himself as a Roman scout.

'Who are you?' he said. He tried to sound commanding though surprise and disconcertion made his throat feel dry and his tongue thick. 'What do you want?'

'You are the stranger here, my friend,' the old man said. An enigmatic smile spread across his thin face. 'I think it is for me to ask the questions.'

He spoke in Latin, like Hagan, however he had a slight accent that Hagan could not quite place. It was not Burgundar though it was not far from it. Perhaps from another Germanic tribe from somewhere more to the east.

'But you are one old man,' Hagan said, levelling the point of his sword at the stranger. 'And there are two of us.'

The old man raised one eyebrow.

'Are you sure about that?' he said. 'You ask me what I'm doing. Do you think I would not be chatting with my friends here?'

He flicked his eyes upwards to where the blackening corpses turned in the wind.

'If you are,' Hagan said, 'I doubt it is much of a discussion.'

'You would be surprised,' the stranger said. 'But what I was actually up to was out training some of the young lads of the warband. Perhaps they should say hello.'

He put two fingers in his mouth and whistled. All of a sudden there was movement all around. Figures rose from the ditches, the bushes, clumps of long grass – any scrap of the terrain that could give any possible cover. There were about twenty of them, all in war gear. They had been concealed so well Hagan had had no idea they were there.

This did explain his earlier feeling of being watched, at least. They wore good mail with no holes in it. It was not rusted, but not polished to gleaming either. That was why no glint of metal had betrayed their presence. They had round shields and every one was painted with a raven.

Hagan's heart soared at the sight of that picture. It was not a bear of the Dagelungs, his clan, nor a wolf, lightning symbol, Sun Wheel or an eagle, but it was painted in the traditional style of the Burgundars, a style he had not seen for fifteen or more years.

They bore spears that were all levelled over the top of their shields, every point directed towards Hagan and Zerco. They wore no helmets and he could see they were young men, between sixteen and nineteen winters old.

There was something else he noticed about them too. In his years in the Roman Army and afterwards Hagan had learned a lot about men in warbands. Many men donned armour and went into battle. Many had to. It was obligatory in return for the protection of a lord. Many joined the Roman Army too but even there, in an organisation whose very purpose was war, there were men who had no real will to kill their fellow men. They would scream war cries, take their place in a shield wall, and even strike at the men they met as opponents in battle. But they had no real *will* to kill their fellow men. They could cause injuries – even kill someone – but it was never really intentional. They delivered death by accident, and the memories of those deeds haunted them for the rest of their lives.

Then there were others – far fewer in number – who always struck to kill. Those who did not hesitate when an opening for their blade presented itself, and who afterwards did not lose a wink of sleep about the lives they had cut short. Hagan had learned they were the ones to look out for in the opposition. You could tell by their eyes: there was a strange, blank look in them, as if their lack of conscience was visible from the outside. In most shield walls, that sort of men was perhaps one in ten and he had learned fast, mostly through the tutelage of his centurions, that they were the ones you needed to kill first.

Looking at the young men around him now, and the cold eyes with which they watched him, Hagan realised with a chill that every one of them were killers. He could also see that none of their hair was shaved at the back, but grew out in long tails that touched their shoulders. If they were Burgundars this confirmed that they had all already taken another man's life.

Hagan sheathed his sword and held both hands in the air.

'I mean no harm,' he said.

'You wear Roman armour,' the one-eyed stranger said. 'Romans are not welcome here. Your little friend wears the armour of a Hun. Those folk are particularly unwelcome in this kingdom. This is a dangerous time, my friend. War is only a heartbeat away. We need to be careful of strangers sneaking into our land.'

'We were not sneaking anywhere,' Hagan said, using his native tongue instead of Latin, resentment making him straighten up in the saddle. 'I am Hagan, son of Godegisil. I am a Burgundar of the Dagelung clan. I was at the fall of Vorbetomagus and was forced to join the Roman legions after that. I did not know my folk had survived that disaster. Then I was told the Burgundars had survived and this was their new kingdom. I have come to rejoin my own folk.'

No one moved. The spear points remained levelled in Hagan's direction.

'Interesting,' the one-eyed old man said. 'You speak the Burgundar tongue but with your short beard and armour you look like a Roman.'

'I am a friend of Gunderic, who I am told is now king here,' Hagan said. 'We grew up together. My father was his father's champion.'

'Anyone can find out the name of our king,' one of the young lads said. 'How do we know you are a Burgundar and not a Roman?'

Hagan pulled off his helmet and tossed it on the ground.

'You can't,' he said. 'But if you kill us you will have to explain to your king – and his sister – why you put one of their oldest friends to death.'

His words did not have the effect Hagan hoped they would. The young men remained unmoved. They looked towards the old man with the one eye.

The one-eyed man in turn cocked his head to one side, regarding Hagan for what felt like a very long time. Once again Hagan felt the strange effect of the other's intense gaze.

Hagan assessed his options. They were few so it did not take long. He was outnumbered twenty to one at least and he had little doubt that the warriors aiming their spears at him would not hesitate to launch them if given a reason. Trying to fight his way out would be suicide. He could spur his horse forward and try to escape but he was surrounded on both sides. He would not be fast enough to get beyond a spear cast and they could not all miss him. There was really only one viable option.

Hagan slid his sword back into its sheath and held his arms wide, palms outward, showing he held no other weapons.

'I see you are no fool at least,' the old man said. 'Now perhaps we can begin our discussion again? You look like a Roman and you speak Latin, but you speak the Burgundar tongue and know a little about the Burgundars from the time before. That suggests you may be more friend than a foe. And I admit I am very curious to hear the story of your dwarf. First though I should make sure you are not here to cause mischief. Let us test your claims. We shall all go and meet the king and we shall see what he makes of you. Grani?'

'Yes, lord?' one of the warriors who looked a little older than the others responded.

'I will take our friends here to Geneva,' the one-eyed man said. 'I'll take eight of the lads with me – that should be enough to keep these two in line. You remain here to finish putting the rest of them through their paces. And keep an eye on this borderland. I want to know everyone who comes and goes.'

Hagan noticed Grani's face fell.

'But what about—' he began to say.

'War does not sleep,' the old man cut him off. 'War does not take a day off. If you want to defeat an enemy then attack him while he's still asleep in bed. Attack him when he isn't prepared. Attack him when he is celebrating his holy festivals. Now, I will take these two to see King Gunderic to see if we should hang them or not.'

The old man counted out eight of his warriors while the others approached Hagan and Zerco and took all their weapons away. Then the one-eyed man and his eight warriors jogged off across the fields. After a short wait in awkward silence – Hagan and Zerco and their captors all eyeing each other with mutual suspicion – they returned, mounted on horses that must have been concealed as well as they had previously been themselves. To Hagan's surprise, he now saw that the old man's feet were bare. The skin on his soles was tough and dirty, suggesting this was normal for him.

Then the old man, his eight warriors, Hagan and Zerco set off down the road. The one-eyed man rode in front, his shoulders slouching from side to side with the movement of the horse. Hagan and Zerco were a little way behind, surrounded by the Raven Warriors.

As they passed through the countryside Hagan tried to question the warriors, asking what clans they were from, who the old man was and if there was any news of other of his old friends and family from the previous time before the fall of

Vorbetomagus. All his questions were met with stony silence, which puzzled Hagan.

'If you young men are Burgundars then our folk have changed much while I've been away,' he said to no one in particular. 'We were always a sociable people, outgoing and welcoming to visitors. What way were you lads brought up that you are so silent and suspicious?'

Even these words provoked no response and Hagan resolved to stop wasting his breath.

As they travelled deeper into the kingdom, the countryside became less deserted and eerie. As they moved further from the borderlands the fields were cultivated. There were cows, sheep and horses roaming. Some hillsides were terraced and lined by rows of vines. They passed a settlement which was ringed with a ditch on top of which sat a palisade of stakes. He could see the roofs of buildings inside and above the gate fluttered a banner with a picture of the Sun Wheel on it, the emblem of the Solung clan.

At the sight of the flag Hagan felt a prick of excitement. Here was the first clear, recognisable sign that this was indeed a Burgundar kingdom. He longed to ride to the settlement and call out to those inside, to sing one of the old songs, but he knew the silent, deadly serious young men around him would brook no such action.

Hagan consoled himself that once he met Gunderic and Gunhild he would be rid of these warriors and everything would be right with the world once more. All he had to do was keep his temper until they reached Geneva, which, after all, was where they intended to go anyway.

Several times on the way Hagan tried to engage the old man in conversation. He was desperate to know as much as he could about this new land. The old man's responses were terse, however, and he always ended any discussion almost as soon as it had begun, either by lapsing into silence or riding on ahead of Hagan.

They came to a small settlement on the shore of an enormous lake. The lake was quite easily the largest Hagan had ever seen. If it were not for the distant outlines of ragged mountains visible on the far side he would have sworn they had reached the sea.

As they rode through the village Hagan smiled at the locals. He did not know any of them but their faces looked somehow familiar. They smiled back but, Hagan noticed, they nodded to the warriors who accompanied him with obvious respect. At the sight of the strange old man, 'respect' was an understatement. The faces of the ordinary people lit up with joy. They grinned and waved at him, apparently desperate for any attention he might throw in their direction.

'Blessings upon you, lord!' one man called as they rode past. 'Thank you for all that you do for us.'

The old man endured all this with a sort of bemused, tight-lipped smile on his face. He nodded and waved to those he passed but never stopped to speak.

Hagan also noticed the distinct signs of preparation for war. Thick smoke rose from the blacksmith's forge and the sound of hammering came from within the round building. Men of fighting age sat outside their houses sharpening blades on whetstones. Some children were polishing their fathers' mail shirts. A party of around ten young men, overseen by an older warrior, were practising shield wall manoeuvres in the middle of the village.

As well as that, a lot of people appeared to be preparing to make a journey. Men were filling leather travel bags and horses were being groomed. They all wore what looked like their best clothes, however, so wherever they were planning to go, it was not to war.

The old man led the way to a long, narrow boat with many rowing benches that bobbed on the water at the end of a wooden jetty. Hagan noticed that around them others were also preparing boats. There were men, women and children in them, all in their best clothes and chatting or laughing. There was a festive mood in the air. Some of the boats had already launched and were heading out into the lake.

Hagan's company got into theirs and soon they were rowing their way along the lake. After a while the sail was hoisted and they picked up speed.

The weather was fine and if he had not been a prisoner Hagan would have found the trip pleasant. The sun sparkled on the water. Wind tugged at their hair as the boat scythed through the water. They passed other settlements on the lake shore and Hagan saw the banners of other Burgundar clans: the wolf of the Volsungs and the lightning symbol of the Leuhtungs. At these sights his heart soared. He really was back among his own people. He was home.

Home. Could he really call it that? His home had been Vorbetomagus. He had grown up among its forests and meadows. This was a different land altogether. A strange one. Then again, his father's generation in turn had likewise called somewhere else, somewhere north of the Rhine, home. Perhaps home was were his people were, regardless of location.

The sun set but they sailed on. The moon rose to shed light on the lake and the lights of shoreline settlements showed them where they were. Across the water Hagan could pick out more lights: other boats on the lake, all sailing in the same direction as they were. The light-hearted, excited chatter of the folk on board the boats drifted across the water. All the while the strange old man with bare feet watched him and Zerco with his one eye, an expression on his face that suggested slight bemusement.

'What is your name?' Hagan said at length. 'We've told you ours.'

'I am known by many names,' the old man said. 'But here they call me Wodnas.'

'You are not a Burgundar,' Hagan said.

'I am not,' Wodnas said. 'But I am a cousin. I came from the east. I lost my kingdom to the Huns, now I am here to ensure the same thing does not happen to King Gunderic.'

'You know that the Huns are coming?' Hagan said.

'Eventually, yes,' the old man said. 'And I am helping Gunderic prepare for that day.'

'I saw men in the village by the lake preparing for war,' Hagan said. 'But also it looks like a festival. Are we all sailing to a celebration?'

The old man did not reply.

'You and your men don't say much,' Hagan said.

'The tongue is the head's bane,' the old man said. 'I teach all my warriors this: watch everything you say. Every word you speak to someone else will bring a reward or punishment in return.'

'Evenings by the fire with your warband must be rather dour affairs,' Hagan said. 'Burgundars have always been sociable folk. This behaviour is not common to us.'

'I have taught them to talk freely only with people you can trust,' Wodnas said.

'And I resent your lack of trust, friend,' Hagan said. Frustration at the man's unforthcoming stance was beginning to boil in his chest. 'You will be sorry when King Gunderic finds out you've treated me this way.'

'We shall see,' Wodnas said. 'The less you speak, the less you tell your enemies about your business.'

'You said you were interested to hear Zerco's story,' Hagan said. It was the last tactic he had to try to force a conversation. 'Yet you haven't asked a thing about him this whole journey.'

For a moment the old man looked at him. Hagan could tell he was biting his tongue. He thought he was finally getting somewhere when Wodnas' eye became hooded once more.

'When we get to Geneva you will tell your whole story to the king,' Wodnas said. 'There is no need for me to listen to it twice.'

269

He got up and walked to the bow, signalling that the discussion was over.

'And that's that,' Hagan said, looking at Wodnas' scrawny back as he walked away from him. 'Another talk done. It's like trying to have a conversation with a ghost.'

Hagan noticed then that one of the young warriors stood beside him, listening. He looked a little older than the others and Hagan had noticed by the way he was treated by them he was some sort of leader, after Wodnas.

'I assume he's more talkative when instructing you young men in war?' Hagan said.

For the first time on the journey, and much to Hagan's surprise, the young man's face lit up.

'The Lord Wodnas is amazing,' he said. 'He knows so much. Not just about war but everything. He is so wise. When he looks at you, you feel like he is looking right into your soul and you feel like you are invincible. I'd fight the world for him. We all would.'

Hagan raised his eyebrows.

'What is he? The War Leader or something?'

'He is the Spirit,' the youth said. 'The Breath. He breaths fire and knowledge into all of us.'

Hagan now frowned, surprised that such strange, almost poetic words should come from someone so young and clad in the raiment of a warrior.

'What's your name, lad?' Hagan said.

'Gunfjaun,' the warrior said.

The conversation ended there, however. The unemotional, guarded mask fell across the young man's face once more. He clamped his lips shut then walked away.

Eventually the fires of what appeared to be a rather large settlement loomed ahead. From the direction of the prow it was obvious this was their destination.

A beacon fire burned at the end of a jetty which speared out into the lake from a large harbour thronged with many other boats. The fires spilled out beyond the harbour, showing that it was so packed others had had to beach their boats in the mud and reeds of the lake shore.

Wodnas steered their boat into the harbour. Hagan was surprised to see that there was one space at the packed jetty that no one had tied up at. Then he spotted a warrior in a dark cloak, minding the space.

'This old man must be important,' Zerco muttered to Hagan, 'if he has his own mooring space in such a busy harbour. What do you think's going on? Why all the crowds?'

Hagan just shrugged but there was something niggling away, deep in his mind; some buried memory that was trying to make itself heard.

Wodnas' warriors tied up the boat and they disembarked. Surrounded by the ever-silent warriors, the old man, Hagan and Zerco plodded up to a wall that looked like it protected the settlement that stretched up the shore behind it. Torches burned atop it and Hagan could see warriors patrolling a platform atop the wall that allowed them to look out over the defences.

There was a large gate in the wall which was guarded by warriors as well. Just beside that was a gallows from which swayed four bodies. Gunfjaun exchanged a few words with the gate guards and they stepped aside to let the company enter.

'Welcome to Geneva,' Wodnas said and went in through the gate.

Hagan, Zerco and the accompanying warriors filed through behind him into the city. They entered a street that was bustling with people. Hagan noticed the same festive atmosphere he had detected in the settlement they had passed through earlier. Torches and braziers lit the night. The buildings were decked with greenery and flowers and the residents were well dressed and chattering in an excited way. People hugged each other as if being reunited after some time.

The paved street, clearly Roman, had fallen into disrepair

but the cracks and potholes had been overlaid with a wooden walkway. As they strode up it Hagan could feel the excitement building in his own heart. The people they passed looked familiar. Not that he knew them personally, but the shapes of their faces, the clothes they wore, the tongue they spoke – all said he was among Burgundars. Many of them showed the same reverence towards Wodnas as in the village and Hagan began to wonder if the man was a bishop or other high-ranking churchman. Yet his thoughts were dwarfed by the emotions churning inside him. Soon he would meet his old friends. Who knew who else was here besides Gunderic and Gunhild? Perhaps more of their friends had survived?

At the same time he felt a tremor of unease. How would they feel about seeing him again? Gunhild especially. Would she even remember him?

Then Hagan saw something else to unsettle him.

CHAPTER THIRTY-ONE

IT WAS A church – or at least it had been one. It looked like any other Roman church: tall, oblong in shape, with large double doors at the entrance. Like any other church, above the door was a metal cross fixed to the wall. Except someone had changed this one. The two arms now bent downwards so it resembled an arrow instead of a cross.

Hagan's time in the Army had lessened his religious convictions, however he still felt a little chill at seeing the holy symbol vandalised. It had been done deliberately, and the fact that the defaced cross was still on the wall said something as well.

Just past the church they entered into a wide square and right in the middle of it an enormous hall. Hagan's mouth dropped open at the sight of it. Its style contrasted with most of the old, brick-built Roman buildings around it. It was long and narrow and at least two hundred paces long, with a roof that rose from not far off the ground at the sides to high overhead at the apex, giving it the look of a huge, upturned ship sitting in the middle of the city.

The roof was covered in shingles that were painted white and glittered in the firelight from ranks of torches set in brackets all around the square. One strange thing Hagan noted was that in the centre of that magnificent roof there appeared to be a gap, through which what looked very like the branches of a tree were poking out.

The square before the hall was slabbed with paving stones and there were lots of people milling around. As their little company pushed their way through the crowds Hagan could not help but note a large, flat rock, that reached to about waist height, right in the middle of the otherwise level square. It was covered in dark brown stains as if some sort of liquid had been splashed all over it and left to dry.

Warriors, their mail polished for show rather than the dull metal worn by the fighters they had met at the border, stood on guard all around. Hagan noted that unlike the strange raven device painted on the shields of the one-eyed man's warriors, these warriors guarding the hall all bore an eagle on their shields: the emblem of the Nibelung clan.

Wodnas led the little company towards the gable wall of the hall where a set of stout wooden double doors, perhaps twice the height of a man, were flanked by a pair of wooden pillars. These held up a short canopy that formed a porch. The doors were covered with ornate carvings of heroes and beasts that twisted around each other in an intricate fashion. The carvings were painted in bright colours. The pillars were the same, some of the decoration even being picked out in shining silver and gold. The building was even more impressive than Gundahar's hall had been at Vorbetomagus.

'There is no shortage of wealth here,' Zerco said from the corner of his mouth. 'I believe we are in the right place.'

He licked his lips.

The guards at the door snapped to attention at the sight of Wodnas approaching. They raised their arms over their heads in a salute. Wodnas nodded then spoke a few quiet words to them that Hagan did not hear. There was a smaller door cut into the left main one and one of the warriors went inside through it. For long moments they stood waiting in the chilly night air, then the warrior returned.

'Enter,' he said, pulling the door wide.

Wodnas went in first, then Hagan and Zerco followed him. The young warriors followed behind.

The inside of the hall was as impressive as the outside and in contrast to the semi-darkness of the exterior was ablaze with light. Torches burned in brackets and oil lamps stood on tall stands. A long hearth ran up the middle of the floor, making the air warm and comfortable, while the smoke from the smouldering wood drifted off through openings in the roof so as not to clog the air.

The roof was held up by two rows of mighty pillars which, like the ones outside, were richly carved and painted with vivid colours. They were also decorated in places by gold and silver leaf which glittered in the torchlight. Long woven cloths hung upon the walls and across the pillars, and over them rode or ran figures from ancient legends: warriors, heroes and monsters. Unlike in the hall of Gundahar, where the tapestries had been ancient and faded, these were new and alive with many bright colours.

In the midst of the hall was indeed a stout, living tree that grew up from the floor. An opening had been created in the roof surrounding its trunk so it continued on above without letting rain or snow in.

The floor was not just packed dirt like in many similar halls; it was paved with countless tiny tiles. They too were many colours and had been arranged to create patterns and pictures in the manner Hagan had seen in great Roman houses and temples.

At the far end of the hall, beyond the hearth and facing north towards the doors, was a dais with three steps, and in the middle of the dais was a great gilded chair. Before it was a table around which a small band of people were gathered.

Despite the years that had passed, Hagan recognised Gunhild straight away. She was no longer the girl she had been when he had last seen her. She was now a mature, beautiful woman but she had the same mane of blonde hair, captivating smile and eyes that seemed to sparkle, even at a distance, enchanting all they fell upon to return their gaze in rapt adoration.

In the gilded chair was her brother. Gunderic too had matured. His torso had filled out and his face had started to resemble his father's. He had a grizzled black beard now and the same aggressive glare that Gundahar had had, though Hagan knew this was more than partly due to the stern arch that by nature his eyebrows made.

Both Gunderic and his sister wore long black cloaks, both with the Nibelungs' eagle embroidered in multi-coloured threads at their left shoulders.

Beside Gunhild was a giant of a man. Hagan knew this could only be the Volsung prince Aetius suspected of stealing the Roman treasure. He was young, handsome and at least a head and shoulders taller than Gundahar, who was a big enough man himself. Like Gunhild and Gunderic he wore a long black cloak, though his had a wolf embroidered on his left shoulder.

There were other men of varying ages at the table but Hagan did not recognise any of them. Hagan's eyes were drawn towards a young woman who sat among them, a big black cat resting on her lap. It was not because she was one of the very few women there but because she was beautiful – as stunning as Gunhild but in a different way. The flash of her eyes as they regarded him, her fine features, and her evidently lithe body accentuated by her tight-fitting blue dress, made Hagan's heart begin to beat faster.

Hagan wondered how Gunhild found having such a rival in her brother's court.

Wodnas walked ahead, leading the way towards the table, his bare feet padding on the tiled floor and the butt of the spear he used as a walking staff clicking out every step. They had barely got halfway when Gunhild rose to her feet.

'Hagan!' she cried. 'Gunderic, look!'

276

Hagan felt himself bursting into a grin. Joy surged in his heart and his eyes became clouded by tears. He realised how much he had missed his old friends, especially now all their other families were gone. Gunhild came rushing down the hall towards him and he ran towards her. He heard the warriors behind him move to stop him but Wodnas said, 'This confirms what he claimed is true.'

Gunhild threw her arms around Hagan. Gunderic came jogging after her and soon all three of them were locked in an embrace.

'I can't believe it!' Gunhild said, staring at Hagan as if he were a ghost. 'After all these years you just turn up and walk in here?'

'I didn't know any other Burgundars had survived,' Hagan said. 'Beyond the ones I was with in the Army.'

Gunderic clapped him on the back.

'Good to see you again, old friend,' he said.

'You too,' Hagan said. 'Or should I say "Lord King"?'

Both laughed, though Gunderic finished laughing before Hagan.

'*High One* is fine,' he said.

'Who is this, my dear?'

Hagan looked around and saw the big young man had joined them. There was an expression on his face that suggested bemused annoyance.

'This is Hagan, Sigurd,' Gunhild said, still looking at Hagan as if she could not believe he was standing there. 'Hagan, this is Sigurd of the Volsungs, my husband. Sigurd, Hagan is a very old friend.'

'Just a friend?' Sigurd said, a half-smile on his face that held no mirth.

'Of course!' Gunhild said. She dropped her arms away from Hagan. Her expression changed to one of consternation that assured her husband that a friend was all Hagan was and that was all he ever would be.

'Sigurd is the new champion of our people,' Gunhild said, 'Just as your father was, Hagan.'

Hagan and Sigurd exchanged cool glances. Sigurd nodded and Hagan returned the gesture.

'So you survived the Army?' Gunderic said. 'I heard the last Burgundars were wiped out by the Goths?'

'I'm hard to kill,' Hagan said.

'And wait until you hear this, Hagan!' Gunhild said. 'Brynhild is still alive too! Soon we will all be back together again.'

'Brynhild?' Hagan's jaw dropped. 'I saw her die!'

'She was only badly wounded,' Gunderic said. 'She recovered. She is a little... different now but still the same fiery Brynhild. Beautiful, too.'

'Is she here?' Hagan said, looking around.

Gunderic shook his head.

'She rules her own realm high in the mountains,' he said.

'I can't believe it,' Hagan said.

'Any more than we can believe you now stand among us, alive and well,' Gunhild said, smiling. 'And who is your little friend, Hagan?'

All eyes turned on Zerco.

Hagan opened his mouth to speak but then hesitated. What should he say? That a Roman general had asked him to bring this dwarf along as a spy? That he was here to try to find stolen treasure? What would his friends think of him then? Perhaps he should just come clean and tell them he had been sent here by Aetius. He would be alright – probably. Then Hagan regarded the suspicious looks of Sigurd and the old man and wondered if that really was the case. Even if Gunderic and Gunhild did protect him, what would happen to Zerco? The little man's life had been miserable enough so far without Hagan now condemning him to a painful death.

'I have heard the Burgundars hate the Huns,' Zerco said

while Hagan was still trying to decide what to say. To everyone's surprise he spoke in the tongue of the Burgundars.

'We do,' Gunderic said. 'They almost wiped our people out at Vorbetomagus.'

'I too hate the Huns,' Zerco said. 'For four years I was slave to Bleda the Hun. He made me work as his jester. You want vengeance on them, right? You are going to fight them?'

'Sooner or later, yes,' Gunderic said, narrowing his eyes.

'When that time comes I can be of service,' Zerco said. 'I lived right at the heart of their court. I know much about them. I know their plans. I know how they fight. I know Attila. Hagan here thought I might be useful to the Burgundars.'

'In that case you are most welcome,' Gunderic said. 'What do we call you?'

'Zerco, lord,' the little man said.

'Well, Zerco,' Gunderic said, 'Welcome to my kingdom. If you prove useful to us – and funny enough – perhaps someday you will be my personal jester.'

Hagan just caught the expression that crossed the little man's face at Gunderic's words. It was a mixture of rage and contempt that flickered like lightning across his visage before Zerco managed to switch it to an obsequious smile.

'It would be an honour, Lord King,' he said in his strange, lisping voice.

Hagan and Zerco exchanged looks. Both knew that they now shared a secret that would be dangerous for both of them if it became known to the others in the hall. Hagan wondered if he had in fact done the wrong thing in not telling the truth about Zerco. But then Zerco may have said things about him that would cause his friends to suspect him in turn. Had he brought a serpent into this new Eden of his people?

'This is indeed a miracle,' Hagan said. 'So many of our folk died yet we three all survived. And Brynhild too! Thanks be to God!'

Hagan felt as if someone had opened the great doors of the hall, letting in an icy blast of wind from the mountains. All around glared at him, their expressions a mixture of consternation and surprise. No one spoke.

'Have I said something wrong?' he said, breaking the awkward silence.

'We no longer honour the God of the Christians here,' Gunderic said. 'We have returned to the customs of our fathers and their fathers. We honour the Thunderer, the Lord Ingwass, Nerthus our mother the Earth and above all the Great God, Tiwass.'

'The old war god?' Hagan said, his voice a little breathless with trepidation. He may not have been the most fervent of believers, but twenty-one years of religious habit were hard to just slough off. An old, half-remembered fear stabbed at his heart as well. The conversion of the Burgundars to faith in Christ had not been bloodless. When he was nine years old, to deny Jesus could have resulted in decapitation.

Gunhild laid a hand on Hagan's forearm. The expression on her face softened again.

'You were not to know, Hagan,' she said. 'Much is different in the new Burgundar kingdom.'

'As you shall see, old friend,' Gunderic said, placing a hand on Hagan's shoulder and steering him towards the table at the top of the room. 'But some things have not. For now it is the second new moon past the winter solstice. Surely you have not forgotten what that means?'

Hagan's jaw dropped open.

'Of course! It's the appointed time for the Great *Thingwas* of the Burgundars. That's why all those folk are gathering here! How could I forget?'

'It starts tonight,' Gunderic said. 'And you will see with your own eyes the greatness of our new nation. Come! You have much to tell us, and we have much to tell you.'

CHAPTER THIRTY-TWO

'I'VE NEVER SEEN the like of this hall, Gunderic,' Hagan said as they walked along the tiled floor.

Unlike the musty, smoky air of many feasting halls he had been in all over the north, the atmosphere in Gunderic's was clear. The smoke from the torches in the wall brackets and the large fires that burned in the floor hearths rose into the apex of the roof but was then filtered out of the building somehow. Nor was it gloomy: light from the torches and lamps reached up to the lofty beams that held the stout wooden roof in place. There was one detail that puzzled Hagan however.

'But why the tree?' he said, nodding towards the thick trunk of what looked like an ash that sprouted from the midst of the tiled floor.

'When we took possession of this hall it was a sorry sight,' Gunderic said with a smile. 'It had been abandoned for years and was falling down. The roof had fallen in and that tree had taken root in the broken floor. When we rebuilt the place I was going to cut it down but then I thought we should leave it. It struck me as symbolic. The rootless tree falls in a storm, but we Burgundars have strong roots. Even though – like this tree – we are now planted in a place where we should not be, we still grow and flourish.'

'I heard you've only been in this land for a few years,' Hagan said. 'You've done a lot of work already.'

'It's been hard work, Hagan,' Gunderic said. 'And the

281

restoration of this hall is just a reflection of what we have been doing with the people. We have been rebuilding the folk, bringing them back together, giving them back their songs, their tales, their customs – and their gods.'

'It must have cost a fortune in gold,' Hagan said.

The king shot a sharp glance at Hagan.

'What does that matter?' he said, eyes narrowing.

'I just mean you've done well,' Hagan said, disconcerted by the sharp change in his old friend's demeanour and deciding to change the subject.

'I could not have done it without this man,' Gunderic said, laying a hand on the shoulder of Wodnas. 'I'm glad you have already met Wodnas. He's a marvel. He has helped us build up our army, taught them tactics and strategies and made them a fighting force. One to be feared!'

'They need to be,' Wodnas said. 'They will be outnumbered in any war that comes to this realm. They will need to kill four men for every one of ours who falls.'

'And they will,' Gunderic said. 'The Alemanni have already felt the sting of our blades on a few raids. But Wodnas is not just a war leader. He has taught us the value of our own gods – the old gods – and he and his people have taught us, *reminded* us, of how we honoured them once. He has become so important in the birth of our new nation that the ordinary people call him the Spirit and the Breath.'

Hagan cast a wary glance at the one-eyed old man who returned his look with an enigmatic smile.

'We are about to ride to the Thingwas,' Gunderic said. 'You must come with us. You will meet the rest of my councillors. Are you still good at hunting?'

'I suppose so. I enjoy it, anyway,' Hagan said with a shrug.

'I have a need for a new Hunt Master,' Gunderic said. 'The last one… let me down.'

He turned and strode off down the hall towards the door. Everyone else followed.

Returning out into the night air, Hagan saw that the crowd thronging the square outside had thinned a bit, and a steady stream of people were now heading towards the street that led to the city gate.

A band of warriors led horses for the king and the others into the square. Their leader was tall and heavily muscled. He wore a black cloak around his shoulders that bore the symbol of the Sun Wheel. He walked up to Gunderic and saluted him.

'Allow me to introduce Geic,' Gunderic said, slapping a hand down on the man's meaty shoulder. 'He is my personal bodyguard and makes sure I am safe wherever I go. Not that I have any enemies within my realm. He is also leader of a special company of men within our war horde you will be very interested to meet.'

The warrior smiled and held out his arm for Hagan to grasp.

'Hagan here is a long-lost brother Burgundar,' Gunderic said, laying a hand on Hagan's shoulder. 'He is the son of Godegisil, the last Champion of the Burgundars from the time before.'

Geic's eyes widened with excitement.

'We sing the old songs about the great deeds of Godegisil,' he said. 'You must come and see the lads. It would be an honour indeed.'

Hagan smiled and nodded. He wondered how they would all feel if he revealed the truth about his parentage.

They all mounted, including Hagan. Then the company made its way across the square, moving with the people down the street towards the gate. Two columns of mounted warriors formed up and rode on either side of them, keeping the mob away from the king and his chosen advisors. The ordinary folk did not seem hostile to Gunderic, indeed they waved, smiled and shouted as he rode past, but, Hagan supposed, it was best not to take any chances. If a foreign enemy wanted the king dead, the press of a crowd would be a good way to get close to him.

Once through the gates they rode along a path that ran between the harbour and the walls that surrounded the city. A gallows, like the one at the border, was set up and several bodies swung below it, suspended from nooses.

The thrill of nostalgic familiarity returned to Hagan's heart. The tradition of the Burgundar Thingwas gathering went back beyond memory. At the appointed time every year the folk – the free ones at least – would all gather in one place. Decisions that affected the whole people were debated and concluded, law courts would hear disputes, important marriages would be arranged, and markets were held, as well the chance for much socialising, dancing and feasting. A large part of the Thingwas also involved religious customs and as they rode Hagan wondered what would happen here. From the age of nine to the fall of Vorbetomagus every Thingwas he had been to had been presided over by Bishop Ulfius. Who would lead the prayers here, and to whom would those prayers be offered?

Despite these slight misgivings he felt glad. Even though this was a strange land, it felt reassuring that the familiar customs he thought were lost forever were still being upheld.

They rode through woods, then a little way from the city the path opened onto a wide clearing in the trees. It was abuzz with activity. The roughly oval clearing was perhaps three hundred paces long and two hundred across. It was lit by many fires. Three large bonfires were ablaze, one in the centre of the clearing and one at either edge, while hundreds of torches were set in the ground all around the perimeter. Many among the crowd of people there also bore torches in their hands. At one end of the clearing was a large earthen mound. It was devoid of grass, making Hagan conclude the mound had been raised for the purpose of the gathering.

At the far end of the clearing three statues towered. They were wooden, each one carved from the single trunk of a mighty tree to resemble a human figure. No, not a human figure, Hagan remembered – a god. The statue on the right depicted Thunerass with his stark, glaring, always angry eyes, his long beard and the stone axe with which he ground out thunder and smashed all his enemies, grasped before him in huge fists.

The figure on the left was Ingwass, the one sometimes just called 'the Lord', the god who made the earth fertile. Hagan noted with a smirk that he had been carved in the old fashion, with a huge, erect male member. He wondered what Bishop Ulfius would have made of all this.

The figure in the middle was taller than the other two, as befitted the status of the supreme god, Tiwass. The huge figure was carved in his war gear: helmet, mail shirt, and with his mighty sword, the legendary *Tyrfing*, held before him. Tiwass the mighty, Tiwass the brave. The god who protected the Burgundars and inspired their warriors to victory. Who kept the wolf from the door.

There was no need for a representation of the fourth deity, Nerthus, for she was all around. She was the earth from whom the crops grew and who covered the dead in their graves.

The sight of the flame-lit effigies was both thrilling and frightening. Hagan felt something primal, savage and beast-like awake deep within his heart. These were the stern images of the Gods of his folk. From his childhood he remembered some of the old ones say that the Gods actually entered the statues and lived in them. Yet Bishop Ulfius had been just as stern and only a hard ruler like Gundahar could have succeeded in pushing the new faith on the tribe. Hagan could still remember the severed heads of those who refused baptism decorating the walls of Vorbetomagus. Ulfius had said the old gods were demons and now, looking at their images in the eerie light of the bonfires, Hagan could understand the sentiment.

Horns blasted and an expectant hush fell on the gathered crowd. The only sound was the crackling of the fires. All attention turned to the mound. There was a man climbing up it with stiff, arthritic strides. He reminded Hagan of a goat. He was very thin, scrawny even, and his pointed beard and long hair were white with age. He was clad in a long white robe that reached to his feet. For a long moment he looked out at the sea of faces below him, then he placed a hand across his chest and closed his eyes.

Every Thingwas began in the same way. The Law Speaker, a wise man of the tribe, recited the laws of the people from memory. Law was what held the people together and no one was supposed to be above it. The Law was the Law. It was the foundation of the land and without it the realm would fall apart.

The goat-like man began pronouncing the laws in a loud, resonant voice that was surprising, given the decrepit frame it was delivered from.

'This is Forsetti,' Gunderic said to Hagan from the side of his mouth. 'He is our Law Speaker. He came to us along with Wodnas and he knows all of the laws and recites them before the district courts sit. He advises all our judges and chieftains on matters of the law.'

'Is there no Burgundar who could be Law Speaker?' Hagan said.

'Alas, my father's Law Speaker was the last Burgundar to hold the position,' Gunderic said. 'And he died at Vorbetomagus. As did his son. If it wasn't for Forsetti to teach us the laws again we'd have lost them forever.'

'If he came with Wodnas, won't they be foreign laws?' Hagan said. 'The Aesir are related to the Goths and Vandals and followed their laws. We Burgundars had our own.'

'Burgundars, Goths and Vandals are cousins,' Gunderic said. 'Both Ostrogoths and Visigoths. Our folk and the Goths are both descendants of Mannus, who first gave laws to men. Their laws are our laws.'

Hagan frowned and looked away. Something bothered him

about this. The unbroken line of Burgundar Law Speakers that had stretched from the distant ancestor, Mannus, had been broken. This was the start of a new line, not the continuation of the old. He began to wonder what else had changed.

As the goat man droned on, a sorry-looking column of nine men were hustled and prodded into the clearing to stand before the statues of the Gods. They were stripped to the waist, their hands bound before them and their legs joined by chains. Hagan felt a growing sense of dread at the sight of them. He had never enjoyed this part of the opening of the Thingwas.

'Slaves?' he said.

'Law-breakers,' Gunderic said, his voice cold with evident distaste. 'Some perverts and a few foreigners we caught who had entered the realm without permission. They are the worst. They say they are merchants but secretly they are spies, working for Rome to overthrow me or steal my gold.'

After a while Forsetti came to the end of his chanting. He raised his arms in the air and pronounced the Thingwas open. Horns blew again and folk cheered.

Then Hagan saw a line of women enter the clearing from the woods. There were ten of them, dressed in long hooded dark blue robes that sparkled and glittered in the firelight from the little seashells and pieces of glass sewn into their material. Each bore a long metal wand in the shape of a spinning distaff. The lead woman was followed by a large cat.

'You have brought back the hellrūnes!' Hagan said. The witches who had guided the magic rituals of the Burgundars had been the first to go when the new faith was introduced. 'You'll be telling me next the Swan Maidens are coming!'

He was grinning with nostalgic delight, but his grin faded when he saw the looks of sadness and dismay on the faces of the king and his sister.

'Alas, no,' Gunhild said. 'They are all gone except for me.'

'And there is something else also missing, old friend,'

Gunderic said. 'You will see soon enough but you must prepare yourself.'

The witches took their hoods down and Hagan saw that their leader was the pretty young woman he had seen in Gunderic's feasting hall earlier.

'This is the Lady Freya,' Gunderic said. 'She is also one of the easterners who came here with Wodnas. She now leads religious practice in our land. Like Forsetti she sits on my personal council.'

Hagan raised his eyebrows at the thought that here was another foreigner of the Aesir in such a key position in the realm but he said nothing.

Men and women with drums, flutes and pipes stood behind the hellrūnes and began a pounding, rhythmical tune that the women in the long blue robes started to gyrate to. As they did so they began chanting, howling *galdrass* – holy prayers to the spirits and the Gods – to the night sky. Some of the crowd joined in. As the song continued it got louder and louder, and the witches spun faster and faster, their long unbound hair trailing through the air as they turned round and round. As they themselves spun, they also began to step around in a circle that ringed the captive men before the statues.

After several verses the galdrass finished with a great, final shout. As the last word echoed through the trees the hellrūnes ceased spinning almost as one. Hagan was astonished that they did not collapse onto the grass, dizzy, in a heap.

The sudden hush that fell on the clearing was almost a shock. It was broken by the whimpering of one of the bound men. Like everyone else he knew what would come next. A stream of urine ran down the leg of the prisoner beside him.

The warriors guarding the captives forced each one to turn so he faced the three towering images of the Gods. The witches gathered into three groups of three. Each group approached a different prisoner.

Freya screeched some inarticulate cry to the statue of Tiwass, then the witches fell upon the men before them. From each group of three, one woman snaked a noose made of animal pelt around his neck and hauled it tight. As he began to choke a second hellrūne struck the prisoner on the crown of the head with a stone axe. As he crumpled to his knees the third woman sliced his throat open with a knife.

'The threefold death,' Hagan said in a hoarse voice. 'I have not seen this since I was a boy.'

'The fitting way to open the Thingwas,' Gunderic said, puffing out his chest. 'Sacrifice to the Gods to give thanks and ask they bless us in the time to come.'

The hellrūnes moved to the next three prisoners and killed them the same way. Then the final three.

'Your father only used to kill one,' Hagan said.

'We have much to be thankful for,' the king said. 'Perhaps if my father had been more generous and not forsaken the Gods he would not have perished at Vorbetomagus. Now come! You shall meet the rest of my council of the realm.'

He led Hagan, Gunhild and Sigurd up onto the mound where Forsetti waited and by now a line of folding chairs had been set out. The seat in the middle of the row was much grander than the others, with gold and silver threads embroidering twisting beasts on the back and sides. Gunderic sat in it. Gunhild took the seat on his left. Wodnas, still barefoot, padded up after them and sat to Gunderic's right. Several others climbed up the mound as well, each one stopping to pay respects to the king as they passed to take their own seats.

First came a thin man with a long grey beard. He was old, older than Wodnas, and had lost a lot of the hair on the top of his head. His eyes were bright though and he looked at Hagan with a curious expression on his intelligent looking face.

'This is Kvasir,' Gunderic said. 'He has been re-teaching our poets and bards the songs of olden times and the sagas of the Gods that were lost when my father made us Christians. He runs a school here in Geneva so the knowledge will never be lost again. While the Thingwas is running he will meet with poets and bards from the rest of the realm and they will exchange more songs.'

The man nodded then went off to take his seat further down the row.

'You have a poet on your council of the realm?' Hagan said in a quiet voice, frowning.

'This is a council of the leaders of the people, not just war,' Gunderic said. 'In all decisions that affect everyone it is imperative that all parts of our society are represented and have a say. Then all will support the action taken. Wodnas has taught me this.'

'Has he?' Hagan said, glancing at the one-eyed man and beginning to wonder just who really ran this new kingdom of the Burgundars.

Next came another man in a brown cloak. His long, straight hair was so blond it was almost white, though he was middle-aged and his hair could well have been changing to that colour. He had no beard and a smooth complexion that was almost like a woman's. He regarded Hagan with an enigmatic smile that was not unlike the one Wodnas often wore.

'This is my old travelling companion, Lokke,' Wodnas said, laying a hand on the man's shoulder. 'He's a devious bastard and great at telling stories. That sometimes gets the better of him so be careful which of his words you believe.'

'Go and ride yourself, Wodnas,' Lokke said, still smiling.

'Like I said, he's an old friend,' Wodnas said.

'Lokke looks after knowledge,' Gunderic said. 'Along with Wodnas' Raven Warriors he gathers information on what our enemies are up to so we cannot be surprised again as we were at Vorbetomagus.'

Hagan nodded, trying to appear as nonchalant as possible. What did this man Lokke know of the plans of Aetius towards the treasure? Was this all just a sham and all these people already knew he had been to Ravenna? Perhaps it was best to admit everything before it was too late, and to Hell with whatever they did with the dwarf.

Lokke took a seat as Freya, fresh from her religious duties, arrived at the top of the mound. She bobbed a curtsey in the king's direction then regarded Hagan with a beguiling smile and quite enchanting eyes. For a moment Hagan felt captivated by her gaze until he noticed the splatters of fresh blood on her cheeks and hands.

This was a strange collection for a council of the realm, a far cry from the band of burly heroes who Gunderic's father would have had in a similar conference. At times of crisis Gundahar had gathered together the hardest men of the tribe and those most experienced in war – noblemen who were the elders of their clans. Gunderic's had a poet, three strange men and two women, all of them, except Gunhild, foreigners.

'And in case you think our folk are now just led by strangers,' Gunderic said, as if reading Hagan's mind, 'the rest of the council is made up of the Lords of the Burgundar clans. Sigurd, Lord of the Volsungs, you have already met. My sister and I represent the Nibelungs.'

The two men who arrived at the top of the mound next wore black cloaks like Gunderic, Gunhild and Sigurd. The first was a sallow-faced, balding man in his thirties with a long white scar down his left cheek and a lightning symbol embroidered on his cloak. The second was a young man who had a Sun Wheel on his shoulder. These were the representatives of the Leuhtung and the Solung Burgundar clans.

'This is Brenwic, Lord of the Leuhtungs,' Gunderic introduced the first man. 'And this is Guntram, Lord of the Solungs.'

Both men nodded then took seats.

'It seems all the clans are represented,' Hagan said, his voice becoming hoarse. 'Except one.'

He turned to the king; his eyes glittered in the light of the fires.

'Be strong, old friend,' Gunderic said. 'I have some sad news to tell you.'

CHAPTER THIRTY-THREE

'THERE ARE NO Dagelungs left?' Hagan said in an empty voice, realising for the first time that there was no one present who represented his own clan.

'I'm sorry, my old friend,' Gunderic said.

Gunhild laid a hand on Hagan's shoulder.

'We have searched the world for the surviving Burgundars, Hagan,' Gunderic said. 'We've sent messengers far and wide, telling the world the Burgundars have a new home and that our folk are welcome here.'

'So far, not one living Dagelung has been found,' Gunhild said.

'Your clan must have borne the brunt of the Huns' fury at Vorbetomagus,' Gunderic said. 'It seems they were obliterated, Hagan.'

The feelings of desolation and loneliness Hagan had become so familiar with over the last fifteen years came flowing back into his heart once more. The memory of his dead brother lying in the mud resurfaced in his mind. His mother's corpse with her head stamped in. Cousins, in-laws, the whole web that made up a clan. The stories particular to his clan. Were they really now all gone?

Then another thought came to him. Was he even a Dagelung? Who knew what clan his real father had belonged to. Anger, resentment and self-pity began to churn within him. His mother was a Dagelung, which made him at least half one, he concluded.

'So I'm the last of the Dagelungs,' Hagan said, blinking to clear the tears that stung his eyes. Whether these were due to the loss of his believed kin or the memory of what the man he had always thought was his father had told him the night before the battle of Vorbetomagus, he could not tell. 'The last blood link to my clan.'

'The last of the *old* Dagelungs,' Gunderic said. 'But the first of the new. Like that tree still growing even though it is now in a feasting hall, you can start your clan anew. You can keep it going. This is indeed a gift from the Great God, Tiwass.'

'And who knows?' Gunhild said. 'Perhaps someday we will find other living Dagelungs. We did not know you were still alive. There may be more like you, beyond the boundaries of the Empire or still serving in the Army.'

'Today you can complete my council, old friend,' Gunderic said. 'You will represent the Dagelungs. At last we will have someone from every clan at the table.'

Hagan just nodded. He decided at that moment his illegitimate lineage should remain his secret. No one living knew of it anyway.

Except, perhaps, the thought ran through his mind, *my real father.* Was he still alive? And if so, was he perhaps even here in Geneva?

'We have kept the memory of the Dagelungs alive,' Gunderic said. 'As you will see.'

There was a shout in the clearing below and Hagan looked to see ranks of warriors were filing in. They walked together with a disciplined step.

Gunderic stood up. He took a deep breath, his chest puffing with pride.

'The Burgundar War Horde,' he said.

Hagan was impressed. Every one of the warriors wore war gear that was new and well looked-after. They wore helmets with cheek guards and long nasal guards, decorated with embossed images of warriors and dragons and polished so they gleamed like silver. So too were the mail shirts that covered their torsos. Each man had a spear, a throwing axe, a sword and a long knife. Gone was the Burgundar horde of his youth where each warrior expressed his own style through his war gear and how it was decorated. Now the only variance was that the black cloak each man wore had the emblem of his clan on the shoulder: eagles, wolves, sun wheels and lightning, though of course no bears for the Dagelungs. Their round shields were slung across their backs; like their cloaks, each was painted with the emblem of their clan, but also with the arrow rune Hagan had seen the cross outside the church twisted into: the symbol of Tiwass the War God.

The warriors formed themselves into three squares.

'An impressive display,' Hagan said. 'The work of Wodnas, no doubt? I haven't seen such discipline since my days in the Roman Army.'

He glanced around at Wodnas, who returned his look with a narrowed eye.

'I don't remember armed warriors being part of the Thingwas, though,' Hagan said. 'All weapons had to be set aside for the duration.'

'This is the new Burgundar realm,' Gunderic said. 'We have new customs.'

Another company of men entered into the clearing.

'Watch, Hagan,' Gunderic said. 'I really want you to see this.'

There were perhaps one hundred of them. They were dressed like the others but they stood out from their comrades because each had a further piece of decoration added to their otherwise uniform war gear. Each man wore a fur pelt around his shoulders like a short cloak. Some were brown, some black, but they were all from the same animal: the Bear.

'These are the men of the *Berh Herjass* – the Bear Warriors,' Gunderic said, beaming with pride as he led Hagan over to meet them. 'They are a special company of warriors we brought together to honour the memory of the Dagelung clan, who we believed to be no longer with us. Only our most fearsome warriors – champions and heroes – can become one. When we are tested by war they will be first into combat and shake the enemy with their courage, their skill and their rage. Geic leads them.'

As Hagan and the others watched, the company of Bear Warriors formed a shield wall. They began to stamp in unison, banging their spears against their shields in a tattoo that matched their steps. They chanted as they stepped first left, then right, then they split into two groups. Each one ran in a circle then reformed their line with a great shout.

Geic stood before them, spear raised in salute to the king on the mound above. Gunderic looked to the side and nodded.

Hagan followed his gaze and saw a warrior coming up the mound. He was a *merkes mann*, a standard bearer. On a long pole he bore a flag that danced in the slight breeze that disturbed the night air. It had seen better days. Compared to the new war gear worn by the warriors the flag was tattered, threadbare and stained. Though its embroidery was faded, the emblem of the eagle was still visible on it.

'My father's battle flag,' Gunderic said, his eyes alight and glittering. 'I saved it from the slaughter field at Vorbetomagus. It remains stained with the blood and earth splattered on it that day. Every year at the start of the Thingwas we use it to remember our glorious dead. With it we keep alive the memory of the old kingdom and what was done to us. One day, soon, the Burgundars will ride into battle once more, and when we do, this flag will lead us. That will be our day of vengeance.'

He took the flag from the warrior and walked down the mound. The rest of the council got up to follow him and Hagan did the same.

Gunderic came to a halt at the bottom of the mound. He lowered the standard so it was almost horizontal. Horns sounded and Geic walked forward. He bowed his head, took a handful of the flag in his right hand and pressed it to his lips. Then he let go and hurried off. Another Bear Warrior came forward after him and did the same.

As Hagan watched, each warrior one by one came forward to kiss the flag. After they had done so they went to Wodnas and knelt before him. The old one-eyed man laid his hand upon their heads and looking up at the dark sky above, called down a blessing upon each man.

It was a strange, yet compelling display Hagan had never seen before. He could imagine the scorn the man he had thought was his father, Godegisil, would have responded with if asked to kiss a flag, but the serious, religious-like reverence with which each of the warriors regarded the standard showed how much it meant to them.

As the night wore on the warriors all came forward. When there were only a few left Hagan began to feel tired and bored. The thought struck him that Wodnas' Raven Warriors did not appear to be among the war horde. Were they some sort of private army the old man kept?

He looked around and, as if in response to his thoughts, spotted Gunfjaun, the raven warrior who had accompanied him from the border. The young man was approaching quickly across the clearing. He went straight to Wodnas and began speaking to him in a low, earnest voice.

Wodnas listened, then nodded. He strode over to Gunderic.

'Lord King,' Wodnas said. 'My Raven Warriors have caught a foreigner crossing the border. He says he has a message for you.'

'They should bring him here to be sacrificed,' Gunderic said.

'Lord King,' Wodnas said. 'He is a Hun.'

CHAPTER THIRTY-FOUR

T HE HUN STOOD in the hall. He had his hands clasped
behind his back and his strangely elongated head was tilted
back as he looked up at the tree that grew from the floor to the
ceiling. He seemed oblivious to the ring of spears levelled at him
by nine Raven Warriors.

Four other Hun warriors, likewise guarded by Raven
Warriors, stood a little way behind him. They had been stripped
of their weapons but the contemptuous smiles and folded arms
showed how little fear they had of their captors.

The main door of the hall banged open and King Gunderic,
his council and Gunfjaun entered. While the raven warrior
joined his comrades, the king strode up the hall, glaring
at the stranger the whole way, until he got to the dais at
the top where he sat in his high seat. For a long moment
he continued to stare at the Hun, who continued to look
unperturbed.

'We do not welcome strangers in this realm,' Gunderic said
at last. 'But most of all we do not welcome Huns. Why have
you come here? Choose your words carefully for they may well
be your last.'

The Hun did not reply but looked puzzled.

Gunderic nodded to Gunfjaun, who prodded the Hun with
his spear point.

'Go forward,' he said. 'Speak.'

The ring of warriors around the single Hun lowered their

spears and he walked closer to the dais. The other four Hun warriors remained under close guard.

'I am sorry but while I understand the Germanic tongue a little, your accent makes it hard for me,' the Hun said, speaking in the tongue of the Romans. 'I am Ediko. I am advisor and emissary to Attila, the Great King of the World and Terrible Punisher of the unbelievers. I have a message from my king to Gunderic, King of the Burgundars.'

'You are speaking to him,' Gunderic said.

'My Lord Attila rides to war at the head of the greatest army ever seen on the face of the earth,' Ediko said. 'He rides at the head of an army of Ostrogoths, Vandals, Gepids, Alemanni and Huns that numbers more than fifty thousand men.'

Hagan saw a look of dismay cross the face of Wodnas. It was the first real emotion he had seen the old man express. He could understand why, though. Impressive as the Burgundar War Horde had been, they were tiny in number compared to Attila's multitudes.

'I come with a demand and an offer,' Ediko continued. 'Attila the Great and Mighty sweeps through the Western Roman Empire like a whirlwind of fire. Everyone who tries to stand in his way perishes like dry grass in a wildfire.'

'We are ready for war,' Gunderic said. 'We don't fear Attila.'

Ediko smirked.

'Many have said that before and found they were mistaken,' he said. 'To their cost.'

Gunderic started to his feet and opened his mouth to speak, but Wodnas stepped before him and laid a hand on the king's forearm. To Hagan's surprise Gunderic sat down again.

Wodnas leaned close to the king and whispered something in his ear. Gunderic sent a sharp look in the old man's direction, but pursed his lips and kept them shut.

'Does Attila not have realms enough?' Wodnas said. 'He already rules everything west of Pannonia.'

'King Attila is only claiming what is rightfully his,' Ediko said. 'The Emperor's sister has sent him a proposal of marriage. As the Emperor's sister she is entitled to half the Empire. King Attila is merely claiming her dowry.'

'Does Attila really believe Justa Grata Honoria was really free to make such a proposal?' Wodnas said.

'King Attila is an honourable man,' Ediko said. 'When a lady calls for help, he responds. But that is not the only reason for the war. Certain treasures which rightfully belong to the Hun people were stolen by someone in Europa when King Oktar was treacherously attacked. They include the Sword of the War God.'

Hagan saw Sigurd stiffen.

'King Attila has been wronged,' Ediko said. 'He seeks redress for serious insults. He seeks the return of the sword and the treasures. How could any king continue to rule if he allowed such wrongs to go unpunished?'

'We care nothing if Attila destroys the whole of the Empire,' Gunderic said. 'We are no friends of Rome.'

'Remaining neutral in the war will not save anyone,' Ediko said. 'King Attila will assume if you are not with him then you are against him and will be treated like any other enemy.'

'Neither are we friends of the Huns,' Gunderic said. 'You speak of wrongs? What greater wrong is there than what the Huns did to my people at Vorbetomagus?'

'My people would say they were just avenging the wrongs inflicted by the murder of Oktar,' Ediko said.

'What is this *demand* of Attila's, anyway?' Gunderic said.

'King Attila will be merciful to any realm who returns what is rightfully his,' Ediko said. 'If you know where the treasure and the sword are, and you tell us, then King Attila will cease to resent the former insult.'

'And what is his offer?' asked Gunderic.

'The Burgundars are renowned warriors,' Ediko said. 'There would be room for you in King Attila's grand army against

Rome. If you don't then King Attila will assume you are an enemy. The Huns destroyed the Burgundars once before. We will do it again.'

'Hello, Ediko.'

A new voice made everyone turn around. Zerco had entered the hall.

For the first time Ediko showed any sign of emotion. His face lit up with both surprise and delight.

'Zerco!' he said. 'You are here?'

'You know each other?' Gunderic said, suspicion in his voice.

'Lord King, I told you I was a slave of the Huns for several years,' the little man said. 'Ediko here was a sworn warrior of Bleda, my master.'

He turned back to Ediko.

'You've done well for yourself,' Zerco said. 'I heard Bleda had an "accident". I'd have thought Attila would've made sure all his men met the same fate too.'

'I am now a trusted advisor of the king,' Ediko said. 'But you don't look pleased to see me, old friend.'

'You remind me of a dark time in my life,' Zerco said, his lip curled in a sneer.

'A dark time?' Ediko raised his eyebrows. 'You were the honoured companion of Bleda, Over King of the Huns. You went everywhere with him. He was very fond of you.'

'I was there to be laughed at,' Zerco said, eyes blazing with anger, teeth gritted. 'A *stupius*! A clown!'

'He looked after your every need,' Ediko said. 'You are missed at the Court of the Huns, Zerco. You can return with me now. Everything could be as it was before.'

'Attila loathed me,' Zerco said. 'He made no secret of that. That's why he sent me back to the Romans. Return with you to Hun Land? Do you think I'm mad?'

'What about your wife?' Ediko said. 'She still waits for you.'

Hagan raised his eyebrows. Zerco had a wife?

'She was a whore Bleda paid to be my companion!' Zerco said.

'I see you won't be persuaded,' Ediko said. Then his expression changed, suggesting he had realised something. 'If you are here then that could mean...'

He turned to look at Gunderic, a broad smile creasing his face.

'I've heard enough of this,' Gunderic said with a snarl. He gestured to the Raven Warriors down the hall. They nodded and without hesitation drove their spears into the guts of the four Hun warriors. The men cried out in surprise and pain. Their faces screwed into expressions of disbelief and agony as the Raven Warriors without mercy twisted the blades of their spears a half turn, then wrenched them out of the Huns' bodies again.

The Huns grasped the wounds torn through their stomachs in both hands, blood gushing through their fingers, as they collapsed to their knees. Four of the Raven Warriors set down their spears, and drew knives from their belts. Each man grasped a Hun by the hair, pulled his head back exposing his throat, then drew his blade across it, unleashing another torrent of blood. Letting go of the Huns' hair, they stood back, letting the men fall on their faces to die on the floor.

Hagan noted that he had been right. The Raven Warriors were trained or born killers. What was also clear was how practised they were at it. The Burgundar War Horde may yet have been tested in war but these youths had been the death of men before.

They began to advance towards Ediko.

With some satisfaction, Hagan saw the self-confident expression on the face of the Hun drop, replaced by wide-eyed panic.

'Wait, Lord King. Wait!' he said, hands held aloft, his voice rising in pitch. 'Don't do this.'

'What's to stop me?' Gunderic said.

'There is nothing to stop you, King Gunderic,' Ediko said. 'But if I do not return from here Attila will descend on this kingdom in wrath. He will turn it to dust and ash as an example to those who disrespect his emissaries. If you choose to stand against him he will do that anyway but if anything happens to me you will be first to feel his wrath.'

Gunderic looked like he was going to say something but Wodnas shook his head. The one-eyed man once more laid a hand on Gunderic's arm and the king closed his mouth again.

'Leave him, lads,' Wodnas said. The Raven Warriors stopped advancing.

'Go back to Attila,' Wodnas said to Ediko. 'Tell him King Gunderic is considering his offer.'

Ediko looked around, looking like he was unsure whether or not this was a trick.

'Escort him back to the border and let him go,' Wodnas said.

The Raven Warriors nodded. They raised their spears and laid their hands on Ediko, steering him towards the door.

'Goodbye, King Gunderic,' the Hun called as they marched him out of the hall. 'Zerco, we will meet again I think.'

When they had gone, Gunderic flopped down in his ornate high seat, his lower lip thrust out in a manner Hagan had not seen him do since he was a boy.

'You should have let me kill him,' the king said.

'We are not ready to fight a full-scale war yet, King Gunderic,' Wodnas said. 'Not alone anyway. And certainly not against the horde Attila commands.'

'You fought the Huns alone,' Gunderic said.

'That was years ago,' Wodnas said. 'They had not subjected as many nations as they have now. Today they can call upon countless warriors to fight with them. And we ended up living in forests and caves, striking them when we could and running away again. It was hopeless. All we were doing was making life difficult for them in the hope they'd give up and go away. They didn't. Which is why we are now here.'

Hagan was taken aback by the bitter passion with which the usually taciturn and placid old man spoke. His display of emotion also had an effect on Gunderic who stared, wide-eyed, mouth slightly open, at Wodnas.

'So what do we do?' the king said. 'I have my council here. Let us decide.'

Hagan swallowed. He had not expected such momentous responsibility to fall on him so soon. He was not sure that either of the titles so far granted to him by the king – Hunt Master or last of the Dagelungs – really qualified him to be part of the Royal Council, certainly in the eyes of others. However, whether or not they did, he was about to take part in a discussion that could seal the fate of the whole realm.

CHAPTER THIRTY-FIVE

HAGAN TOOK A seat and looked around at his fellow councillors.

'We must fight Attila sooner or later,' the king said. 'Why not now?'

'We don't have enough warriors, Lord King,' Geic said. 'You heard Ediko: Attila commands fifty thousand men.'

'A lot of whom are cavalry,' Wodnas said. 'I'm sure you saw the havoc Hun horse archers can cause at Vorbetomagus. We have no mounted warriors to counter them.'

'Really?' Hagan said. 'The rest of the war horde seems complete. It's almost Roman in its discipline and organisation.'

'It takes years to build a war horde and we were starting almost from scratch, with mere boys,' Gunderic said. 'We needed to start with the basics and that meant foot warriors. We haven't had the time or enough people with knowledge of mounted warcraft to move on to that yet.'

While Hagan had learned the value of cavalry support in the Roman Army, he knew the previous Burgundar horde of his father had not used mounted warriors. They had also been devastated by the Hun horsemen.

'Even if we had cavalry, our forces cannot match fifty thousand,' the lord of the Leuhtungs said.

'Perhaps our only choice,' the man called Lokke said. 'is to accept Attila's offer and join him?'

'We will never join the Huns!' the lord of the Solungs declared, slamming his fist on the table.

'Agreed,' the king said. 'You heard the emissary: Attila wants our treasure.'

'I did not hear that,' Lokke said. 'I heard that he was interested in a sword.'

'Well, let him come and try and take it,' Sigurd said, patting the hilt of the sword. 'Or perhaps *you* want to try?'

'Sometimes, Lokke,' Wodnas said, shaking his head, 'I think you just say things to see what sort of reaction you can get. I know you cannot be serious. We both lost our homeland to the Huns.'

'And perhaps this is a way to return there,' Lokke said.

'Don't be childish,' Wodnas said. 'We cannot trust Attila. He only says he will accept us into his horde. He will take our warriors, perhaps, but we, their leaders, will all be put to the sword. Either that or humiliated, degraded and treated no better than his hunting dogs. I have seen these so-called kings who submitted to Attila. They quake at his every word lest it brings punishment down on them. They jump at his every command. They do whatever he orders, no matter what the cost to themselves or their people, because they fear torture and death. I'd rather die than live like that.'

'I certainly don't want that,' Gunderic said.

'So what do we do? Hide in the mountains and let Attila and his horde sweep through our land?' Gunhild said. 'Let him take everything we've built here, everything we've worked on for the last eight years?'

'Attila will not just sweep through this realm and head on to Ravenna,' Wodnas said with a heavy sigh. 'He means to take the whole Roman Empire. When he's done he means to rule everything from the Western Sea to the Danube and the Don. Attila will leave officials and warriors to make sure this realm remains part of his Empire. I once thought my land was free but now it is just another part of Hun Land.'

'It sounds like we must fight Attila either on our own terms or his,' Freya said. Hagan marvelled that even her voice was captivating, almost like the pealing of little bells.

'He must be defeated,' the lord of the Leuhtungs said. 'It is the only way for us to remain free.'

'Have you not been listening?' the lord of the Solungs, a man in his early twenties, said. 'How can our war horde of perhaps a thousand men – with no cavalry – defeat Attila's army of fifty thousand?'

Hagan was surprised and dismayed at how fast this council of the realm appeared to be falling into conflict with itself. Then he realised this could be an opportunity. Since leaving Ravenna he had been wondering how he would present Aetius's message – message? More ultimatum – to his folk but now it seemed Fate had given him the chance.

'There is perhaps another way,' Hagan said. 'I came here from Ravenna. The Romans are preparing to fight Attila.'

'They will lose,' Wodnas said. 'Until a couple of years ago the Huns made up half their army.'

'Aetius, the Roman Magister Militum, is creating an alliance with other kingdoms to make up for that,' Hagan said. 'He intends to offer battle in Gaul. We could join this alliance.'

'Fight alongside Rome?' the young lord of the Solungs said with a sneer. 'You must be dreaming.'

'I spent ten years in the Roman Army,' said the lord of the Leuhtungs, 'That was enough for me.'

'I too was in the Roman Army,' Gunderic said. He talked as though deep in thought. 'I was rewarded for brave deeds. Perhaps if we help them defeat the Huns we will be rewarded. Perhaps this is a way for this realm to remain free.'

'You forget what we did to our Roman officials, brother,' Gunhild said.

'Why would we willingly put ourselves under Roman command again?' the lord of the Leuhtungs said. 'It would bring dishonour. Shame.'

307

'We would not be the only folk to do that,' Hagan said.

'Who else has pledged to fight with Aetius?' Gunderic said.

'King Sangiban of the Alans, Hegelac of the Saxons as well as the Armoricans and Franks,' Hagan said. 'And Theodoric, King of the Visigoths.'

A gasp went around the gathered councillors.

'The threat from Attila must indeed be great,' Gunderic said. 'If it can compel Theodoric to hold his nose and fight alongside Rome.'

The Western Goths and the Western Empire had been at each other's throats for most of one hundred years, and had of course sacked Rome some decades ago. Theodoric had since taken great swathes of Hispania and Southern Gaul away from Rome and made his own kingdom there.

'There would be no shame in joining the army that opposes Attila if Theodoric the Goth was also part of it,' Gunhild said.

The lord of the Leuhtungs stroked his chin as he considered this. He turned the corners of his mouth downwards and cocked his head to the side.

'Just say we did join this alliance,' Gunderic said. 'I would want us to fight as one unit within the larger army. That way if we perform great deeds everyone will see it was the Burgundars who did it, not the Romans.'

'I believe all allied peoples will fight in their own formations,' Hagan said. 'Aetius will be in overall command though.'

'You seem to know a lot about Aetius's plans,' Lokke said to Hagan, eyes narrowed. 'What if we lose?'

'No one should ever go to war expecting to lose, Lokke,' Wodnas said with a smile. 'The way I would prefer to look at it is that if we join Aetius it will swell the ranks of those opposed to Attila and make it less likely they will lose.'

'It seems we may have little choice in this matter,' Forsetti spoke for the first time. 'Either we join the Roman Alliance or we risk perishing alone.'

'You've been very quiet, Kvasir,' Gunderic said to the old man with the grey beard. 'What are your thoughts?'

'A hero needs to perform great deeds for a poet to sing his praises,' Kvasir said with a shrug. 'A war would give the chance for our heroes to perform great deeds. The poets could write new songs. On the other hand, if we lose this battle we could all be annihilated by the Huns. What use is glory if there are none to sing of it?'

There was a moment of silence as everyone considered his words.

'Attila is the greatest threat to the world,' Wodnas said. 'His greed and viciousness know no bounds. If he is not stopped he will enslave all of humanity. Theodoric can see that. The other kings can see that too.'

'Yes,' Gunderic said. 'And if we are among many others it is also a chance to show what we can do. Wodnas. You have been saying lately how it is only a matter of time before we need to strike out at someone. All nations must do it. We cannot just remain within our borders and think we shall have peace. If we don't strike out then others will think they can strike us. What better way to show our power and prowess to all than if we take part in a battle that every other kingdom is part of? If we win glory then all other nations will think twice before they attack us in the future. If we stand up to Attila and he is defeated we remain free and we keep what is ours.'

Hagan felt a little panic enter his heart. Was he doing the right thing? Since leaving Ravenna he had come to the conclusion that the right thing for his folk to do was fight Attila, and their best chance of success was to join the alliance Aetius was putting together. Aetius had made it clear he would be as ruthless as Attila towards the Burgundars if they did not choose to join him. It looked like things were going to go that way. However, Aetius was as greedy for the Burgundar treasure horde as Attila.

'We still have no horse warriors,' Wodnas said. 'Even if we

are part of a larger army I wouldn't want to fight the Huns without cavalry of our own to counter theirs.'

'What about Brynhild?' Gunhild said before Wodnas answered. 'Her mounted warriors helped us defeat the Romans once.'

'True,' Wodnas said. 'They would be excellent. Well-trained. Disciplined. Bloodthirsty. I'd certainly rather they were on our side than against us.'

'But aren't they all...' Gunderic began to say but trailed off.

'What? Aren't they all women?' Gunhild said, raising an eyebrow. 'Is that what you were going to say? It wasn't a problem the last time they helped us against the Romans.'

'Except now we would be asking for them to fight *for* the Romans,' Gunderic said. 'We would need to offer them something to make it worth their while. Something to their advantage.'

'Perhaps it's time to offer an alliance?' the lord of the Solungs said. 'We need to expand the realm anyway.'

'I agree,' Wodnas said. 'Gunderic, you realise what that means? A marriage.'

'You think I should marry Brynhild?' Gunderic said. 'That would not be a chore.'

'That's the usual way two realms are united,' Wodnas said.

'There may be a problem with this,' Lokke said. 'Brynhild's realm cut themselves off from the world a year or so ago. They don't let anyone in. Several other kings have offered Brynhild an alliance but she has set some sort of test of skill and courage and vowed to only marry the man who completes it. So far no one has.'

'I have an advantage, though,' Gunderic said. 'I am an old friend of hers. And when we were younger I am pretty sure she had an eye for me, if you know what I mean?'

He grinned. Hagan opened his mouth to say something but hesitated.

'It really is time you were married anyway, King Gunderic,'

Wodnas said. 'We have talked about this before. A king should have a queen, and she should give him children. That way there is stability in a realm.'

'If we can secure Brynhild's cavalry then I would support the war on Attila,' the lord of the Leuhtungs said with a sigh.

'We have talked enough,' Gunderic said. 'Everyone has had their say. Wodnas, what should we do?'

Hagan raised his eyebrows. Surely a decision such as this should lie with the king?

'Let me consider everything for a moment,' the old man said.

He stood up and walked away from the table. When he was about thirty paces away he sat down on a side bench and set the leather satchel he always carried on his lap. Wodnas unlaced the straps and peered inside. He began to mutter something but he spoke so quietly and was too far away for anyone at the table to hear. To Hagan it looked like he was talking to something inside his bag.

Hagan looked around the table. No one else seemed surprised by the old man's odd behaviour.

'What's he doing?' Hagan mouthed at Gunhild.

'He always does this when he has an important decision to make,' Gunhild said.

Hagan caught the looks of approbation from all the others around the table and realised he had made another impropriety by questioning this man's behaviour. He blushed but could not dispel a sense of unease that the fate of the Burgundars now lay with an old man who talked to a bag.

After a while Wodnas stood up and rejoined the others at the table.

'I think we should fight Attila as part of the Roman Alliance,' he said. 'He must be stopped. If we don't fight him now as part of a larger army we will have to fight him alone later.'

The others all nodded. Hagan noted that even his fellow Burgundars who had previously objected, no longer did so.

'If it looks like Rome is losing then we withdraw as fast as possible,' Wodnas continued. 'And we leave all the rest to their fate.'

Everyone around the table cheered, even Hagan who felt himself carried along with the enthusiasm of the others.

Gunderic clapped his hand on Hagan's shoulder.

'You have come at just the right time, my friend: we're going to war and I'm getting married to Brynhild!'

'Soon our little group of friends will finally be all back together,' Gunhild said.

CHAPTER THIRTY-SIX

THE NEXT MORNING Gunderic, Gunhild, Sigurd and Hagan, with Wodnas, Geic, Lokke, Brenwic, Lord of the Leuhtungs, and a warband of Burgundar warriors prepared their horses for the trek to the icy realm high in the mountains ruled by Brynhild.

Zerco was left behind, something he was more than happy with. He told Hagan that several pretty slave girls in Gunderic's hall had caught his eye, then muttered from the side of his mouth that it would be easier for him to ferret out where the treasure might be while the king and his councillors were out of the way.

Gunderic's war gear was even more impressive than his warriors'. His mail was burnished black and his shoulders and breast were also protected by segmented strips of iron of the same colour. Like his warriors he wore a black cloak but his was trimmed with fur.

He too had a decorated helmet but his had plates of gold as well as silver, a visor that covered the top half of his face, while a veil of mail protected his mouth, chin and throat.

'I had this made for me,' Gunderic said when Hagan expressed his admiration for the headpiece. 'This will be the new Kin Helm of the Burgundars. My father's was lost at Vorbetomagus. When I wear this no one would mistake who the king of the Burgundars is.'

Sigurd also wore his distinctive armour which was made up

313

of countless small rectangular iron plates polished to shine like mirrors. His huge sword swung in its jewelled scabbard under his left arm.

Compared to his companions, Hagan felt rather inadequate in his tired old, army war gear.

At the blaring of horns, the company mounted and set off.

'It seems to me, Gunderic,' Hagan said later as they trotted along the flat plain beside the huge lake towards a wall of jagged mountains, 'that all the most important positions on your council are held by Aesir. Are there no Burgundars fit to fill those roles?'

He had found himself a little away from the rest of the company and beside the king, so judged this was an opportune time to ask.

'I can understand why you think that, old friend,' Gunderic said. 'But they have the experience and knowledge we need. Such crafts were lost to our people in the massacre fifteen years ago. And they are not wholly foreigners. They are Aesir, a sub-clan of the Thingvi and cousins to us Burgundars. We all descended from the holy Mannus. Don't worry, though. Every one of Wodnas' folk has a Burgundar who is learning from them, ready to take over when the time comes.'

Hagan took another look at the warriors around them.

'Well they've done a good job with the war horde, I have to admit,' he said.

'Everyone has to fight,' Gunderic said. 'Every boy when he becomes a man must join the horde. They are trained in warcraft by the older men and Wodnas.'

'Not everyone is a fighter, though,' Hagan said.

'They are not,' Gunderic said. 'But an army needs all sorts of men. Men who prepare armour. Men who sharpen weapons. Men who cook. Men who tend the horses and, if there is a need, those men can still stand in a shield wall if they know what to do. This way everyone is ready for war. We are not a numerous people, but our warrior army is strong. We can call on every man of the folk if we have to. Once we have Brynhild's cavalry we will be complete.'

'Everyone is riding today?' Hagan said, gesturing to the column of mounted warriors they rode alongside.

'Oh, everyone can *ride*,' Gunderic said. 'We can ride to the battle. But we can't fight on horseback. There has been neither the time nor the expertise to train cavalry. Now war is upon us there never will be time. That's why Wodnas advises that we should make this alliance. Brynhild's warriors are trained cavalry. Their cavalry can augment our warriors on foot when we strike the Huns. They can foil them when they charge at us.'

'Do you really need to marry her, though?' Hagan said.

'We will still need her fighters, even after the battle,' Gunderic said. 'They can train a new generation of cavalry for us. And my realm will grow bigger once hers is included.'

'Why do you think Brynhild will agree to marriage?' Hagan said.

'We are old friends. It makes sense for us to combine our realms,' Gunderic said, as if that was all it would take. 'Besides, like I said last night, I think she always had a thing for me.'

Hagan did not reply.

'One thing I ask of you, old friend,' Gunderic said, leaning in his saddle so he was closer to Hagan. 'I don't mind you calling me by my name when we're alone. When others are around, however, let's remember I'm the king. Alright?'

He winked and turned his horse to ride back closer to the rest of the company.

Hagan frowned. Gunderic's words were more admonishment or order than request.

They rode on, crossing the plain as the snow-capped mountains grew ever taller. After a while they came upon another ghost fence of stakes and severed heads like the one Hagan had seen on entering the kingdom.

'We are now leaving my realm,' Gunderic said.

Hagan took a deep breath as he looked at the rotting heads. A shiver ran down his spine.

'Who are they?' he said.

'Enemies, foreigners who enter the land without permission. Criminals, deviants and traitors,' Gunderic said. 'Cowards and shirkers. Those who refuse to fight.'

'There are a lot of them...' Hagan said, looking at the line of posts that disappeared far into the distance.

'Wodnas and his people have taught us the importance of the rule of Law,' Gunderic said. 'Forsetti oversees the courts and they sit every week. Justice is swift and hard but fair and equal and the folk respect that. Unfortunately there is no shortage of law-breakers. But in death they can contribute in a way they could not in life. Their ghosts guard our realm.'

'So you really have rejected God?' Hagan said. 'Aren't you worried He will be angry?'

'The God of the Romans was never really our god,' Gunderic said. 'He was imposed on us. Now we have Tiwass back. Our own god.'

'How can you be so sure you've done the right thing?' Hagan said, deciding not to point out that it was Gunderic's own father who had 'imposed' Christianity on the Burgundars.

'Tiwass himself has shown his approval,' Gunhild said. She and Sigurd now rode alongside her brother and Hagan. 'The fact that he has allowed his famous sword, Tyrfing, to fall into the possession of my husband, is proof of this.'

Hagan raised his eyebrows. Tyrfing was a sword of ancient legend. It was forged by dwarfs when the world was young; not those who wandered the world now like Zerco but the magical creatures of mystical skill who had forged all the great treasures of the earth. It was said that when it was drawn it shone and gleamed like the blade was on fire.

'I thought Tyrfing only existed in lore,' he said, glancing at the large sword slung under Sigurd's left arm. 'Can I see it?'

'The sword bears a curse,' Sigurd said. 'Whenever it is

316

drawn it must draw blood. So if I draw it now to show you, I'd also have to kill you with it.'

The others laughed but Sigurd looked Hagan directly in the eyes, only a half-smile on his face, and Hagan could tell his words were only half a joke. They were the first thing Hagan had heard the big man say since their meeting the night before. It was clear he was still not comfortable with Hagan's presence. Hagan felt a further shiver at the thought that he was now the potential enemy of a giant warrior who bore the sword of a god.

They rode out of the realm along a dilapidated Roman road then turned south-west along a valley where the land was flat beside a meandering river but on either side sheer cliffs rose up like impossibly high walls.

They rode in a long column past some villages where the locals went running at the sight of a warband riding by their settlement. The landscape changed to woods and they kept riding, sticking to a long straight path through them. Hagan mused that it was perfect territory for an ambush but it seemed Gunderic had enough confidence that the size of their warband was enough to deter any would-be attackers.

All along the way they found Burgundar warriors with ravens painted on their shields already waiting for them. They reported what lay ahead and any potential dangers or obstacles that would slow the rest of the company down. Hagan began to realise these Raven Warriors played the same scouting and reconnaissance role that the exploratores and speculatores did in the Roman Army. Yet again Hagan wondered if Wodnas had served the Romans. If he had not, he certainly seemed to have learned a lot from them.

The Raven Warriors always delivered their messages directly to Wodnas, accompanied by looks of total devotion, and once again Hagan wondered who the real commander of the Burgundar army was: Gunderic, or Wodnas?

Night fell and they made camp. Hagan was impressed by

the discipline of the Burgundar warriors who, like Roman legionaries, first dug defences to secure the campsite before anyone either ate or put up their leather tents. The party of warriors was small in number but unlike many hordes of what the Romans called barbarians they were well-trained and self-controlled. As the Roman Army had proved time and again when fighting outnumbered against barbarian hordes whose overwhelming culture was one of boastful individuality, it was such discipline that usually brought victory.

A strange smell like rotten eggs pervaded the air and what looked like smoke was seen drifting through the trees. This led to some anxiousness that the forest was the haunt of demons or similar otherworldly creatures but Wodnas' Ravens reported that there were hot springs nearby. Hagan who was missing the Roman baths already, took himself off to find them and even though he was aware that he was exposing himself to potential danger, spent an enjoyable few hours wallowing in the pools of hot water that bubbled up from the ground amid the forest.

As he relaxed in the warm water, feeling the warmth of the water soaking into his bones, he lay back and looked at what could be seen of the sky through the canopy of leaves.

The sound of laughing women came to his ears. Looking up he spotted Gunhild and several other women approaching. Feeling a rush of embarrassment, Hagan pulled himself out of the pool and began rubbing himself dry with his cloak. He had no desire to be caught naked by a band of women.

'We thought we would try out this miracle of the hot waters,' Gunhild said when they arrived. 'Have we disturbed you?'

'I was just finishing up,' Hagan said, pulling on his britches.

Gunhild caught sight of the amulet with the stylised horse and bird on it that Hagan wore. She frowned.

'Where did you get that?' she said. 'I don't remember you wearing jewellery when we were young.'

'I took it from my mother's corpse at Vorbetomagus,' Hagan said, blushing. 'It was hers.'

'Your *mother's*?' Gunhild seemed incredulous.

Hagan felt confused and uncomfortable at Gunhild's reaction. He pulled his jerkin on over his head, covering the offending amulet from view.

'I should go,' he said, hurrying off into the trees.

As he went he glanced over his shoulder. Gunhild was still watching him.

CHAPTER THIRTY-SEVEN

IN THE MORNING they dismantled their camp and set off again. Their ride was taking them ever higher along a river valley that carved its way between two ranges of mountains, a gap that got narrower the higher they climbed. At a certain point they turned off the valley floor and took a path that wound its way up the heavily wooded mountainside, twisting and turning until the incline became too steep for riding and everyone had to dismount.

'You said Brynhild's warriors are cavalry?' Hagan said to Gunderic as they puffed and panted beside their horses up the steep hill. 'Do they ride goats or horses?'

'We know very little about them, to be honest,' Gunderic said. 'Like our kingdom they do not welcome visitors and as you can see, her realm is not easy to get to.'

'How do you know where it is then?' Hagan asked.

'Wodnas came by this path on his way to my kingdom,' Gunderic said. 'He and his Ravens know the way.'

They climbed on. Hagan could smell the cold in the air as they got higher. The trees and path began to be dotted with patches of snow. They stopped to put on fur cloaks and boots, mittens and other things to keep the cold out, then resumed the punishing climb. Hagan noticed that Wodnas still went barefoot, despite the freezing air and frost-covered ground. The skin on his feet must have been tougher than leather.

They marched along, shields slung across their backs, mail

clinking and weapons clanking so it was impossible to move with anything like stealth. The trees kept the path from being submerged in snow but they also blocked the view so it was impossible to see very far ahead or around. Hagan began to get the old familiar feeling like his skin was crawling that told him that somewhere in the surrounding undergrowth eyes were watching them as they passed. He reasoned that they could belong to bears, wolves or boars and knew there was little point in raising an alarm over what was, after all, just a sensation.

At long last the column of warriors halted. A young man came running from the front. Finding Gunderic he stopped and bowed his head.

'Lord King, we have arrived at the gates of Queen Brynhild's realm,' he said. 'There is a problem.'

Gunderic and his bodyguards, plus Hagan, Gunhild, Geic, Wodnas, Lokke and Sigurd pushed their way through the halted column of warriors until they got to the front. There the trees ended and they found themselves on a ledge at the edge of a ravine. It looked as if some giant had ripped the two sides of the mountain apart, leaving a narrow gap between two cliffs that fell away to a dizzying depth filled from edge to edge by the rushing waters of a mountain river. Hagan felt his stomach lurch as he looked down the sheer drop to where the water frothed over boulders and fallen tree trunks far below. There were branches tangled and clogged in the river too, caught in rocks and blanched white by the ever-running water.

There were the beginnings of a stone-built bridge, but it ended abruptly in mid-air, perhaps the length of two horses out into the chasm. There was a matching construction on the other side, but nothing in between but air.

There appeared to be a line of sticks and hay piled across the end of what would have been the far end of the bridge. It was like a little barricade, but given the missing centre of the bridge the only thing it would hold back would be birds.

Beyond it was a large wooden gate in a palisade fence. The tall pine forest Hagan and the others stood in continued on the other side. Smoke rose from behind the palisade in several places, suggesting there was a settlement beyond it. Beyond that the mountainside rose in a steep slope.

'How did you get across when you came this way before?' Gunderic said to Wodnas.

'There was a wooden bridge between those two stone lintels,' the one-eyed old man said. 'It was lightweight so they must be able to pull it away when they are not in the mood to welcome visitors. It's a sound strategy. I've never seen such an effective drawbridge.'

There was no one on the other side. Gunderic and the others tried shouting but their words were carried away by the wind and the crashing water below. Geic unslung his large hunting horn and blew several blasts on it. This was more successful. A small door opened in the wooden gate and a figure stepped out.

To Hagan's surprise it was a woman. This in itself was not unusual but she wore breeches like a man, her hair was braided and pulled back behind her head, and there was a sword sheathed on a baldric under her left arm.

'Who are you who comes here surrounded by warriors?' she called across the divide.

'I am Gunderic, King of the Burgundars,' Gunderic shouted back. 'We mean you no harm. I wish to offer an alliance.'

'I know who you are, Gunderic,' the woman said. 'We came to save you from the Romans a few years ago.'

Gunderic frowned and Hagan could see the clouds of anger forming on his face. He opened his mouth to retort but Wodnas laid his hand on Gunderic's forearm, distracting him. The king looked at the one-eyed old man who shook his head. Gunderic nodded.

'I wish to speak to your queen,' he shouted. 'I have an offer to make to her.'

'There is no queen here,' the woman on the other side

replied. 'We have no king either. No bishops, lords, counts or generals. This realm is a haven for women. Many who have suffered at the hands of men. Brynhild is our leader though.'

'Can we cross?' Gunderic said. 'Will you put the bridge out for us?'

'No,' the woman shouted back. 'We will not let men over the bridge.'

Gunderic looked at Wodnas.

'Did they let you over?' he said.

'It was years ago,' the old man said with a shrug. 'Perhaps something has changed.'

'Look, we just want to talk,' Gunderic shouted back across the ravine. 'Can you tell your... leader that Gunderic is here. He is with her old friends Gunhild and Hagan. We wish to discuss an alliance of our realms.'

The woman turned and went back inside the gate.

There was an awkward wait then the gate opened again. A line of people came out. They were all dressed in war gear with shields, helmets and spears. At first Hagan thought they were boys but then he realised they were women. They divided into two and lined up on either side of the gate, behind the small barricade of sticks and hay bales. After that Brynhild emerged.

It was fifteen years since Hagan had seen her. She looked a lot different but he still recognised her. She was no longer the girl he had seen supposedly dying on the grass outside Vorbetomagus. Now she was a tall woman with a body that was lean and muscled from exercise. Despite the cold her arms were bare. Her long black hair had black bird's feathers – crows' or magpies' – tied through it. It tumbled around her shoulders and mingled with the sable pelt of a bear that she wore as a cloak. Her legs were clad in men's leather riding britches. Her eyes were surrounded by black paint that made them stand out in stark contrast. A blonde-haired woman in similar garb stood beside her.

'Who comes here with an army?' Brynhild said, her voice echoing off the rocks of the chasm below.

'We mean no harm,' Gunderic said. 'We have come to request an alliance.'

'Brynhild! It's us: Gunhild and Gunderic,' Gunhild said, waving across the divide. 'Don't you recognise us?'

'I recognise you, Gunhild,' Brynhild said. 'And your brother the royal Nibelung too.'

'What sort of a welcome is this for old friends?' Gunhild said. There was bewilderment and hurt in her voice.

'This is the welcome we give to everyone,' Brynhild said. 'There are no exceptions. No one can enter. Especially not men.'

'What has happened?' Gunhild said. 'You and your warriors once rode to help us. We need your help again.'

'Once we were open to helping others,' Brynhild said. 'But the Alemanni used that against us. They sent a woman here claiming she was a nun. She said her nunnery was under siege by Alemanni raiders who wanted to rape them all then carry them off to slavery. We rode to their rescue, or so we thought. But instead we rode into an ambush. We fought them off and only just escaped. We lost many good warriors and it was not the nuns who were raped, it was those of my warriors who the Alemanni managed to capture. Women who had fled to the sanctuary of my realm because that very thing had happened to them in the first place. Women who I had offered protection to.'

Her Ie, which had been strong and defiant, cracked at this.

'I let them down,' Brynhild continued. 'The only thing I can do by way of restitution is ensure the same thing doesn't happen again. The gates of my realm are closed.'

'And what if the Alemanni decide they want to come in?' Gunderic said. 'If they come with their warrior horde? Can you fight them off?'

'They will have to get across this ravine,' Brynhild said. 'The only other way in is over the mountains. It is dangerous and freezing, even in summer. They would lose half their force on the journey.'

'But they could still come,' Gunderic said. 'My spies tell me they are planning to attack both our realms.'

'Your spies, Gunderic?' Brynhild said, her voice betraying her scepticism. 'Has your new kingdom grown so Roman already that you have spies?'

'I have had some help,' Gunderic said. He stood aside and the old one-eyed man stepped forward. 'Tell her.'

'It's true, Lady Brynhild,' Wodnas said. 'My Raven Warriors range far and wide. They scouted deep into the Alemanni territory. They returned with news that the Alemanni have made an alliance with the Huns and are now preparing to attack first your realm then King Gunderic's.'

Hagan frowned and glanced sideways at Wodnas. This was the first time he had heard this mentioned. Looking back across the gorge he saw Brynhild's expression had changed. Some of the hardness had gone.

'Is that you, Hagan?' she said.

Hagan stepped forward, then realised he was close to the edge of the precipice and stepped back again.

'It's me, Brynhild,' he said. 'I thought you were dead.'

She regarded him for a moment, her hard expression completely gone now and a little of the open, playful innocence he had known to be in her when she was a girl resurfaced for a moment. There was an odd wistful expression on her face, as if she were looking at something that once was important to her, that still mattered a little but now belonged to the past. Then it was gone and her face clouded over with suspicion, contempt and challenge once more.

'As you can see I am very much alive,' she said. 'No thanks to you, who left me alone and bleeding on the riverbank fifteen years ago.'

'You—' Hagan began to speak but consternation clogged his throat.

'I have come to offer an alliance,' Gunderic interjected. 'I wish to propose we unite our two realms.'

'Unite our realms, Gunderic?' Brynhild said. 'What would that gain us?'

'Our war hordes would be one,' Gunderic said. 'Together we will be stronger and the Alemanni will be deterred from attacking. My foot warriors would complement your cavalry and vice versa.'

Even at a distance Hagan could see Brynhild's sneer at Gunderic's use of the Latin phrase.

'Persuading her to fight alongside Rome is going to be a challenge,' he muttered out of the side of his mouth. 'Perhaps this is a lost cause.'

'Get her married then subjugate her to your will,' Sigurd said, speaking in a low enough voice that his words would not carry across the chasm. 'That's how it usually works.'

'Really?' Gunhild said, raising one eyebrow.

'You and I are different,' the big man said with a shrug and a smile. 'I am not a king. As yet.'

Hagan saw the look that passed between them and realised for the first time that the pair cared much for each other. He felt the ache of loneliness return.

'We could carry the war to the Alemanni together,' Gunderic continued. 'We will hit them before they hit us. Apart we are strong but together we will be even stronger again. We will be a fighting force the world will fear. We will be strong enough to resist anyone who tries to attack or enslave us.'

Hagan had to admit he was impressed by Gunderic's rhetoric. He had learned much about the power of words and the crafts of persuasion in the years since they were last together. Or perhaps he had always known these arts. His father was a king after all.

'The fact that we are old friends is not enough for my people to trust outsiders,' Brynhild said. 'Especially men. There are women here who have suffered terribly at the hands of men. They will not believe you come here with good intentions.'

'I come with an offer of marriage, Brynhild,' Gunderic said. 'I did not think I would do it this way, but I ask for your hand. What better way to unite our two realms and show my good faith than with the union of we two, the leaders?'

Hagan saw Gunderic was doing his most disarming smile and trying his best to look her in the eyes, even though they were separated by the ravine. For a moment it felt like they were young lads in Gunderic's father's hall once more, trying to impress the girls.

'Lady Brynhild,' Wodnas said. 'I urge you to consider this offer. The Huns are coming like the great cascades of snow that tumble down these mountainsides. The trees that stand alone are swept away. The trees that stand with others stop the avalanche.'

'Lord Wodnas, I know you are a very wise man,' Brynhild said. 'And I respect you and your folk, but I have my own people to think of. And for all Gunderic knows I could be married already. He did not deem to ask.'

She put her arm around the shoulder of the blonde woman who stood beside her.

'Such alliances as these always end up with the king ruling both realms. You are not the first king to come here offering such an alliance, Gunderic. For that reason I have set a challenge to anyone seeking my hand in marriage. I have sworn before my people that I will only marry the bravest of men. Someone who has proven his right to rule through courage and skill by completing this challenge.'

'I never shirk a challenge,' Gunderic said, spreading his hands. 'Tell me what it is. Whatever it is, I will do it. I accept your challenge. I will prove before all these people – my warriors and yours – that I am worthy.'

'Wait—' Hagan began to say but it was too late. He felt his heart sink as he saw Brynhild smile for the first time. Gunderic had walked into whatever trap she had set for him. Gunderic's arrogance had always got him into trouble. Now he had to either complete the challenge or be humiliated in front of Brynhild's warriors and worse, his own.

Brynhild took a ring from one finger and placed it on the ground before the gate.

'Whoever wishes to marry me must jump this ravine, on horseback,' she said. 'I leave my ring here. If you make it across, pick it up and come to me. Oh and just to make it more interesting...'

She nodded to one of the women around her. The woman dashed inside the gate and returned almost immediately with a flaming torch in her hand. She passed it to Brynhild.

Brynhild tossed the torch onto the little barricade. The sticks and hay that made it up must have been soaked in oil as it exploded into flames, creating a line of fire from one side of the far end of the bridge to the other.

'Good luck,' Brynhild said, with a taunting smile.

The women around her all laughed and grinned. They filed back behind the palisade, closing the gate behind them.

CHAPTER THIRTY-EIGHT

'**B**Y TIWASS!' GUNDERIC said, his face ashen. 'It's impossible.'

'To jump across that chasm into fire?' Gunhild said, shaking her head. 'It's too difficult!'

'I believe that is the point,' Lokke said. 'To put people off from trying. I *did* warn you there was a challenge to overcome.'

'Some more details might have been useful,' Wodnas said, looking sideways at Lokke. 'It hasn't put everyone off trying, I see.'

He pointed the spear he used as a walking staff down into the gorge. Hagan once more felt his guts lurch as he looked over the edge, down the sheer walls of rock to the river churning over the rocks far below. With a start he realised that what he had previously thought were whitened sticks were actually bones. There were two long columns tangled in a fallen tree, one longer than the other, which Hagan recognised now as backbones, one of a horse and one of a man. There were several skulls lodged among the rocks and fallen branches too. A few scraps of tattered cloth, the remnants of the clothes of previous men who had attempted Brynhild's challenge, washed back and forth in the running water.

'It's unfortunate that you accepted the challenge so publicly,' Wodnas said.

Gunderic looked around. Hagan followed his gaze as he looked on the many Burgundar warriors who watched on from among the trees behind them. They all had the same look on their faces: one of expectation.

'Perhaps we should discuss this elsewhere?' Wodnas said, flicking his eyes towards the watching men.

They all nodded and trekked a little way back through the forest until they came to a clearing far enough away from the eyes and ears of the rest of the company of warriors.

'This Brynhild is a clever one alright,' Lokke said. 'She has created a double-edged sword. If a king attempts the challenge, there is a high likelihood he will die. If he turns it down, he will lose the respect of his men, who will then look for another king to replace him. Either way a rival to her realm is removed.'

'That bitch,' Gunderic said, gnashing his teeth. 'To think we used to call her our friend!'

'Things happen to change people,' Lokke said.

'To try that jump would be suicide,' Geic said.

'It's not that bad,' Sigurd said with a shrug. 'I could do it.'

All looked at Sigurd, unsure if he were joking or not. The jump was very difficult and any mistake would mean certain death.

'You showing off, husband, won't get us anywhere,' Gunhild said. 'It has to be Gunderic.'

'I'm supposed to keep you alive, lord,' Geic said. 'For that reason I can't allow you to try this.'

'But I have to!' Gunderic said. His voice was higher than normal and Hagan saw a look of panic on the king's face. 'You heard Lokke. If I don't I risk losing the allegiance of our warriors.'

'Lord, I'm saying this not just for your sake but for the sake of all the Burgundars: don't do it,' Geic said. 'Your realm is still new. To lose its king so early on could result in it falling apart completely. You have no son. Who would take over the throne?'

All of them looked at Wodnas. The old man, impassive, pursed his lips.

'It would be whoever you say it should be, King Gunderic,' he said.

'I can't say who when I'm dead!' Gunderic said.

'Perhaps you should say now,' Gunhild said. 'I am your sister, Gunderic. And the last of our royal Nibelung family. The throne should pass to me.'

'Nibelungs have not always ruled,' Brenwic, Lord of the Leuhtungs said. 'There was a time when Leuhtungs guided the destiny of our folk.'

'Before the Nibelungs the Volsungs ruled,' Sigurd said. He placed his hand on the hilt of the great sword sheathed beneath his arm. 'Tiwass has blessed me. It makes sense that Gunhild and I should rule together.'

'Stop it! Stop it!' Gunderic said. There were tears in his eyes. 'You're arguing like I'm already dead.'

Sigurd glared at Brenwic, who looked back in defiance. Hagan felt dismay that their company that had left Geneva in such high fettle, with combined purpose, should fall apart so fast.

'This is exactly what I mean, lord,' Geic said. 'If you fall into that ravine the rest of this company will be at each other's throats, fighting for the throne, before you even hit the bottom. That is why you can't do it.'

For a moment there was silence as each person in the clearing looked at the others around them. Those who until moments before had been allies, comrades and fellow-folk had changed to rivals, even potential enemies as the chance of gaining power had appeared.

'The choice is up to the king,' Wodnas said. 'Do you want to attempt this challenge, lord?'

'No,' Gunderic said in a quiet, hoarse voice. He bit his lower lip. 'I don't want to die.'

He looked at the forest floor and another silence descended.

'Perhaps there is another way,' Hagan said when he could stand the uncomfortable atmosphere no longer. He was not sure where the idea came from but he was desperate to avert further confrontation. 'Let me speak to Sigurd and the king alone.'

The others hesitated but Gunderic nodded and they filed away.

'Sigurd, if you really do think it is easy, then why don't you do it?' Hagan said when they were alone.

The big man started, blinked, then frowned.

'Because it has to be Gunderic who does it,' Sigurd said. He spoke in a tone of voice like someone criticising a child who had said something stupid. 'I'm already married to Gunhild. I don't need to marry this other woman. She is pretty though.'

Hagan lifted the Kin Helm from where the king held it in the crook of his arm. He pointed to the visor and chain-mail veil.

'You could wear the king's armour,' Hagan said. 'And ride his horse. With this helmet on, and his cloak, no one will know it is you instead of him. At least the women on the other side won't anyway. That fire burning over there will obscure their view as well.'

'It's brilliant!' Gunderic said. He was smiling again, his eyes alight. 'Hagan, perhaps you should be my chief councillor.'

Hagan could feel Sigurd glaring at him.

'I do not mean to push you into this,' Hagan said. 'I only ask you to do it if you think you can. I've no wish for you to throw your life away without need.'

'I'm sure you don't,' Sigurd said, his lip curling into a sneer. 'Unless you too think you have a claim to the kingship?'

Hagan felt a surge of genuine terror in his guts. The big man's sheer physical presence was intimidating enough but when the full weight of his glare was added the effect became

332

withering. For a moment Hagan wondered if Sigurd was about to draw his blade and strike him.

'I do think it's easy,' Sigurd said, his voice almost a growl. 'If you have enough willpower and determination of your own to push the horse. And I *could* do this deed that you fear to do, my king.'

Gunderic sucked in his breath through his teeth. The derision was evident in Sigurd's voice.

'But leaping the chasm is a feat of bravery that will live in the memory of all who see it and the stories they tell others about it for ever. If I do it dressed as you, no one will know it was me who did it.'

'That's the whole idea,' Hagan said.

'But then I do the deed but get no glory,' Sigurd said. 'Where is the advantage for me in that?'

'Whatever you want,' Gunderic said. 'Name your price – within reason.'

'You name me as your successor,' Sigurd said.

'Of course,' Gunderic said. 'My expectation was that my sister would rule if anything happened to me anyway.'

'Your sister will rule as my queen,' Sigurd said. 'But I shall be king. I want to make that clear.'

'Gunderic, to agree to this is dangerous,' Hagan said.

Sigurd planted his large forefinger on Hagan's chest.

'Shut your mouth, Dagelung, or I will teach you the meaning of real danger,' he said. Hagan once more felt the burning weight of the big man's fiery eyes. 'Well, King Gunderic? What do you say?'

'I agree,' Gunderic said. His eyes flicked sideways then back again.

'Very well,' Sigurd said. He was now smiling a wolf-like grin. 'Let us get changed.'

Hagan checked no one was watching then returned to help the king and Sigurd strip out of their armour. Sigurd unclasped his cloak and removed it.

'Unbuckle this, will you?' Sigurd said to Gunderic, turning his back to the king. As he did so Hagan noticed that the back of Sigurd's unusual scale-like armour did not meet. It was buckled together down the back but the big man's torso was so large it pulled the sides too far apart to join together, leaving a gap between them. This meant the armour had not been made for Sigurd.

When he pulled on the king's black mail shirt the same thing happened, even more noticeably. Even with both of them hauling at the straps, Gunderic and Hagan were unable to make the mail shirt meet at the back at all. In the end Sigurd shrugged them away and pulled on Gunderic's cloak, sweeping it around his shoulders and covering the gap in his mail. He took Gunderic's helmet and squeezed it onto his head. The iron visor amplified his heavy breathing.

Gunderic, on the other hand, had no problem fitting into Sigurd's scale armour. Indeed the arms were loose and the tunic, which came down to Sigurd's thighs, almost reached Gunderic's knees.

'Perhaps you should hang back out of the way when Sigurd rides,' Hagan said, beginning to doubt if his plan would work. 'I will get the horses.'

Gunderic looked at the drooping sleeves of the armoured jerkin he wore and nodded.

Hagan ran out of the clearing and back to the Burgundar company waiting at the edge of the precipice and along the track back downhill from it. Seeing the questioning looks of Gunhild and the others he nodded to them then went to find Gunderic's horse.

It was a magnificent beast – a Hispanic stallion with a slick black coat. The sight of the creature returned some of the hope in Hagan's heart. It was strong and feisty which looked promising if carrying the weight of Sigurd across that yawning chasm.

Hagan led it and Sigurd's own horse back to the edge of the clearing where the king and Sigurd waited.

'I'll use my own horse,' Sigurd said. 'She is used to me and we trust each other.'

With misgivings churning in his stomach, Hagan handed the reins to Sigurd.

'Right,' Sigurd said. 'Let's get this over with.'

He jumped onto the back of his horse and trotted off down the track in the opposite direction to the ravine. The warriors standing on it jumped out of the way as he galloped downhill. A little way down the track Sigurd halted, reining his horse to a sudden halt. The beast reared on its hind legs and wheeled around to face back up the slope.

'Ya!' Sigurd cried out, kicking his heels into the horse's flanks and thrashing the reins. The horse started forward and began galloping up the hill. Sigurd shouted and kicked, goading the horse onwards. It went ever faster, picking up speed despite going uphill. He leaned forwards, yelling words of encouragement into the creature's ears as he continued to drive it onwards. From inside the metal cage of the helmet his voice sounded strange and metallic, which added to the disguise. As he rode up the hill the warriors who lined the track began cheering, their noise swelling the closer he got to the ledge at the top.

The shouting attracted the attention of the women in the settlement across the ravine. Hagan saw Brynhild and several others appear above the palisade that surrounded the settlement. The view of her shimmered in the heat rising from the fire below, but at the sight of the horseman galloping towards the precipice, Hagan thought he saw Brynhild's face fall into a look of consternation.

He clenched his teeth and fists, breathing through his nose and trying not to hold his breath. Sigurd in Gunderic's armour galloped across the last thirty paces to the ledge at the edge of the gorge.

Sigurd gave one last cry, forcing the horse onwards. The creature – no doubt frightened out of its mind but more in awe of its master – gave out a loud whinny as if in response.

Total silence fell on the watchers so the only sounds were the drumming of the horse's hooves on the soft, pine-needle covered floor of the forest track and the rushing of the river over the rocks far below.

The horse reached the edge of the precipice. Sigurd gave one more shout and kicked his heels then the horse took a huge leap. The drumming of its hooves ceased, but its feet still thrashed as if it were on the ground and for a moment it looked like horse and man were riding across the air to the other side. A great gasp went up from everyone watching on both sides of the ravine.

Then the horse's forehooves crashed down on the far side. Its back legs followed and it skidded forwards, momentum pushing its rear end around in a semi-circle.

'He's made it,' Wodnas said.

The horse let out another frightened whinny but Sigurd, remorseless, drove it on towards the fire. He did not even attempt to leap it – there was no time – but instead ploughed into the burning barricade, kicking it aside. It shattered and fell apart, toppling blazing sticks in every direction.

Before the horse even came to a stop Sigurd was off its back and stooping to pick up Brynhild's ring. He held it aloft, grasped between the forefinger and thumb of his mailed right hand.

Cheers of triumph, pride and relief burst from all the Burgundars in the woods around Hagan.

Then a realisation came to Hagan. Sigurd could not keep Gunderic's helmet on for ever. And when Brynhild and her people came out of the gate in the palisade they would realise just how tall he was. The ruse would be discovered.

The same thought appeared to occur to Sigurd. With the cheers of the Burgundars still ringing across the ravine, he leapt back onto his horse. With a cry and kick of his heels he began to ride back towards the edge of the precipice. In a moment he was galloping straight for the ravine. The cheers died in the throats of the onlookers, replaced by a collective gasp as the horseman leapt into the air once more, completing the deadly jump again in the opposite direction.

As Sigurd's horse landed on their side of the gorge the Burgundars went wild with elation. As far as they were aware their king had been set an impossible challenge and not only had he met it but he had done it twice. Hagan felt himself carried along by the emotion, clenching his fists and stomping his feet as Sigurd rode past him.

Despite the clear dislike Sigurd had for him Hagan could not help but admire the courage, skill and strength of the man.

Sigurd rode back to the clearing where Gunderic awaited, having already stripped out of Sigurd's armour. Hagan trotted to the edge of the clearing and stood guard while Sigurd tossed the ring to the king then pulled Gunderic's helmet, mail and cloak off. Gunderic pulled it on and not a moment too soon as floods of Burgundars came rushing on foot after Sigurd, eager to congratulate the king.

Gunderic, holding Brynhild's ring in his fist, pushed his way through the thronging warriors who clapped him on the back and cheered him all the way back to the ravine.

On the far side Brynhild and her warriors had filed out once more from behind the palisade and now stood on the edge of the cliff. They all looked upset. Brynhild herself was aghast.

Gunderic motioned for silence and his warriors settled down. When relative quiet was restored, the king held up Brynhild's ring for all to see.

'Well, Brynhild?' he said, a broad grin on his face. 'I have completed your challenge and I repeat my offer. Let us unite our two kingdoms and our war hordes. And to seal this alliance we shall be married.'

Brynhild looked at the ground, then heaved a heavy sigh.

'I swore an oath that I would only marry the man who was brave enough to jump this ravine,' she said. 'Most were too frightened to try and the few who did are now at the bottom of that river down there. I am a woman of my word and I must accept your offer or break my oath.'

The blonde woman at her side grasped her arm. She said something that the Burgundars on the other side of the ravine could not hear. She had a pleading look on her face.

Brynhild shook her head.

'I must,' she said. 'If I break my word then who will ever trust it again?'

'Will you put over the bridge then?' Gunderic said. 'Let us cross.'

Brynhild shook her head.

'My oath did not include letting men into my realm,' she said. 'That still stands. I will come to you in Geneva in a week.'

Head bowed, she turned and went back through the gate in the palisade.

Hagan watched from the edge of the clearing. Gunderic clapped hands with those around him, a broad grin on his face as he accepted their plaudits and congratulations. He was his old, arrogant self and a far cry from the anxious wreck who thought he was going to have to jump the chasm himself not long before.

He felt the weight of a large hand on his shoulder and turned to see Sigurd standing beside him.

'Well, friend,' Sigurd said. 'It seems we both know something about the king that could be very dangerous for both of us.'

'So you bear me no ill-will for suggesting you make the jump?' Hagan said, hope lifting his heart that he had perhaps not made an enemy of one of the most powerful warriors he had ever met.

Sigurd raised an eyebrow.

'Right now you are the only witness to what Gunderic said back there about the royal succession. For that reason I will make sure you make it back to Geneva alive so it can be made official. If it wasn't for that you'd already be dead.'

CHAPTER THIRTY-NINE

'**I** HAVE BEEN SLEEPING my way around the slaves,' Zerco said, waving around a wine goblet that was too large for him. 'They are by and large wonderful girls and can be most obliging if you pay them enough.'

It was late in the evening. The fires in Gunderic's hall burned low and most people had gone to bed. Hagan and the others had returned from Brynhild's realm a few days before and there had been a couple of nights of celebration. After that feasting everyone had been busy preparing Geneva and the great hall for the king's upcoming wedding. Floors were swept, flowers and greenery brought in from the meadows and forests to decorate walls and tables as servants began brewing ale.

Hagan set off on a quest in the hope of finding some old friends or perhaps even surviving relatives. After a few days however, it became apparent that what he had already been told was true: he was indeed the last of the Dagelungs. Many of the folk had heard of Godegisil, the mighty champion of the tribe, or his beautiful wife Gunteka. A few had even known some of his old friends, but all of them were sure none now dwelt in the new kingdom of the Burgundars.

Resigned to the fact, Hagan took on his new responsibility as Hunt Master and led the huntsmen into the forests to find game for the tables. Now all was ready and, tired from the preparations and feasts, most folk had retired to bed. All that had to be done now was wait for the bride to arrive.

With that waiting came the question: would Brynhild turn up?

Now, in the quiet of the hall, Zerco and Hagan sat at a bench, sharing a jug of wine. Despite the efforts of a day's hunting, Hagan found it hard to relax. He had, without meaning to, made an enemy of Sigurd, so he had made it his habit not to go to bed until well after everyone else had, in order to make sure he was the last to fall asleep. He did not think Sigurd would try anything in Gunderic's hall, but neither did he want to take any chances.

This was the first time Zerco and Hagan had been alone since arriving in Geneva and Hagan was interested to know what the little man had been up to while he and the others had been away. Perhaps it was the journey they had made together, or the fact that they shared the secret knowledge of Aetius's interest in the treasure, but despite his previous discomfort in the presence of Zerco, Hagan found it strange that he felt more comfortable in his company than among those supposed to be his own folk.

Zerco was only too happy to share with Hagan what he had been up to while everyone else had been away.

'Slaves are also useful if you want to know things,' he said. 'People ignore them. They forget they're human beings and talk freely in their presence. A slave also can go anywhere in a house. Trust me: if you want to get close to an emperor or a king, use a slave.'

'I hope you didn't abuse the power you have over these poor girls,' Hagan said. 'Remember those not free are at the mercy of those who are.'

'You forget that I've been treated no better than a slave all my life,' Zerco said. 'They see me as one of them. They take me into their confidence and if I happen to reveal I have some gold or silver to share, well...'

He left the rest to Hagan's imagination.

'So what did you learn from these slaves?' he said.

'The treasure is here in Geneva for sure,' Zerco said, leaning close and speaking in a conspiratorial tone. 'There is wealth aplenty.'

'Anyone can see that,' Hagan said. 'Where is it, though? I've seen no sign of a treasury or strong room anywhere.'

'No one knows,' Zerco said. 'But it's widely believed the big man, Sigurd, possesses it, or at least is the keeper of it. That makes sense to me. I told you I saw the man who led the raid on Aspar's cohort and he was a giant. He had a helmet on but I'm pretty sure it was him. Have you not noticed his armour as well?'

'The odd metal scales?' Hagan said. 'Yes I have. What about it?'

'It's Byzantine,' Zerco said. 'Soldiers of the Eastern Roman Army wear it. It's the most effective body protection in the world. The dragon troopers who accompanied Aspar were all wearing coats of it when we were ambushed. He must have taken it from one of their corpses.'

'It certainly wasn't made for him,' Hagan said and told Zerco about how Sigurd's armour did not meet at the back.

'Two coincidences? I don't think so,' Zerco said. 'He took that treasure. That sword he bears must be the one Attila is after.'

'Gunhild said it was the Sword of Tiwass,' Hagan said. 'Tiwass is our war god, not the Huns'.'

'Tiwass, Mars, Ammon, Jehovah – what does a name matter?' Zerco said. 'Everyone will call it by the name of whatever bloodthirsty deity they claim demands they slaughter their neighbours and steal their land. Sigurd found that wealth and he has it hidden somewhere. He shares it with Gunderic, probably to buy favour. They say he is touchy about having spent time as the slave of a blacksmith and is desperate to erase what he sees as that blight on his nobility by achieving a crown himself.'

Hagan nodded, thinking how fast Sigurd had come up with

his request to be Gunderic's successor as the price for him leaping the ravine.

'That he shares it with the king is certain,' Zerco continued. 'You can see that with your own eyes. The Burgundars are a rich folk. The war gear for their horde, the jewellery the noble women wear, the food they have, it all comes from Gunderic, but Gunderic got it from Sigurd. Only Gunderic, Sigurd and his wife know where the gold is hidden.'

'Really?' Hagan said. 'That's hard to believe.'

'When they need to draw gold from wherever the hoard is hidden they always go together,' Zerco said. 'Probably in case one of them runs off with it. They trust each other so little. Sometimes they take slaves with them to help load up horses. When they do those slaves never return. The rest of the slaves tell me they dread being picked to go if it's announced that Gunhild, Gunderic and Sigurd are going on an expedition together. Once the previous Burgundar Hunt Master, Heiric, stumbled over them by accident while chasing a deer.'

Zerco leaned closer to Hagan.

'The next day he was seized by Gunderic's warriors and accused of treason,' the little man said from the side of his mouth. 'They *say*, he tried to fight them and was killed in the process. But we both know what that means, right? Gunderic had him killed.'

Hagan frowned, thinking of Gunderic's comment when he had been appointed chief huntsman. Had his old friends really become so ruthless, so corrupted by gold?

'No,' Zerco said, shaking his head. 'No one knows where the treasure is but those three, and they are thick as thieves.'

'So they've replaced me with Sigurd,' Hagan said, with a sardonic grunt. 'The three of us – and Brynhild – used to be close friends.'

'Used to be, eh?' Zerco said, raising an eyebrow as if he found this information very interesting. 'Friendship tends to wither fast when power and gold come into play. Well, I can tell you another thing. We aren't the only people sneaking around asking about the treasure.'

'Who else is?' Hagan said.

'The old man,' Zerco said. 'The one with only one eye. He plays the loyal servant but he's creeping about, poking his nose around, looking for the gold.'

'I'd have thought he could have used his Raven Warriors to find it,' Hagan said.

'Then he'd have to share it with them,' Zerco said, shooting a glance at Hagan that suggested he regarded Hagan as slow-witted. 'But those raven fighters are a fearsome lot, I can tell you. Wodnas has turned every one of them into stone-hearted killers. They're completely loyal to him and everyone fears them.'

'Warriors usually need blooding in battle to become that way,' Hagan said. 'The Ravens are young men. I didn't think the Burgundars of this new kingdom had been in any real wars yet. A few raids maybe.'

Zerco glanced around, then leaned even closer.

'They say,' he said, his voice little more than a breathless whisper, 'that when Wodnas completes the training of a band of new Raven Warriors an initiation ritual takes place. Wodnas takes them into the forest by night. A hunt takes place. Except they don't hunt animals. They hunt *people*. The new raven warriors must find a victim and kill them. It doesn't matter who it is. If they don't kill someone they cannot join the Raven Warriors, so every one of them makes sure he does.'

'Ah. *They* say, do they, Zerco,' Hagan said rolling his eyes. 'Is this more slaves' gossip? Are you seriously saying that Gunderic allows Wodnas and his Raven Warriors to ride around the forest at night murdering folk?'

'Take it as you will,' Zerco said, jutting out his lower lip. 'But the local folk all know that on nights when Wodnas' Wild Hunt is abroad, they should stay indoors.'

'Well this is all very interesting,' Hagan said. 'It seems there's a lot more going on in Geneva than meets the eye.'

'Or the *one* eye,' Zerco said, in a poor attempt at humour. He sat back, the smile on his face showing how pleased he was with himself. 'But if we're going to find the treasure we need to keep both our eyes open. The chance might come soon, too.'

'Really?' Hagan said.

'The king's wedding – if Brynhild actually arrives – will need to be paid for,' Zerco said. 'Marriage feasts are expensive and Gunderic will need gold and silver for his new bride. They will need to visit the treasure hoard before the wedding to draw on its wealth. When he does, we can follow them.'

Hagan nodded. He was not sure why he was still playing along with this treasure hunt and potentially betraying his own folk, but the trip to the mountains and his recent confrontation with Sigurd had left him uneasy. All was not as rosy as it seemed in the new kingdom.

'I'll tell you another thing,' Zerco said. 'The war is starting. Rome is on the march. Aetius has gathered his army in south-west Gaul – just outside Arelate. Then they are moving to Lugdunum to pick up more allies: they will be right beside this kingdom. Meanwhile Theodoric is leading his Visigoths north from Tolosa. They aim to meet at Aurelianum and stop the Huns there. Aetius thinks if he does not stop them there the war is lost. Old one-eye knows this too but there is no talk of it.'

'How do you know this?' Hagan said. 'Slaves again?'

'I heard this one myself,' Zerco said. 'I am like a slave in the respect that people ignore me, or dismiss me as stupid, ignorant or incapable of understanding their language. Even if I can, of what consequence is a freak like they think me to be? So they talk freely as if I am not there. I was nearby when one of Wodnas' Raven Warriors came to him to report it. That strange man Lokke knows it too.'

Hagan scratched his chin. Unlike Zerco's other gossip,

which just confirmed what they had already suspected, this was news indeed. Also, while he had no doubt others looked on Zerco as inconsequent, from what he had seen of Wodnas the old man likely would not. He was too crafty, too calculating to allow anything to happen by chance if he could avoid it, and if something did, then he would be very sure to exploit it to his own advantage.

'Zerco, my friend,' Hagan said, finishing his goblet of wine. 'I do not think any of those things of you, but now I also know that not only are you perfectly capable, you are downright dangerous. I am glad you are on my side.'

'All depends on this wedding then,' Zerco said with a self-satisfied smirk.

'What do you mean?' Hagan said.

'If Aetius was on the march then time is running out for the Burgundars,' the little man said. 'The wedding might give us the chance to find where the treasure is. Also it will bring the cavalry the Burgundars say they won't go to war against Attila without. If they don't join the alliance against Attila, Aetius will regard them as an enemy and march the legions here first. This new Burgundar kingdom will be annihilated. I don't care how good their warriors are. There aren't enough of them to fight off the whole Roman army.'

Hagan nodded, thinking back to that dark day outside Vorbetomagus.

'You're right,' he said. 'This marriage is crucial. So let's just hope Brynhild turns up for it.'

CHAPTER FORTY

HAGAN WOKE WITH a gasp from the clutches of a nightmare. For a few moments he lay in the dark, panting, eyes wide, as the last vestiges of the dream dissolved from his mind. Within moments he could not remember what it had been about, but the unease the dream caused in his heart lingered on, stopping him from falling straight back to sleep.

Gunderic had granted Hagan a room in an old Roman tenement across the main square from the feasting hall. It was a generous space for one man, having been originally built to accommodate an entire family. For someone like Hagan who had spent years sharing a *contubernium*, a Roman army tent, with other soldiers, then sleeping in the halls of kings, quartered with the rest of the warriors on the floor, being alone at night in this big empty room was a little unnerving.

He knew this was not what had caused his nightmare, though. Something else was disturbing him. Hagan lay staring at the dark above him trying to work out what it could be. The events of the last few weeks churned in his mind. The Burgundars' new kingdom, Brynhild, the strange old man, Wodnas. Sigurd's crazy jump across the chasm. Gunhild's strange reaction to his amulet...

He sighed. The darkness told him it was still the middle of the night, but with all this going on in his head there was no chance of getting back to sleep.

Hagan swung his legs out of bed and walked to the window,

nightmare-induced sweat cooling to chill his skin. The shutters were open a crack and let in a shaft of moonlight that sliced across the floor. Hagan swung the shutters fully open and took a deep breath of the night air. He leaned on the sill, taking in the view outside.

The old tenement was three storeys tall and stood along one side of the main square at the centre of Geneva. To his left was the great feasting hall. Facing it, to Hagan's right, was the former Roman palace with its impressive marble steps and columns that now served as the personal residence of King Gunderic.

It was the contrast of a dark figure against the whiteness of those steps in the moonlight that caught Hagan's eye. The square was empty, as far as Hagan could see, as befitted the middle of the night. Any warriors on guard would be at the gates, on the walls of the town or outside the bedrooms of whoever they watched over.

The figure on the steps was wrapped in a long black cloak with the hood pulled up, and from the way they scurried Hagan could tell they were being furtive. For an instant he wondered if he should grab his sword and run down to confront this person before they did any harm. Then he reasoned that the person was coming down the steps of the king's residence. If he was an assassin, he had already done his work.

Anyone running around like that in the middle of the night could be up to no good, so Hagan resolved that he had to check what they were up to.

He was about to dress when another movement below caught his eye. Coming across the square from the shadows around the great hall was another figure in a similar black cloak. This person's hood was down and Hagan could see they had long hair bound in a knot, which meant this was either a married woman or a warrior. From his vantage point high above it was not possible to see their face so he could not tell if the figure had a beard or not.

The newcomer was hurrying across the square to meet the other person coming from the palace.

Hagan's exploratores' training told him that sometimes the best thing to do was to wait and observe, and act only when as much information as possible had been gathered and you were sure of the situation you were rushing into. Aware that the light of the moon might illuminate him to the people below, he stepped back a little from the window. He could still see what was going on below but now the shadows of the room hid him from the sight of those below.

The two cloaked figures met in the middle of the square. They began talking but spoke in low voices, so despite the quiet of the sleeping city, Hagan could not hear what they said. This confirmed to him that they did not intend anyone else to know what they were up to.

Hagan felt a tingling sensation in the back of his neck, a weird thrill that he was watching something no one was supposed to.

Then the figure that had come from the hall looked up, glaring directly at the window Hagan stood at. Despite knowing those below could not see him, instinct made Hagan flinch back further into the shadows, losing sight of the scene below as he did so.

The instant before he moved back, however, was enough for Hagan to have seen Gunhild's face, bathed in the moonlight, peering up at his window as if either double-checking there was no one listening or had she somehow sensed he was watching?

Nonsense, he told himself as he stood in the darkness of the room, trying to control his breathing so it did not give his presence away. There was no way she could have spotted him. Perhaps the presence of his open window had just drawn her suspicion.

After a few more agonising moments of silence, Hagan inched forward again. He moved on his toes, ready to jump back into the dark if he had to. To his relief he could see

Gunhild was no longer looking up. Now she and the other cloaked figure were hurrying across the square, away from the tenement. Hagan watched them for a moment. He had not seen the face of the second cloaked person but from their size and the way they ran – and the fact Gunhild was there – he guessed that it was probably Gunderic.

What were they up to? Sneaking around in the dark in their own city?

The king's wedding will need to be paid for. They will need to visit the treasure hoard before the wedding to draw on its wealth. Zerco's words surfaced in Hagan's mind. Was this a chance to find out where the treasure was? Sigurd was not with them, but what else would Gunderic and Gunhild be up to?

As fast as he could, Hagan dressed in his hunting clothes. Casting his own dark hooded cloak around his shoulders, he ran for the stairs.

CHAPTER FORTY-ONE

IN HIS TIME in the exploratores, Hagan had learned skills in tracking, infiltrating and how to observe without being observed oneself. This, combined with his experience and inherent skills in hunting meant that he had little difficulty following the two cloaked figures.

After charging down the three flights of stairs in the tenement as fast as it was safe to, he crept out the front door then hurried around the edge of the square, careful to keep to the shadows to reduce the chance of his being seen. By the time he reached the far side Gunhild and her companion were gone, but from their previous direction he could judge which street they had left by. Sure enough, as he started down it himself, he glimpsed the two hooded figures in a shaft of moonlight at the far end.

Hagan rushed as fast as was prudent along the dark, silent street as the two figures ahead disappeared around the corner. He had no fear of being seen, his biggest concern was falling into a gutter in the dark. When he got to the end of the street himself he turned the same way as the others and found himself amid the dense gloom of a side street that ran parallel to the walls that surrounded the city.

A light flared up ahead. Hagan froze, then pulled his dark cloak around himself as he sank to a crouch. As he watched from the shadows he saw that about fifty paces further along the street, Gunhild had lit a torch. She held it aloft as her companion went down on one knee and began working at something on the ground. The torchlight fell on his features, confirming that it was indeed Gunderic who accompanied Gunhild. After a few moments the king raised what looked like a heavy wooden trapdoor in the ground.

Hagan felt a thrill pass through his heart. Was this where the treasure lay hidden – in some secret hole under the streets of Geneva? Had it been resting right under his very feet since he got here?

Then Gunderic and Gunhild clambered down into the hole the trapdoor had covered, taking their torch with them. The street plunged back into darkness as they pulled the trapdoor closed behind them.

Hagan hurried after them. When he judged he was about where they had been he fell to his hands and knees and began sweeping his hands across the ground. His fingers slid over cold stone flags, laid by the Romans untold years before, then he felt the wood of the trapdoor. It was made of stout planks bound with iron strips. His finger made out a bolt and what felt like a large key hole.

This could not be the entrance to a treasure hoard, Hagan realised. Though it was sturdy and made to keep people out it was in the middle of a street. Folk must know it was there.

Hagan raised it a crack. Peering down he could not see much except the faint orange glow of flickering torchlight reflected on what looked like stone steps. This was the entrance to some sort of passage. Hagan looked up at the city walls that loomed above the street. He realised that Gunhild and Gunderic had gone into a secret tunnel, the sort that existed in most walled towns and cities. It would run under the walls and some way away underground from the town, where at last it would open in some out of the way or secluded place. In times of siege it could be used to smuggle food into the town or to launch surprise attacks on the besieging warriors. In times of peace, when it was not guarded, it was perfect for what it was being used for now by those who had a key for it – to sneak in and out of the town without anyone knowing.

Hagan pulled the trapdoor open, confident Gunderic could not have locked it behind him. The tunnel was for keeping people out so all locks, bolts and security would be on the city side of its entrances and exits. The faintness of the retreating torch glow told him that the other two were already some way along the tunnel, so without hesitation Hagan went down the steps and pulled the door shut above him. At the bottom of the steps he could see the passageway leading off. Perhaps sixty paces along it Gunhild and Gunderic were hurrying away, the flames of the torch licking the dank, slime-covered stones that made up the roof overhead.

He set off after the others. The air was chilled and smelled of damp earth and he tried to not make too much noise as his feet splashed through puddles on the floor.

Before long the light ahead once again vanished, which told Hagan that Gunhild and Gunderic had left the tunnel. Plunged back into total blackness, Hagan had to slow down once more, though his training meant he knew how to keep moving even in the dark. He kept his left arm outstretched before him to detect anything he might walk into, while he swept his feet along the ground rather than lifting them, so as not to trip over some hidden obstacle.

After some time his left hand touched the stone of a rising staircase and he knew he was at the other end. Hagan scrambled up the steps and found they ended in what felt like the wood of another trapdoor. As with the entrance, the latch and bolt were on the inside, so Hagan knew it would not be fastened shut from the outside.

With aching slowness, he lifted the trapdoor a little.

Hagan froze.

He could hear Gunderic's voice. He was not far away. Mere paces from the trapdoor by the sound of it. Fearful of making a movement the other two might spot, or the trapdoor crashing shut with a bang, Hagan remained still where he was, holding the door open a little with the top of his head.

'Where is that husband of yours?' he heard Gunderic say. His voice was tetchy. 'He should have been here to meet us. We don't have all night!'

So Sigurd is part of this too, Hagan thought. This confirmed that they were going to the treasure, just as Zerco had surmised they would.

Hagan could not see Gunderic or Gunhild through the narrow gap the raised trapdoor left, but their burning torch illuminated the grass and the trunks of surrounding trees. He surmised the tunnel ended in a sheltered copse among the woods not far from the city walls; the perfect place to come and go from Geneva without being seen.

After a short but ever more uncomfortable wait for Hagan supporting the trapdoor with his head, as he was, the soft thump of horses' hooves on damp earth heralded the arrival of someone else.

'There you are, dearest husband,' Hagan heard Gunhild say. 'My brother was starting to complain.'

'I had to have these horses taken from the reserve stables then saddled and prepared. That's why I took so long,' Sigurd said. 'When I went to the stables the ready horses had all been taken. The old man and his raven fighters are out on one of their hunts in the woods tonight.'

'What did you tell the grooms you needed these ones for?' Gunderic said. Hagan could hear the concern in his voice.

'I told them I was joining Wodnas in his hunting,' Sigurd said. 'Which put the fear of Tiwass into them. They didn't ask any more questions after that.'

He gave an evil-sounding little chuckle.

'If Wodnas is hunting the woods tonight could that hinder us?' Gunhild said.

'We've nothing to fear from him or his black bird soldiers,'

Sigurd said in a derisive voice. 'He won't touch us. He wouldn't dare. Don't worry your pretty head about that, dear.'

'But he might *see* us,' Gunhild said. Hagan could hear the exasperation in her tone. 'He might try to follow us.'

'Then we'll just have to tell him to mind his own business,' Gunderic said. 'Besides, I knew he would be hunting with his men tonight. I gave him two criminals due for execution for his quarry.'

'Do you think it's wise to let him continue these hunts, Gunderic?' Gunhild said, still sounding dubious. 'If the ordinary folk find out you know of it and allow it to happen they may start to look on you as a tyrant.'

'Wodnas hunts law-breakers, perverts and prisoners of war,' Sigurd said. Hagan could picture the sneer on his lips without needing to see it was there. 'Men who will die anyway.'

'Most of the ordinary folk think the hunt is supernatural: led by the Devil – if they're still Christian – or some *jötnar* or other monster,' Gunderic said with a little snort. 'The ones who know it's Wodnas are too scared of him to do anything about it. Anyway, the old man insists that it's necessary. He needs to harden his warriors. So if a few prisoners dying is the cost of making our war horde more deadly, then that's a price I'm prepared to pay. And it's all the better that he is abroad tonight, it will keep the ordinary folk indoors. They're terrified of the Wild Hunt. There will be less prying eyes who might catch sight of us. Now let's go.'

Hagan listened to the creaking of saddle leather and straps as the others mounted. This was followed by the receding sound of hooves as the trio rode away. The glow of the torch went with them.

Hagan waited as long as he thought necessary, then pushed the trapdoor fully open and scrambled out of the tunnel. He was indeed in a grove of trees outside the city walls. There was no one else around except for Gunderic, Gunhild and Sigurd who were riding away down a path through the woods.

Crouching low, Hagan closed the trapdoor then prepared himself to follow the others. It would not be easy tracking mounted quarry, but the darkness meant that they could not ride too fast. Even trotting could lead to a trip and resulting fall and a gallop would be suicide. With the sound of the horses he would not have to be too careful about any noise he made himself. All the same, he would have to run to keep up.

Taking a few deep breathes through his nose, Hagan wrapped himself in his cloak, pulled his hood down and set off, jogging along the path after the riders.

The path led uphill and it was not long before Hagan was panting and sweating, despite the chill of the night. His lungs began to burn and his legs felt heavy but he knew from experience – long forced marches with the Roman Army – that he had to keep going and push through it. If he did, then soon he would find himself in a state where his breathing was easy and he would feel like he could keep on going for miles, or at least until exhaustion began to set in.

The three riders followed the path until it emerged near an old Roman road. Here they turned left and began following it. Hagan did the same, though he kept to the side of the road in the gloom of the woods so as not to be easily spotted. There was enough moonlight to see that the road went perpendicular to the great Lake Geneva, bisecting woods that rose above the city and denser forest that covered the rising ground on the other side of the road that rose up to eventually become mountains that towered against the night sky.

After following the road for perhaps a Roman mile or more, the party on horseback stopped. Gunderic jumped off his horse and examined something beside the road, perhaps some hidden sign or secret marking. Then he remounted and led the other two off the road on the other side, onto a path through the forest that led to the mountains.

Hagan picked up his pace to catch up and followed them into the forest. Soon he found himself in the dark bosom of the surrounding pine trees. The darkness closed in and his feet moved over a soft carpet of fallen pine needles. Hagan began to fear that he might trip over a root or fallen branch.

Gunderic's torch was visible ahead, unhindered by trunks, so Hagan kept following, confident that he was still on a path rather than struggling through undergrowth. The further they went, the steeper the ground became and the denser the gloom of the forest. Hagan's breath began to get ragged once more and he knew he would soon have to stop for a rest.

He noticed that up ahead Gunderic's torch had stopped moving. Grateful for the reprieve, however short it turned out to be, Hagan stopped jogging and stood, hands on hips, trying to regain control of his breath once more.

Then he heard voices.

They were coming through the trees from his right, along with the sound of the feet of many men moving through the undergrowth, snapping dry branches and twigs.

Then the blast of a horn came through the trees. It was the unmistakable note of a hunting horn and it sent a thrill of terror through Hagan's heart.

Zerco's words swam into Hagan's mind: *Wodnas takes them into the forest by night. A hunt takes place. Except they don't hunt animals. They hunt people.*

CHAPTER FORTY-TWO

A MAN BLUNDERED OUT of the trees further up the path, between Hagan and the others. Directly behind him came four more men. Hagan could see their spears. Behind them came riders.

'No!' the first man just had time to cry out before one of those pursuing him drove his spear into his guts. With a strangled cry of anguish the hunted man dropped to his knees.

'That's one of them,' Hagan heard one of the riders say.

'Look,' one of the men on foot said. Even in the gloom Hagan could tell the man's raised arm was pointing in his direction. 'There's the other one!'

The hunting horn blew again and the company began moving down the path.

Hagan did not need to think about what to do. In the Army he had often had to travel unobserved into enemy territory. Several times Hagan had been in the situation of needing to escape an enemy force and the one thing he knew was that the fastest way to get caught – and die – was to freeze while you worked out your next move.

He ran for his life.

Hagan pounded downhill along the path, back the way he had come, heedless now of the danger of tripping in the dark. Caution was irrelevant. If he fell they would catch him. If he slowed down to avoid falling they would catch him as well. His fate was now completely at the mercy of whatever whim the *Dísir* who wove his destiny had in their great minds at that moment.

His first priority was to get as much distance between himself and his pursuers, as fast as possible. Later, if he got away, he could stop and think about what to do. Right now it was all about speed and luck.

Hagan pushed himself on, ignoring the burning in his already tired thighs and his lungs. Behind him he heard excited shouting and guessed he had been spotted. The horn blasted once more. This time it was joined by a second horn and the soft thrumming of hooves on the earth as horses broke into a trot.

He knew he could not stay on the path much longer. The horses would run him down. It was time to move to the trees where branches, tree trunks and the uneven ground would remove their advantage.

Hagan shot sideways off the track and scrambled down the bank into the forest. As the trees closed in around him the darkness did too as their branches cut out what little light filtered down from the moon and stars above. He kept going while there was some ambient light near the path but soon that was gone and he was forced to slow down. Then his foot struck a fallen branch and he went sprawling headlong to the ground.

He gritted his teeth, closed his eyes and tried to twist sideways as he fell, attempting to limit any injury he was about to sustain. His left shoulder struck the ground but the landing was soft as he crashed into damp earth and countless years of fallen pine needles. Throwing his hands out he felt around until his left palm struck the rough bark of a tree trunk. Hagan rolled across the forest floor, turning himself around so he lay behind the tree trunk, putting it between him and the way back to the path behind him.

He peeked around the side of the tree trunk to see what was going on behind him. While he lay in darkness the ambient light from the night sky now lit the track for him to get a clear view of it.

The hunting party, four on horseback, perhaps twenty on foot, were still on the trackway. They went past where Hagan lay and for a moment he felt elation at the thought they might not have seen him come off the path and continue on down it. This died almost immediately, however, as they stopped just a little further down the hill.

'He went in here somewhere, lord,' one of the men on foot said.

'Fritigern has already blooded his spear tonight,' one of the riders said. Hagan recognised the voice of the strange, one-eyed old man, Wodnas. 'Athaneric, Gundioc and Sigismund: you too have completed your training. Now prove you are worthy to join my Raven Warriors. Go in there. Find this man and bring me his head.'

Hagan swallowed. The rumours were true. Wodnas really did blood his warriors by having them hunt down human quarry.

Four of the men on foot began to scramble down the bank from the track into the woods. Hagan could see they wore hooded cloaks and carried spears. Every instinct screamed at him to get up and run but his training told him to do the opposite. The hunters were perhaps thirty paces away. Any movement on his part would make noise and alert them to where he was. The other thing he needed to do, was cover his face.

For some reason men can always see your face, Faustus, the centurion who had trained him had said. *It's something men are born with. No matter how dark it is, or how well you think you're hidden, men can always spot a human face.*

As quietly as he could, Hagan grabbed a handful of wet earth, heedless of the pricking of hundreds of pine needles, and smeared it over his face. He had no idea how effective it was but he needed to do something to obscure his pale visage.

Then he pulled his cloak around himself and lay as still as he could.

The candidate Raven Warriors entered the trees. Hagan could tell they were trying to move with stealth but in this terrain it was impossible not to make some noise and he could work out where they were by the crack of fallen branches being stepped on and the occasional heavy thump of a stumbling footfall.

Hagan, lying in the dark wrapped in his cloak, ears straining for any noise that might indicate one of the Raven Warriors was approaching him, felt as if every nerve in his body was stretched to breaking point.

As he listened, he heard the hunters go past where he was, moving deeper into the trees. They were good, he judged. Most men would be crashing and flailing around in the dark, making a racket and telling everyone where they were. All he heard from these four were the occasional snap of a random branch, the odd soft footfall or sharp intake of breath. It was enough though for Hagan to judge their positions.

After a little while longer, Hagan dared to peek out. By now his eyes had become accustomed to the darkness and he was able to make out some things in the Stygian gloom, especially if he used the edge of his vision and did not look directly at whatever he was trying to see.

He caught sight of movement perhaps forty paces further into the trees. Looking back at the track he saw that the rest of the hunting party still waited. This really was a test of the new lads.

Well, my friends, Hagan thought to himself, *this is one test I will do my utmost to make sure you fail.*

Now at last it was the time to move. Sooner or later the men in the woods would come back, or the ones on the path would come into the trees. It was now or never.

With careful movements, Hagan rose to a crouch behind the tree trunk. He felt around him on the ground until his fingers found a broken branch that was just about large and heavy enough to use as a cudgel. Then, judging that his hunters had gone deeper into the forest perpendicular to the path, Hagan set off in an uphill direction, walking at an angle away from the path rather than straight away from it. He walked with slow, deliberate steps, planting his toes first and rolling forward onto his heels. If he felt a branch he was careful to avoid bending or breaking it. That would result in some of the loudest noises that could be made in a forest and immediately announce his position.

Every ten or so steps he stopped, standing still and peering into the dark around him. At the same time he listened for any sound that meant someone was nearby. Finally he breathed in through his nose, trying to detect any smells that meant one of the hunters was close. If all was clear he moved on another ten paces.

He had not gone too far when the sound of running water came to him. There was a river somewhere nearby. Rivers could be dangerous for men on the run. They tended to be a gathering point for people and animals. On the other hand he could perhaps use it to hide any tracks he might be leaving. Hagan decided to move in the direction of the sound.

He had only travelled seven paces when he froze. His nostrils twitched. There was a faint smell in the air that was familiar and did not belong in a forest. Then he realised what it was: butter. There was someone close by who had either been eating butter or had, as some of the younger folk liked to do, smeared their hair with it in order to make a style.

Hagan stood still as a stone, his ears straining for the slightest noise. A branch snapped mere paces away. Hagan lashed out with the branch, swinging it as hard as he could in a vicious arc. His shoulder jarred as the branch connected with something solid. He heard a man's voice cry out and knew he had hit his target. The fact that he could still cry out meant he had not hit him hard enough, however.

Hagan rushed towards the source of the cry. He raised his left hand, grasping in the darkness until he felt the unmistakable touch of human skin. He felt a nose, lips and something warm and wet – either blood or snot. Now sure where the man's face was he unleashed three more hard blows with the branch in short succession. Then the man was not there any more. Hagan's fifth blow swiped thin air and he almost fell off balance. There was a crash of breaking sticks and a heavy thump which told Hagan his opponent had fallen down.

He didn't wait to see if the man was out of the fight or not. Cries from his companions floated out of the dark to Hagan's right and he heard their footsteps coming closer. Hagan started to run away then stopped almost straight away.

He had to think. The hunters were close. He could stumble off into the dark but how far would he get before they caught up with him? He could well fall himself and break a leg or ankle and then he was done for. He could fight them but there was three of them, with spears. He could not take all of them by surprise.

He dropped to his hands and knees and felt around the forest floor for the spear of the man he had felled but it was nowhere to be found. He felt the man's legs and could tell he was lying flat on his back. The hunter began to moan and Hagan cursed to himself. The noise would bring the lad's friends to him even faster.

Hagan briefly thought of dealing the fallen hunter a few more blows to shut him up but realised he did not have the time. The others would be here in moments. If Hagan was going to survive this the only way would be if he could out-think his opponents. He had to do what they would not expect.

Trackers always look down, the voice of old Faustus surfaced in Hagan's mind again. *They look for footprints, trails and traces of the person they are hunting. No one ever looks up.*

Hagan felt around him for tree trunks. The nearest was too

thin – a stripling that would not be able to bear his weight. There was another close by that was much bigger. Hagan reached up, found branches above him and hauled himself up. Once he got his feet onto the branch he reached above himself again, finding another branch to haul himself up higher.

He did this twice more until the sound of rushing footsteps came from below. Hagan stopped moving and hugged the tree trunk, bracing his feet on the branches below. Then he just stood still.

'Gundioc? Is that you?' Hagan heard one of the hunters below say.

'There's someone on the ground,' a second voice said.

There then came a mumbling half-groan from the man Hagan had struck.

'It is him,' a third voice said. 'The bastard must have jumped him.'

'Either that or the idiot ran into a tree in the dark,' the first hunter said.

'Not Gundioc,' the third man said. 'He's the best of all of us.'

'Come on,' the second hunter said. 'The bastard can't have got far.'

Then the unmistakable sound of branches cracking underfoot drifted from further off amid the trees, the sound of someone with no training in stealth craft moving through the forest.

'There he is,' the third hunter said, dropping his voice to a low whisper.

Thanking his lucky stars, Hagan listened as they moved off. He did not know who the newcomer was, but most likely it was the second of the two unfortunate prisoners Gunderic had gifted Wodnas that night for his deadly hunt.

Taking advantage of the respite he hauled himself on up the tree further, until he came to a stout branch growing out from the main trunk that was big enough for him to straddle with some comfort. He threw his arms around the trunk and rested his head against it.

The men below might be back, or their quarry might lead them off. It was impossible to tell. All Hagan could do now was stay where he was and wait. If his luck held then sooner or later they would give up and leave or move on to try to find other quarry. Then he would climb down and there would be nothing to do but walk back to the city.

Either way it was going to be a long night.

CHAPTER FORTY-THREE

GUNHILD FELT EXCITEMENT growing in her heart as she clambered over the slippery rocks. She had visited the treasure three times now, but for some reason each time she returned the feeling got more intense rather than diminishing with familiarity.

They had ridden up the path away from Wodnas' hunting party, going on through the forest and further uphill. They had switched paths several times before eventually emerging from the trees amid the rock-strewn slopes and towering cliffs that marked the start of the mountains. By then it was deep into the night and Gunderic was on his third torch, the previous two having burned out.

They rode up the path of a river that tumbled from the heights above over boulders and rocks, until at last they came to a sheer cliff face about five times the height of a man. A waterfall gushed down from above into a wide pool at the head of the river. Here they had dismounted and tied up their horses, each of them unstrapping a leather saddlebag from their steed.

Gunderic, holding the torch high, led the way around the edge of the pool towards the waterfall. The rocks were wet and slippery and the spray of the water freezing, making all of them huddle under their hooded cloaks. As they reached the side of the waterfall the torchlight revealed that it tumbled from a slight overhang above, which left enough of a gap that they could walk behind the curtain of falling water, something that was not visible from the front.

Behind the waterfall was a narrow gap in the rocks, just wide enough for each of them to pass through one at a time. On the other side of this they found themselves in a cave that led downwards, deep into the cliff.

With Gunderic in the lead, they scrambled down, clambering over boulders and navigating around amazing columns of pointed rocks. Water dripped from above and the walls of the cave at times appeared to be covered in shimmering crystals or multi-coloured glass. Eventually the walls of the cave widened and they entered a large chamber. The flames of Gunderic's torch cast ghastly flickers around the walls, illuminating strange paintings on the rock – stylised depictions of people and animals, as well as weird geometric patterns.

When the Burgundars had first arrived in Geneva an old man, one of the very few remaining of the Allobroges the Alemanni had not frightened away, had shown Gunderic this cave. He said the paintings were ancient: the work of witches or devils from deep within the earth. Realising he had the perfect hiding place for the Burgundars' treasure, Gunderic had killed the old man and now only he, Gunhild and Sigurd knew of the cave's existence.

Gunhild felt a little shiver at the sight of one of the cave paintings. It depicted a man in a sort of half-crouch, as if he were preparing to leap as high as he could into the air. Instead of a normal face, however, he was painted with two large spirals where his eyes should have been, and the horns of a stag sprouted from the top of his head. As with the last couple of times she had been here, Gunhild found the picture a little disturbing, as if this strange human-stag creature was watching from above, the sole witness to the secret the three people below kept within this chamber.

Then the torchlight fell on the treasure and Gunhild forgot about everything else.

Gunderic and Sigurd had hauled it up here themselves, doing the work twenty men had done for her father when he had stolen it from the Huns and brought it back to Vorbetomagus. Coins, necklaces, arm rings, amulets and jewels lay in heaps around the cavern. The torchlight danced across rubies, emeralds and garnets. The flames glinted on silver and their glow was reflected from the heaps of gold, bathing everything in a warm, orange hue. Her father had taken four wagonloads of treasure and most of it still remained, its vast wealth hardly even dented, even by the expense of repairing Gunderic's hall and building a new kingdom.

Gunhild gazed at the treasure, feeling a strange fascination with it that made it difficult to look away. The thought flickered through her mind that there was enough wealth here for her to live as a queen for the rest of her days. A queen in her own right, not beholden to the crumbs a brother or husband deigned to throw her, and free of their whims and petty jealousies. The gold held her in a strange fascination. It was not just precious metal. It was freedom. A means to live life as she wanted to, not as a decoration possessed by some man. If she had it all to herself...

She glanced at Gunderic. He was glaring at the treasure, eyes wide, mouth ajar, his face wearing an expression not unlike the one she had seen on King Half of the Danes when he had regarded her naked body. His eyes rolled around, first towards Sigurd who was already shovelling gold coins into one of his saddlebags, oblivious to all else, then to Gunhild. They had a wild, savage look in them, as if he were about to lose all control.

Gunhild reached inside her cloak, her hand grasping the hilt of the dagger sheathed at her waist. Then Gunderic's face relaxed. Gunhild let go of her knife.

'Come on,' he said. 'Let's get started or we won't be back before dawn.'

Gunhild nodded and set her saddlebags down. She stooped

and began scooping handfuls of gold and silver into them as her brother did the same.

She had just finished filling the first saddlebag when a gold horse trapping caught her eye. It had the image of a bird stamped into it, depicted in the Hunnish style. Gunhild picked it up and regarded it for a moment.

'Hagan wears something very like this, you know,' she said, holding the round metal disc between her thumb and forefinger. 'He says it was his mother's.'

Gunderic stopped filling his own bag and looked up. Gunhild flicked the ornament to him, sending it spinning through the air. Gunderic caught it then looked at it, frowning.

'His mother? How on earth did she...?' he said, then looked up, meeting Gunhild's gaze.

Then Gunderic stabbed his hands into the pile of treasure before him, grabbing two fistfuls of gold. He rose to his feet, letting the gold and silver coins, amulets and bracteates run through his fingers and clatter back into the pile.

'I will not share my treasure with anyone,' he said, as if forgetting the others were there. 'No one, do you hear me?'

Then, like someone waking from a dream, he looked up again, seeming puzzled at the looks that both Gunhild and Sigurd now levelled in his direction.

'What?' Gunderic said. 'Don't just stand there looking at me. We need these bags filled.'

Gunhild stooped to begin filling her second saddlebag. As she did so she shot a sideways look at her brother. In her heart she knew something had just changed. She could no longer be sentimental. Here was the wealth of half the known world at her fingertips and she had as much right to it as her brother had. She wanted it, and if the cost of that was the death of old friendships and trusted relationships, then so be it.

It was time to start looking out for herself once more.

CHAPTER FORTY-FOUR

BRYNHILD KEPT HER word. The next morning she arrived at the gates of Geneva, accompanied by a contingent of her Valkyrjur warriors.

Hagan felt as though his eyes had been rubbed with handfuls of sand. His thighs and calf muscles ached from his exertions of the previous night. He had had very little sleep. Wodnas' warriors had taken a long time to give up their hunt. At last however, Wodnas had called the prospective Raven Warriors back to the track, no doubt to deliver the bad news that they had not passed the test, and the company had moved off down the track.

After waiting a prudent amount of time Hagan had clambered down from his perch. When the company had at last moved off, Hagan had clambered down from the tree. Any hope of tracking Gunhild and the others to the treasure was long gone and there was little left to do but to get back to Geneva. This meant another gruelling run. He could not take the chance of getting back after Gunderic, Gunhild and Sigurd as they would most likely lock the trapdoors behind them, leaving him stuck outside the city walls. The sun was up as he had crawled into bed and it seemed to Hagan like he had only closed his eyes when the trumpets began blaring in the square outside his room, announcing the arrival of Brynhild and her entourage.

He had to admit he was impressed by the Valkyrjur. Unlike the expensive war gear of the Burgundars, their armour was repurposed, repaired or improvised. Still, it was well-maintained and fit for purpose. It was meant for use rather than show. The company of riders all wore leather jerkins and mail shirts, visored iron helmets, leather riding britches, and greaves to protect their lower legs from blows from the ground. Each trooper bore a long spear – a *lancea* – and had a great round shield slung across her back. The shields were all painted with the rune of Tiwass, the one Hagan had seen the cross on the church in Geneva twisted into, except Brynhild's riders bore it upside down, which Hagan knew some saw as a symbol of death. They had decorated their helmets with the black feathered wings of birds – ravens and crows by the look of it, one nailed to either side. The women's eyes were surrounded by black paint so the visors of their helmets looked like the hollow eye sockets of a skull. Each rider wore the pelt of an animal – a bear or a wolf – around their shoulders as a cloak. Their long hair was worn in braids down their backs. Some of them had bones woven through their tresses.

'I don't know about you,' Hagan said to Zerco who stood beside him as they watched the riders file through the gates of the city, 'but I've never seen such fearsome women.'

'I find them exciting,' Zerco said, licking his lips. 'They're magnificent. So proud and haughty. And with a hint of danger. Though to look at them you'd think they were coming to a funeral rather than a wedding.'

'I'd steer clear of them if I were you, Zerco,' Hagan said. 'I doubt they will stand much for your lecherous ways. The way your hands wander you're likely to get them chopped off.'

The procession made its way to the centre of Geneva where Gunderic's hall stood. The king, his sister and Sigurd, as well as all the members of Gunderic's council stood waiting. Everyone was dressed in their finest clothes: long robes, tunics and dresses embroidered with gold and silver threads. Even Wodnas was wearing a new tunic and a blue cloak that reached to his knees. Despite this he was still barefoot.

371

A company of Wodnas' Raven Warriors and another of Burgundars, all decked out in polished armour and spotless cloaks, were lined up across the square. Beyond them, ordinary folk had come out to see the spectacle unfolding in the middle of their city.

In a makeshift pen nearby, a great brown bull snorted and kicked at the wooden boards that confined it. Just in front of the pen was the wide, flat stone Hagan had noted on his first arrival in the city. A long-handled axe rested against the side of the stone and a large, copper bowl sat on top of it.

'Hail, Brynhild,' Gunderic said. 'You are most welcome to our city.'

'I'm so glad to see you again,' Gunhild said, smiling at her old friend.

Brynhild looked at both of them and made a little bow of her head. She unlaced her helmet and took it off.

'I have come as I agreed to,' she said.

Wodnas stepped forward and raised the spear he used as a staff.

'Hail, Brynhild,' he said in a loud voice. 'Ruler of the ice realm. I too am glad you have come. You do the right thing. Uniting these two realms will make one almighty one.'

'Thank you, All Father,' Brynhild said with a wistful smile. 'If you approve of this then I am happy to go through with it. I submit my will to your wisdom. When you and your folk stayed with us in our realm, before you came here, you taught us the value of the old ways and the traditions we had lost.'

'Then you will be comfortable with our marriage ritual,' Gunderic said. 'It will be presided over by Wodnas and the Lady Freya and blessed by the Sword of Tiwass. Normally I would preside at a noble marriage but I cannot do that at my own wedding.'

'I know the Lady Freya well too,' Brynhild said, smiling warmly now as she nodded to the woman with the cat on her shoulder standing beside Wodnas.

Hagan noticed the blonde-haired woman who had stood beside Brynhild at the edge of the farther precipice rode beside her.

'So shall we get on with it?' Brynhild said.

'If you wish to prepare and don your wedding clothes we have hot water for you and your company,' Gunderic said.

Brynhild smirked. The women around her laughed.

'We have no desire to deck ourselves out to please the gazes of men,' Brynhild said.

'There is no shame in having some pride in your appearance,' Gunhild said. 'We have dresses and robes as well if you wish to borrow them.'

'We are in our finery already,' Brynhild said. 'Our war gear is our proudest attire. I shall prepare my hair though.'

Brynhild dismounted, as did all her Valkyrjur. The blonde-haired woman took off her helmet and Hagan saw the black paint around her eyes was smeared and streaked down her cheeks as if she had been crying.

'Greta will be my wedding maid,' Brynhild said.

'I thought I could be your wedding maid,' Gunhild said. 'We are old friends.'

Brynhild just shook her head. Greta, the blonde woman, approached Brynhild and began to arrange her hair. She split her one braid into three then wound them around the top of Brynhild's head so they made an arrangement like a crown. When she was done, Greta smiled and kissed Brynhild on the cheek. Hagan spotted Gunhild casting a concerned look at her brother. Gunderic seemed unconcerned or oblivious.

Brynhild turned to address her troop of horse warriors.

'I do this because I swore an oath that I would marry the man who met the challenge of courage I set,' she said in a loud voice. 'If I broke my word I would be nothing in your eyes and lose your respect. Why would you follow me if you cannot trust in my pledges?'

She paused.

'And I also do it because with the help of the Burgundar War Horde I can keep my people safe,' she then said. She lifted her head and spoke even louder. It was clear that this message was directed at the wider crowd in the square. 'The Alemanni and the Huns threaten us and mine is too small a realm to stand against them alone. Together we shall be stronger.'

She turned around once more.

'Let us get started,' she said.

'Very well,' Gunderic said. He signalled to some of his warriors who lifted up some ropes that lay on the paving slabs of the square. The bull in the pen stopped kicking and began to bellow with rage. Heaving like a tug of war team the warriors pulled on the rope. As they stepped backwards the bull's head, to which the rope was attached, was drawn out of the pen and over the large flat stone. Its protests became high-pitched and strangled as the noose tightened around the creature's neck.

Gunderic lifted the long-handled axe and Hagan realised just what the brown stains on the rock he had seen on his first arrival in Geneva actually were. The bull let out one more cry as Gunderic raised the axe above his head in both hands.

'I give you to Tiwass!' the king shouted.

Then he brought the axe down on the back of the bull's neck.

It was a mighty blow. The polished blade severed the bull's spine and almost decapitated it completely. Its bellowing stopped dead. The creature dropped to the ground as if all the bones in its legs had turned to water. Bright crimson blood welled up from the wound and gushed all over the stone below.

Wodnas stepped forward, manoeuvring the copper bowl to catch as much of the blood as possible as Gunderic, panting from the sudden exertion, set the axe down beside the stone again.

Wodnas lifted the copper bowl by its handle. It was now brimming with hot blood, its coppery smell mingling with that of the bowl itself.

'Come, Gunderic,' Brynhild said, a wistful smile on her lips. 'We shall be married.'

She held out her hand. Frowning, Gunderic took it, then he strode off, determined to be seen as the one leading the way across the square to the *Hov*, the building that had formerly been the church of Geneva but was now a pagan temple. Gunhild and Sigurd followed them, then Wodnas, Lokke, the lords of the Burgundar clans and Hagan and all the rest of the Royal Council. A contingent of the senior leaders of the Burgundar War Horde and Brynhild's Valkyrjur fell in behind. They all jammed into the building. Any remaining space was taken up by Burgundar nobles and other important folk.

The crowd of ordinary people pushed forward but Gunderic's warriors formed lines around the edges of the square to keep them from swarming around the Hov.

As they were entering a sacred space, all weapons had to be left outside. The warriors and nobles all set spears, swords and shields against the walls. Hagan noticed that Sigurd carried the sword Tyrfing as usual and wondered if perhaps as it was the sword of a god it was acceptable to bring it into the temple.

For a moment when he entered the former church Hagan thought he was stepping back into his childhood. His memories of the former, pre-Christian customs of his folk were dim, more like dreams than recollections. Now however, the smell of smouldering herbs that hung in the air and gloomy interior of the building, lit only by the flickering flames of torches, brought much of it rushing back.

The building, an old Roman basilica, retained its overall tall, narrow shape, but the interior no longer resembled a Christian church. At the far end, on the raised platform where the priest and choir once would have stood, there were now four very tall wooden statues carved from the trunks of trees. They were images of the Gods: Tiwass, Nerthus, Ingwass and Thunerass. The Sky, the Earth, the Folk and the Storm. They had snarling lips, gnashing teeth and almond-shaped eyes that glared down on the congregation in fierce domination. The walls were draped with long tapestries covered with embroidered scenes from myth and legend.

Before the Gods, a great round fire pit was sunk into the stone flags of the floor. In it blazed a fire that, Hagan recalled, was never supposed to go out. It symbolised the spirit of the Burgundar folk and it was the duty of all to keep it alight.

The alter still stood but all crosses and Roman writing had been chiselled off or painted over. There were runes carved into it now and painted. Its flat top had been sheeted over with iron. Instead of a chalice there was a great silver arm ring set on it, and a short tree branch which Hagan knew was from an ash tree, the tree from which all men were supposed to have been born.

Now he thought of it, the last time Hagan had been in a Hov was for a wedding too, when his aunt had been married. King Gundahar himself had presided over that ceremony. Hagan could not help noticing that the Hov had the same sort of atmosphere now as then: hushed but bubbling with an undercurrent of animated chatter, reverent of the sacred surroundings but excited about the occasion.

Freya, the one they called 'The Lady', entered through the main doors. She was dressed in a long blue hooded robe that sparkled as she walked. Hagan knew this was due to little shells and pieces of glass that were sewn into the material and caught the firelight as she moved. She had a long metal staff that looked like a distaff in one hand. Her cat trotted behind her. Behind her came eight of her hellrūnes in pairs, side by side, all dressed the same as her. They marched to the top of the Hov and fanned out into a semi-circle before the statues of the Gods, facing the congregation.

Wodnas followed the women, carrying the bowl of steaming blood before him. He set it on the altar and the women behind him began to chant in a loud, raucous manner that took Hagan by surprise with its volume. Their words echoed around the vaulted ceiling high above. Hagan felt the hairs on the back of his neck rise as he recognised the *Galdr* and the Ward-Lock from the days of his childhood, sacred prayers that called down the favours of the good spirits and held off those of the bad. Two of the women beat goatskin drums, enhancing the rhythm of the chanting.

Gunderic and Brynhild stood before the altar. Sigurd stood to the right of Gunderic and Greta stood on the left of Brynhild. Gunhild was behind all of them. Wodnas nodded to Sigurd, who unstrapped his sword and laid it on the iron top of the altar.

The women's chanting rose to a crescendo then ceased. In the silence that followed Wodnas began pronouncing the ancient words of the marriage ritual. Gunderic handed Brynhild a ring. After that Wodnas picked up the silver arm ring and passed it to them. Brynhild held one side while Gunderic held the other, and they swore oaths that they would be faithful to, care for and look out for each other until one of them was dead.

Wodnas then set the ash branch into the bowl of blood. He picked up the sword Tyrfing, still sheathed, turned around and held it aloft in his arms.

'Great Tiwass, fertile Ingwass and thundering Thunerass,' he cried to the watching statues. 'Accept the blood and spirit of the bull we have sacrificed to you and bless this union, not just of two people, but of two realms. Let them weather the coming storm and prosper as free peoples in the future.'

He turned around again and laid the sheathed sword first on the shoulder of Gunderic, then on the shoulder of Brynhild. Hagan remembered the sword was drawn at his aunt's wedding, but then also remembered the curse of Tyrfing that Sigurd had scornfully told him of. Wodnas and the others took this legend very seriously, it seemed.

The one-eyed man then set the sword back on the altar. He picked up the ash branch and flicked it at the bride and groom, sending a shower of bull's blood over them to speckle their faces and clothes.

'Blessings on you,' Wodnas said. 'Brynhild, you are now the wife of Gunderic. Gunderic, you have entered the house-bond: it is now your duty to serve the needs of your wife.'

Cheers erupted from those watching, though mostly from the Burgundars and not Brynhild's Valkyrjur. However Hagan did spot the ghost of a wistful smile cross Brynhild's lips.

The newly married couple turned. Hand in hand they walked back down the aisle of the Hov, the crowd of onlookers parting to let them through. Wodnas walked behind them, the bowl of blood in one hand, the ash branch in the other. As they walked to the door he flicked showers of blood on the onlookers, conferring the good luck of the blessed blood on all it fell upon.

Hagan and the others followed them. The cheers of the onlookers echoed around the building.

'It seems our folk are pleased with this union,' Gunderic said to Brynhild. He was grinning broadly. 'If you think this is loud, wait until you hear the people outside.'

He pushed open the doors. To everyone's surprise they were not met with a wall of cheering from outside. In fact there was just silence, a silence which washed into the former church and caused the cheers of those inside to die in their throats.

There was a horseman sitting mounted in the middle of the city square, beside the blood-splattered sacrificial stone. He wore the uniform of a Roman Army messenger.

CHAPTER FORTY-FIVE

THE ROMAN WAS mounted on a white horse. He seemed impervious to the silent hostility with which hundreds glared at him from behind the lines of warriors who kept them back. Likewise he paid no heed to the nine Raven Warriors who stood around him, spears levelled and ready to skewer him at his first wrong move.

The crowd from the Hov crossed the square to meet him. As they approached, the rider was prompted to dismount with a few prods from the spears around him.

'We intercepted him riding over the border, lord,' the lead raven warrior said. As usual he spoke to Wodnas. 'He says he has a message for the king. We thought we should bring him here as you asked us to be on particular alert for Romans.'

Wodnas nodded.

'This is our king, dog,' the raven warrior said to the Roman. 'Show some respect.'

'He won't understand you,' Hagan said.

'I know your tongue,' the Roman said. 'That's why I was sent here. I am an emissary from General Flavius Aetius, Magister Militum of the Western Roman Empire. I am here at his behest. I wish to speak to King Gunderic.'

'I am Gunderic,' the king said.

The emissary removed his helmet and raised his right arm in salute. He also bowed his head, which Hagan saw pleased Gunderic.

'You have courage to ride alone into our kingdom,' Gunderic said. 'Outsiders are not welcome here. Especially Roman outsiders.'

'You wouldn't dare kill a Roman emissary,' the Roman said with a barely concealed smirk. 'Even the wildest of barbarians know that to do that will bring a storm of retribution down on themselves.'

'We founded this kingdom by killing a bishop, a Roman official, and a commander with his two turma of cavalry,' Gunderic said. 'An emissary will be just one more dead Roman to us.'

Now it was the turn of the Burgundars to smirk. The emissary tried to smile, but Hagan could see his arrogant confidence had been dented a little.

'King Gunderic,' the emissary said. 'General Aetius demands your answer.'

'What is this, Gunderic?' Brynhild said, frowning. 'What is he talking about.'

'My answer to what?' Gunderic said.

Hagan felt his guts lurch, knowing what would come next. That bastard Aetius could not have waited until he or Zerco could have sent a response more discreetly. The general had had to push the issue. Now, with this happening so openly, he would look like a mere lackey of the Romans.

'The general sent messengers here weeks ago,' the emissary said. 'They were to request you join the military alliance against Attila the Hun, the Scourge of God.'

'What is this man talking about?' Brynhild said again.

Gunderic glanced towards Hagan and Zerco.

'We got Aetius's message,' he said, ignoring Brynhild's protests.

'So will you join the Alliance against Attila?' the emissary said.

'*Our* alliance was to fight off the Alemanni!' Brynhild said.

'And *then* defend ourselves against the Huns. Not to join the Romans.'

Gunderic tutted and shook his head.

'We shall speak more on this later,' he said, his voice tetchy.

'Lady Brynhild,' Wodnas said in a more placatory tone. 'Attila is rampaging through the world, burning towns, cities and villages. He is killing men, women and children who stand against him and enslaving those who surrender. The Alemanni have joined his cause. By fighting him we will also fight them.'

'But if we march off with the Romans we will leave our own realm unprotected,' Brynhild said. There was a note of panic in her voice.

'The Alemanni will not attack now,' Wodnas said, turning to the emissary who nodded. 'Tell her.'

'He is right. The Alemanni War Horde is with Attila,' the Roman said. 'As are the Ostrogoths and Gepids. General Aetius has Visigoths, Saxons and Franks and now he hopes you Burgundars as well. An unlikely alliance, I grant you, and we can all only pray it holds together long enough to fight Attila. All the world is gathering outside Aurelianum. The battle will be immense. The Churchmen are saying this could be Armageddon, the battle that will end the world.'

'But you said—' Brynhild began to speak.

'Things change,' Wodnas said, cutting her off.

Brynhild looked around her. Her eyes were wide and her face pale. Hagan felt a stab of pity in his heart for his old friend. She had agreed to join Gunderic because of the threat of the Alemanni to her people and now that threat seemed to be gone. She must be wondering just how big a mistake she may have made, or if she had been lied to. His pity was overshadowed by a wave of guilt that he had had a part in deceiving her as well.

'We accept General Aetius's proposal,' Gunderic said. 'We will join the Alliance against Attila.'

'No!' Brynhild said.

'Brynhild, you are now my queen,' Gunderic said, heaving a sigh. 'But you are also now my wife. There are hard decisions to be made and now I must make them for both of us.'

'You make a wise choice, King Gunderic,' the Roman said, a smile creeping across his face. 'If your answer had been no, then Aetius's first action was to march the legions into your kingdom. He cannot leave a potential enemy at his flank.'

'He would lose many men if he did that,' Gunderic said.

'Perhaps,' the Roman said. 'Your warriors look capable enough. But Aetius marches with the entire interior army. Your little kingdom would have been annihilated. Happily that will not now be the case. I will ride back and tell the general you are with us. Attila is heading for Aurelianum. If he takes it all Gaul will be lost. Then...'

The Roman shrugged. 'Expect more messengers with your marching orders.'

He saluted Gunderic once more. Gunderic nodded to the Raven Warriors who stood back while the emissary swung himself up into the saddle then rode off, the hooves of his horse clicking over the paving slabs of the square.

Brynhild glared at Gunderic, who raised his hands in a conciliatory gesture.

'You heard what he said, Brynhild. If we don't join this alliance we will be wiped out.'

'A glorious death would be better than the shame of joining with Rome,' Brynhild said through clenched teeth.

'A corpse on the pyre is useful to no one,' Wodnas said. 'This way you get revenge on the Huns, who decimated your old kingdom and mine. Attila must die.'

Brynhild's eyes flashed but she did not say anything more. The words of the one-eyed man were enough to silence her for a moment.

'Come, this is our wedding day,' Gunderic said, spreading his hands wide and smiling. 'There are hard times coming but today is a day for celebration. Let us feast!'

They set off for the great feasting hall. Hagan could see Brynhild was brooding like a thundercloud on the horizon. There would be feasting to come but there would also, he had no doubt, be a storm.

CHAPTER FORTY-SIX

THE FEASTING HALL was ready for the wedding feast. The floors had been swept, the tiled parts washed and scrubbed and the rest strewn with fresh straw. The walls and pillars were decked with flowers and early spring greenery from the woods.

Three very long tables ran parallel up the hall floor alongside the fire pits. Benches flanked the tables and they were already crammed with many men and women. At the end of the hall another table was set with chairs behind it facing the entrance. This table was where the most important people would sit.

The air was filled with the aroma of roasting meat, the tang of ale and the babble of joyous conversation. The remaining spaces at the long tables were quickly filled by Brynhild's Valkyrjur and King Gunderic's warrior company. Gunderic sat in the high seat at the centre of the top table with his new queen Brynhild on his left. Sigurd and Gunhild sat beside her and Wodnas, the Burgundar lords, Lady Freya and Lokke took the next seats. The rest of the seats were taken up by nobles Hagan had not yet met.

When everyone was seated, two slaves approached. One of them set a huge bull's horn rimmed with silver and supported on curled iron feet in front of the king and queen. The second laid a large wooden ladle before the queen then stepped back. For a moment all at the table looked on with expectant smiles. When after several moments had passed and Brynhild had still not lifted the ladle, Gunderic gave a little cough and turned to her.

'Perhaps you have forgotten, my queen,' he said. 'But it is customary for our folk that a newlywed husband is served his first ale by his bride.'

Brynhild tossed back her head and laughed.

'I may now be your wife, Gunderic,' she said. 'But I'm not your slave. I've no doubt you have plenty of servants who can get you a drink.'

There were a few gasps from around the table. Gunderic's face flushed a deep red but he motioned to the slaves who took the horn and ladle away to the entrance of the hall where great vats of frothing ale stood. One slave dipped the heavy wooden ladle into the vat and filled the horn with foaming amber liquid. Then they brought it back to Gunderic.

As soon as he was served, slaves began moving around the hall delivering filled drinking horns to the guests at the tables. Wodnas sat a few places from Hagan, and Hagan saw him wave the slaves away when they approached with a frothing ale horn for him.

'You know I only drink wine,' the old man said in stern remonstrance. The slaves hurried away to get him some.

When all had a drink in their hands, Gunderic rose to his feet. As he did so the conversation that bubbled around the hall died away and an expectant hush descended. Hagan felt a nostalgic glow of recollection. It was almost like being back in the hall of Gunderic's father at Vorbetomagus, all those years ago. He knew that what would come next was the tradition of toasting.

Gunderic held up both hands.

'Friends, old and new,' he said, voice raised so it boomed around the interior of the hall. 'Kin folk and our new allies from the icy realm in the mountains. We are here to celebrate my marriage to Brynhild and the union of our two peoples. Together we shall be a mighty force, far stronger together than either was apart.'

Cheers erupted around the hall. Hagan could tell Gunderic

385

was using all his political craft to bring people along with him but it was not quite working. Looking around, he saw a few people, mostly Brynhild's, shaking their heads.

'Yes, there are dark days ahead,' Gunderic continued. 'Most of us are uncomfortable with the people we will fight alongside, but just as our two peoples are stronger together, the Romans cannot fight off the Huns without our help, just as even together we are not big enough to fight the Huns alone. Yes, a glorious death that will live forever in the sagas is something to be admired...'

He glanced at Brynhild.

'But as Wodnas says, *a corpse is no use to anyone*. Why choose death when there is a way we can fight the hideous people who brought shame and degradation on our folk and win? We can face them and we can defeat them. We will gain glory. We will rain down vengeance on them and folk will sing of our glory for generations to come!'

This time the cheers that echoed around the rafters of the hall were louder as more folk joined in. Brynhild still wore a sour expression but many of her people who had previously been sceptical now grinned and cheered with the others.

'Now let us commence the feast with the holy pledges,' Gunderic said as the cheers abated. A revere silence fell. 'To Tiwass! Grant us victory in war!'

He raised the great horn above his head then put it to his lips and took a long, deep draught. Hagan watched his throat work as he swallowed gulp after gulp. He was impressed by just how much Gunderic was quaffing and began to wonder if he would ever take a breath. It seemed Gunderic was keen to set an example for everyone else. At last he lowered the horn, cuffed the froth from his mouth with the back of his right hand and let out an explosive sigh of satisfaction.

The rest of the guests then raised their horns to those seated around them and echoed the toast. 'To Tiwass!' all roared in an enthusiastic babble.

As the cries and belches echoed around the rafters, Gunderic handed the horn to Brynhild. This move was a surprise, including – as was obvious from the expression on her face – to Brynhild.

'As queen, will you propose the next toast?' Gunderic said.

A great hush descended on the feasters. Brynhild looked around her. Seeing all the expectant eyes gazing at her from around the hall she slowly stood up. She stood in silence for a moment, collecting her thoughts. Then she began to speak.

'Our customs tell us that when we are born, three powerful spirit women, the Dísir, visit our cribs,' she said. 'Some wish us good. Some are evil. They give us gifts – courage, humour, fears – which will either help or hinder us in our lives. All we can do is make the best of what we are given. And all our fates are determined by the *Nornir*, the Three Holy Women. Giants of great power who sit by a well at the roots of the world, somewhere northwards and netherwards. They weave a great tapestry that depicts the lives of everyone. Because they are weaving it, no one knows what the threads will tell in the future. We do not know why the Nornir have brought us together, and we can only hope it is for the best. So my toast is to the Dísir, the Nornir and all the women who guide our Fates.'

She drank a deep draught from the horn then handed it back to Gunderic.

'The Dísir,' – the toast was echoed all around the hall.

Gunderic's face grew serious, as did the expressions of everyone in the hall. A reverent silence then settled on the feasters as Gunderic raised his horn a final time.

'In remembrance of those who have passed. The glorious dead,' he said.

His voice was raised but his tone respectful in contrast to the raucous roars that had preceded. All those in the hall drank a reverent toast in memory of the worthy departed. Of all the toasts drunk, the hard glassy looks they exchanged and the set of their faces showed the memory of their slaughtered kinsfolk at Vorbetomagus was still raw.

After a suitable pause, a slave hurried to Gunderic and refilled the great bull's horn from a jug. The king spoke once again.

'Now it is time for the Bragging Cup. Does anyone wish to make an oath before me and this gathered company?'

'I do, High One,' a young lord said, raising his hand.

Hagan settled down into his seat as a series of young Burgundar warriors and nobles each took turns to boast how they would perform great deeds in the coming war and gain bloody revenge on the Huns. Each brag was accompanied by more cheers and quaffing. They were all very serious, but after the sixth or seventh claim one tedious boast merged with the next. Hagan also found himself getting quite drunk.

After the bragging cups were drunk it was finally time to eat. The wedding guests feasted on game, fruits, vegetables and bread, all accompanied by yet more beer and wine.

As the evening wore on the noise of voices, raised in volume by drink, became overwhelming. At times Hagan had to shout just for those around him to hear what he said, which of course just added to the cacophony.

Music and dancing followed then as children were ushered away to bed and the formal arrangements of the hall dissolved into multiple groups formed around tables based on friendships or allegiances rather than where they had been placed. The drink continued to flow, and the laughter and occasional shouting got ever louder.

Through a pleasant fog of ale, Hagan looked around him and realised a lot of the others at the top table had now left it. Brynhild was sitting at one of the long tables, surrounded by her Valkyrjur warriors. They were drinking, laughing and singing songs of their own. Brynhild was right in the centre of everything, leading the choruses of her warriors. It was clear they adored her. She had her arm crooked around the necks of whichever ones happened to be sitting beside her. The more demure Burgundar women looked on with disapproval but many of the young Burgundar warriors were gathering around, eager to join in. Freya was there too.

'You should be careful, Gunderic,' Lokke said, a faint smile on his lips. 'Or folk might mistake just who is the king here.'

The king and his council remained at the high table, though they were barely able to make themselves heard above the raucous shouting, singing and laughter. As the party around Brynhild got ever louder, the king became ever more brooding and the conversation became strained. Hagan watched Brynhild's group with envy. They looked like they were having a lot more fun than those around him at the top table but loyalty to Gunderic and Gunhild, and the disapproval with which a move to the other group would bring, kept him in his seat.

Gunderic tutted and took a drink from his horn. His face was flushed and like most other folk he was now very drunk.

'For one born into so noble a family as she was,' Gunhild said with a sniff, 'she certainly has the common touch. Our old friend has changed quite a lot in the last fifteen years.'

'It seems the morals in her realm are more relaxed than they are here,' Brenwic said.

'They are warriors,' Wodnas said with a shrug, 'If your warriors were here alone, Gunderic, without the social restraint of having women present, they would not behave much different.'

'But Brynhild's warriors *are* all women,' Gunhild said. 'I don't think that is an excuse to forget how a noblewoman should act.'

Some of the Valkyrjur produced musical instruments: a bagpipe, a flute and a drum, and began to play lively tunes. Soon they and the Burgundars around them were chanting and singing and stomping their feet.

'She has been living among rough, wild women in the mountains,' Gunderic said, his expression becoming a little more philosophical. 'I suppose it is to be expected. To lead them she must be as tough as them.'

Brynhild was now on her feet, downing a horn of ale in a drinking competition with one of the young Burgundar warriors. Gunderic's knuckles were white as he clutched his own horn of ale.

Brynhild finished the horn of ale moments before the warrior. He shrugged in good-natured acceptance of his defeat. Then they embraced. Brynhild's warriors cheered.

'You might need to control your wife, King Gunderic,' Sigurd said. 'Remind her who is king.'

'Is that what you did with my sister, Sigurd?' Gunderic said through clenched teeth.

'Brynhild was raped by the Huns,' Hagan said. He had thought long and hard about whether he should reveal this, but the way the conversation was going he decided that it was now justified. 'They stabbed her and left her for dead on the riverbank outside Vorbetomagus. I found her there but thought she then died. I left her there…'

Hagan coughed. He felt his eyes stinging with tears. He clamped his jaw shut to stifle a sob that threatened to come out and betray his lack of manliness to everyone around him. He stared at the table and shook his head. He had not realised he was so drunk.

When he looked up again he saw looks of consternation on the faces of the others around him.

'So she is not a virgin, then,' Sigurd said, looking sideways at Gunderic.

'I was married and widowed before we were wed,' Gunhild said to her husband.

'Married to a *king*,' Sigurd said, raising one eyebrow.

Brynhild climbed up onto the long table and, hand in hand with the blonde-haired Greta, began dancing a jig.

'I think perhaps it's time you took your new wife to bed,' Lokke said, the smile still on his lips.

'I think you're right,' Gunderic said.

He stood up, swaying a little, then strode down the hall to where Brynhild and the others were. The rest of those at the top table exchanged glances. Due to the racket in the hall they could not hear what words were exchanged but from the anger on Gunderic's face and the scorn on Brynhild's they did not look pleasant. Then Gunderic grabbed Brynhild's wrist and led her towards the doors. All the warriors at the table – Brynhild's included – erupted in a lecherous cheer at the sight. Halfway to the door Brynhild shook off Gunderic's grasp but she still followed him out of the hall.

In their wake the loud carousing continued.

Not long afterwards, Gunhild announced she was going to bed. Most of the noble ladies and the more refined men were doing the same, leaving the hall to the noisy drinking and singing of the warriors.

Sigurd said he would stay on for more ale, then he, Lokke and the others drifted off towards the other tables where it looked like the party was continuing.

Hagan sat at the top table alone, which suited him fine. He had never been comfortable on social occasions like this. His conversation often let him down and if he did not know someone well he often descended into an awkward silence that was usually only ended by the other person walking away. As he watched the drunken revellers shouting like fools and clinging onto each other to stop themselves falling over he was more than content to stay away from it.

Despite being once more at the heart of a Burgundar kingdom, something he had thought would never happen again, Hagan felt the old lonely ache steal into his heart. Now he was actually among Burgundars once again he was struck by how little fellow feeling he had for them, how lacking he was in any desire to go down and join the others.

He took another drink, wondering if perhaps the longing that had dogged him throughout his years wandering the world had not just been false nostalgia, for a time and place that he had actually spent most of his time trying to get away from.

'So now there is just we two outcasts.'

A voice made him turn around and he saw Zerco had come up to the top table. Hagan, unnerved, consoled himself that it was probably because he had drunk so much wine that the little man had been able to sneak up on him. Though Zerco did seem to have an uncanny ability to move around without being noticed.

'What do you mean?' Hagan said. 'Outcasts?'

'Everyone else seems to be enjoying themselves,' Zerco said, reaching for a goblet and filling it with wine. 'Or are already off in bed with their wives or husbands.'

'Speak for yourself,' Hagan said.

Hagan sat back. His eyes felt heavy and the ale and wine were taking their toll. His fingers went to his throat and he began his absent-minded habit of fiddling with his mother's amulet.

'Well I suppose at least we've learned one thing,' he said. 'The treasure hoard is kept somewhere near Geneva.'

'I've always meant to ask you,' Zerco said. 'For someone who hates the Huns so much, why do you wear that amulet?'

'What do you mean?' Hagan said.

'The artwork on it,' Zerco said. 'It's Hunnish. That style of engraving a horse is the way their craftsmen work. The real giveaway is the bird, though.'

'How so?' Hagan said, frowning.

'It's a *Turul*,' Zerco said. 'A mythical bird of prey. The Huns believe their War God flies over battlefields in the shape of one, watching the deeds of the bravest warriors below. You'll see that soon enough: Attila has one on his personal war banner.'

Hagan shook his head. Why did his mother have the amulet of a Hun? Did that mean his real father was a Hun? One of the loathsome folk he had spent the last fifteen years hating? Did that mean he was half Hun himself?

His head spun, and it was not just from effects of the ale. He stood up, swaying a little.

'I'm going to bed,' he said.

'Suit yourself,' Zerco said. 'But it looks like this is turning into quite a party.'

Hagan staggered off down the hall towards the door. Out of the hall the night air hit him making him feel even more dizzy. Across the deserted square the sound of shouting reached his ears. He stopped for a moment then, dismissing it as probably some stupid drunken argument, he stumbled on, off to bed.

CHAPTER FORTY-SEVEN

FROM HIS VANTAGE point on the dais, Zerco immediately spotted Geic entering the hall. Even at a distance Zerco could see the concerned look on the bodyguard's face.

Geic stood for a moment looking around the hall, checking the faces of the revellers. Then clearly not finding who he was looking for, he approached the top table. His expression of disappointment and concern increased when he saw only Zerco.

Zerco set his goblet down and leaned forward.

'Is something wrong?' he said.

The bodyguard pursed his lips and glanced around again.

'It's alright,' Zerco prompted him. 'You can tell me. I am the right-hand man of the Hunt Master and leader of the Dagelungs, after all.'

'No,' Geic said. His expression suggested he was both surprised and alarmed that someone who looked like Zerco could speak at all, never mind use the Burgundar tongue. 'I need someone from the king's inner council. Have they all gone?'

'All except Sigurd,' Zerco said, gesturing down the hall to where the big man was in deep conversation with a particularly pretty member of the Valkyrjur. She was smiling at Sigurd and he at her in a way that Zerco guessed Gunhild would far from approve of.

Geic nodded and went off in their direction.

Now here is something I should perhaps pay attention to, Zerco thought to himself. The bodyguard was worried and if it involved him it most probably involved the king. Perhaps there was something he could learn that would be to his advantage in the future.

Zerco slid off his seat and followed Geic from a discreet distance. As he was little more than half the height of everyone else, he did not have to do much to stay out of sight as he weaved his way around the legs of the drunken revellers.

When Geic reached Sigurd he stopped.

'Come with me, will you?' Zerco heard him say. 'There's a problem. Gunderic needs our help.'

'What with?' Sigurd said. 'It's his wedding night. We can't help him with that.'

The woman warrior laughed.

'It's... sensitive, Lord Sigurd,' Geic said, looking around to see if anyone might overhear him. He did not spot Zerco lurking a few paces away. 'I think we need to keep this among the king's council if possible.'

He tugged Sigurd's sleeve to move him away from the woman.

'Get your hands off me,' Sigurd said, scowling as he snatched his arm away. 'Don't you see I have something going here?'

'Please, lord,' Geic said. 'It's terrible. The king is in trouble. I need your help.'

Sigurd turned down the corners of his mouth. He turned back to the woman and shrugged.

'I have to go,' he said.

'Don't you have a right to enjoy yourself like everyone else?' the woman said, in mock sympathy.

'What can I say? My king needs me to help him out. Again,' Sigurd said with a wink. 'When you're as important as I am, there's no time off. I'll be back when this is sorted out. Stay right here.'

Sigurd then followed Geic out of the hall. Zerco waited until they had left then trotted after them to the door. Going out, he saw they were already halfway across the square, heading for the former Roman palace that now served as the personal residence of the king. They went up the marble steps, passed the columns that flanked the entrance and into the atrium of the building.

Apart from a few patrolling warriors the square was empty and lit by torches and braziers. If either Sigurd or Geic turned around they could not fail to see him, so Zerco let them go inside. Then he sped across after them.

They had not closed the door behind them properly and it now stood ajar. Zerco could hear raised voices from inside. For a moment he lurked outside, his ear cocked to the gap.

'Upstairs,' he heard the bodyguard say.

A loud crash came from the next storey of the building. Then came the sound of shouting. A man and a woman were arguing. Then there was a smash of shattering pottery. This was followed by the sound of feet pounding on steps.

Guessing this meant Sigurd and Geic had gone upstairs, Zerco pushed the door open a little further then slipped into the gap. The atrium had a cracked marble floor. It had once been very grand but without the skills of Roman masons to maintain it the room, like the rest of the stone buildings in the town, was starting to fall into disrepair.

A white stone staircase swept up to the next floor from the atrium and Sigurd and Geic were at the top of it. Also standing there were two female slaves, but the angry voices were not coming from them. They were coming from behind a closed door the girls lurked outside. Zerco could make out that one of the voices was Gunderic's. The words he spoke were muffled by the door but he sounded enraged. There was something else to it too: was it fear?

Gambling that everyone would be too busy to notice him, Zerco tiptoed up the stairs after them. At the top was a landing that led to the door which the others were now gathered around.

Zerco spotted a dark corner under a table to the left and slid himself into it. From there he would be able to watch everything that went on.

To Zerco's surprise, and in contrast to the look of trepidation on the face of Geic, both the slave girls were tittering with laughter. When they saw the bodyguard glaring at them, however, their expressions changed to the fearful looks of children caught being naughty.

Then the sound of Brynhild's laughter came from behind the door. Zerco would not have said it was gleeful, more mocking. Then came another crash of breaking pottery. Geic flinched.

'You two can go,' he said to the slave girls. 'Do not say a word about this to anyone. Understand?'

The girls nodded, then hurried away down the stairs, heads down, doing their best not to laugh. When they had gone Geic turned to Sigurd, a distraught expression on his face.

'They'll be gossiping this all over the slave quarters,' he said. 'It will be the talk of Geneva by the morning.'

'What's going on?' Sigurd said.

Geic cocked his head towards the closed door.

'It started just after they came in,' he said.

'Is that the bedroom?' Sigurd said.

'Yes,' Geic replied.

Sigurd tried the handle. It was locked.

'Let me go!' they heard Gunderic shout from inside.

Sigurd pounded the door with his fist.

'Brynhild! Gunderic!' he shouted. 'It's Sigurd. What's going on? Let me in.'

The only response was another smash from inside.

The big man stepped back and launched his boot into the door. With a crack of splintering wood he smashed it open.

For a moment there was a stunned silence.

The bedroom beyond was a mess. The sheets were pulled off the bed, torn and scattered around the room. The shattered remnants of at least two wine jugs littered the floor and their contents formed pools that looked like blood.

Gunderic was hanging from a cloak hook on one wall. His wrists and ankles were bound behind him by torn sheets which were also tied together so his feet nearly touched his hands. His jerkin was pulled over the hook so he dangled from it. His nose was bloody, there was a cut on his forehead and his right eye was bruised and swelling. There was blood on his teeth. He was struggling to get free, each movement making him swing back and forth more violently.

Brynhild stood a little way away. She had a drinking horn in her left hand and an orange in the other. Judging by the other pieces of fruit lying on the floor under Gunderic she had been throwing them at him like he was a target hanging from a tree.

'Lord, I am sorry!' Geic said gaping, open-mouthed at the scene. 'I was unsure what to do. I thought perhaps you were chastising your wife, not...'

'Get me down!' Gunderic squealed. He sounded on the verge of hysteria.

Sigurd turned to Geic.

'I think you should go too,' Sigurd said. 'I will handle this from here on.'

The bodyguard, his face ashen, hesitated for a moment, then nodded and staggered off down the stairs. He looked relieved at not having to stay.

'Help me,' Gunderic said, seeing Sigurd at the door.

The big man went into the room.

'He said he wanted to have some fun,' Brynhild said in a mocking voice. Her words were slurred and she swayed back and forth, leaning to one side. 'So I am having fun.'

'She's mad!' Gunderic said. 'I thought she was just drunk but she's out of her mind.'

'He tried to force himself on me!' Brynhild shrieked. Her composure had switched in an instant from mocking humour to rage. Her eyes narrowed and her white teeth flashed as she hurled the orange at Gunderic. Unable to get out of the way, all he could do was close his eyes tight as the fruit bounced off his head.

Brynhild raised her right arm. It swayed up and down as she tried to level it at the hanging king.

'He put his filthy, lecherous hands on my body,' she said. 'I said I did not want to but he wouldn't stop.'

'I was demanding what is my right as your husband,' Gunderic said. 'It is our wedding night. I have a right to expect my wife to lie with me.'

'That would be hard to do from up there, King Gunderic,' Sigurd said. There was a noticeable smirk on his lips.

Zerco, under the table, did his best not to laugh and give himself away.

'She put me up here!' Gunderic said.

'And you let her?' Sigurd said. He folded his arms.

'Of course not,' Gunderic said. 'She attacked me. A lucky punch. I was dazed. When I came around again I was tied up and hanging from this hook.'

Brynhild put her hands on her hips, threw back her head and laughed.

'The mighty King Gunderic,' she sneered, swaying back and forth. 'Yet his wife knocked him out and trussed him up like a prize chicken. It wasn't one lucky punch, Sigurd. You think his face got that way from one little slap?'

Her face fell into an expression of drunken confusion.

'And yet he had the courage and skill to beat the challenge I set,' she said. 'It's almost like he's a different man now.'

Sigurd and Gunderic exchanged glances.

Sigurd then sighed and shook his head.

'Look, I can't stay here all night trying to help you two sort out your problems,' he said, reaching up to start untying Gunderic. 'I have better things to do back in the feasting hall.'

'No!' Brynhild snarled. She staggered towards Sigurd and began trying to pull the big man's arms away from their task.

'Leave him there. If he gets down he will only start pawing at me again.'

Sigurd, a look of annoyance on his face, shoved Brynhild away. She went stumbling backwards as he returned to his task. The torn sheets came away, freeing Gunderic's arms and legs. There was a tearing sound as the king's jerkin finally gave way and he fell to the floor from the cloak hook, landing on his backside on the floor.

With an inarticulate scream of rage Brynhild staggered forwards, both hands outstretched, fingers hooked like claws. Gunderic let out a little cry of fear and crouched behind the bulk of Sigurd's body.

'You are my champion,' Gunderic shouted. 'Don't let her near me. She'll kill me.'

'I *will* kill you,' Brynhild said, trying to push past Sigurd to get at him.

'Do something, Sigurd,' Gunderic said. His voice high-pitched with new panic.

'You want me to protect you from your wife?' Sigurd said. His voice held as much scorn as Brynhild's and his expression had changed from drunken bemusement to irritation.

'I want you to protect your king!' Gunderic said.

'Very well,' Sigurd said.

He turned and in a swift movement smashed his large right fist into Brynhild's jaw. The blow was a heavy one, enough to make Zerco, watching, wince. Brynhild went flying backwards through the air. She landed in a crumpled heap on the floor beside the bed. She did not move.

'Some people should never be allowed to drink ale,' Sigurd said, looking down at the now unconscious woman. 'That, Lord King, is how to deal with your wife if she gets out of hand.'

'Yes, well,' Gunderic said, struggling to his feet. 'I would never have hit a woman like that. That is how the mad bitch got the better of me.'

He gave Sigurd a sheepish glance.

'You won't... tell anyone about this, will you?' Gunderic said.

Sigurd did not reply for a moment. Then, just as the king was starting to look worried, he spoke.

'It will be our secret, Lord King,' he said. 'That is another thing you owe me. And I will expect recompense. Though there are a few others – your steward and two slave girls – who saw what happened. Right now I am going back to the hall. There is someone waiting for me there. Your wife should give you no more trouble. You can do what you want with her now.'

The big man turned and strode out of the room. Zerco pressed himself as far into the shadows beneath the table as possible as Sigurd walked past and headed down the stairs. When he judged it was safe to look out again he saw that the door to the bedroom was still open. Gunderic had dragged the unconscious Brynhild to the top of the bed. He had hauled her arms above her head and tied them to the bed frame with the same torn sheets she had used to bind him.

Now he stood above her, unlacing his britches.

'Now I will teach you who is king,' Gunderic said.

He kicked the door shut with his heel.

CHAPTER FORTY-EIGHT

HAGAN WOKE EARLY the next day. He did not have much choice thanks to the racket going on outside.

Hagan rolled out of bed and went to the window. He swung open the shutters, wincing as the early spring sunshine battered his eyes; he had a great view right across the square to the great feasting hall opposite. It was filled with people already.

The Burgundar War Horde was gathering in preparation to march north. Hundreds of men with shoulder bags, blanket rolls, cloaks and felt hats – the gear of an army going on campaign – mingled and chatted. The noise was considerable.

There were ordinary folk gathering around the square to wave the warriors goodbye.

Hagan knew he needed to get his own gear together and meet the rest if he did not want to be left behind.

As he started to gather his belongings he wondered for the first time since arriving if perhaps being left behind might not be a bad thing. He could slip away before anyone noticed. His old friends were not who they once were. He had no doubt Gunderic was ruthless, and given Hagan now knew a few things that the king would prefer were not widely known, it was a dangerous position for him to be in.

Gunhild was wrapped up in her life with Sigurd and Sigurd hated Hagan. Brynhild's spirit seemed to have been twisted by what happened to her at Vorbetomagus. Wodnas, Lokke and the other strangers were unnerving. The Burgundar folk themselves he had so long ached to be among were similarly different, like strange reflections of the folk he had grown up among.

Then again, he had no one else. Changed though they were, the company of his old friends was comforting in comparison to those years of aching loneliness he had spent wandering. And there was still much he might learn by staying with the Burgundars.

He thought again about Zerco's comment that his mother's amulet was Hunnish. With Gunderic's war horde he would once again face the Huns. Had it been a Hun who raped his mother? How could that be, though? And would it not mean... Then all was lost as a surge of anger poured into his heart. Revenge on the Huns would be most sweet and he did not want to miss that.

He pulled on his jerkin and breeches then stuffed his few clothes and belongings into his leather travelling bag.

Gunderic had supplied him with new war gear: mail, a helmet and a new shield. His mail shirt hissed into his saddle-bag along with his other gear. Then he donned the new black cloak with the emblem of the bear embroidered on the shoulder, slung his shield over his back, lifted his spear and, struggling under the weight of everything, staggered down the stairs and out into the square beyond.

Gunderic, Sigurd, Gunhild and Lokke were preparing horses outside the great feasting hall. Most of the rest of the king's council were there too. The previous late and drunken night had resulted in a lot of grey faces and red-rimmed eyes.

'Never again, eh?' Hagan said with a weary smile. 'Is everyone as hungover as I am? This isn't the best start to the campaign is it?'

His jaded smile faded on his lips. The strained atmosphere showed there was more than hangovers to worry about.

Gunderic looked worse than everyone else. His face was

flushed, there was a bruise on his left cheekbone and his nose looked swollen.

'What's going on?' Hagan said, becoming serious.

'A dreadful thing has happened, Hagan,' Gunhild said.

'Last night,' Gunderic said. 'I was attacked in my bed.'

Hagan looked around, aware then that Brynhild was not there.

'The queen,' Hagan said. 'Is she—'

'She is alright now, thanks be to Tiwass,' Gunderic cut him off. 'But she was knocked out during the incident. She is also quite shaken by the ordeal so will be travelling by covered wagon, like the other noblewomen.'

Hagan frowned. The thought of Brynhild being upset or even just sitting placid in the back of a wagon instead of leading her warriors into war – however reluctantly – did not seem right.

'What happened?' Hagan said.

'Treachery!' Gunderic said through clenched teeth. His eyes flashed with anger. 'My own bodyguard, Geic, tried to kill me and the new queen while we slept last night. He bribed two of my slave girls to let him into the house and attacked us in bed. It was lucky I woke up or he'd have killed us both.'

'What?' Hagan said. 'Why would he do such a thing?'

'Who can understand the mind of a traitor?' Gunderic said, anger blazing in his eyes. 'Perhaps he hated the idea of fighting alongside the Romans. Or he wanted our treasure. Personally I suspect he was perhaps in the pay of the Huns. I woke up and managed to fight him off. Thanks to the Gods, Sigurd happened to be passing by outside and heard the commotion. He ran in and between us we put an end to their little scheme.'

'Where are they?' Hagan said.

'They're dead,' Gunderic said. 'We had no choice. Geic had a sword and refused to surrender.'

'And the slave girls?' Hagan said, frowning.

'They were caught up in the fighting,' Gunderic said. 'They were killed too.'

Hagan looked at Sigurd, who smiled.

'I thank Tiwass that I was able to get to them in time to help,' the big man said. 'Otherwise we would have lost both our king and queen.'

'And you would now be king,' Hagan said.

Both Sigurd and Gunderic glared at Hagan.

'What's that to do with anything?' Gunderic said.

'Nothing, lord,' Hagan said, realising he was playing with fire. 'I too thank the Gods you survived this.'

'Right, we've dawdled enough,' Gunderic said. 'Let's get underway.'

He walked away to talk to one of his captains before Hagan could ask anything else.

Hagan slung his saddlebags onto his horse and tightened all the straps in preparation for the long journey ahead. They would ride north towards Aurelianum to meet the Romans and the Visigoths, a journey that would take several days.

As they stood around waiting, a farmer leading a donkey cart laden with sacks entered the square. Seeing Hagan the farmer took off his hat.

'Is the Lord Wodnas here?' he said.

'He should be here somewhere,' Hagan said, looking around but not spotting the one-eyed old man.

'Well I've got what he asked for,' the farmer said. 'I've travelled all over the realm collecting them from farmsteads. I need to know what he wants me to do with them now.'

'Well you'd better find him then,' Hagan said. 'I don't know what you're talking about.'

'One thing's for sure: the sheep will be shaggy by the time you get back,' the farmer said, which puzzled Hagan even more.

The man led his cart off. As it went Hagan heard it jingling and rattling. Whatever was in those sacks, it was metal.

After some time horns blasted and drums were struck, announcing that it was time to leave. The company mounted their horses and as the watching crowds cheered and waved the company moved off. They formed into a long column so as to fit through the streets and the city gates.

Hagan watched the faces they rode past. Military wives were riding with the war horde, but everyone else was left behind. There were boys too young to go to war, their eyes alight with excitement as they waved to the warriors riding by. Behind them stood a very few old men who had survived the massacre at Vorbetomagus who looked both nostalgic that they were now too old to go to fight and at the same time, having seen war for themselves, relieved that they were no longer expected to. Then there were women – mothers and unmarried girls – who were both proud of their menfolk and dreading that this could be the last time they would see them.

The company filed out of the city gates where the rest of the war horde were gathered in the fields beyond. As they rode out of the gates of the city Hagan thought his eyes were playing tricks on him. The gallows beside the gate had three new bodies swinging from it. The first two were the corpses of two young girls. Their eyes bulged and their tongues protruded from their mouths. Their faces had turned purple but not black, which meant they had been hanged only that morning. The third was Geic.

Before them two men, warriors in black cloaks, looked like they were arguing. Forsetti, the old goat-like Law Speaker, stood between them, stroking his goatee beard and listening with interest to the words of the others.

'What's going on there?' Hagan wondered aloud.

'They're holding Geic's trial,' Gunderic said.

'But he's dead!' Hagan said.

'True,' the king said. 'But I want everyone in the kingdom to know that in my realm everyone is entitled to a fair trial. Even the dead. I don't want people thinking I'm a tyrant. We hanged his corpse as an example to others, but Geic wasn't summarily executed.'

Hagan opened his mouth but did not reply. The world was going mad and his old friend seemed to be slipping away with it. Whatever had happened the night before, Hagan doubted that it did involve treachery, at least not on the part of Geic. Being close to the king was becoming a very dangerous position.

PART V

ARMAGEDDON

'And I looked, and behold a pale horse: and his name that sat on him was Death, and Hell followed with him. And power was given unto them over the fourth part of the earth, to kill with sword, and with hunger, and with death, and with the beasts of the earth.'

Book of Revelation, chapter 6, verse 8

CHAPTER FORTY-NINE

THE BURGUNDAR WAR Horde, along with its new contingent of Valkyrjur cavalry, rode first west then north. They moved away from the mountains that surrounded Geneva, through foothills to the rolling plains of south-central Gaul.

By day they rode along the Via Helvetica travelling west. At night they dug a large rectangular ditch and used the earth from it to create a defensive rampart, then pitched their camp inside. It was just what a Roman legion would do when on campaign and yet again Hagan wondered if Wodnas, who had taught them to do this, had spent time in the Army of the Empire.

One difference from a Roman army was the presence of women. Burgundar wives travelled along with servants in a baggage train that followed the mounted warriors. In former times when the Burgundars went to war the whole tribe had travelled too, and the families of the warriors screamed their support for their menfolk from the edge of the battlefields. They were also there to encourage, witness and remember the deeds of the warriors. Hagan knew the young women who accompanied the war horde now were a continuation of that tradition, but like all the others it was changed, different from the past.

With a train of wagons and pack horses it meant progress was slower than if the warriors were riding alone, but it also meant they were more comfortable and better equipped.

The road passed through forests, vineyards and meadows, alongside meandering rivers and past settlements. The weather was getting ever warmer with the waxing summer and the hundreds of horses kicked up a cloud of dust that filled the air and covered the riders in a thin brown coating.

The war horde moved in a disciplined fashion. As when they went to the realm of Brynhild, the Raven Warriors went ahead, ranging through the countryside, scouting the way for the main force. In the main body of the horde the Bear Warriors rode at the front, ready to charge at any potential threat that showed its face. Behind them rode the rest of the warriors with the king and his council at the centre. Brynhild's Valkyrjur were divided in two and rode on either side of the main column, protecting its flanks. Behind all lumbered along the train of wagons and carts carrying provisions, baggage, slaves, servants and the noblewomen who had chosen to accompany their husbands to the battlefield.

Geic's death had left Hagan with an uneasy feeling in his heart and he felt uncomfortable being around Gunderic and Sigurd. The feeling was mutual, as they both seemed gruff and aloof. There was no sign of Brynhild either. Gunderic continued to say she was shaken by the attack and remained in a wagon at the rear but Hagan could not help feeling the king was evasive and short-tempered whenever anyone asked about his queen. Hagan's suspicion of what had happened deepened. Gunhild mostly stayed with the women at the rear and Hagan once more felt alone with no one to talk to.

A few days into the journey Hagan ran into Gunhild by chance one evening on one of her rare journeys to the fore of the company. She was looking for Gunderic.

'Have you seen Brynhild?' Hagan said. 'I haven't seen her since we left. Do you think she is alright?'

Gunhild pursed her lips.

'I haven't,' she said. 'I was a bit worried, but two of the women tell me they have met her in the last few days. She

412

seemed fine, though the odd thing is they both said Brynhild kept herself wrapped up in that long black hooded cloak of hers, despite the weather. She definitely is keeping herself out of the way.'

'I suppose we shouldn't be surprised,' Hagan said with a shrug. 'With what happened on her wedding night, coming on top of all the other unfortunate events that have blighted her life, she probably needs some time to herself to get over it all.'

A little more reassured, Hagan parted from Gunhild. He remained wary of what Sigurd might try and made sure he slept both with a knife under his bed roll and in a tent with others. If the big man or anyone else wanted to try something they would have to do it before witnesses.

After a week of travelling nothing had happened, and Hagan began to relax a little, at least enough to start leaving the tent in the dark at night if he needed a piss instead of lying there holding on until the morning.

One night he was relieving himself against a dry stone farm wall. The camp for the night had been made on top of an unfortunate farmer's settlement. Hagan was looking up at the stars, a little cloud of steam from his urine rising into the chilly night air, when he caught sight of movement from the corner of his eye.

Hagan tensed, his flow ceasing immediately. Then he saw who was lurking a little way off.

'Zerco?' Hagan said, squinting to make out the little man's shape in the shadows. 'You're here?'

'I followed the war horde,' Zerco said in a hoarse whisper. 'And caught up with the baggage train. You aren't travelling that fast so it was easy enough. I need to tell you something.'

'I thought you'd be taking advantage of everyone being away from Geneva to search the place for treasure,' Hagan said.

'I have to warn you,' Zerco said. 'I was in Gunderic's house the night of the wedding. Geic had nothing to do with it.'

Hagan looked around to see if anyone was within listening

range. Seeing the nearest people awake were some warriors on watch on the rampart about fifty paces away, Hagan grasped Zerco's sleeve and led him deeper into the shadows near the wall.

'Tell me everything,' Hagan said.

Speaking in a whisper, Zerco related all he had seen in Gunderic's house that night.

When he'd concluded, Hagan sat for a moment in silence. He felt heavy with this knowledge rather than enraged.

'So I was right,' he said after a few moments, 'there was something strange about that whole story. You should be careful, Zerco. If Gunderic or Sigurd find out you know this you will be a dead man.'

'I know that,' Zerco said. 'That's why I have decided to go back to Aetius. I will ride ahead and join the Romans at Aurelianum.'

'What about the treasure?' Hagan said.

The dwarf sighed.

'For a long time the gold was all I thought about,' he said. 'Really. Night and day. What I would do with my cut. What I would buy. How I'd never have to suffer the scorn of others once I was fabulously wealthy. But I look at Gunderic and the others and see the sickness this gold brings with it. You need treachery to get it and then you must become even more treacherous to hold onto it. Do I want to live my life that way? I look at you and realise the answer is no.'

'Me?' Hagan said.

'Yes,' Zerco said. 'You've had as bad a life as I have yet you never let it twist your heart.'

'Not quite as bad a life, I'd say,' Hagan said.

'You see what I mean?' Zerco said. 'Your life has been shit. You lost your homeland, your family and people were massacred. You found out your father was not your father. You were never after the treasure when you went to Geneva, you wanted to help your people. You wanted a new home but when

414

you got there it turned out to be a den of snakes. Through it all you carry on. You were not lost in bitterness. You still try to do right when others do you wrong.'

'You're right. I'm an idiot,' Hagan said.

'I used to pity you,' Zerco said.

'*You* used to pity *me*?' Hagan rolled his eyes.

'But now I realise you are to be admired,' Zerco continued. 'You have what the Romans call *virtus*. You are like their stoics. I was only fooling myself anyway. If I had become wealthy the smiles and praises of others would just have been masks, hiding what others really thought of me, which would be no different from what they think of me now. So I will give up on this dream of gold and return to Aetius. There is something rotten in Geneva and I'd rather be alive and poor than dead and rich.'

'Aetius won't be pleased if you return without the gold,' Hagan said.

'All the same, I will feel safer with the Magister Militum,' Zerco said. 'And I can at least assure him the treasure is in the Burgundars' lands, should he want to go and find it himself someday. Now I must go. I came here so you would know the truth and that you must be very careful for your own safety. Look after yourself.'

He touched his forehead in salute then slunk off into the darkness.

Hagan watched him go, then went back to his tent and went back to his leather sleeping bag, careful not to step on any of the others snoring around him. He lay down but did not sleep the rest of the night.

CHAPTER FIFTY

EARLY NEXT MORNING Hagan hurried through the camp as it was being dismantled, seeking out any of the Raven Warriors who might still be there.

After a search he spotted Gunfjaun and another raven warrior talking to Wodnas near his tent. Like Hagan they were red-eyed and had been up most of the night scouting the forests ahead. They were now delivering a report on what they had found.

'I want to join your scouting forays for the journey,' Hagan said. 'It's boring riding along with the rest of the warband and the women. At least there is some danger in what you do.'

Gunfjaun and the other raven warrior folded their arms. There was scorn and scepticism on their young faces.

'We are a specialised company,' Gunfjaun said. 'Wodnas has taught us many crafts particular to our work that others do not know. I don't want to find myself trying to move silently through a wood to attack an unwitting enemy with you crashing along behind me like a bison.'

'I am an expert hunter,' Hagan said. 'I have been since I was a boy. I can move through a forest silent as a cat. And in the Roman Army I was a scout. I learned similar skills to you.'

He looked sideways at Wodnas.

'If not the same skills,' Hagan said. 'Give me a chance. If I let you down you can just tell me to return to the main column.'

The Raven Warriors looked at Wodnas, who looked at

Hagan for a long moment. Hagan felt the intensity of that one blue eye that seemed to search his very heart.

'Let's see how he does, lads,' the old man said after a moment, a faint smile brushing his lips. 'But don't go easy on him.'

The others nodded, though still looked far from happy.

'Meet us at the gate,' Gunfjaun said. 'Don't take too long.'

Hagan ran to grab his gear and horse then rode to the gate in the rampart of the camp which was being taken down as the two Raven Warriors sat on their horses beside it. The three of them rode off, out of the camp and away from the main army.

Hagan felt relief as they left the rest of the Burgundar War Horde behind. He was now in the company of killers, but they were warriors not murderers. If Gunderic or Sigurd wanted to cause him any harm he was, with any luck, beyond the reach of anyone they might send to do it. All he had to do was impress his new colleagues so they would let him stay with them.

It did not take long. Once Hagan had displayed his knowledge, the lads became more welcoming, recognising someone who shared the same skills.

The further north they rode the more it became clear they were riding towards a war. The settlements they passed that were large enough to have walls had their gates closed and armed warriors on ramparts regarded the passing warband with wary eyes as it rode by. The closer they got to Aurelianum the busier the roads became, though all the traffic was going in the opposite direction. Great crowds were trekking down the road. There were some rich people in litters or wagons but most were ordinary people struggling along with only as many of their belongings as they could carry. Once they even saw a whole convent of nuns, walking barefoot and empty-eyed down the road. They were all the eternal victims of war: those who could not defend themselves. Many of those who passed a few words with the Burgundars told tales of horror – massacres of innocents, defeats of armies and the sacking of cities. Attila was on the rampage and it seemed no one was able to stop him.

The weeks wore on and the further and further they got from Geneva, the countryside grew ever more flat while the weather got warmer. Soon the days were spent trudging through countryside under a baking hot sun.

Among all this Hagan heard people calling the king of the Huns by a new name he had heard only once before: the Scourge of God. The world had grown wicked, perverse and corrupt and the Almighty had sent Attila to deliver His judgement and punish the sinners. So many cities had fallen already and now he was riding to take Aurelianum.

'Why there?' Hagan wondered as he sat around the campfire one evening with a few of the other Raven Warriors.

'It's nearly in the centre of Gaul,' Gunfjaun said. 'Aurelianum is the gateway to the west. The way the roads run, if Attila can take this city then he could cut Gaul in two. The West is already rebellious so he is gambling that, if cut off from the threat of the legions, the Bacaudae, the Armoricans and thousands in other tribes will declare themselves free of Rome and willing to pay Attila tribute. Then all he has to do is ride south and take Ravenna. Attila will rule nearly all the world.'

Hagan looked at him for a moment, then said, 'For one so young, you are very wise.'

The lad smirked and shook his head.

'That's what Wodnas told us,' he said. 'I'm just here to kill Huns.'

They all laughed, though Hagan's mirth was not as unrestrained. He had been thinking about the battle that was coming and how the Burgundars might be deployed. The Romans often tried to use 'barbarians' as shock troops, warriors who would either lead the attack or absorb the initial fury of one from the Huns while the legions watched until enough casualties had mounted on both sides for them to march in. They then finished the job against a weakened enemy with minimal casualties to themselves. It was a proven tactic. He had learned about it the hard way.

If Aetius did that with these warriors it would be a waste of good men. The lads around him were good, there was no doubt of that, but they were few in number. The special skills they had would count for nothing against thousands of mounted, charging Huns. If deployed in the right way, however, they could cause real havoc among the enemy.

Hagan made up his mind that if he got the chance to talk to Aetius again he would try to impress this on the Roman, instead of thinking of ways to kill him.

After eleven days the raven warrior scouts came in sight of Aurelianum. The countryside was mostly flat but there were occasional woods and a few rolling hills. The Raven Warriors were about a day ahead of the main war horde. When they crossed open ground that offered no cover to launch a surprise attack, they rode. When they came across nearby woods, glens, hills, or anything that might hide an ambush force, they dismounted and worked their way through it in silence until they were satisfied it was clear.

They had come upon a perfect place for an ambush – a wooded hill just beside the road – and the company had dismounted to check it out. Hagan was making his way through a thicket, spear ready, walking with careful, deliberate steps so as to make as little noise as possible, when he heard the sound of a deer bleating coming from uphill of him.

While it could have been a deer, it was also the signal the Ravens had agreed among themselves before they began searching the forest. Hagan began tracking uphill towards where the sound was coming from. The hill was not high and he made it to the top in a short time, despite moving with caution in case he was walking into a trap.

On the summit he found Gunfjaun in a little clearing. The trees opened up to give a good view of a city that must have been Aurelianum. It was a large settlement, rectangular in outline and surrounded by walls built in the Roman fashion with defensive towers at three of the four corners and defending every gate into the city. The towers had conical roofs covered in red tiles. The same tiles covered the roofs of many of the buildings visible beyond the wall. At one last corner with no tower the walls curved around the massive bulk of an amphitheatre. There were no games that day however as even from this distance the glint of sun on weapons showed the top tiers of the theatre seating was lined by warriors.

A river curled around two sides of the city. Until recently the settlement must have spilled out beyond its walls, but now the houses, shops or whatever had been built beyond the walls was just piles of smouldering rubble. Hagan reasoned they had either been destroyed by Attila's forces or torn down by the defenders of Aurelianum to remove any cover for attackers reaching the base of the walls.

Right around the city was a system of trenches, ramparts and palisades. These were newly built as Hagan could see that the earth taken up in digging them was still a dark brown.

'We're too late,' Hagan said. 'Attila got here first.'

CHAPTER FIFTY-ONE

'ARE YOU SURE about that?' Gunfjaun said.

Hagan looked again and realised the ramparts faced away from the walls of the city, not at them. The ditches faced outwards. They were also quiet and not thronging with besieging warriors.

'Those are defences!' Hagan said. 'Attila must not have made it here yet.'

He was almost right. After some wary negotiations with the defenders on the walls of Aurelianum, the gate opened and a little man with a large belly, dressed in the robes of an important Roman churchman, came out to meet them. The suspicions of the defenders were emphasised by the speed with which they slammed the gate shut as soon as the churchman was clear of it.

He introduced himself as Anianus, Bishop of Aurelianum, and he was eager to tell them of what had occurred over the last few weeks. He was particularly keen to relate his own, crucial role in keeping up the spirits of his flock within the city as they waited for the arrival of the Huns and impending fire and death. Hagan could see these events were the most exciting thing that had happened to either the city or Bishop Anianus for a very long time, and the fact that the axe had not fallen on Aurelianum made it all the more thrilling.

'I'm sad to say our king, Sangiban of the Alans, was not in favour of holding out,' Anianus said. 'He wanted to surrender to Attila. But the people did not. They knew what awaited them at the merciless hands of the Huns. So it fell upon me, by the grace of God, to take on the mantle of authority.'

'Lucky for God you happened to be here,' Hagan said.

'The people were at the end of their wits,' the bishop went on, oblivious to Hagan's sarcasm. 'They were cowering in dread at the coming terrible chastisement. I did my best to prepare everyone. Then just a week ago we saw a great cloud of dust on the horizon. There was great lamentation among the women of the city: it seemed Attila was finally coming. I sent a messenger to see and, like the messenger of Elijah, he came back, covered head to toe in dust and told us the wondrous news that it was not Attila approaching, but the army of Rome! We were saved.'

The Roman-Visigothic army had arrived without a moment to spare. They had set to work throwing up defences, working day and night to pull down the buildings around the town and build the ditches and ramparts that now augmented the city's walls. They were still finishing them when the horde of Attila rode over the hill.

'You should have seen the look on his face when he saw a Roman army waiting for him!' Anianus said, beaming with pride.

'Attila came close enough that you could see his face from the walls?' Hagan said, raising an eyebrow. 'It's a pity there were no archers alongside you or they'd have shot him and we could all go home.'

The bishop gave Hagan a black look.

'So I was told,' he said. 'But seeing the forces of Christ arrayed before him, Attila turned tail and retreated the way he came, back to Tricassium.'

After waiting a day or so for their final reinforcements, Aetius had taken the Roman army and set off in pursuit.

Hagan and the rest of the raven warrior scouts rode back along the Roman road until they met the main body of the Burgundar horde.

'So Attila is on the run already?' Gunderic said when they told him what had happened. 'I wonder: did he hear we are coming?'

'I very much doubt that,' Wodnas said. 'It is the Romans who are being forced to fight, remember. The Huns are horsemen. Sieges and attacks on a heavily defended city is not what they are good at. No, if I were Attila I would try to draw my enemy away to a place of my choosing. Somewhere where I can use my cavalry to most advantage.'

'You think Aetius is marching into a trap?' Hagan said.

'Perhaps,' Wodnas said. 'But he must fight Attila. He has to stop him here and now. He's pulled together a coalition of enemies that will not hold together for long. Aetius is not stupid. He must know what Attila is up to. Perhaps if you are going to march into a trap then it's best to do it with your eyes open.'

'Well let's go and find out, shall we?' Gunderic said. 'Hagan, we miss your company. Why don't you join the main company again?'

'I was enjoying myself with the raven warrior scouts,' Hagan said.

'All the same, I'd prefer it if you were closer by,' the king said. His tone made it clear this was not a request.

Hagan nodded and the company set off again, this time following the Roman road north-west towards Tricassium. Unlike the relaxed atmosphere among the raven warrior scouts, Hagan found the mood strained around the Burgundar leadership. Sigurd acted as if he had no time for Hagan, sometimes looking at him like he wondered why he was there. Gunderic was guarded and suspicious and tended only to speak to Gunhild. Lokke and Wodnas seemed to be in constant, private conversation. Brynhild still remained in her wagon the whole time.

At one point Gunderic sidled his horse closer to Hagan, who was riding as usual a little way away from the others.

'What were you doing with Wodnas' men anyway,' Gunderic said. 'Anyone would think you didn't want to be with your old friends any more.'

'I was bored,' Hagan said. 'The raven warrior scouts get to ride ahead and flout danger.'

'Oh, really?' Gunderic said. His tone of voice suggested he was far from convinced.

Hagan bit his lower lip. He yearned to blurt out that he knew what Gunderic had done. That he was appalled by what had happened to Geic and all the other lies, just so Gunderic could keep his greedy hands on a pile of gold.

'The thing is, Hagan,' Gunderic said. 'You are part of my Royal Council. You are close to me and know some of our secrets. Because of this I need to know I trust you.'

Hagan looked his old friend straight in the eyes. Anger flared in his heart.

'What are you trying to say?' he said.

'Some have pointed out to me,' the king said, 'that what that Roman emissary said after my wedding was very similar to what you said the night the Hun came. Very similar indeed.'

'Who are these people?' Hagan demanded. 'What are they insinuating? I was open about how I met Aetius in Ravenna. What is it? You think I'm working for him?'

Hagan felt rising panic in his chest to mix with the anger. Did someone else know the truth? Had they told the king? Yet again he cursed himself for not coming clean about everything the moment he arrived in Geneva. Now it looked like he had been hiding something all along.

'Calm down, old friend,' Gunderic said. 'I don't think that. What sort of a king would I be if I had welcomed a spy into my own council? Who knows what his real purpose might be?'

Hagan's panic deepened. Was this just suspicion or did Gunderic know the truth. If so, how?

'A king who found that out would have to act with complete ruthlessness,' Gunderic said. 'And make himself rid of that spy. But I would never do that to you, Hagan. You are one of my oldest friends. And what would the people think? You are the last of the Dagelungs and son of our greatest champion from the former days. So you are special to me, and that is why I prefer you stay close instead of roaming through the forests.'

And within striking distance, Hagan thought as the king rode away from him again.

Gunderic's tone had been so matter-of-fact it was impossible to tell his true thoughts. Had he just delivered a threat or did he mean what he said?

Either way, Hagan resolved, he needed to remain vigilant.

The journey ahead was an uncertain one. They did not know how far Attila had gone and at any moment they could stumble upon his warriors. For the first few days of the journey they travelled through close country where the horizon was never too far away. At times it was heavily forested and there were lots of low hills, ridges and valleys where a lurking enemy could await for an ambush. The raven warrior scouts were kept busy ranging ahead of the main horde to thwart any such attacks.

From the state of the countryside it was clear that not one but two great armies had passed through it in the last few days. The road itself was intact, but for at least one hundred paces on either side the grass was trampled down and the undergrowth flattened by the tramp of marching feet, the tread of horses and the wheels of rumbling wagons. They passed campsites with burned-out fires, heaps of rubbish and stinking latrine pits that had only been half covered. Fields of beans, the only crop in season in the baking early summer heat, had been stripped of their crops. Every settlement too small to have walls was burned to the ground. Those large enough to defend themselves had their gates shut and their ramparts manned.

'Attila has not stopped to raid these towns,' Wodnas said, stroking his beard in thought. 'Which means he is in a hurry.'

'I did not think Attila would be so cowardly,' Gunderic said as they rode along.

'I would see it differently, Lord King,' Wodnas said. 'The leader who chooses the ground on which a battle is fought is usually the winner. Attila has somewhere in mind that will give his warriors the most advantage over the Alliance, and he is hurrying there to make sure he gets there first. I imagine General Aetius is pursuing him just as hard to try to stop that happening.'

The next day they came across evidence of just how hard and how close that pursuit was. The smell caught Hagan's nostrils before they arrived at the site. As the road snaked past a long ridge beside a river, the aftermath of a fight was scattered all around. There were arrows everywhere, either broken on the ground or embedded in it like hard grass. Broken weapons lay all around and there were splatters and pools of maroon in the dust and across the road: dried blood, some of which was deep and fresh enough to not yet have clotted.

There were two mounds of dead men. Stab wounds, hacks and slashes all yawned in their bodies, the red and purple gashes contrasting sharply with white skin made more pale by death. Severed limbs were piled alongside them.

One group of them had been gathered with respect and arranged in rows, lying on their backs, a throwing axe grasped in each man's dead hands before him, in a shallow pit that was perhaps fifty paces across by fifty long. A relatively small band of slaves and warriors sat resting beside it, the shovels they had dug the pit with sitting nearby. In the hot sun that was climbing into the sky above it must have been heavy work.

The second pile of dead men were just piled in a heap. They were stripped naked and there was no sign of any grave for them. The stench of death clogged the air and the warm summer sun meant hordes of black flies now buzzed over the corpses.

'*Vae Victis*,' Wodnas said. 'Woe to the defeated.'

From the men digging the mass grave they learned that the Alliance's vanguard, a contingent of Franks, had run into Attila's rearguard, a warband of Gepids. The Franks had got the better of their enemies but the skirmish managed to delay the advance of the Alliance by a day, which meant Attila had more time to make it to wherever he was heading for.

'The Franks and the Gepids are all sons of Mannus,' Hagan said as he surveyed the piles of corpses amid the clouds by buzzing flies. 'Just like we Burgundars. Yet now they fight each other on the behalf of foreign masters.'

'The bitterest fights happen within a family,' Wodnas said. 'The Ostrogoths and Visigoths are direct cousins, lad. But they will fight each other in the coming battle. War is war. There is no need to get sentimental about it. If you do, you are lost.'

They resumed the journey, now even more careful than before. Every rock could hide an enemy. On every rise beside the road a company of Huns could be waiting to ride down and attack.

Gradually the ground got flatter, the trees became less dense. The weather was hot and the road dusty, and the Burgundar company halted to take water at the river that the road ran alongside.

As the sun began to sink towards the horizon, a raven warrior came galloping back along the road and announced that the armies lay just up ahead. Suitably refreshed, the war horde mounted and resumed the journey.

A little further down the road the forest petered out and the countryside opened up before them. In the very far distance they could make out an encamped army. It was like a dark smear on the landscape, a huge indiscriminate mass of men, horses, tents and wagons. Grey smoke rose from countless cooking fires to collect into one giant cloud that smudged the sky above.

'That must be Attila's camp,' Lokke said.

'That looks like a huge army he has,' the lord of the Leuhtungs said.

Nearer to where the Burgundars were was the Roman camp, immediately recognisable by its formal layout. Around and about it though were countless other tents, fires, wagons and shelters of the other allies.

On the right was a sharp ridge, but from that on there was nothing but flat open ground as far as the eye could see. It was covered in grass that was turning to yellow straw in the summer heat.

'Perfect ground for Attila's cavalry,' Wodnas said.

CHAPTER FIFTY-TWO

THE BURGUNDARS HAD no need to ask directions to find the tent of Aetius in the Roman camp. In times of relative peace Roman soldiers were now billeted among the population – a far from popular policy. When on campaign, however, from time immemorial, every Roman army camp, no matter where it was, how permanent it was, or how many men it was designed to accommodate, was always built to exactly the same plan. It was a well-tested strategy that had served the Empire for centuries with no need for change.

A huge rectangle was marked out and a ditch dug around its periphery. On the inside of the ditch the legionaries erected a rampart topped with a palisade of sharpened wooden stakes. Hagan knew they would have brought these with them, carried in wagons in the baggage train, lest there not be enough wood in the countryside to make new ones. The cohorts of the legions arrayed themselves in ordered 'streets' of tents inside the defences. There were four gates, one in each rampart: the *Porta Principalis Dextra*, the *Porta Principalis Sinistra*, the *Porta Decumana* and the main gate, the *Porta Praetoria*.

Two tracks ran through the camp between the gates, the *Via Praetoria* and the *Via Principalis*, which intersected in the very centre of the fortification where the *Praetorium*, the headquarters, lay. Here the slaves pitched the tents of the commanding officers, and outside the biggest tent – that

429

belonging to the general – they erected the standards of the cohorts and the legions.

The arrival of a strange war horde had already caused a commotion amid the allies and a flurry of scouts and emissaries had shuttled from the camp to the Burgundars until who they were and what their intent was had been established. Eventually General Aetius had sent word that the leaders of the Burgundars should proceed to the Praetorium but the rest of the war horde had to remain outside.

'It seems like trust within this Alliance does not extend to sleeping together,' Lokke said with a sniff.

'Gunhild, you will not be able to accompany us into a Roman camp,' Gunderic said to his sister.

'I am aware of the Romans' hatred of women,' Gunhild said. 'I will attend to the setting up of our camp.'

The rest were admitted through the Porta Praetoria and led up the Via Praetoria by soldiers of Aetius's personal bodyguard. Outside the tent there were perhaps twenty warriors standing, leaning on spears or sitting on the ground, looking bored. They had the look of Franks, Visigoths and others who probably made up the personal hearth-warriors of the kings who made up the Alliance.

'You can bring only three with you,' Aetius's lead bodyguard said to Gunderic. 'No one else has more than that in their delegation and General Aetius has left strict orders we are not to upset any of the others. Please choose who you bring in.'

The expression on the Roman soldier's face and his tone of voice made it plain that he disapproved of this bowing to the sensitivities of barbarians.

Gunderic sighed and looked around at those who surrounded him.

'Wodnas and Sigurd,' he said without hesitation. Then he took another look at the expectant faces of his councillors.

'And Hagan,' he said.

Hagan blinked, surprised he had been chosen. He saw the

looks of consternation, hostility and even suspicion on the faces of the others.

'Good,' the lead bodyguard said, 'now you can enter.'

As they made their way through a short tunnel that formed an entranceway to the big tent, Hagan tugged at Gunderic's sleeve.

'Why me?' he whispered from the corner of his mouth. 'Aren't I a little new? The others will be offended.'

'It's because you are new that I chose you,' Gunderic said. 'You don't command a faction in my realm. If I chose one of the rest over another it could cause offence between them. Apart from that, I'd like to check something.'

He turned and walked on before Hagan could ask what that 'something' was.

Inside the spacious Praetorium tent a group of men were gathered around a table. Aetius was in the middle of it all, clad in his ceremonial leather armour which looked a little old-fashioned. Hagan mused that it was probably an ancestral heirloom and wondered just how much longer such uniforms would continue to dominate the world.

Beside Aetius stood three men who resembled one another. The first was a tall, barrel-chested man with white hair and ruddy cheeks. He was richly dressed in long robes decorated with twisting beasts embroidered in many-coloured threads. He was almost as large a man as Sigurd but was much older, perhaps sixty winters old. Beside him stood a young, black-haired man dressed in a similar manner and with a facial resemblance to the older man that could only mean he was a son or nephew. Another son or nephew stood on the older man's other side. All three of them had curly hair that receded towards the crown but hung long at the back. They had bushy eyebrows and long, aquiline noses, though one of the younger men's was twisted from a past bad break. All three of them wore the same, slightly odd style of facial hair that involved leaving their temples, cheeks and upper lip unshaven but removing all hair from their chin and square, heavily muscled necks. This style was particular to the Western Goths, or the Visigoths as the Romans called them.

On the other side of the table was a man in his middle years. He was dressed in white silk robes and baggy trousers and Hagan could not tell if his skin was naturally dark or if he was deeply tanned by the sun. The way his gaze darted back and forth as he ran his tongue over his lips suggested to Hagan he was nervous about something. With a battle ahead against a warlord who had never lost, who could blame him?

Next was another big, blond-haired man who reminded Hagan both in looks and dress of the Saxons he had fought alongside. There was also a man dressed like the Burgundians who was probably a Frank and finally, to Hagan's surprise, a warrior who had the curly black hair and dress of a Briton.

Behind them all, away from the table, lurked others similarly dressed who had the air of seconds-in-command, advisors or councillors. Hagan was surprised to see Bishop Anianus from Aurelianum was also there.

Aetius and these others were peering at a large piece of parchment which showed what Hagan deduced to be a drawing of the nearby countryside. There was a long blue line at the top with a large black circle denoting the camp of Attila. The ridge to the right was drawn in, and a square in blue at the bottom depicted the Roman camp. In between, various lines and arrows were painted in red and green. The scribe who had painted them stood beside the table, brush and paint pots ready if more was needed.

As the Burgundars came forward everyone straightened up. Hands fell to hook thumbs into belts as most of the men puffed out their chests at the sight of potential rivals.

'King Gunderic,' Aetius said, as if greeting an old friend. 'Good to see you again after all these years. I'm glad you've seen sense and decided to join us. At times like this people start to realise the value of the Empire. We're stronger together.'

'I have been led to believe this is an alliance of equals, Aetius,' Gunderic said. 'Let's not talk of the Empire.'

Hagan noted some of the others around the table exchanging glances.

'This is truly a remarkable coalition, I can assure you of that,' Aetius said. 'And who is this accompanying you?'

'This, general, is Sigurd Volsung,' Gunderic said, gesturing to the big man who stood beside him. 'He is my champion and leader of the Burgundar War Horde.'

'So this is the young prince I heard so much about?' Aetius said. 'Your fame travels before you, young man.'

Sigurd looked delighted.

'The one who bears the famous sword?' the older man with the white hair said.

'What do you know of my sword?' Sigurd said. His smile disappeared. He grasped the hilt of his sheathed weapon.

'We know Attila wants it badly enough to go to war for it,' the old man said. 'And we know you took it from a hoard stolen from King Oktar of the Huns. Who do you think we are? Children that you can hide things like this from? You're not in your little kingdom among the mountains now, lad. Aetius has told us all about it.'

'Has he?' Sigurd said. 'And how does he know about all this?'

He flashed a glare laden with anger and suspicion in the direction of Hagan.

'If Attila wants this sword so badly, why don't we just give it to him?' the sallow-skinned man in the white tunic said. 'Then he will go away.'

'Go away, perhaps,' Aetius said. 'But then he will be back next year, wanting something else. And the year after. Wolves like Attila do not just go away. They attack and attack until they have bled the land dry.'

'This is Wodnas, my special advisor,' Gunderic said, nodding towards the one-eyed old man. Wodnas stood,

433

impassive as usual, leaning on the spear shaft he used as a walking staff. Hagan caught sight of the look of consternation on the Magister Militum's face as he glared at Wodnas' bare feet, no doubt bemoaning how far the might of Rome has sunk if she now depended on alliances with such barbarians.

'And this is Hagan,' Gunderic said.

'Oh, I've met this man already,' Aetius said, beaming at Hagan in a way that made him cringe inside.

Hagan blushed a deep crimson. He could feel the eyes of the others boring into him. Did they think he was a Roman agent? If so he was as good as dead. He glanced up and saw Gunderic looking at him, his upper lip curled in distaste.

'That is what I wanted to check,' Gunderic said in a low, even voice.

Hagan yearned to blurt out that he had been open about having met Aetius on the way to Geneva – indeed he was the reason why he was there – but somehow he knew that would make him look even more suspicious.

'He was in the Army,' Aetius said. Hagan felt a rush of relief that the Magister Militum had sensed the awkward atmosphere. 'We met several times. He's an excellent scout as I recall. But you've arrived just in time. We were just discussing the battle plans for tomorrow, which you can now play a part in. Come, let me introduce you to the other leaders of this Alliance.'

Aetius clapped a hand on the shoulder of the white-haired man beside him.

'First and very much foremost is Theodoric, King of the Visigoths, or the Western Goths as I believe you call them,' Aetius said. 'He commands fifteen thousand warriors. Who would have thought he and I would have ever fought alongside each other?'

The king of the Visigoths smiled, a gesture that increased the wrinkles around his eyes tenfold.

'Greetings, my friends,' King Theodoric said. He spoke in the Gothic tongue which was not that far different from

Burgundar that they could not understand him. 'Welcome to our little festival.'

'King Theodoric, it is an honour to meet you at last,' Gunderic said. 'Your mighty deeds and many wars against Rome are legendary and an inspiration to us all. I'm glad we Burgundars will at last fight on the same side as your warriors.'

'Likewise, King Gunderic,' Theodoric said. 'Your father was a terror to all who stood against him. And I mean that in a good way.'

He winked.

'Now our forces are combined,' he continued, 'we cannot fail to gain victory. Then who knows who we will fight next?'

'I do speak your language, remember?' Aetius said in a cold voice, much of his former civility gone.

'I know you do, Aetius,' Theodoric said, and winked at Gunderic again.

'Then let us stick to speaking Latin,' Aetius said. 'Out of courtesy for everyone here. It is the only common tongue everyone can understand.'

It was clear to Hagan that the general was trying as hard as he could to assert an air of command. This would be difficult, given the unlikely alliance represented by the men gathered in the tent. Until Attila's invasion they had been enemies, rivals engaged in endless bitter wars with each other. The only things that united them were their opposition to Attila and a hatred of Rome, the very empire whose soldiers they would all fight alongside the next day. Hagan wondered if this fragile alliance would hold together even that long. For the first time he began to feel nervous about the upcoming fight and the prospects for success.

'Allow me to introduce my sons, Thorismund and Theodoric the younger,' the Visigoth King said, beaming with pride at his offspring. 'Tomorrow we three shall ride into battle together. We will lead our warriors to victory.'

Sigurd made a derisive snort.

435

'You find something funny?' King Theodoric said.

'You don't mean personally, do you?' Sigurd said. 'Aren't you a bit... old?'

Others in the room gasped.

'Sigurd, show some respect!' Gunderic said.

Sigurd, eyes wide with surprise, made a puzzled expression.

'You actually mean it?' he said.

'Listen to me, boy,' Theodoric said, his voice a low growl. 'I've fought more battles than your mother had lovers. If I was the sort of coward who ordered his warriors into battle then sat back and watches them do the fighting then I would not deserve to be called king. Nor would they follow me. I will lead my men into battle tomorrow just as I have done countless times before. And I will not stand for snide remarks from a boy wearing someone else's Byzantine armour that doesn't even fit him!'

Sigurd's expression turned to one of consternation and his right hand dropped to the hilt of his sword. Theodoric's two sons reached for their own weapons. The Saxons and Franks grinned, entertained by the thought of seeing some violent sport.

'Sigurd, no,' Gunderic said, laying a hand on the big man's forearm. 'We are all on the same side here.'

Aetius rolled his eyes.

'King Theodoric, our apologies,' Wodnas spoke for the first time. 'Our champion is hot-headed at times. You must admit it is unusual to see a man of our age still fit enough to fight. My compliments to you.'

Theodoric nodded, appearing a little placated.

'*If* we could get back to discussing the battle plan?' Aetius said, pointing to the map.

They all turned their attention back to the table, though Sigurd and the three Visigoths cast sideways glances at each other.

'In the morning we will offer battle in the open Catalaunian fields beside the ridge,' Aetius said, pointing to the area on the map. 'We will form up on the open ground with the ridge to the east.'

'You intend to march off the high ground onto the flat of the plains?' Wodnas said. 'Isn't that giving away whatever advantage we might have?'

'We must fight Attila here and now,' Aetius said, through gritted teeth. 'If we sit on the high ground he might simply pack up and withdraw. If we move down onto ground more advantageous to him it will provoke him to fight.'

'Why is it so important to fight Attila here, now?' Gunderic said.

'This Alliance is extraordinary but it cannot hold,' Aetius said. 'Let's be honest, the chances of us sustaining it much longer are low. Fighting has already broken out between the Franks and the Saxons on two occasions, on the way here from Aurelianum. Right now we have an army capable of beating Attila. We must defeat him. If we let him slip away then he will lick his wounds, regroup his forces and come back stronger. He'll fight us one by one instead of together. And then he will defeat us. It's us or him.'

'But the terrain?' Wodnas said. 'I can't think of anywhere more suitable for Attila's warriors.'

'True,' Aetius said. 'But this is our only chance and if our shield wall holds firm we can win. Attila is rattled. We know he was shocked to find we had beaten him to Aurelianum and he is worried about the battle. He will make mistakes.'

'How do you know Attila is worried?' Gunderic said.

'Spies tell us he is consulting soothsayers,' Aetius said. 'Attila is a great general but his one weakness is superstition. Our Saxon friends here tell me that he has sent out for German witches – those hellrūnes of yours – to come and divine his future. He has become convinced only they can truly see the future. Does that sound like the actions of a man confident of victory?'

437

The others all looked at each other. Hagan could sense the atmosphere change in the tent as each of the war leaders, like hunting dogs catching the scent of blood, realised perhaps for the first time that victory over one of the greatest war leaders who had ever lived, was within their grasp.

'When we reach the plains we will fan out into a long front,' Aetius said. 'Behind us we have the high ground we are currently camped on and the woods which will protect our flank. With the ridge to the right of us there is no effective way Attila can get around us. If things go badly we can retreat back up to the high ground. The Romans, Saxons, Franks and Armoricans will form the left wing. I will command there.'

The mention of Armoricans explained to Hagan the presence of the dark-haired men he had thought were Britons. Many were migrating from Britannia to Armorica, enticed by promises of rejoining the Empire, provided they help to manage the rebellious local Bacaudae there.

'Our newly arrived Burgundar friends can join us on the left,' Aetius went on. 'Theodoric's Visigoths will form the right wing. King Sangiban here will lead his Alan cavalry to the centre.'

He nodded towards the nervous-looking, dark-skinned man in the silk tunic.

'It seems he had a crisis of faith in our prospects of defeating Attila,' Aetius said. 'And was prepared to open the gates of Aurelianum and surrender the city to his forces. He assures me now that he has realised his mistake and his loyalty is not in question. I have decided to give him a chance to prove this by placing him right at the heart of our formation.'

And the place most likely to bear the full force of any charge Attila would mount, Hagan thought. Also, surrounded by troops whose loyalty was not in question, there would be no opportunity for Sangiban and his men to slip away from the fight. No wonder the Alan king looked so nervous.

'What about Attila's forces?' Wodnas said.

'He has a great horde, both Huns and warriors collected from the nations he has conquered so far,' Aetius said. 'Perhaps twenty-five thousand Huns, then another twenty-odd thousand Alemanni, Gepids, Thuringians, Scirians, Heruli and a sizeable contingent of Ostrogoths under their king Valamir.'

'An even match, then,' Gunderic said. 'This could be a close-run thing.'

'Indeed,' Aetius said. He continued looking at the map as if trying to see into the future. 'But this is our last chance. We must defeat Attila or fall.'

'General, I would like to ask a favour,' Gunderic said.

'Go ahead,' Aetius said.

'King Sangiban has only cavalry, I believe?' Gunderic said. 'We have a company of great fighters. Our finest champions. They are called the Berh Herjass – the Bear Warriors. They will never flinch from combat. If we deployed them alongside the Alans they would add some steel to the centre of the army.'

Hagan frowned. This did not seem the best way to deploy attacking warriors like the Berh Herjass. In that position they would bear the brunt of Attila's attack. They were bound to suffer casualties, perhaps heavy ones.

'Very good,' Aetius said. 'Let's do that. But only if you are sure. It's bound to be hot in that position. If these are your best men then perhaps you don't want to throw their lives away.'

'These men should be wherever the fighting is hardest,' Gunderic said. 'I have full confidence in them and the man who will lead them tomorrow.'

He clapped a hand on Hagan's shoulder.

'That man will be none other than my oldest friend and son of my father's last champion: Hagan.'

CHAPTER FIFTY-THREE

HAGAN FELT HIS heart sink in dismay. If the Bear Warriors were going to be at the centre of the Hun attack, whoever led them would be the first to enter that storm. He looked around him and saw the various leaders all knew this too. He was not sure but he thought he saw a look of concern cross the face of Aetius, though the Roman changed his expression very quickly to be more impassive. There was a mocking smile on the lips of Sigurd. Gunderic's jaw was set in a stony expression.

'King Gunderic,' Aetius said. 'I am grateful for your offer of your best warriors but perhaps they would be best deployed elsewhere? Perhaps somewhere they are not likely to incur as many casualties?'

Gunderic's expression turned to one of triumph. Hagan knew he was congratulating himself that his suspicions of Hagan and the Romans had been proven true.

'I want my warriors wherever they can gain most glory for our folk,' the king said.

'If I may suggest something?' Wodnas spoke. All eyes turned towards him.

'The Berh Herjass are excellent warriors, and can fight wherever they are sent,' the old man said. 'Perhaps we should think of moving them around? Place them wherever the greatest need is?'

Gunderic smiled.

'I like the idea of that,' he said. 'And the first place they will be most needed is alongside the Alans.'

Hagan rolled his eyes. Of course Gunderic was smiling. If he was not killed in the shield wall he would be moved to wherever the next place of higher peril – and higher chance of his death – was.

'Very well,' Aetius said.

Then he dismissed everyone with a final toast of wine to victory. Outside, Hagan and the others were reunited with the rest of Gunderic's council who had waited there. They tramped back out of the Roman camp to where the Burgundars had set up their own encampment. No one spoke on the journey. When they reached Gunderic's tent the king began to speak to the councillors, delivering orders. Hagan listened with only half an ear, his mind fixated on the battle to come. His memory flew back to the day he had faced the Huns at Vorbetomagus, except tomorrow he would be in the front, not the third rank of the shield wall. He was not scared of dying, but he had a strong feeling that he was being pushed into this situation.

They gathered around the fire that had been lit outside Gunderic's tent. Gunhild came and joined them.

'How did the meeting with Aetius go?' she said.

Gunderic and Sigurd told her.

'Victory sounds far from assured,' Gunhild said, frowning, when they were done. 'If anything it sounds like Aetius is rolling the dice.'

'I agree,' Wodnas said. 'This alliance too sounds very fragile. I can see why Aetius is desperate to fight now. In a few more days everyone will be at each other's throats.'

'You think we should leave?' Gunderic said.

'No,' Wodnas said. 'If we do, then we will run the risk of revenge from Aetius if he does happen to win. We should still fight Attila, but we need a strategy for if things do go wrong.'

'I don't like the way Aetius knows so much about us,' Sigurd said. 'You heard them talking about my sword. How does he know all this? If he knows about the sword he probably knows about the—'

Sigurd broke off, though Hagan guessed his next word would have been *treasure*.

'Spies,' Lokke said. 'He must have managed to get spies into the realm.'

'We hang all foreigners trying to enter the country,' Gunderic said.

'Then it must be someone who isn't a foreigner,' Lokke said.

All eyes turned to Hagan. He felt a surge of indignation run down his spine and he straightened his back.

'I'm not a Roman spy, if that is what you are thinking, Gunderic,' he said.

'And why would I think that?' the king said. There was sarcasm in his voice.

'Why else would you have put me in a position that means almost certain death?' Hagan said, blazing with indignation. His skin pale, his eyes wide.

'What is this, Gunderic?' Gunhild said. 'What does Hagan mean?'

'He means, sister, that I have honoured him with the most sought-after position in our war horde,' Gunderic said. 'That of leader of the Bear Warriors. However, it seems that is not good enough for him.'

Hagan realised Gunderic's statecraft was as slippery as it always had been. For Hagan to deny the honour of the appointment was to insult the honour of the company, something he could not do without causing huge offence to all gathered around him. And if he continued to try to talk his way out of the position it would make him sound like a coward trying to worm his way out of a dangerous situation. Everyone would have nothing but contempt for him. Worse, they might kill him outright. Perhaps there was one more route to try.

'Lord King,' he said, fighting to control his breathing. 'I am flattered to be named the new leader of the Berh Herjass, but surely there are others more worthy of this honour?'

'Who would be more worthy than you?' Gunderic said. 'The warrior band was formed to preserve the memory of the Dagelungs, and you are the last of the Dagelungs.'

The king's voice was cold. He looked Hagan in the eyes with a steady, unflinching gaze that left little doubt he was as good as condemning the Dagelung to death.

Hagan shook his head.

'And after Attila's charge there will be no more Dagelungs,' he said, his voice sharp with bitterness.

'Hagan why would you not want to lead the champions of the Burgundars?' Gunhild said. 'Just as your father before you did? I remember when you were young and we were all friends. You were always talking about the day you would ride out with the warrior horde, leading it like Godegisil did then.'

Hagan looked at the sky for a moment. He heaved a heavy sigh, then looked at Gunhild once more.

'That's just it,' he said. 'Godegisil was not my father.'

'What?' Gunhild's face was screwed up with incomprehension.

'He treated me like a son,' Hagan said. 'But he was not my real father. My mother was raped while he was away at the wars.'

'Godegisil killed the rapist, I am sure,' Gunderic said. 'As he deserved.'

'No,' Hagan said. 'My mother never said who he was. She said that was to protect Godegisil.'

Hagan dug his mother's amulet out from under his tunic and held it up.

'This is the only clue I have of his existence,' he said. 'My mother snatched it from the man as he attacked her.'

Gunhild's eyes widened.

'That's the amulet I told you about!' she said, looking at Gunderic. The king remained impassive.

'So for all we know you are not even of noble lineage!' the king said. 'And to think we used to all be friends! Well, tomorrow you will atone for everything. Your deeds on the battlefield at the forefront of the Berh Herjass will ennoble you. The Folk will remember you as a great man.'

'Atone?' Hagan said. 'For what?'

'For betrayal,' Gunderic said, his teeth clenched and eyes flashing. All pretence on his behalf was now gone. 'For coming to my kingdom and using our friendship to spy on your own folk and try to steal away my gold!'

'Our gold,' Sigurd said. 'And my sword.'

Hagan shook his head.

'It was never about that, don't you see? All I ever wanted was to be back with my own folk again.'

'Well, now I am giving you the chance to live in their hearts and memories forever,' Gunderic said. 'As a legend who died fighting bravely against insurmountable odds. Or perhaps you'd rather just be hanged like a common criminal?'

'Like Geic, you mean?' Hagan said.

Gunderic glared at Hagan for a long moment.

'You think Geic is the only man I've ever had put to death?' Gunderic said. 'Didn't I tell you? A king must act with ruthlessness when his position is threatened.'

He let the words hang in the air for a moment. Then he glanced at the others around him and shook his head.

'I think everyone is getting overwrought. We should all get some rest,' he said. 'Tomorrow we go to war. Hagan, I will send some warriors to guard your tent to make sure you have a good night's sleep.'

CHAPTER FIFTY-FOUR

HAGAN FOUND IT very hard to sleep. The night was hot and sticky and he lay on his bedding, dry-mouthed and bathed in sweat, but it was not the discomfort that kept him awake.

He was tired but the events of the evening repeated themselves over and over in his mind. He was angry with himself and at the unfairness of the situation. He was not scared to fight – he had fought in many battles – but his days of being in the front line should have been over. Gunderic said Hagan had betrayed him but it was really the other way around. Gunderic had betrayed his friendship. So what if Aetius had sent him to Geneva to spy on the Burgundars and find the treasure? He had not actually carried out the orders. He, Hagan, had betrayed no one.

He cursed himself for not telling them everything as soon as he arrived. Then again, what might that have achieved? Perhaps they would have killed him outright there and then.

He was also angry at how he had let Gunderic manipulate him. It had always been the same since they were children. Gunderic always knew what to say or do to get the others to do what he really wanted.

Hagan knew he could run from all of this, slip away into the night and turn his back on the whole Burgundar tribe. Gunderic knew, however, that Hagan would not want to leave a reputation behind that he was a coward who shirked the responsibilities handed to him in time of need. What stopped Hagan running away was his pride.

That, and the ten warriors Gunderic had posted outside his tent.

Then there was Gunhild's reaction at the sight of his mother's amulet. The more Hagan thought of it, the more he felt there was something strange about the way she had looked at it then looked at Gunderic, as if expecting some sort of reaction from him. Had she seen it before? Did she know something about his father?

The crushing loneliness that had dogged him during his years wandering had returned. All that time he had yearned to be back among his folk. Then he had found them again, but the new Burgundar realm was not the old kingdom he had known. Everything was strange and his old friends suspicious and conspiratorial. The homeland of his childhood was gone for ever.

Haunting memories of screaming Huns charging towards him at Vorbetomagus surfaced in his mind and he wondered how he could manage to escape what seemed like almost certain death. Perhaps he could fight his way out of it? Battles were chaotic situations where all sorts of unexpected things happened. Who knew what he might be able to achieve?

The thought made him feel better. He focused on the thought of slashing his way through Huns to finally stand before Gunderic, covered in their blood, watching the expression of dismay on the king's face that his plan had not worked out the way he had intended.

Then he would kill him.

With this thought finally giving him some respite from the inner turmoil, Hagan drifted off to sleep at last. He woke with a start. It was pitch dark but he sensed something was different. Someone was in the tent with him.

His first thought was that Gunderic had decided not to leave his death to chance and sent assassins to kill him in the dead of the night. He slid his hand under his bed roll to grasp the hilt of the knife he had left there. If someone was here to kill him he would take as many of them with him as he could.

Hagan squinted. He could make out a figure standing above him. There was something familiar about the outline. Whoever it was, he was tall and slender. Hagan could just about make out the man's long sleek hair and the spear shaft he carried. Somehow he knew it was Wodnas.

'What do you want?' Hagan said. The strange presence of the old man was as unnerving as usual.

'I need you to help me,' the old man said. He spoke in a quiet voice.

'Did Gunderic send you?' Hagan said, pulling the knife from under the bed roll.

'No,' Wodnas said. 'He doesn't know I'm here. I wish to keep it that way. Come with me now and you could greatly increase your chances of seeing the sun set tomorrow night.'

'How do I know I can trust you?' Hagan said.

'You don't,' said Wodnas. 'But the way I see it, you don't have much choice.'

'What do you want me to do?'

'I have need of your special hunting crafts,' Wodnas said.

'Tonight? How will we get past the guards?' Hagan said.

He could not see in the darkness but he got the distinct feeling like the old man was looking at him with his one eye, an expression on his face that suggested Hagan had just said something stupid.

'I am Wodnas,' he said. 'These folk practically worship me. Do you think they will question what I say?'

Hagan pulled on a dark woollen hooded jerkin and britches, put his boots on then followed Wodnas out of the tent. As he had predicted, the guards just nodded when Wodnas told them he needed Hagan to perform the initiation rite of the Bear Warriors and Gunderic knew all about it.

Then they hurried off out into the dark. Despite the late

hour, the Burgundar camp was not starting to quieten down. Men sat around fires, talking or checking their war gear, unable to sleep and preparing themselves for the battle that would come in the morning. It was still hot despite the darkness, and the high ground they and the rest of the Alliance were camped on was dotted with the light of countless campfires so that it looked like a mirror of the star-pocked sky above. Far away, as if on the other side of a sea of darkness, fires also burned in Attila's camp on the far side of the flat plain.

There was no moon, so once away from the camp it became very dark despite the fires. Hagan let his eyes become accustomed to the darkness. Just outside the camp he saw a hooded figure waiting for them. As they approached he was surprised to see it was Freya. She was dressed in her dark ceremonial robes of a hellrūne. She bore her metal distaff in her right hand.

Together they all set off again, following Wodnas downhill and into the dark beyond the camps. They passed through the guards and scouts posted to stop any surprise attacks. Before long the ground levelled out and they continued out across the plain.

'If I didn't think it was madness,' Hagan said in a low voice, 'I would say we were heading towards the camp of Attila.'

'We are,' Wodnas said. 'I know you have special skills learned in the Roman Army. My raven warrior scouts speak of your crafts with great respect. And I have seen for myself your ability to disappear in the night. That night we hunted you outside Geneva my best men were unable to find you.'

'So you knew that was me in the forest?' Hagan said.

Hagan saw the outline of Wodnas' head nodding.

'I suspected it was you,' Wodnas said. 'I thought there was someone else there that night, and when he escaped from my Ravens I knew whoever it was had great skill. The sort of skills only an expert hunter could have... or perhaps someone who has spent time in the Roman exploratores. What I've heard about you during your time spent with the Raven Warriors on the journey here confirmed my suspicions.'

Hagan shook his head in disbelief.

'Tonight I need you to get the Lady Freya across to Attila's camp,' Wodnas said. 'Once inside it she will do the rest. All I ask is that you use all the skills you have to get her over there and then safely back here without being caught by the Huns.'

'You want me to take her into the Huns' camp?' Hagan said. 'Are you mad?'

'Some think that, yes,' Wodnas said.

'Why me?' Hagan said. 'Why not send one of your Raven Warriors? Gunfjaun is every bit as good as I am.'

'I don't want anyone to know we're doing this,' Wodnas said. 'If it works, it could be key to victory over Attila. If that happens I want the Burgundars to believe they won the day by their strength and battlecraft, not because of an old man, a girl and one warrior creeping around in the night. Even if it was. Besides, I know how good you are at scurrying around in the dark.'

Hagan could not see it, but he somehow felt the old man's one glittering eye was gazing at him.

'Very well,' Hagan said with a grunt. 'Though it seems all I've gained by following you here is the chance to die tonight instead of in the morning.'

CHAPTER FIFTY-FIVE

THEY MOVED THROUGH the long grass. Hagan was confident that for the first half of the journey there was no need for caution. When they got past the midpoint to the Hun encampment however, they slowed down. The Huns would have advance guards, pickets and scouts out in the fields in case anyone tried to sneak up on the camp in the night, just as Hagan and the others were trying to do now. Hagan had no desire to stumble over armed warriors in the dark so he led the others in cautious, creeping steps, careful to make as little noise as possible. The closer they got to the camp the lower they dipped, moving crouched over in case their outlines became visible above the grass. Twice Hagan detected warriors not far off. The first one gave himself away by a cough while the second was whistling to himself. On both occasions they changed direction and moved off, silent and careful, giving the warriors a wide berth lest they detect their own presence.

When they got closer Hagan saw that the Huns had drawn their wagons into a large semi-circle around their camp, forming a perimeter every bit as effective as an embankment. Torches and braziers had been set a little way out from the wagons to create a lit space where anyone coming from the fields could be spotted approaching. Warriors walked back and forth at intervals along the illuminated area. Behind the wagons fires blazed and he could make out glimpses of tents and moving figures. There was the sound of voices, some laughter and some high-pitched shrieks. Through it all came the noise of wild drumming, flutes and horns.

'It sounds like they are having a party,' Hagan said in a whisper.

'Excellent,' Wodnas said. 'This is exactly what I had hoped for. I will go no further. I am an old man and might hinder you if I continue to accompany you. Freya knows what to do once you are in there.'

Hagan nodded. The next part of the journey – getting through the well-lit perimeter – would be the most difficult. While the old man padding along in his bare feet was silent as one of Freya's cats, it would still be easier to get two people rather than three into the camp. However he was not ready to go along with the plan without knowing more about it.

'I want to know what I'm getting myself into,' Hagan said. 'If I'm walking into certain death I want to do it with my eyes open. What is Freya going to do? If you think she can kill Attila and get away alive you're madder than you look.'

'Nothing so drastic, my friend,' Wodnas said with a little chuckle. 'I will leave suicidal bravery to your friends in the Berh Herjass. Attila is consulting hellrūnes and other witches. He has sent word all over the north for tribes to send him their best. It is well known that Attila is a superstitious man – otherwise why is he so obsessed with the Sword Tyrfing? Freya here is one of our own witches. I want her to deliver a message to him that will worry him further. A shaken leader can act rashly, or make mistakes. He might hesitate to send his warriors into action at a crucial moment or send them in too early. Perhaps we can provoke Attila to do something that makes our victory more certain.'

Hagan nodded. It was a very good idea, if rather dangerous.

'Sometimes, my friend, you can fight without actually fighting. Good luck,' Wodnas said, and disappeared back into the darkness.

Hagan looked at Freya. Her dazzling eyes reflected the nearby firelight and to his amazement she smiled. Did she not realise what danger they were in? If they made a noise or were spotted creeping up on the camp it would mean certain death yet she did not seem the slightest bit concerned.

She presented her hand as if accepting an offer to dance. Hagan took it and led her forwards towards the pool of light outside the Hun camp. Despite the peril they were both in he found the touch of her skin exhilarating and he could smell her scent on the warm night air. The effect of being this close to her was intoxicating. For a brief moment he felt like he might lose all control, grab the beautiful young woman and pull her close to him, pressing his lips onto hers and his body against her lithe one. Then he remembered that in a dark field outside an enemy encampment there were more important matters to attend to.

When nearly at the edge of the torchlight, Hagan stopped and crouched down, pulling Freya down with him. For a few moments they watched the men guarding the space between the wagons and the darkness of the fields. Hagan reckoned they stood about thirty paces apart. There was no way into the camp here. Even if he could distract some of them, others would catch sight of him and Freya as they dashed across the open ground. Even if the ones outside did not, there were bound to be more watching from behind the wagons.

With a motion of his head he gestured to Freya that they should move on. Crouching low and staying in the dark beyond the arch of the firelight, they hurried around the camp, following the perimeter of wagons in its large semi-circular path. After some time they came to one end of it and found that Attila had made his camp against a river. That made sense. Both horses and men needed to drink and the flowing water would provide some protection from any attack from the rear.

It also gave Hagan a way to get into the encampment.

The row of wagons ran all the way to the river's edge but

stopped there. Hagan and Freya followed the river upstream a little further.

'We need to get in,' he said in a low voice. 'Then drift downstream into the camp.'

'I can't do it in my robes,' Freya said. 'They will soak up the water and pull me under.'

Hagan realised she was right. The same would apply to his heavy wool cloak.

'We'll have to—' he started to say but Freya, her enigmatic smile on her lips, was already stripping off.

'We need to hurry,' she said. 'I don't want to miss the ceremony.'

Wondering what she was talking about, Hagan took his own clothes off. They tied their clothes into bundles then slipped into the water and pushed out to the middle of the stream. Despite the warmth of the summer night the water was chill and Hagan realised they could not stay in it too long. Nor could they swim, as the splashing would be heard by those in the Hun camp. All they could do was hope the current carried them downriver as swiftly as possible.

They drifted, making the occasional kick or arm movement under the surface to keep them going in the right direction. After a time they reached the end of the half-ring of wagons that marked the edge of the camp. Inside it the camp was a blaze of light and noise.

Hagan nodded to Freya and they both kicked as gently as they could towards the riverbank. If they continued to float downstream someone was bound to spot them. They crawled up the bank and rolled under the nearest parked wagon. Under there they scrambled to pull their damp clothes back on without making too much noise.

'We need to find Attila,' Freya said in a hissed whisper.

'The best thing to do is act like we are supposed to be here,' said Hagan. 'If we walk around with confidence then no one will suspect we are from the enemy.'

Freya arched an eyebrow but nodded.

'Very well,' she said. 'Let's go.'

They rolled out from under the wagon and stood up. Both were brushing dust and grass off themselves when a voice called out in a tongue Hagan did not understand.

He turned around and saw a Hun warrior striding towards him. He had a spear in one hand, pointed at him and Freya.

CHAPTER FIFTY-SIX

HAGAN SHRUGGED, SHOWING he had not understood.
'What were you doing under that wagon?' the Hun
demanded, switching his tongue to that of the Ostrogoths. It
was a language similar to Burgundar if with a strange accent.

'I was bringing this Saxon witch to the Lord Attila,'
Hagan said, doing his best to imitate the lilting accent of the
Ostrogoths. 'But I thought I might enjoy her charms first.'

The Hun looked Freya up and down, a lascivious grin on
his face.

'I can't say I blame you,' he said. 'She's a fine piece. But you'd
better hurry. The king has already started his consultation
while you've been swiving under there.'

'Where do we go?' Hagan said.

'Follow the noise,' the Hun warrior said, pointing further
into the camp.

Hagan and Freya hurried off. They crossed through lines
of tents with men huddled around fires outside them. It was
late but the Huns and their allies clearly had as much trouble
sleeping as Hagan had. He had camped alongside Huns in the
Roman Army and knew what to expect. It was not the wild,
lawless chaos some Romans might believe a barbarian camp to
be. There was a huge enclosure beside the river where the horses
were penned. The Hun tents were round with conical tops
rather than the rectangular ones of the Goths and the Romans.
There were countless campfires with groups of people gathered

around them, not just warriors but women and children too, as the Gepids, Ostrogoths, Alemanni and other Germanic allies had all brought their families with them. The men were busy checking equipment and war gear for the coming battle. As they passed by tents of Germanic warriors Hagan could not help but notice there was little difference between them and the men in the Alliance camp.

Hagan also noted there was none of the wild intoxication that often happened in Germanic tribal camps the night before a battle, where men and youths tried to quell the butterflies that crowded their stomach with strong wine and ale. Indeed, the Romans had been known to 'accidentally' let contingents of wine fall into the hands of enemies they were due to fight, so that the next day, when the tribesmen stumbled out of their tents, hungover and weak, they presented much less of a threat.

Attila had fought alongside Romans for many years and knew all this. He must have left strict orders there would be no carousing. When the morning came his warriors would be ready for war, not ready to throw up.

There was a commotion going on somewhere in the camp, however. There was a great blaze sending sparks and smoke roiling into the night sky from somewhere towards the centre of the camp. The sound of wild drumming and discordant flutes, along with high-pitched shrieking that could have been singing, reached their ears.

'That sounds like where we need to be,' Freya said.

Like in the Roman camp, the closer they got to the centre of the camp the larger the tents became. Those of Hun and Ostrogoth kings and nobles were pitched at the heart of the temporary settlement, well out of range of arrows shot from beyond the perimeter of wagons and buffered from any potential assault by the rows of tents of the lesser ranks around them.

Right in the centre of the camp was a clearing in which a huge bonfire blazed. The heat from it was oppressive and it

456

drove winds that picked up dust and tugged at the hair of all near it.

A ring of people were gathered before the fire. Many Hun nobles and their allies watched a lurid scene unfolding before them.

A motley crowd of bedraggled men and women beat on goatskin drums and played on flutes. They were almost naked, their modesties just saved by scraps of ragged cloth. Their skins were slick with sweat in the firelight. They beat the drums in a wild, erratic rhythm, none of them in time or beat with any of the others, while the flutes sounded out jarring notes. It was a cacophony rather than any sort of tune.

Another group of women dressed in long dark robes shrieked and wailed. It was only because they did this in unison that Hagan could tell the racket they made was on purpose. They were *Galdring*, chanting the holy prayers that called down the powers of spirits and gods. Before all of them another band of women danced and swirled, trailing their arms and long hair as they spun in circles. Some were dressed in sparkling blue robes like Freya's, some were in different dresses, but all carried some form of distaff in their hands. Hagan knew this meant they were *Hel-Runae* – witches who could speak to the spirits and divine the future.

A gory pile of butchered corpses lay on the ground. Three men and four women had suffered the threefold death: strangled, hit over the head and stabbed. Then their stomachs had been ripped open so their insides tumbled out. Several of the witches were now scrabbling around in the loops of white, blue and green guts, studying them with great interest.

All this was set against the garish flickering of the flames of the bonfire which somehow made the scene all the more like something from a nightmare.

There was a wooden platform erected before the fire. On it was a high seat with a canopy of silk above it. A short, barrel-chested Hun with an elongated skull sat there, watching the proceedings with interest. Unlike the other noblemen around him who were bedecked with jewellery, gold rings and armlets, he was dressed in simple clothes: a plain linen tunic, leather breeches and latched Scythian shoes. Nevertheless from the deference with which all others treated this man, and from the fact that he was the only person sitting, Hagan deduced this must be Attila himself.

A white banner hung from a pole behind the seat and as the wind caught it Hagan gave a start as he recognised the emblem on it. Just as Zerco had said, it was the same stylised bird as the one on his mother's amulet.

Attila said something to a nobleman who stood nearby. With another start Hagan realised it was Ediko, the Hun emissary who had come to Gunderic's court. Hagan stepped back a little, away from the firelight, in the slight chance Ediko might recognise him.

Ediko raised his horn to his lips and blew. The drumming, caterwauling and dancing came to a gradual stop. From the confused, blank or frightened expressions on many of the dancers and musicians, Hagan judged they were either very drunk or, more likely, under the influence of the herbal or mushroom concoction he knew the witches drank so they could see into the spirit world.

'King Attila orders that you make your prophesies now,' Ediko said in a loud voice, translating Attila's words into that of the Goths. 'Which of you has seen anything?'

'Looks like I'm just in time,' Freya said in a low voice to Hagan. 'I've got to get out there.'

She pulled up her long hood then stumbled out into the cleared area into the crowd of magic women, as if she had spun into the crowd and was now returning. In the confusion of dancing shadows, the light of the great fire and the swaying movements of the witches and the musicians, Hagan could see how she might get away with not getting recognised. He just hoped no one had counted them.

Several of the women stood up and began spouting gibberish. Spittle flew from their mouths as they chanted in a tongue known only to themselves. Attila looked at Ediko who shrugged. The king frowned angrily.

'I see blood and death!' another witch howled. 'The winds of doom will sweep these fields tomorrow. Warriors will battle warriors. Shields will be sundered. Helmets will be hacked. A tide of blood will be unleashed. Many will die. Wolves will feast on the corpses of thousands.'

Attila growled something to Ediko.

'The king knows men will die,' the nobleman said. 'He wants to know who will win the battle.'

'That I cannot see, lord,' the witch said.

'What about you?' Ediko pointed to another hellrūne. 'Can you see who will have victory tomorrow?'

The woman shook her head and scurried away.

'The future is murky, lords,' another witch cried. 'The Dísir and the land spirits do not want to speak tonight.'

'You've all been well paid already! Surely someone must be able to see something?' Ediko shouted. 'This had better not be a ruse to get more silver.'

'Lord, I can see one thing,' another of the witches said. She was pointing at one of the piles of human entrails. 'In the liver of this one. It tells me that the leader of the enemy will be killed in the battle tomorrow.'

Those who understood the German tongue all cheered. Ediko translated for Attila and his straggling black beard, flecked with grey, split in a broad grin. The other witches all nodded and smiled, eager to show they now saw the same thing.

'I too see something, lord!'

Hagan stiffened. This time it was Freya who spoke.

'You will not win victory tomorrow,' she said.

Silence descended all around. In moments all that could be heard was the crackling of the fire. Attila's grin became fixed as all eyes turned to him.

For a moment the king looked back at them all. Hagan could feel the strength of the man's presence and the power of his will. It was like they were all captive to him. Then he spoke. His words were a short, staccato burst in the tongue of the Huns. The Hun noblemen who stood around the fire cheered once more.

'We still fight tomorrow, the king says,' Ediko said for the benefit of those who spoke the Germanic tongues. 'Who knows if the prophesies of witches are to be believed or not? But if they are, the death of Aetius is victory enough for me. For he stands in the way of all our plans. However, think about this, King Attila says: why would Fortune have made the Huns victorious over so many of the nations of the world if she were to turn against him now? No! Tomorrow will bring us victory.'

The Goth, Alemanni and Gepid noblemen cheered then, though their cries were nowhere near as lusty as those of the Huns. Yet Hagan noticed the way Attila's eyes flicked around the crowd. Perhaps it was his own wishful thinking but the Hun King looked unnerved.

Hagan felt someone touch his arm and he turned to see Freya beside him. Somehow she had slipped away from the other witches again while all attention was on Attila.

'We had better go,' she said in a low whisper. 'I think we've tried our luck to breaking point already.'

CHAPTER FIFTY-SEVEN

GUNHILD PICKED HER way carefully down the riverbank towards the stream that flowed past the camp. She and her maidservants had walked some way upstream to a quieter part of the river, both to avoid the sewage and detritus that flowed from the encampment and to minimise the chance of any men accidentally walking by when she was bathing.

It was early morning and the baking sun was only starting to rise over the horizon. It formed a blazing red ball that was smeared by the mist rising from the water. Gunhild looked at it for a moment, remembering that some saw a red morning sky in the morning as an omen of impending disaster.

There had not been many chances to wash on the long journey north, and the days spent in the dust and heat had left her feeling sweaty, dirty and uncomfortable. This had been compounded by the night spent in the camp, living close to so many warriors and all their detritus. She now felt filthy. She was not the only one who felt that way, as several other noblewomen were also making their way to the water. From their excited chatter she could tell they were all Visigoths, Saxons and Franks.

Once at the river she took a final look around in case any men or others had arrived, then, seeing none, she stripped off her dress and waded into the water. Despite the chill it felt invigorating to be rid of the grit and dirt of the roads and be clean again. She swam a little out into the stream, then came back to wash herself, running her hands over her body to wipe away the remainder of whatever still clung to her. As she did so she looked down at herself, proud that her body was still lean and attractive.

She lay back in the water, letting its coolness strip away her cares for a moment along with the dirt. There would be a battle that day, perhaps the greatest the world had ever seen, yet Gunhild was not especially worried.

Yes, it was true that many men would die and that was sad, but that was just the way of things. Men fought and men died. That was all men seemed to do. The world was a constant struggle between men's kingdoms. At least this fight would happen well away from her new homeland. Her brother had at least learned that from the disaster their father had overseen at Vorbetomagus. Today, if it all went badly wrong for the Roman Alliance, the Burgundars could always flee south again to their new realm. Surrounded by the mountains, perhaps they could huddle down and let the world outside kill itself.

There was always the chance Gunderic might be killed, of course. That too would be sad, but then again, it would leave her and Sigurd as rulers of the kingdom. And the treasure belong to two instead of three. Or rather, it would be all hers. Sigurd she could control. She was sure of that.

She had no fears for her husband in the coming battle. Who could kill him? Sigurd was indestructible. He had fought and killed who knew how many men. He was strong as a giant and the Byzantine scale armour he wore was as impenetrable as the hide of a dragon. He was one of those lucky men, the sort who could walk through the war at the end of the world and come out of it without so much as a scratch.

She loved him, she had to admit to herself. In her own way, of course. At first she had thought he was just big, strong and stupid and therefore easily controlled. However she had soon seen that was not the case. She had grown to understand and appreciate the dogged determination with which he approached everything. His indomitable spirit and drive for power were infectious, and despite himself, she believed he loved her. He was proud of being married to a woman thought to be the most beautiful in the world. She knew perhaps he had had some dalliances with other women, but they were unimportant and never noble enough to threaten her.

The one thing that disturbed her heart was Hagan's words and the sight of the amulet he wore around his neck. She had always seen Hagan as the boy they used to run around Vorbetomagus with, the slightly built son of her father's champion. He was of no real consequence, he was just Hagan. He was not a player in the power games she and Gunderic had been involved in. He was just an ordinary lad.

Now, perhaps, he was a threat.

Movement from the top of the riverbank caught Gunhild's eye and she looked up. Another woman stood there, the blood red ball of the rising sun just behind her. Gunhild squinted as the woman began to clamber down the bank. She wore a long hooded robe but as she got closer to the water Gunhild recognised her.

'Brynhild!' she said, raising her hand from the water to beckon to her old friend. 'I am so glad to see you. Where have you been all through the journey? We have so much to talk about.'

She smiled but Brynhild just looked at her with her dark eyes from the shadows of her hood. She did not reply. Then she turned and picked her way along the riverbank, moving further upstream.

Gunhild frowned. There was no question that Brynhild had seen her. She had looked right at her.

Brynhild, further up the river now and with her back to Gunhild, pulled down her hood and got undressed. She slid into the water and began to bathe.

Gunhild stood up and waded towards her old friend.

'How was your wedding night?' she said.

As she got closer Brynhild turned around.

Gunhild gasped. There was the remnants of a huge bruise across Brynhild's right cheek and jawline. It was in its final yellow and purple stages of dispersal. Her top and bottom lips had also been split but were scabbed over and healing. The rest of her body was covered in welts and fading bruises too. Her eyes were narrowed, whether through hate or anger Gunhild could not tell.

'I am sorry. I was foolish to ask of your wedding night,' Gunhild said. 'I forgot Geic attacked you and Gunderic. Did he do this to you?'

She reached out a hand to touch her friend's face. To her astonishment Brynhild slapped her hand away.

'Let me wash you,' Gunhild said. 'Why are you bathing upstream from me? You are the king's wife now and I am his sister. We are equals at last.'

'I am upstream from you in case some of your filth washes down in my direction,' Brynhild said through clenched teeth. 'You are married to *him*. You are the other bastard's sister. Their crimes stain you as well as them.'

'Surely you could not mean my husband Sigurd?' Gunhild said. 'He saved you and Gunderic that night, thanks be to Tiwass.'

Brynhild's upper lip curled.

'Is that what he told you?' she spoke as if her throat was full of river gravel. 'Well, it's a lie.'

'What?' Gunhild said.

'It was your husband who did this,' Brynhild said. She raised a finger to her bruised face. 'Your brave hero punched me in the face. He knocked me to the ground so your brother could rape me.'

Gunhild's eyes widened.

'How dare you say such things!'

'You don't believe me?' Brynhild said. 'Do you think I did all this to myself?'

'I don't know,' Gunhild said. Her own anger was rising. 'For all I know, maybe you did. You've hidden in your wagon since we left Geneva. Who knows how you got them.'

'You would deny this?' Brynhild said, glaring at Gunhild with angry astonishment. 'I "hid" in my wagon because I was so ashamed. I felt so utterly defeated. When the Huns raped me at Vorbetomagus and left me for dead it took me years to recover. But I did. I swore a vow to the Gods that I would not let it happen to me again. I grew strong. I learned to fight. I prepared. I formed my own realm where women like me could live and be free. But men are men. Kings are always looking to expand their realms and I always knew suitors would come, pretending to want me but really wanting my lands. So I set that challenge of leaping the gorge. I set it because it was impossible. No one was supposed to be brave – be *stupid* – enough to complete it. Then along came Gunderic and he did. I have to admit, such courage impressed me. It made me actually want him. Then... then he did this.'

She trailed off. She was looking down at the dark river water, a desolate expression on her face as the reflected light of the rising sun dappled and danced across it. After a moment she sucked in a breath that was almost a sob.

'You said you wanted Gunderic,' Gunhild said. 'Are you sure it was rape? It was your wedding night. You were both very drunk.'

Brynhild's faraway expression disappeared in a flash.

'Don't you dare try to suggest that,' she snarled, pointing her forefinger at Gunhild. 'Don't you dare say it was my fault! Yes, I was impressed by his deed. Yes, I probably still bore some remainder of my girlish infatuation with him deep inside. But that night, when he came fondling and pawing at me, drooling like a dog as he tried to unlace my dress, it brought back all the memories of that bastard Hun at Vorbetomagus. I told Gunderic no. I told him to stop. Perhaps I went too far in making my point but that doesn't give him an excuse for what he did.'

Gunhild looked up, frowning as if unable to comprehend the other woman's words.

'I was knocked out by your husband,' she said. 'Your brave brother – the man who jumped the chasm – was too cowardly or too weak to fight me and needed Sigurd to help him. When I came around I was tied up. My dress ripped away and Gunderic was...'

She shook her head and looked at the river again silently.

'Well,' Gunhild said, her cheeks flushed. She did not know if Brynhild's words were true or not but she was angry that her old friend had said them. They also unsettled her. Not because of the deeds themselves but because she had been brought up in the Royal Household. It was ingrained in her that at all times the most imperative thing was to maintain outward appearances. Family members could commit the most vile deeds but they were always dealt with in private. The folk, the rest of the world, should only see an outward facade of virtue.

'You say Gunderic was weak but others would say he was too noble to strike a woman,' she said.

Brynhild spat into the water and turned away. She began washing her arms, rubbing them vigorously as if she were trying to scrub the very skin off them.

'And you know what my little brother is like,' Gunhild said. 'He's still a spoiled little prince. Perhaps if you had not denied him what he wanted—'

'Get away from me,' Brynhild said, wading further upstream. 'I want nothing more to do with you or your family.'

'Don't you turn your back on me!' Gunhild felt fury boiling in her heart. 'How dare you wash upstream from me. I am the daughter of our last king. I am the sister of the new king.'

'You said we were equals a moment ago,' Brynhild said, turning back to face Gunhild. 'I was the queen of my realm! I am *your* queen. I am your superior.'

'How dare you even think that!' Gunhild said. She levelled her forefinger at the other woman. 'You think you were a queen? By whose right? Tiwass? Jesus? You pronounced *yourself* a queen.'

Brynhild was staring at that forefinger. The black-haired woman suddenly reached out and grabbed Gunhild's hand. She pulled it closer to her face and Gunhild realised she was examining the ring she wore.

'Where did you get this?' Brynhild said. She spoke in a quiet, even voice now.

'Sigurd gave it to me,' Gunhild said. 'Why do you want to know?'

'When did he give it to you?' Brynhild said.

'Why, just a few weeks ago,' Gunhild said, her brow furrowed, perplexed at yet another sudden shift of the other woman's mood. 'Just before your wedding.'

Brynhild let go of Gunhild's hand, dropping it as if she had forgotten she was holding it. Her mouth was half open. Her dark eyes were empty, as if the fierce soul that blazed within her body had left it. Gunhild knew the old legends of the *draugwass*, the after-walkers, dead folk who returned from their graves to haunt the living. Looking at Brynhild now, she resembled exactly how Gunhild had imagined those dead yet walking creatures to be.

'That is my ring,' Brynhild said. 'I laid it on the ledge for the challenger to pick up.'

She looked up, meeting Gunhild's gaze.

'I have been deceived,' she said in the same, hollow tone. 'It was not Gunderic who leapt the ravine. It was Sigurd. The whole thing was a lie.'

Gunhild gasped. She felt a pang of unease that – if this was true – Sigurd had not told her. At the same time she also felt a thrill of pride that in fact it had been her husband who had been the only one brave enough to meet the challenge.

'So that is what Hagan's idea was,' she said, remembering the day at the chasm when Hagan had asked to speak to the king and Sigurd alone.

'Hagan too?' Brynhild said. There were now tears running down her cheeks. 'All my so-called old friends: Hagan, you, Gunderic. All of you conspired to deceive me.'

'We didn't conspire,' Gunhild said. 'This is all just... accidental.'

'I was not *accidentally* raped!' Brynhild said, her lip curling into a snarl.

Brynhild waded to the shore. She pulled on her dress then turned around to face Gunhild.

'Today I will lead my Valkyrjur into battle,' she said. 'We will kill many Huns. I will take my revenge for what was done to me at Vorbetomagus. Then—'

She looked up at the sky as if speaking to someone up there instead of Gunhild in the river.

'Then I will take my revenge on all who have deceived me.'

She spun and stalked up the riverbank.

From the water Gunhild watched her go. Her previous feeling of contentment was gone.

CHAPTER FIFTY-EIGHT

20TH JUNE, AD 451

JUST AFTER DAWN the sound of horns woke those who had managed to sleep. Warriors scrambled out of their tents and gathered their equipment. Some chewed scraps of stale bread but most did not have the stomach for eating and made do with water. The meekest were terrified at the thought of the coming battle while the hardest and most experienced were gruff and short-tempered. Everyone's nerves were on edge.

Hagan felt a strange sense of unreality as he watched the warriors form up at the edge of the Burgundar camp. Across the hillside the Romans and their other allies were all doing the same in their own encampments. It was a beautiful morning with not a cloud in the sky. The air was already full of the perfume of lavender and other aromatic trees and shrubs. Insects buzzed around. It was odd to think he might be living the last moments of his life.

Would there be another life after death? Was there a heaven? If so, would he get there? Would there be endless life in green fields like the Romans believed, or would he go under the earth to the misty realm his forefathers had believed in?

Signalled by other blasts of Roman horns, the war horde of the Alliance mounted their horses and began filing out of their camps. Everyone apart from the Roman soldiers would ride to the battle then, if they were to fight on foot, dismount and take their positions.

Gunderic stood before his warriors.

'Men,' he said in a commanding voice, 'today we fight for the honour of our people. Some of you will not be happy that we fight as part of a Roman army – the people who slaughtered our folk at Vorbetomagus. But I ask you to put that from your minds. We fight for our kin today. The men who fight by your side are blood of your own blood – your clan folk. We are all sons and grandsons of the Burgundars who the Huns slaughtered, whose blood now cries out for vengeance! Today is the day we take that revenge.'

Hagan listened with bitterness in his heart as Gunderic continued. His speech was full of noble words and fine sentiments as he told the warriors how they would win glory today for the honour of the folk, but Hagan was unable to stop his upper lip rising in a sneer.

Gunderic had decided to stay with Aetius during the battle rather than lead his warriors in person. Hagan thought of the men of the Berh Herjass, supposedly the best of Gunderic's warriors, sacrificed by being placed in a dangerous position just to put Hagan in the same position, and that just to protect Gunderic's reputation and his treasure.

He thought of Geic, swinging from the gallows, his reputation blackened forever by a lie.

Hagan knew he could probably run away but he would not. Unlike his king he would bear his responsibilities and fight alongside his own folk.

As the Burgundars began to move out of the camp they were joined by Brynhild's Valkyrjur cavalry. They looked magnificent. Their mail shirts and helmets gleamed in the sun. They held their spears high and their shields were slung across their backs. Each rider's cloak, black like the Burgundars', flowed in the breeze behind her like the wings of a raven. Brynhild rode at their head. Hagan was pleased to see her at last. She sat upright in the saddle. Her visored helmet with a raven's wing nailed to either side shone in the early morning sunlight.

The Valkyrjur joined the Burgundar column and together they lurched downhill towards the flat plains, where the hot summer sun had already bleached the grass to hay.

Attila's army consisted of many fast-moving mounted archers. The greatest danger with that type of enemy was that they could raid around you and attack the flanks and rear. To counter this threat, as they rode the army of the Alliance divided into two huge columns. The cavalry and foot soldiers of the Visigoths, led by Theodoric and his sons, headed eastwards along the road towards Tricassium. The second column, led by Aetius and consisting of the Romans, Saxons, Alans and Franks, proceeded north-east downhill. Hagan and the rest of the Burgundars went with them. This meant if the Huns tried to ride around one column, they would be exposing their own flanks to the second column.

Once at the bottom of the slope they had rejoined and deployed in the long arc that Aetius had described the night before. The Roman soldiers kept marching beyond everyone else, then turned to form the left wing of the army. Their cavalry formed up behind them in support. Beside the Roman foot soldiers the Franks, Saxons and Burgundars dismounted then spread out to continue the line. Right in the centre were the Alan cavalry. The Visigoths' foot warriors formed the whole right wing of the army. Their cavalry stood behind them, ready to counter-attack if required.

The leaders of the Alliance gathered on horseback near the centre, behind the Alans. When battle came they would ride to their various positions with their own men but until then they sat watching the plains before them, surveying their troops and issuing the occasional order to messengers who relayed them to the intended recipients. Hagan was with this group. Gunderic had insisted he stay close by and had assigned several warriors to ensure he did not wander off.

'So here we all are,' Aetius said, 'Now all we need is someone to fight.'

There was no sign of the Hun army. Far away, on the opposite side of the plains, Attila's camp was still there, its edge marked out by the line of wagons, but his warriors remained inside it.

They watched and waited. The sun rose ever higher and got hotter. Soon everyone, arrayed as they were in their heavy war gear and standing in the open, was sweating. Men began to sit down, hunkering behind their shields to get some shade from the blistering sun.

At one point Aetius sidled up beside Hagan. Still gazing out at the empty grassland before them, he said in a quiet voice as if he were enquiring about the weather, 'Tell me, did you ever find out anything of what we talked about in Ravenna?'

'You mean the treasure?' Hagan said.

Aetius flinched and looked around, checking no one else had heard. Then he nodded, frowning at Hagan's lack of discretion.

'Yes, I suppose I have,' Hagan said.

Aetius nodded again. He gave Hagan a knowing look then casually walked away again.

Now and again there was a flurry of movement and riders burst forth from out of the Hun camp. Every time this happened the warriors of the Alliance got to their feet and made ready for any potential attack. They proved to just be scouts however, and once they had ridden close enough to the Alliance lines to get a good look at them they wheeled their horses and galloped back across the plain to their own camp. The warriors went back to waiting again.

The sun rose towards the middle of the sky. Hagan, feeling his skin starting to burn in the heat, began to wonder if Wodnas' plan of the previous night had worked. Perhaps Attila was superstitious enough to believe Freya's fake prophecy and now was too concerned to join battle.

'What are they waiting for?' Sigurd said.

Hagan stood a little way off but not too far that he could not hear what the war leaders said. The big man was not the only impatient one. They had all been waiting a long time, and with every moment that passed the sun got hotter and the warriors of the war horde got thirstier, hungrier and more restless.

'He's softening us up,' King Theodoric said. 'If our warriors stand here much longer in this heat they'll be too tired and thirsty to put up much of a fight when Attila finally attacks.'

'Well, if that is what he is planning,' Aetius said, 'he did not figure on the organisational skills of the Roman Army. It's what we are best at, after all. We've had centuries of practice, after all.'

The general spoke to one of his aides who hurried off. Soon signal horns blasted and columns of servants and auxiliaries laden with amphorae and baskets came from behind the lines and began making their way through the ranks, doling out water and bread. There was watered-down wine and roasted ducks for the war leaders.

Now the waiting and the heat had turned his initial nervousness to boredom, Hagan, like the others, found himself ravenous and he tucked into the food and drink with passion. Afterwards he felt much better.

When they had finished refreshing themselves it was past midday and there was still no sign of the enemy. Hagan's heart began to lighten at the thought that perhaps there would be no battle after all.

He looked around, seeing that Wodnas was deep in conversation with Theodoric. After a while they broke off and Wodnas walked back over to rejoin the Burgundars. The king of the Visigoths began speaking to some of his aides, who hurried off in the direction of the Visigoth lines.

'What were you two conniving about?' Gunderic said. The sun appeared to be making him tetchy. 'You're supposed to be *my* special advisor, remember?'

'I was just telling King Theodoric about the special training we have been doing,' Wodnas said. 'In preparation for fighting the Huns. I was also remarking how amazing it was that for

473

most of the last twenty years the left and right wings of this army, Theodoric's Visigoths and Aetius's Romans, have fought against each other. Now they stand together against a common enemy.'

'I'm starting to think that the enemy has lost his nerve,' Aetius said.

As if in response to the Magister Militum's words, Hagan caught sight of movement at the far end of the plain. Horsemen were filing out of the Hun camp.

'More scouts, do you think?' Gunderic said.

More and more kept coming. They spread left and right, forming a long line that stretched across the plain. Before long their formation stretched from one side to the other, mirroring the long battle line of the warriors of the Alliance. The bright sunshine glittered and danced across helmets, spear points and polished mail.

'Not scouts this time,' Wodnas said. 'Attila is coming for battle.'

All signs of relaxation vanished. Horns began blasting. The warriors who had been sitting on the ground jumped to their feet and began readying their arms. Men took up the positions they had been designated, making one last check of their war gear while there was still time.

'Alright, everyone,' Aetius said, swinging himself up into the saddle of his horse. 'It is time to take our positions for battle. May God protect you all and grant us victory. King Sangiban, you should join your men now.'

The king of the Alans, who looked green with nerves, nodded and swallowed. He climbed onto his horse and set off towards the Alan cavalry in the centre of the allied formation.

Satisfied Sangiban had gone, Aetius made the Roman salute, kicked his heels and galloped off in the direction of the Roman lines.

'God's blessings on you all,' Theodoric said, then he and his two sons rode off towards the Visigoth wing of the army.

'Hagan, it is time you took your new command with the Berh Herjass,' Gunderic said. 'Good luck and may Tiwass smile on us all today.'

Hagan just grunted.

'I will go with you,' Wodnas said, to Hagan's surprise. 'I have something special for them.'

CHAPTER FIFTY-NINE

HAGAN NOTICED FOR the first time that one of Wodnas'
Raven Warriors was standing nearby holding the reins of
a pack horse. The beast was laden with packed saddlebags. At
a signal from Wodnas the lad handed the reins over to the old
man.

Hagan and Wodnas set off, Wodnas leading the pack horse.
From the clinking of its every step Hagan deduced whatever
was inside its saddlebags was metal. The rest of the Burgundar
horde with the other smaller warbands – the Saxons, the
Armoricans and the Franks – lined up beside the Roman army.
The Bear Warriors on the other hand were in the centre of the
line, separated from the Romans and the other Burgundars by
the Alans – and sandwiched between the Alans and the huge
Visigoth warband who formed the whole of the right wing.

Hagan and Wodnas rode down the lines, following in the
tracks of King Sangiban who was riding in the same direction.
After a while they arrived at the centre of the Alliance army
line where the Alan cavalry and the Burgundar Bear Warriors
stood. All were readying themselves for battle. Across the other
side of the plain the Hun army spread out.

Hagan looked at the gathering horde. It was enormous, a
dark line running from one side of the horizon to the other,
bristling with spears. The hooves of thousands of horses kicked
up a cloud of dust from the dry earth that hung above Attila's
army like smoke.

Wodnas handed a goatskin to Hagan.

'Take a drink,' he said.

'It's a bit early, is it not?' Hagan said. 'I'd like to keep a clear head.'

'This is not wine,' Wodnas said. 'It is a special drink I make with herbs and other ingredients. It is an ancient mixture and Freya has had it blessed by the Gods. Drink it. It will do you good.'

Hagan took a swig. The liquid was fiery and bitter, like very strong wine mixed with wormwood. He coughed, blinking away the water that had sprung into his eyes.

'Good stuff, eh?' Wodnas said with a smile. 'Trust me, this will help with your tiredness. Take another drink, please. For my sake.'

Hagan frowned at this strange request and took another drink, forcing the obnoxious liquid down his throat.

'Keep the rest,' Wodnas said. 'Use it when you need it.'

Hagan tucked the goatskin into his belt, thinking the most likely thing he would do when out of sight of the old man was dump the foul stuff.

The Bear Warriors were winding themselves up for the coming fight. They had pulled the heads of their bear skins up over their helmets as they screamed and roared in each other's faces, goading their comrades into ever higher states of rage. Some punched their chests with their fists. Some punched their fellow warriors.

They were all big men, their tall frames packed with muscle. Nearly all had had their noses broken at least once in the past. Some had scars on their faces. Just as he had recognised the type of men who made up the Raven Warriors, Hagan was also familiar with the sort of men who made up this company. They were the sort who believed the solution to any problem was violence. Men who flew into a rage at the slightest perceived disrespect. The sort of unthinking brutes who would laugh with you one moment then punch you in the face the next.

'You don't approve?' Wodnas said to Hagan. Hagan realised the expression on his face must be giving away his inner thoughts. 'These are the finest champions of the Burgundars, brought together to honour your now extinct clan. To honour your father.'

'He was not my father,' Hagan said. 'And I mean no disrespect. It's just that I know of warriors like this. They are all bluster and bullying. They lose their minds with rage and can be as much danger to their fellows as the enemy. Attila's army is mostly cavalry and the best way to counter that is with a firm shield wall. These type of hotheads are more likely to throw away their shields and try to fight the horses, just to show how tough they are. Besides, if they are so valued why is their king sacrificing them in the most dangerous part of the battle line?'

'Sometimes to win the favour of the Gods you must sacrifice that which is most valuable,' Wodnas said with a shrug. 'Or perhaps Gunderic has placed his best warriors in the position where they will have the greatest effect. The Alans don't look like they have much heart for this battle. Their King Sangiban looks like he would prefer to be anywhere but here. If they collapse the whole line could be lost. Having the Bear Warriors beside them will put some steel in the Alans' spines.'

'I suppose I shouldn't be so disparaging towards men I'm about to lead into battle,' Hagan said, blushing. 'And who I could well die alongside.'

'General Aetius is anxious to keep you alive,' Wodnas said, looking at Hagan from the corner of his eye.

'Why do you care what the Roman general thinks?' Hagan said.

'What do you think?' Wodnas said.

'I got very little sleep last night, old man,' Hagan said with a heavy sigh. 'So I don't have much patience for your enigmatic answers this morning. The way I see it there are two possibilities. One, Gunderic has sent you to pretend to be my friend to find out if I am a Roman spy or not. Two – and this one I've been wondering about for some time – are you a secret Roman soldier, in the pay of Aetius? Which one is it?'

'There is a third option,' Wodnas said. 'I have spent a long time training these men and the rest of the Burgundars. I've changed them from a defeated, disorganised band to a disciplined fighting force, with a folk behind them who believe in something worth fighting for. I've acted as a mentor to Gunderic in the art of kingship. Now you have been placed in a crucial position that could sway the outcome of everything. I need to know what sort of man you are. Aetius seems to think you are important. I've heard him arguing with Gunderic about moving you to a safer position. This just makes King Gunderic more suspicious of you.'

'I don't know what sort of a man I am,' Hagan said. 'I don't even know who I really am. My mother was raped. I went to Geneva half hoping to find out who my real father was. I had no choice in going to Ravenna to meet Aetius, but when I got there I saw him as a way to get to the new homeland of my people.'

He watched Wodnas for any sign of reaction but the old man was impassive, as always.

'The king of late,' Wodnas said after a moment, 'has perhaps made some strange choices. Unfortunately this can happen sometimes. The power or gold that comes with kingship can sometimes cloud a man's mind and blacken his heart. Blinded by these distractions, he can sometimes make errors of judgement. At times like those, it is the duty of those who advise the king to make corrections, so that the people he rules do not suffer the consequences of one man's foolish decision.'

He was now looking at Hagan with his one eye. Hagan felt captivated by its dazzling blue. It felt as though the old man was looking into his very soul. At the same time he felt energy and excitement flowing into his tired limbs. Perhaps it was the drink Wodnas had given him but his head, which had been foggy from lack of sleep, now felt fine, his mind sharp. His eyes had been crusted and dry but now felt clear.

'Today I need you to lead these men,' Wodnas said. 'I know you must feel angry about being pushed into this situation but sometimes the Three Great Women who weave all our fates weave us into a certain place at a certain time where we can make a difference. I need you to make a difference today.'

'This is war,' Hagan said. 'One hundred thousand men will fight each other today. What difference can one man make?'

'Is that what Godegisil, the man who raised you, would have said?' Wodnas said. 'Look at it this way. The enemy we can do nothing about. Victory for us depends on every single man doing what is asked of him today and not shirking his responsibility. No one man can ensure every other man in our army will do that, but we can all make sure the one person we can control – ourselves – does the right thing. And if enough men all do that, then it's no longer a matter of one man in an army of fifty thousand.'

Memories of Godegisil surfaced in Hagan's mind. He heaved a sigh. Godegisil had been a good man. Not his natural father but his true father. He had not been gentle, but then that was not what was needed to protect kin and folk. He had been the sheepdog who drove away the wolves from the flock. Hagan remembered his last moments, riddled with arrows shot by the very same horsemen who would soon come thundering across the plain towards him. Anger started to simmer within his heart.

'I will do it,' he said through gritted teeth.

'Good,' Wodnas said. 'Now let's introduce you to your new command.'

At the sight of Wodnas, the Bear Warriors all turned around, expectant looks on their faces.

'For the sake of these men,' Wodnas said to Hagan, 'this afternoon we shall keep up the pretence that your father is the man everyone thought he was until recently.'

Hagan nodded. He halted his horse and swung himself off.

Wodnas clambered down from his mount too. The men of the Berh Herjass gathered around, an excited babble rising from them. Wodnas held the spear he used as a walking staff above his head and silence fell. The nearest ones puffed their chests out and hooked their thumbs into their belt, looks of cool, arrogant appraisal on their faces that Hagan had no doubt could in a moment turn into glares of outright aggression.

Hagan could see the looks of devotion in the eyes of the sweating, panting men when they looked at Wodnas. The same could not be said for himself. Most cast suspicious or dismissive looks at him. He knew why. Most elite warriors saw all other fighting men as lesser beings, and with good reason. These men were the best of the best.

'Warriors of Tiwass!' Wodnas said in a loud voice. 'Today you will face the greatest challenge yet. But I know you will be victorious. I have no doubt whatsoever. Not just because I have trained you and the great god of victory has blessed you, but because on top of all that, this day you will be led by the son of the great Burgundar champion in whose honour this company was formed. Geic has gone, but who better to replace him than the last of the Dagelungs, the bear clan: Hagan, son of Godegisil?'

He clapped a hand on Hagan's shoulder and the eyes of the warriors shifted to Hagan. He could see expectation and curiosity on their faces. He could almost feel the weight of the responsibility he had been given, pushing down on his shoulders. Today some – perhaps many – of these men would die, depending on decisions he would make or orders he would give.

'Men, we do not know each other,' he said. At first his voice was gravelled and he stopped to cough. 'But I am truly honoured to lead such a fine company. My father would have been proud of every single one of you and deeply honoured

481

to know the Burgundars formed this company of the finest and best warriors of our folk in his memory. Today his spirit will fight alongside us. Today we fight against the Huns, the bastards who killed him and who massacred our people at Vorbetomagus. You're all probably too young to remember that day but every one of you will have an uncle or father who died that day. An aunt or sister who was raped. A cousin who was butchered.'

Hagan could see the light igniting in the eyes of the men who stood before him. Before they were angry, now they were ready for war. It made his own heart start to beat faster.

'If Attila is not stopped here today he will ride on south,' Hagan said. 'Devastating all in his way. He will take Geneva and your wives, daughters, parents will be slaughtered or enslaved. The Burgundar realm will fall again, perhaps this time forever. But we stand in his way. We shall stop him. We shall take bloody vengeance for Vorbetomagus!'

The men cheered and Hagan's heart soared. He did not know where the words had come from. He felt like he had uttered them in some sort of trance. He had opened his mouth and they had flowed from somewhere deep within his soul.

The Bear Warriors crowded round, eager to shake Hagan's hand or clap him on the back.

'We know many songs about your father,' one warrior said. 'He was a great man.'

'I saw him fight the bastard Alans,' another said, seemingly oblivious to the Alan contingent who stood nearby. 'He was a one-man army. A real giant of a man.'

'This is a sign from Tiwass,' one of them said. 'He is sending his blessings. You can drink with us anytime.'

Despite their warm words Hagan could tell by the looks in their eyes they were a little surprised Hagan was not taller or bigger in frame.

'What are your orders for battle, lord?' one of the Bear Warriors said.

'I need you to stand firm,' Hagan said. 'We need the shield wall to hold fast. It's more important than anything today.'

A groan rose from the men. Hagan knew they were full of pent-up anger, ready for a fight, their legs aching to charge into the enemy first. Now they were as much as being told to stand and let the enemy hit them.

'Lord, we are most effective when we charge,' the same Bear Warrior said.

'I have no doubt about that,' Hagan said. 'But until the right time comes to do that, victory depends on every last one of you standing firm and keeping the shield wall intact. When the time comes you will charge and you will cut a bloody swathe through the enemy like the hounds of vengeance you are.'

'And when will that be?' another warrior asked.

'When I tell you,' Hagan said.

The men nodded.

'Men, remember the special training I have been doing with you,' Wodnas said. 'Now, take the equipment from the pack horse.'

The men nodded then filed around the horse, unbuckling the packs and taking out what looked like arches of metal. On further inspection Hagan saw they were blades, joined together by a half-loop of steel.

'Are those sheep shears?' he said to Wodnas.

'They are,' Wodnas replied. 'There is not a pair left in the whole of the Burgundar realm. We took them all for the men fighting today.'

'Why?' Hagan said.

Wodnas did not get a chance to reply. Signal horns began to blast from further down the lines.

'Into position!' Hagan shouted.

The men of the Berh Herjass jogged to their place in the lines, spreading left and right in three ranks to form a shield wall and support. When they were in position Wodnas pulled a long piece of material from under his robe. He shook it out and Hagan saw as the breeze caught it that Wodnas held the tattered, bloodstained battle flag of the Burgundars with its threadbare embroidered eagle.

The old man began walking among the warriors. He stopped before each man. Wodnas placed his hands on either side of the warrior's head, one hand holding the battle flag against the Burgundar's cheek. He looked each warrior straight in the eyes with his single eye. In a loud voice Wodnas called down blessings and protection of the Gods. Hagan noticed that as he spoke each warrior's back straightened as if he had been given more strength and belief.

Hagan unslung his shield, took his spear from his saddle and then took his place in the very centre of the shield wall formed by the Bear Warriors. He looked left and right and the two warriors on either side nodded to him. They were ready.

When Wodnas had reached the end of the line he returned to his horse and mounted.

'Good luck to you all,' he said. 'Victory will be yours today.'

As he rode off, the sound of distant horns reached their ears. Out across the flat plain, through the shimmering haze of the heat, the dark line that was the enemy began to move. The distant drum of thousands of horses' hooves sounded like thunder in the far-off mountains, the threat of a coming storm.

'They're coming,' Hagan said.

CHAPTER SIXTY

The Hun army rumbled closer and closer. Hagan looked at the men to his left and right but they were focused on the approaching menace. Their jaws were set and their faces pale though there was no sign of fear.

The shimmering heat on the horizon meant it was difficult to make out the approaching horsemen and Hagan wondered if that was why Attila had waited until the middle of the day to attack, so as to confuse the Alliance further. Before long they could feel and hear the approaching horses though. The ground underfoot thrummed with hoofbeats and the air began to fill with their drumming sound, the whinnying of excited horses and the distant war cries of their riders.

Hagan waited with the rest, feeling like his nerves were stretched to breaking point. It was unbearable. For a moment he felt exhausted. The lack of sleep from the night before had taken its toll, as had waiting all morning in the baking heat. He was unsure if he even had the strength to hold up his shield. The overwhelming thirst returned to clog his throat and dry his mouth, though he was not sure that this was due to the heat.

Remembering the drink Wodnas had given him, he pushed his spear butt into the hard, dusty earth as far as he could, leaving the shaft to rest against the inside of his shield. Taking the goatskin from his belt he uncorked it. It tasted foul but it would have to do. Hagan drank several swallows of the bitter liquid then, grimacing from the taste, put it back in his belt and took up his spear again.

The plain was perhaps three Roman miles across – Hagan knew because he had crossed it the night before – so it took some time for the enemy to cross it, and they were not charging, so as to not exhaust their horses. In that time each man had plenty of time to think about what lay ahead.

Then the horsemen emerged from the shimmering haze. They were more visible now. Hagan could see their fur-rimmed helmets, their glittering mail and the glint of gold and silver off the ornaments they decorated their horses' bridles with. He saw they had bows in their hands. His mind flew back fifteen years to when he had seen those riders coming at Vorbetomagus, except now he was standing exactly where his father had been standing that day.

A low noise began to rise from the men all around Hagan. At first it was just a murmur, a growl at the back of their throats, but it got louder and louder until it became a chanting. There were no words, just a sound that somehow every man knew how to create and which somehow raised in volume in a steady way even though no one was directing it. With a thrill Hagan realised they were making the *baritus*, the Germanic war cry that had terrified Roman soldiers since they first tried to cross the Rhine centuries before. As the noise built to a deafening roar he joined in, feeling the hairs on the back of his neck rise. Despite the summer heat the flesh on his forearms was standing in gooseflesh too.

Some shouted into the backs of their shields, amplifying the sound even more. He could hear it from other places in line too: the Visigoths and the Saxons were joining in. He could hear it from somewhere across the field too. The Ostrogoths, Gepids and the other Germanic warriors in the Hun army were chanting the same war cry.

As he looked out across the fields, it seemed as though all the colours had become sharper, more vibrant. The sky was as bright a blue as the sea he had sailed over north of Ravenna and the sun-dried grass was a fierce yellow. All his fears, doubts and tiredness melted away, driven out by the deafening roaring of the warriors around him, a roar that also came from his own mouth.

He also wondered for the first time what really was in the drink Wodnas had given him.

The line of riders that seemed to stretch from horizon to horizon began to part, splitting into discrete sections at some unheard command from signal horns drowned out by the screaming warriors around Hagan.

They were about three hundred paces away.

Then, all at once, they charged.

The Alliance's men snapped their shields together, clamped their jaws shut and dug their feet in, ready for the impending impact.

The Hun archers divided into wedge-shaped formations. Hagan felt as if the whole of the enemy army was galloping straight at him.

'Hold the line!' he shouted to those around him. 'Stand firm. Their horses won't charge into our formation if the shield wall stays solid.'

At about one hundred paces the Hun archers loosed their first arrows. They rose high in the air like a dark wave. As they began to descend the riders were already notching their second arrows.

Hagan crouched behind his shield, trying to get every inch of protection he could from it. Then it grew dark around him and he saw that the men in the second rank were holding their shields up high in both hands, as if trying to set the bottoms of their shields against the top of the front rank's shields, but tilted back so they provided cover both for the man in the front and the man holding the shield. He only had time to wonder if this was part of the 'special training' Wodnas had referred to before the first arrow storm arrived.

The shields thrummed and bucked under the impact as countless arrows smashed into them. The shields tactic worked well, however. His own shield had protected his body while the man standing behind him had covered Hagan's head and shoulders with his shield.

The hail of arrows petered out and Hagan just had time to peek out and see that the Huns were even closer now. Then the second arrow storm hit. Again the world was drowned out by the frantic drumming of arrows landing on shields all around.

Somewhere further down the line a man cried out in pain and surprise as an arrow found its way through the cover of the shields to strike flesh and bone beneath.

As the din of arrows subsided the sound of hoofbeats was ominously closer and getting even nearer by the moment.

'They're nearly on us,' the warrior beside Hagan said. 'They're going to ride straight into us!'

'Not if we keep our spears out,' Hagan said. His own protruded through the narrow gap between the top right of his shield and the top left of the man next to him. 'No horse in its right mind will ride onto a line of spears and shields. That's why we need to stand firm.'

A third hail of arrows came crashing down, shot now from mere paces away. This time there were more screams from along the lines. This close, the Huns had time to aim for gaps in the shield wall and had sent their arrows through them to strike the men behind.

At almost the same time Hagan heard Roman *bucinae* blaring and again the air was filled with the whoosh of arrows, but this time it came from behind. The Roman archers had loosed, and their deadly shafts rained down on the Hun horsemen as they were preparing to shoot one more volley themselves.

Men and horses screamed as the shafts pierced them. Crouched behind his shield, Hagan heard the crunch and clatter of them falling. He felt fierce joy at the Huns' pain.

Peering through the small gap in the shields Hagan saw that though some had fallen, the rest of the mass of horsemen were nearly on top of their line. They were still galloping at full speed. He gritted his teeth, fighting the rising panic that the huge mass of horseflesh, thrashing hooves and bristling weaponry was about to smash straight into the other side of his shield.

He had said himself that no sane horse could be made to do that. He had believed it but now, facing the onrushing riders, the flaring nostrils of the horses mere paces away, the thunder of their hooves drowning out all else, doubt stabbed into his heart. Could the Huns, with their iron discipline, have somehow trained horses to smash into shields?

Every instinct within Hagan screamed to get out of the way. To drop out of position and jump out of the way of the charging horses.

He knew that if he did that he would open up a hole in the shield wall that the horsemen *could* ride into. Then, with the Huns in behind their defences, the whole shield wall would collapse. He was also supposed to be the leader of the men around him. If he broke they would break too. The whole line would dissolve like parchment touched by fire and the battle would be lost.

Hagan dug his feet in and took a deep breath. On the other side of his shield a horse snorted and Hagan swore he could smell its hot, stinking breath.

At the last possible moment the charging horsemen broke left and right, wheeling their horses and charging away from the shield wall.

The Burgundars cheered. A few stood up from behind their shields to taunt the retreating Huns.

'Get down, you fools!' someone along the line shouted. 'Remember your training.'

The warning came too late. Even though the Huns were now galloping away, each one turned in his saddle and shot a

489

final arrow as he went. The men who had stood up were struck in the head, the neck and the chest – anywhere exposed above their shield.

Some were saved by their war gear. Others were not so lucky. They cried out, blood spurting from their transfixed wounds, as they fell backwards.

Straight away men from the second ranks moved forward to fill the gaps left by the wounded or dead even before the casualty had been dragged out of the way. Repairing the shield wall was the utmost priority.

'Good work, lads,' Hagan shouted to the Bear Warriors.

He felt some elation to have survived the first assault. Though he was under no illusion that this was nothing but the opening clash of what would be a great battle, the discipline shown by those he had thought of earlier as violent madmen gave him some encouragement that perhaps they would make it through after all.

Gunderic would be disappointed.

The Huns withdrew to a hundred or so paces away, far enough to feel safe from any more Roman arrows, then they turned around once more.

'Here they come again,' Hagan shouted and he and his men hunkered down, pushed out their spears and braced themselves for another attack.

The Huns came thundering back in almost a replay of their previous attack. This time they again managed three volleys of arrows before reaching the shield wall. Hagan again felt as if his heart would not be able to stand the strain as he crouched behind his shield, unsure how far away the enemy was, anticipating being battered into the dirt by horses' hooves at any moment.

The Romans again showered the Huns with arrows while they were in range and more bodies of horses and men piled up before the shield wall. Again the Huns turned at the last moment and retreated back out of range.

This time no one jeered their retreat. Those wounded by arrows were dragged out of the line and any gaps in the shield wall closed by others from the rear. Hagan noted that their losses were not great, but if this went on all day they would be worn down. Eventually there would not be enough men in the rear to replace those who fell at the front. This could well be Attila's tactic. If so, they would have to come up with a way to counter it or suffer a long slow defeat through the death of one warrior at a time.

The Huns began a new charge. Hagan and the others braced themselves again. The first salvo of arrows came raining down, clattering and banging against the shields. When a second one did not arrive Hagan peeked out through the gap at the shield's corner and saw that the Huns had put their bows into their hide holsters on their saddles and now brandished spears and swords. Every fourth Hun rider held a hide noose.

Hagan remembered Godegisil, ensnared by their nooses, unable to raise his arms or fight back as they riddled him with arrows. It seemed the next attack would be like the one that killed him.

This time the riders came right up to the shield wall. They prodded with spears and hacked with their swords, trying to find any weakness or gap they could get their weapons into. Hagan's shield bucked with the battering of Hun blades.

Then the point of a spear came lancing in through the small gap between the top corners of his shield and the shield of the man to his right. It flashed through the gloom just to the right of Hagan's right ear. He heard the anguished cry of the man in the second rank who stood behind him, holding his shield over Hagan's head.

The spear gouged into the warrior's thigh and he fell backwards, taking his shield with him. Hagan felt himself suddenly in the full glare of the bright sunshine. This was not the only thing he was exposed to.

Before Hagan could react another Hun cast his noose. It fell around Hagan's shoulders and pulled tight in an instant. Before he could do anything he was already being hauled to his feet as the Hun holding it started riding away.

CHAPTER SIXTY-ONE

H AGAN SCREAMED. IT was not from terror or pain but from pure frustration.

He was being dragged out of position and there was nothing he could do about it. He would be trailed across the dust to be finished off like a lassoed cow while other Huns punched through the gap in the shield wall he had left behind.

Then without warning the noose came free. Trailed behind a horse and rider, it shot away, leaving Hagan behind. As it flew through the air he just had time to see the two parts of the noose had come apart. Had it broken?

Without waiting to be shot or stabbed, Hagan lifted his shield again and dropped back into position.

A loud snip sounded close to his ear. Hagan turned and saw the grinning face of the warrior to his right, who had set down his spear and now brandished a set of sheep shears. The significance of the shepherd's tools Wodnas had brought now became clear. A single blade slid across the surface of the hide the Hun's nooses were made of, but two brought together in the shears would slice it like it was the softest of cloth.

'Old Wodnas taught us about this,' the warrior beside him said. 'He fought the Huns for years and knows all their tricks.'

A torrent of arrows and spears from Romans in the rear of the Burgundars began raining down on the Huns attacking the shield wall. They continued trying to open gaps but many more nooses where cut by sheep shears wielded by the Burgundars. The wall remained intact. After a time signal horns blew and the Huns withdrew once more.

Hagan poked his head up. He looked left and right. The shield wall of the Alliance stretched in a continuous, unbroken line as far as he could see.

So far, so good.

The Huns returned to their first tactic of approaching the Burgundar shield wall, shooting arrows and then retreating. Hagan judged they had decided to spend more time wearing down their opponents through archery. They would then attack later, when they felt they had weakened the warriors of the Alliance enough.

The attacks continued and the day drew on. The blazing sun beat down and the warriors were soaked with sweat which the dust then stuck to. Their mail became hot and uncomfortable. Just when Hagan thought his thirst was getting unbearable, Roman auxiliaries arrived with water and bread. While the Huns were withdrawn the front ranks were changed and Hagan and the others took a welcome break. The second rank replaced the front one. The third replaced the second and the reserves took the rear. The men from the front rank withdrew behind the ranks of archers to drink and eat.

As they did so they passed ranks of dead warriors laid out on the ground behind the archers. They had been dragged away from the front line. Most had been killed by Hun arrows. The wounded sat beside them. Hagan was dismayed at the number of casualties – more than he had thought they would have at this stage. If wearing down the Alliance with wave after wave of archer attacks really was Attila's strategy, it looked like it was working.

'They're coming back,' someone shouted from the front lines.

Hagan looked and saw the Huns were starting to charge again. With a sigh he stood up and prepared to put his helmet back on. Then, as he watched, the Huns turned. They headed off to the left instead of straight at his part of the lines.

'It looks like the Romans are going to get all their attention this time,' one of the Bear Warriors said.

'Good,' another grunted. 'They deserve each other.'

Hagan squinted against the heat haze on the plain. It was strange. It seemed like the Huns had galloped off but yet were also still where they had been before. Then he realised they had indeed headed off to attack the Roman lines, but this had revealed another line of horsemen behind them, perhaps just as long as the one that had been attacking them all afternoon. He felt a moment of despair at the thought of how vast Attila's army must be.

The second line trotted forwards, crossing to the midpoint between Attila's camp and the lines of the Alliance. Then they stopped and dismounted.

'These aren't Huns,' one of the Bear Warriors said. 'They would never dismount to fight. They must be King Valamir's Ostrogoths.'

The enemy warriors began to march forward, forming a shield wall of their own as they came.

Hagan frowned. He wondered if his ears were playing tricks on him. He felt sure he could hear something but when he tried to listen he could not identify what it was. Then it got louder and he realised it was a low growling. It seemed to resonate through his chest and head. The Ostrogoths were starting the baritus.

In response a similar growl came from the Visigoths on their right.

'It might get difficult to work out what side a man is on,' one of the Bear Warriors said.

Hagan could see what he meant. The designs and emblems on the oval shields and banners of the advancing Ostrogoths portrayed different things, but they were of the same style as those of the Visigoths who formed the right wing of the

Alliance army. Their conical, visored and plumed helmets were the same too.

'There is nothing so vicious as a fight between cousins,' Hagan said. 'We should probably get back into the shield wall. They might need our weight now.'

Tired but refreshed by the water and bread, they laced their helmets back on, gathered their weapons and jogged back to join the lines.

Hagan pushed his way back to the front. He did not have to but somehow he felt it was his duty. The welcome looks the Bear Warriors to his left and right gave him when he took his place in the shield wall made him feel glad he had. They locked their shields together and faced the oncoming Ostrogoths.

The roar of the baritus from the enemy got ever louder and it was matched by the warriors in the Visigoth shield wall. Those around Hagan began battering spears and sword hilts against their shields to add to the racket until it all became almost overwhelming.

The Ostrogoths got closer and closer. They did not run but marched in step, keeping their shield wall aligned. When they came into range the Roman archers loosed a hail of arrows. The Ostrogoths paused, holding their shields up to protect themselves from the hail of barbs from above. Then they recommenced their advance.

Next the Visigoths launched a tide of spears at the advancing enemy. The weapons took their toll, bringing some of the advancing warriors down. The Ostrogoths closed the gaps they left, stepped over the fallen bodies and kept on coming.

Hagan could see the flaring nostrils and screaming mouths of the men coming towards him. Their eyes were wide with hate but he did not feel intimidated. Instead he felt a fierce joy as he roared his defiance back at them.

These men would not be like the Huns, who shot arrows and rode away again. The time had come to fight man to man; toe to toe and face to face.

When they were twenty paces away the Ostrogoths suddenly changed pace and charged, closing the gap in moments. Javelins and light spears flew overhead. Hagan gripped the shaft of his spear and braced himself.

Then with a deafening crash the two shield walls met.

Hagan felt the impact as it rattled along the shield wall of the Alliance. His left shoulder bucked under the concussion. His back foot skidded backwards a little but the formation held.

In a moment Hagan found himself in the midst of a crush of men. He stood shoulder to shoulder with the Burgundars on his left and right. Behind him the other ranks shoved the front rank forward. On the opposite side of the locked shields was a crushing mass of the enemy. An Ostrogoth with a grizzled face and iron helmet pressed his shield directly against Hagan's, his mouth wide open in a scream.

The Ostrogoth jabbed a spear over the top of Hagan's shield, probing to find a target. Hagan struck back with his own spear, holding it overhand, trying to hit his opponent in the face. The spear blade skidded across the man's helmet instead. Hagan pulled his spear back and jabbed again. This time the point went through the right eye hole of the Ostrogoth's helmet. Blood gushed from beneath his visor and the man collapsed like a rag doll.

Hagan could not see where the body fell but for a moment there was no pressure on his shield. Then another Ostrogoth moved in to fill the gap. He had less distance to charge so this time the impact was not as great. The Ostrogoth shoved his spear over the tops of the shields, its shaft grating over the rims. Hagan saw it coming and ducked his head sideways. The blade punched through nothing but air mere finger breadths from Hagan's right eye.

For a moment Hagan thought about trying to strike his opponent under the shield but realised he was jammed between the men on his right and left and there was no room to move his arm down.

The enemy struck again. This time his spear point hit Hagan on the brow of his helmet. Hagan's head bucked backwards under the blow and he felt a rush of fear mixed with anger. He stabbed back blind with his spear. The blade checked as it drove into the man's outstretched forearm. There was a rattle of metal as the blade parted the rings of his mail shirt and tore the leather jerkin under it. The man cried out as Hagan's spear sliced into the skin and muscle beneath.

With a curse the Ostrogoth dropped his spear. He wrenched his injured arm back and tried to push himself away. The press of his own men coming behind meant he could go nowhere. Hagan struck at him again and this time caught him on the chin. The spear opened up a red streak but the man jerked his head away before serious damage could be done.

The Ostrogoth then bent over to try to retrieve the spear he had dropped. The press of his own men behind him pushed him over. Hagan felt him crash against his shield then disappear under the crushing, tramping feet of the men behind him pushing forwards. Whether he screamed or not Hagan could not tell.

The noise was unbelievable. All around men screamed in rage, pain or terror. The clang of blades rang out as they clashed against shield rims, mail and other blades. Shields clattered as they battered off each other in a constant, rolling thunder. Through it all, from close inside his helmet, Hagar could hear his own breathing, loud and rasping under his visor. Sweat ran down his cheeks, neck and back. The air was filled with the stench of bad breath and sweat from the men fighting around him. It mixed with the metallic tang of blood and the odour of shit from spilled entrails and the emptied bowels of the dying, the dead and the terrified.

Another Ostrogoth slammed into Hagan and he found himself shield-to-shield with the enemy once more. The press of men became thick as both sides shoved against each other, each one trying to push their opponents backwards. Hagan could feel men behind him driving him forwards and for a moment he thought he was going to lose his footing and go down. Panic surged into his heart. To fall under all those trampling feet, where men did not heed what they stamped on as they battled for their own survival, would be certain death.

Hagan gritted his teeth, set his feet as best he could, and drove his shoulder into his shield with all his might. The pressure around him was enormous and the front ranks were unable to strike effective blows. With no room to swing, the two sides just prodded and stabbed at each other. Their main efforts now went into pushing as each tried to drive the other back.

Hagan kept his head ducked behind his shield and concentrated on trying to shove his enemy backwards. The press became so great Hagan started finding it hard to breathe.

A great whooshing sound swept overhead, followed by the cries of injured men. Arrows began to rain down just beyond the front rank of the Alliance where Hagan stood. They landed on the heads and shoulders of the men in the second and third ranks of the Ostrogoths, causing many to fall. The Roman archers had begun shooting again. It was a risky tactic. With the shield walls locked so tightly together they were in danger of striking their own men as much as the enemy. Though perhaps that did not matter to the Romans, Hagan thought.

The shower of arrows moved on down the line and it had some effect. With the sudden disappearance of men behind them shoving them forward, many Ostrogoths in the front rank were thrown off balance and staggered backwards.

The consequent removal of pressure on his own shield made Hagan stagger forwards. For a moment he thought he might fall but just managed to steady himself in time.

Hagan braced himself for another attack but it did not come straight away. Dead men now lay heaped before him. It caused a gap that meant the attacking Ostrogoths now had to reach forward to strike him.

He felt a tap on his shoulder. Hagan looked to the left and saw a Bear Warrior standing behind him.

'Take a break,' the man screamed into his ear.

Hagan nodded. He pulled back and the other man went straight into his place. Along the line others were doing the same wherever the chance occurred.

Hagan went to the back rank. Now out of immediate danger, tiredness hit him like a hammer. The heat, exertion and constant peril had his muscles aching and nerves feeling like someone had scrubbed them with a wire brush.

Hagan heard another voice, calling from the rear. He looked and saw King Theodoric, riding his horse along behind the Visigoth ranks, shouting encouragement to his men. The old man's voice sounded reedy and high-pitched compared to the throaty roaring of the fighting men but that somehow made it carry over the din of the rest.

Hagan's throat was so dry it felt like it was lined with sand. The awful-tasting drink Wodnas had given him would do nothing to slake his thirst. He looked around but there was no sign of any Roman auxiliaries with their welcoming amphorae of water. There was however a little stream running along the base of a slope that rose behind the Visigoth lines at the edge of the plain.

Hagan hurried over to it as best he could. He was tired but anxious to not be away from the fighting too long in case he was needed. When he reached the stream he went down on all fours and dipped his cupped hands into the water. He was raising it to his lips when the colour caught his eye.

With a grimace Hagan opened his hands, letting the cool liquid fall back into the stream without tasting any of it. His tongue and throat burned for water but the water of the stream was red, tainted by the blood of who knew how many men whose corpses lay bleeding into it upstream.

With a sigh he stood up again.

'What's the matter?' a voice made him turn around. 'Don't like the taste?'

Hagan turned and saw Wodnas mounted on his horse not far off. He walked over to meet him.

'I came down from the hill to get a closer look at how the battle is going,' the old man said. 'Aetius wants reports. It was lucky I did. Someone needed to tell those archers to get to work.'

'So how is the battle going?' Hagan said.

'Good so far,' Wodnas said. 'The line holds. The Huns are pressing the Romans and the other Germanic tribes hard but the shield wall has not broken. If that continues they can shoot all the arrows they want and ride away again but they'll never be able to win.'

'The Ostrogoths are pushing us hard here,' Hagan said. 'But we're holding them. For now anyway.'

At just that moment a new shout came from their left. It was different from the war cries of the Goths hacking away at each other not far away and seemed as if many men all let out a great groan of dismay all at once. A moment later this was drowned out by cries of bloodthirsty triumph that sent a chill down Hagan's spine.

Wodnas stood up in his saddle, using the height of the horse to let him see over the heads of the fighting warriors before him. A look of concern fell across his face.

'What's happening?' Hagan said.

'I spoke too soon,' Wodnas said. 'The Alans have broken. They're fleeing the battlefield. They've left a hole in our line. The Ostrogoths are pouring into the gap. If we don't stop them the Alliance army will be split in two!'

CHAPTER SIXTY-TWO

A BOVE THE ROAR of voices and the clash of weapons, Hagan heard the sound of signal horns blowing frantic warnings.

The Visigoths' line started at the edge of the plain where a steep ridge rose, protecting their right flank. The Alliance line then continued across the plain along the bottom of the slope that led down from the Roman camp. The Visigoths had stretched almost halfway across the plain, then came the Burgundars, then the Alans in the centre of the line. Beyond them were the Saxons, Franks, Romans and Armoricans.

Now the Alans were galloping hard away from the battlefield, leaving a gap right in the centre of the line.

The Hun cavalry had not failed to notice this and now pounded in a long wedge formation straight for the hole. Their signal horns blasted and banners waved and bobbed as they charged.

Hagan felt a chill run down his spine. If the Huns could get through the gap in the line they could turn and – now behind their defensive shield wall – attack the flanks and rear of the Alliance warriors in the now divided Alliance lines. With the Ostrogoths pressing in front and the Huns attacking from the side and then rear, the Burgundars and Visigoths would be cut off from the rest of the army, surrounded and then finished off.

King Theodoric had seen the danger as well.

'Wheel to the left!' he shouted, grabbing hold of one of the signaller's nearby. 'Sound the order.'

The signaller raised his horn and began to blow a series of loud blasts.

As the Burgundars were now at the left end of the shield line, they were in most immediate danger. The urgency of the present danger drove Hagan's thirst and weariness away and he ran back to the ranks of the Bear Warriors.

'Wheel left! Wheel left!' he shouted to the men in the third rank as he ran along it, thumping their shoulders and pulling them to the left. 'The Alans have run away. Pass it on.'

The Hun cavalry was pouring into the gap in the lines already, shooting arrows left and right. On the far side the Roman line was already starting to rotate to keep their shield wall facing the enemy.

With agonising slowness, the Burgundar and Visigoth line began to move as well. It was not easy. The Ostrogoths were still pressing their attack on the shield wall so warriors had to continue to defend themselves while starting to take steps backward and to the left.

Hagan could see they were not moving fast enough. It would not be long before the Huns were swarming around their flank and riding in behind them.

He looked around. The rest of the Visigoth line was managing to move but they were just as slow. What had once been a single continuous shield line stretching across the plain was now starting to resemble a V, broken in the middle.

'Stand firm, my warriors!' King Theodoric cried. 'Fight hard. Show these bastard Easterners who are the true Goths! Don't let them—'

He never finished the sentence. An Ostrogoth spear came sailing over the shield wall and pierced his throat. The great leaf-shaped blade erupted from the back of his neck in a spray of blood. The old king, eyes wide in surprise, open and closed his mouth for a moment but all that came out was a gush of crimson gore. Then he dropped to his knees and fell to the earth.

A moment later a great cry arose from further along the line as someone in the front rank lost their footing and fell, pulling those around him down with him. The Ostrogoths surged forward and fell as well. Soon there was a mass of men sprawled on the ground, intertwined but desperate to extract themselves from each other, still trying to fight with frantic hacks and stabs. All three ranks of the Ostrogoth line at that section fell over, each man knocking the man behind him over. At the very back the body of the king was trampled underfoot and disappeared under the other falling bodies.

Hagan's heart sank. The Burgundars' shield wall was intact but now detached from the rest of the Visigoth line by the mass of fallen men. It would not be long before they were surrounded and massacred. No amount of bravery, skill or training could save them from the overwhelming numbers of attackers.

The sound of a horn blaring out a series of staccato blasts rose over the cacophony. It was obvious this was some sort of signal but Hagan did not know what it meant. He glanced around and saw that it was Wodnas who was blowing the horn.

In response, the Burgundar warriors tensed and stopped shifting left.

'Ready?' the man at the far left called.

'Yes,' the others shouted back.

'Three, two, one, go!' the first man yelled.

Almost as one, the Bear Warriors shoved their shields forward. At the same time they stepped back. The two ranks behind them fell back, turned and ran. The front rank, now with no one behind them, spun around and did the same. The Ostrogoths they had been pushing against were taken by surprise. One moment the Burgundars had been pushing against them with all their might. The next they were gone. Some Ostrogoths stumbled forwards onto their shields. Others staggered sideways.

Hagan, equally surprised, just had time to turn and run after the others otherwise he would have found himself surrounded by the enemy. It was obvious that the Burgundars were executing a well-planned, much practised move. The only problem for Hagan was that had not been part of those practice sessions.

The Burgundars ran as fast as they could, making the most of the brief time they had before the Ostrogoths recovered and ran after them. If they did, it would be all over. The end of the shield wall was gone and the enemy could outflank the rest of it.

The Bear Warriors ran back but then skidded to a halt. They reformed their line as they did so, creating a new shield wall at right-angles to the existing one, from the end of the Visigoth line to the bottom of the steep slope that rose up to the ridge behind them. In doing so they sealed off the way that the Huns and the Ostrogoths could use to get behind the Alliance lines. The bottom of the ridge was too steep at that point to climb up without great difficulty.

They made it just in time. Moments after they set their shields together, the jumbled mass of Ostrogoths on foot and Huns on horseback crashed into them. Hagan had ended up at the rear again. He felt the impact of the charge and shoved his shoulder into the man in front of him, lending his weight to help keep the enemy back. There was still a contingent of Roman archers behind the Visigoths, now cut off from their fellows. They began raining arrows down on the enemy warriors.

The new shield wall held. After a time the Huns, realising there was no way to outflank the Visigoths after all and taking casualties from arrows and spears, extracted themselves from the crush of men and rode off across the plain to attack the Roman lines.

Hagan, feet braced in the dirt and shoving with all his might to keep the shield wall from moving back, felt a tap on his shoulder. He turned around and to his surprise saw Gunfjaun the raven warrior standing behind him. The young lad cocked his head towards Wodnas, who sat a little further back on his horse.

While he had no doubt his weight helped the men at the front, Hagan was under no illusion that if he left it the shield wall would collapse. He nodded to Gunfjaun and they both jogged over to join Wodnas. The usually impassive old man had a look of concern on his face.

'That was a great move,' Hagan said. 'I take it you taught them that? It saved us.'

'It may have been for nothing,' Wodnas said. 'I'm not sure how long the Visigoths can continue to hold out. If the Huns start diverting men from attacking the Romans to join the Ostrogoths attacking us here they'll outnumber us many to one. Look for yourself.'

He gestured with his spear to the piles of dead and wounded who lay behind the Visigoth shield wall.

'They've lost a lot of men. It's been a long, hot day,' Wodnas said. 'They're exhausted.'

'It's been the same day for the enemy,' Hagan said.

'The enemy hasn't lost their king,' Wodnas said. 'When word of Theodoric's death gets around it will take the heart from his warriors. Will they go on fighting? Meanwhile the Huns continue to wear down our numbers with their arrows.'

'All the more reason I should be helping back at the shield wall then,' Hagan said. There was anger in his voice. 'Did you pull me over here just to tell me you think we're going to lose?'

'My Raven Warriors have been ranging around the battlefield, fighting where needed, scouting elsewhere,' Wodnas said. 'Gunfjaun and some others were on the ridge behind us. He says there is a contingent of Hun cavalry approaching the ridge from the other side. If they get up there they can get down this side and attack our rear here. Then it really will be all over.

Someone needs to get up there and stop them. The job really needs cavalry and I've sent for some but they will need warriors on foot to support them. The Bear Warriors and my Ravens are perfect for this sort of fight so I want you to lead some of them up there. Try to get to the top before the Huns and if you do, try and hold them until the cavalry arrive to drive them off.'

'By taking men away you'll weaken the shield wall,' Hagan said.

'I've thought it through,' Wodnas said, patting the leather satchel he carried everywhere. 'It's a risk worth taking. Either we make sure we take the ridge or have the Huns coming down on us from behind.'

Hagan remembered the old man talking to whatever was in the satchel while trying to decide if the Burgundars should join this alliance or not. Was he mad? Had all their fates been decided by the choices of some crazy old man who talked to a bag?

'In the meantime I'm going to try to make things harder for the Huns,' Wodnas said. 'If they can't see us they can't attack us.'

'You're going to blind them?' Hagan said, frowning. Was this further evidence of the old man's madness?

'In a way, yes,' Wodnas said. 'If the Huns can continue to ride freely across the plains, hitting the Romans then us, shooting arrows and riding away again, then I believe Attila can win. Gunfjaun and some of the others are going to start setting fires. The grass is dry as a bone and will burn easily. If we're inside a cloud of smoke the Huns won't know what they are shooting at.'

Crazy or not, there was some reason to what Wodnas said. The old man's concerned expression told Hagan the situation was indeed perilous. He nodded.

'I know you will succeed in this,' Wodnas said. 'You're a lucky man. I knew that from the first time I saw you.'

'Lucky?' Hagan said. 'I don't feel very lucky.'

'Think of how many times you should already be dead and perhaps you will change your mind,' Wodnas said, his enigmatic smile returning. 'May your luck hold now, for all our sakes. You will need it.'

CHAPTER SIXTY-THREE

HAGAN JOGGED UP the slope. He and thirty of the Bear Warriors ran as fast as they could, desperate to get to the top before the Huns.

He felt as if his mail shirt was weighing down his shoulders, making every breath of the hot air an effort. His thighs burned and sweat stung his eyes. His battered shield, slung over his shoulder, bounced and bumped his back with every step. The rim of his iron helmet dug into his forehead and the back of his neck.

The ridge that ran along the side of the plains had a long, gradual slope on one end and a much sharper drop at the other so it looked like a great whale, rising from the sea.

Hagan and the others were climbing the steep end. It was a shorter distance, but much harder work. The terrain of the ridge was rocky and covered with scrub and grass like the plains below, all of which made the going tougher.

It did not take them too long to make it to the top however, and when they did Hagan was relieved to see the Huns were not already there. Panting, he unlaced his helmet and took it off, wiping away the sweat that ran freely from his brow. The ground on the top of the ridge consisted of a short plateau scarred with gullies filled with brush and other hardy bushes. After their breathing returned to somewhere close to normal he and the others loped their way across the top of the ridge to the edge of the plateau and looked down the long slope that led to the Hun encampment.

There were indeed horsemen making their way up the hill. About fifteen scouts dressed in light armour were riding hard, ahead of a much larger band of armed heavy horsemen. They were on the back side of the ridge and out of sight of the army in the plain below.

'Sneaky bastards,' the Bear Warrior who stood nearby commented.

'Let's give them the welcome they deserve,' Hagan said.

He told the others his plan then ordered them to find hiding places, crouching in the gullies or behind bushes, then they waited for the Hun scouts to arrive. Hagan himself found refuge behind a large boulder near the end of the plateau.

As they waited for the enemy to arrive, Hagan caught the whiff of burning in the air. He glanced towards the plain and saw long tendrils of grey smoke begin to creep towards the sky. It mixed with the clouds of dust kicked up by Hun cavalry riding this way and that. Wodnas' fire-setting plan had begun.

The sun was starting to sink in the sky and to his amazement he heard the chirp of birds that were flitting around the top of the ridge. The plains below were now scattered with the corpses of dead men and horses. The din of the battle continued but up here it was nowhere near as deafening. Hagan closed his eyes, enjoying this brief moment of peace and rest – however short it proved to be – in what had been an exhausting, brutal day.

The noise of hoofbeats broke Hagan's reverie and he pressed himself against the back of the boulder, drawing his francisca throwing axe from his belt. He did not dare look over the top of rock. To do so would give away his position, so he resolved to wait and try to judge by sound when the scouts were all on the plateau and in the trap.

He heard the sound of more horses coming and the shouts of the Huns calling to each other. He could not understand their words but the tone of them suggested they were delighted to find the top of the ridge empty of their enemy, or so they thought.

When he judged he had waited enough, Hagan rose from behind his rock.

'Now!' he shouted and the others all rose from their hiding places as well.

Hagan just had time to see most of the Hun scouts had made it onto the top of the ridge. They glared, startled and frozen by the sudden appearance of warriors all around them.

Hagan picked the nearest one and hurled his francisca at him. The axe tumbled through the air, making a whooping noise like the beating wings of a swan. It crunched into the Hun's chest, its blade slicing through the man's light leather armour and cleaving through his ribs deep into his chest beyond. The Hun cried out and tumbled backwards off his horse.

The other Bear Warriors also rose from their hiding places and threw their own axes. The scouts did not stand a chance. Some were hit by two axes at once. In a moment eight of them had fallen from their saddles. They had barely hit the ground when other Burgundars swarmed around them and finished them off.

Two of the remaining scouts raised their bows and sought targets. Hagan could see the panic on their faces. The Bear Warriors were scattered all around and moving fast. It would look to the Huns like they were coming from every direction at once. The Huns had to pick a target and take careful aim, which in turn delayed their shots.

Hagan was already charging at the nearest enemy, his shield held before him, spear in the other hand. One of the Huns saw him coming and levelled his bow at him. Hagan crouched as he ran so only the top half of his head, which was protected by his helmet, was visible above his shield rim.

The Hun lowered his bow, switching to aim at Hagan's lower legs. Hagan leapt forward as the man shot. The Hun's arrow thudded into the rocky ground where Hagan's right foot had been an instant before. The shaft shattered on impact. The

Hun now had no time to notch another arrow and shoot before Hagan got to him. The Hun dropped his bow and reached for his sword. He had just grasped the hilt when Hagan drove his spear into the man's guts. The Hun let out a high-pitched cry, doubling over as the spear punched through him and burst from the centre of his back. The man flew backwards out of his saddle, wrenching the spear embedded in his body from Hagan's grasp as he did so.

A Bear Warrior to Hagan's right cried out and fell over, an arrow transfixing his shoulder. Hagan, his spear gone, had a knife and sword but no time to draw them before the Hun notched another arrow. He turned his shield sideways, took it in both hands and hurled it at the second Hun archer. The round shield spun through the air. The Hun was looking to his right and already drawing his bow to shoot another arrow. He never saw the shield coming. Its metal rim smashed into the man's right cheek, splitting the skin and smashing his teeth into pieces. His head rocked wildly to the left then he dropped his bow and toppled from his saddle. As he hit the ground two Bear Warriors fell on him and cut his throat.

Hagan looked around. Others of the Berh Herjass had killed two more of the Huns. The remaining three enemy had just been arriving at the top when Hagan had sprung the trap so had just time to wheel their horses. They were now galloping away back down the way they had come.

The Burgundars on the hilltop cheered. They all rushed to the edge of the plateau and looked down. Seeing their scouts – or at least three of them – galloping hard as they could back down the ridge, the main Hun cavalry contingent had stopped and now waited for the surviving scouts to rejoin them. It was not a large force, but still easily outnumbered the Burgundars on the plateau at the top of the ridge.

'What do we do now?' a Bear Warrior said. 'They know we're up here now. We can't take the rest of them by surprise.'

'Well, if I was one of those scouts,' Hagan said, 'I wouldn't want my comrades thinking I'd just panicked and run away from a small band of tired, thirsty men like we are. I'd be down there telling my mates that half the Roman army is up here, which hopefully will put the rest of them off. Even if they tell them the truth I doubt those three had time to see how many of us there actually were. With any luck the rest of them will give up on the idea of coming up the ridge. At least until they can get more men. No one wants to attack a well-defended hilltop. Fighting uphill in this heat? No thank you.'

'I hope you're right,' the Burgundar said.

'Let's try and make sure,' Hagan said. 'Everyone over to the edge of the plateau. Someone grab those loose horses and get on them. Let's make them think we have cavalry up here too.'

Hagan took hold of one of the Hun horses himself and pulled himself into the saddle. Then he rode back to the edge of the plateau.

'Try and make yourself look as big as you can,' he said to the others. 'They are looking up the slope. There's no way of them telling how many are standing behind us up here.'

'But there's no one standing behind us?' one of the other warriors said, a puzzled expression on his face.

'They won't know that,' Hagan said. 'They can't judge our true numbers from below.'

'Will they really fall for this?' one of the warriors said.

'I hope so,' Hagan said. 'Otherwise we're all dead.'

The Burgundars all began shouting and waving their spears. Some battered their shields with sword hilts or spear butts. Hagan and the others on the horses wheeled them around, sometimes rearing up on their back legs and generally putting on a fine show.

After a little time the Huns down the slope did indeed turn around and began trooping off back towards their own lines.

'They bought it!' one of the Bear Warriors said, grinning and looking at Hagan with new admiration.

'Sometimes you can win a fight without actually fighting,' Hagan said. 'I'm surprised Wodnas didn't teach you that.'

'What now?' asked another warrior.

'We wait for the cavalry to arrive,' Hagan said.

CHAPTER SIXTY-FOUR

THEY WAITED. HAGAN regretted the fact there had not been time to get water before they had climbed the ridge. There was little cover on the plateau at the top and the sun beat mercilessly down on him and the others, though at least they could be thankful that it was moving down the sky and the blistering heat of midday was long past.

They took the opportunity of getting some rest but once Hagan had recovered a little he found himself beset by a strange mixture of boredom and anxiety. He was bored because after the intense activity and terrifying excitement of battle, they were now sitting around with nothing to do. All the while though, there was the very real danger that the Huns would return with reinforcements to take the ridge.

From the distance of the height of the ridge, Hagan was able to take a detached look at the battlefield below. It was turning into a mess. The single battle line of the Alliance that had stretched from one side of the plain to the bottom of the ridge he stood on was now split in two. The Romans, the rest of the Burgundars, the Franks, Saxons and others had been pushed back and now stood at an angle, half facing the ridge he was on top of. Gepids and Hun foot warriors attacked them in waves. Wave after wave of Hun cavalry rode to and from the shield walls, swirling in great movements that made Hagan think he was watching the movements of whirlwinds across the plain instead of horsemen. The Roman archers shot back, driving the Hun cavalry away whenever they got too close.

The Visigoths who had started with their right flank to the ridge had been pushed right around so now their backs were against it. Attila's Ostrogoth foot soldiers were pressing them hard and the Visigoths had lost so many men that the right end of their line now only stretched perhaps halfway along the length of the ridge below.

The bodies of men and horses were scattered all over the plains. The smoke from the fires Wodnas and his men were setting drifted in the wind across the plains, obscuring parts of the conflict so it was hard to get a clear picture of what was really happening.

Hagan hoped the old man knew what he was doing. The smoke was drifting towards the enemy but if the wind changed it was just as likely to confuse, choke and blind the Alliance warriors as Attila's.

Hagan could see the Visigoths were struggling and the Ostrogoths were pressing them hard. More and more Hun cavalry were concentrating their attacks on them too, like hounds scenting blood on a hunt. The Visigoths were cut off from the rest of the Alliance army, outnumbered and would be near to exhaustion. It was only a matter of time before they collapsed.

'Horsemen approaching,' a Bear Warrior shouted.

There was a brief moment of anxiety that the Huns were returning, then Hagan saw that the horsemen were riding up the steep end of the ridge, which meant they must belong to the Alliance. As they got closer Hagan could make out the white eagle banner flying about them, which confirmed they were Visigoths. There was another contingent with them as well. As they got closer Hagan saw it was Brynhild's Valkyrjur cavalry. Riding at their head was Brynhild herself. All the troopers had scratches and slashes on their shields and some had wounds to their forearms or thighs, bound with bloodied bandages and showing that they had already been in action that day.

Hagan was relieved to see that this combined force was more than enough to hold off the Huns if they decided to try to take the ridge again.

The leader of the Visigoths pulled off his helmet, unleashing a tumble of sweaty black curly hair. Hagan recognised the young man as Thorismund, the son of King Theodoric of the Visigoths.

He and Brynhild dismounted and approached Hagan as he looked out over the plains below.

'Good work holding this place,' Thorismund said. 'My God. It looks like Hell down there.'

He stared at the panoply of battle unfolding at the bottom of the ridge.

'Your folk are doing well,' Hagan said. 'They are holding their own but they're under a lot of pressure. If Attila sends any more men against them I wonder if they can continue to hold out.'

'My father is down there with them,' the young man said. There was both pride and concern in his tone of voice. 'I hope he can help encourage them. I'd like to get down there to help him rather than sitting up here where it is safe.'

'Lord Thorismund—' Hagan started to speak then stopped. It was clear that the young man did not know his father was dead and he wondered how he might begin to break the news to him. Then he decided there was no easy way to go about it.

'Lord Thorismund, your father is dead,' Hagan said. 'I am very sorry.'

Thorismund looked at him for a long moment. His mouth was half open. He looked as if he were trying to decide if Hagan's words were true or not.

'How did he die?' the young man said. He looked away, his voice thick.

'He was killed by an Ostrogoth spear,' Hagan said. 'I saw it with my own eyes.'

Thorismund nodded. He wandered a little way off. It was obvious to Hagan that the young man was struggling to come to terms with this news and he did not want his men to see that. Hagan was amazed that among all this death, one more could strike someone as being so personal.

'So you've survived, Hagan,' Brynhild said, sauntering up to stand beside him. 'Despite Gunderic's best efforts.'

'He has let his queen ride into battle?' Hagan said, raising an eyebrow. 'I would have thought he would not have allowed you to upstage him.'

'I don't care what Gunderic thinks,' Brynhild said. 'He doesn't know where I am anyway. He believes I still hide in my wagon, too cowed and intimidated to come out. But I'm not. Not now. I will never hide again. Today I ride for my revenge.'

'Revenge?' Hagan said. For the first time he caught the strange glint in her eye. It was more than anger. Brynhild seemed a little unhinged.

'I know what you did,' she spat. Her white teeth were clenched. 'You and the other two: the treacherous Nibelungs. My so-called old friends. How you must have laughed about it! *Stupid old Brynhild. She'll never know the difference.*'

'I don't know what you are talking about,' Hagan said.

'You do,' Brynhild said. 'Gunhild said it was all your idea. You tricked me into breaking my oath. Now I must act like it was all true, or seem an oathbreaker – a nothing – to my own people.'

Her voice was cracking a little. Hagan's face flushed crimson.

'Brynhild, I am sorry,' Hagan said. 'Telling Sigurd to switch places with Gunderic to leap the chasm was something that came to me in an instant. I hoped Sigurd would fail in the attempt. I did it for the sake of Gunderic, who I thought was our old friend. I did not realise then what Gunderic was really like...'

Shame choked the rest of the words in his throat.

I've known what he was really like since Vorbetomagus, Hagan thought.

'Well you know now, don't you?' Brynhild said. 'And do you really think he's any different than the spoiled brat of a boy we used to play with in Vorbetomagus? Did you help him rape me, as well as that big buffoon of a Volsung?'

'Rape you?' Hagan held up both hands. 'Now wait, Brynhild—'

'Hun cavalry, lord,' one of the Bear Warriors shouted from the edge of the plateau. 'You'd better take a look.'

For a moment Hagan and Brynhild glared at each other.

'We shall finish this talk another time,' Hagan said. 'There are more pressing things to deal with right now.'

Brynhild nodded. They both jogged over to the end of the plateau. Thorismund joined them. The Burgundar warrior who had shouted was pointing with his spear to a large band of horsemen riding out from the Hun encampment at the far end of the plains.

'They must be Attila's reserve cavalry,' Thorismund said. 'He is making his last play. This ridge must be important to whatever his strategy is.'

'They'll be fresh then,' Hagan said. 'Look at how hard they are riding. Those horses haven't been running around in the sun all day. If they take this ridge and attack the Visigoths from behind, it will be the end for your folk, Lord Thorismund.'

'There are more of them than we have up here,' the Bear Warrior who had called them over said. 'Can we stop them taking the ridge?'

'They have to fight uphill,' Hagan said. 'That could take away the advantage they have in numbers.'

The Huns disappeared into a swathe of drifting smoke. When they emerged again they were almost halfway across the plain.

'Wait,' Brynhild said. 'I don't think they're coming up here.'

519

They all watched and saw that though the Huns were riding their way, their trajectory meant they would arrive perhaps halfway along the ridge, well past the long slope the Huns had previously approached the ridge from.

'It's too steep to climb up down there,' Hagan said. 'They can't be coming to attack this ridge.'

'They're going to join the attack on the Visigoths' shield wall,' Brynhild said.

'Attila must believe my people are at breaking point,' Thorismund said. 'His scouts will have told him.'

'I'm sorry to say he may be right,' Hagan said.

Thorismund clenched his fists. Then he turned to Hagan and Brynhild.

'If my people fall there is little point in us defending this ridge,' he said. 'We will all be cut off from the rest of the Alliance army anyway.'

'So what do you intend to do?' Hagan said.

'If we ride down the back of the slope they won't see us coming,' Thorismund said. 'Then we can cut left and hit them in their flanks. We can take them by surprise and stop them. And we'll be to the rear of Attila's warriors. We can hit them all from behind.'

Hagan looked at the vista below. Thorismund was right. The Huns and their allies had pushed the Roman Alliance so far back they now were to the left of him and the others on the top of the ridge. If they could get behind them they could cause all sorts of chaos.

'We don't have much time,' Hagan said. 'Mount up.'

He and eleven of the Bear Warriors took hold of horses they had taken from the dead Hun scouts, then they joined the Visigoth cavalry and the Valkyrjur at the edge of the plateau. Beneath them the chaos of the smoke-streaked battlefield lay.

'My father's spirit cries out for vengeance,' Thorismund shouted. 'I hear him calling on the wind. Let us ride down on these filthy Huns and Ostrogoth bastards and wreak havoc on them.'

Hagan tied the laces of his helmet and looked around. To his surprise Brynhild was grinning.

'You said it looked like Hell down there, Thorismund,' she said. 'So come. Let us all ride into Hell together.'

CHAPTER SIXTY-FIVE

THEY STARTED SLOWLY, doing their best to keep a line as their horses picked careful footsteps across the sloping ground. At first it was very steep, then as the incline became more moderate, they picked up speed. The horses reached a gallop and the wind began to roar in their ears as the horses' hooves beat a tattoo on the ground.

Hagan clenched the reins in his left fist. His spear was couched under his right arm. He narrowed his eyes against the wind that rushed into them. He gripped his horse with his thighs, knowing that to fall off would most likely mean death, his bones first smashed against the hard, stony ground then ground beneath the pounding hooves of the horses following behind.

The ground rushed by in a blur. His horse's head dipped and rose as it galloped. When they reached halfway down the slope their speed was now beyond control. The horses barrelled on, their weight and momentum carrying them as much as their legs. Riding in close formation, all it would take was one to slip and everyone would go down in a great tangled mass of horses and men.

Despite the danger and the fact that they rode into battle, Hagan felt the fierce battle joy, an elation like his heart was flying along somewhere above his body. The sheer thrill of the speed they travelled at made him laugh out loud. He felt like an eagle, swooping from a mountaintop, to fall on far-below prey.

Others around him, also carried away by the moment, were laughing, shouting or yelling war cries.

Thorismund rode in front of all of them, sword in hand. Hagan and Brynhild were directly behind him then the rest of the cavalry rushed on behind. The battlefield was hidden from view by the bulk of the ridge they rode down the back of. When they were almost three-quarters of the way down the slope, Thorismund began turning his horse to the left. The rest followed and the cavalry now swooped across the slope back towards the battlefield.

They crossed the centre of the ridge slope and Hagan saw the beleaguered Visigoth line, beset by the Ostrogoth foot warriors, come into view. The contingent of fresh Hun cavalry was riding to join the attack, no doubt expecting to deliver the final hammer blow that would shatter the exhausted Visigoths' shield wall.

With a thrill of excitement Hagan realised that the Huns were directly ahead. Thorismund had timed it perfectly. They would smash right into their flank. The Huns, intent on their own charge at the Visigoths, were unaware of the new danger to them.

Hagan began screaming at the top of his lungs. Others around him did the same. They were so close now it no longer mattered. He heard a chilling, high-pitched wail. Glancing around he saw it came from Brynhild who was riding hard, her sword held before her, ready to strike.

The galloping Huns were thirty paces away. A moment later twenty. Some of them began to look around. Hagan saw the surprise and terror on their faces and it ignited the bloodlust inside his own heart. He and his folk at Vorbetomagus must have looked just as shocked when the Hun cavalry had ridden at them from the forest all those years ago. Now the shoe was on the other foot.

Hagan gritted his teeth and clenched his spear. A moment later he and the Alliance cavalry ploughed into the Huns.

The sound was incredible. A great crashing of metal on metal, breaking bones and screams of terror and pain from horses and men filled the air. Hagan's spear, driven by the whole weight of the galloping horse and man behind it, drove into the side of a Hun's chest. The blade smashed through the rings of the Hun's mail shirt, carried through him and burst from the far side, pieces of the man's entrails trailing from the point.

Hagan wrenched the spear back as the Hun flew out of his saddle. All around him Huns were going down, either killed by weapons or just smashed out of their saddles by the impact of being ridden into. Horses fell, pitching their riders from their backs. Hagan and the others rode on, ploughing a bloody swathe through the Hun formation. He stabbed left and right, opening wounds wherever he could. The Visigoth and Valkyrjur riders slashed with their swords and stabbed with spears. They trampled fallen Huns beneath their hooves.

The Hun cavalry formation split asunder. Men began riding in all directions, desperate to escape the sudden onslaught that had fallen on them seemingly from the sky.

Hagan managed to spear one more Hun through the back, then there were no more targets before him. The Hun cavalry had completely scattered.

Through the din and the noise the sound of a horn blaring came. Smoke was now drifting around him and Hagan had to peer through it to see it was Thorismund who was blowing the horn.

The riders gathered around the young prince of the Visigoths.

'We've broken their cavalry attack,' Thorismund shouted above the noise. 'Now let's hit the Ostrogoths!'

He levelled his sword at the ranks of warriors assaulting the Visigoth shield wall.

'Have no care that they have their backs to us,' Thorismund

shouted. 'Remember what they did to your forefathers. Stab them. Slash them. Kill them all! Onward! Into glory ride!'

The gathered riders cheered and wheeled their horses.

As one, they charged into the rear of the Ostrogoth ranks besieging the Visigoth shield wall. Hagan almost felt sorry for the men he cut down first. They had no idea what was coming. But there was a fire in Hagan's blood that incinerated all pity. Instead he felt nothing but contempt as his spear drove into the back of an Ostrogoth warrior, transfixing him and bursting from his guts at the front. The shaft of the spear shattered into three pieces and Hagan ripped the sword under his left arm from its sheath.

He began hacking to his left and right. Raining blows down on shoulders, arms, heads, anywhere he could find a target. After one strike across a man's head that split the steel of his helmet the warrior put both his hands on top of his head, as if trying to hold the helmet together, Hagan struck again and watched as the man's severed fingers tumbled to the ground. A small voice within him told him the memory would return to haunt him in the future but at that moment all he felt was hate.

All the anger that had built up from fifteen years of exile and the frustrated hopes that he had found his people and friends once again rose within his heart like a black tide that drowned out all pity, compassion and empathy. He stabbed and slashed, cut and hacked, felling warriors with his blade as his horse battered others beneath its hooves like it was mowing down long grass. He knew he should be tired – exhausted even – but his arm felt imbued with power.

Soon panic spread through the ranks of the Ostrogoths like the fires Wodnas had set in the dry grass as they realised that they were under attack from the rear. Those who could turned to try to meet the new threat, though those in the front ranks were still engaged with fighting the Visigoths.

Hagan felt the press of men around him ease a little. He saw warriors starting to flee on foot, trying to avoid being struck from one of the horsemen assaulting them as they went.

With a surge of triumph Hagan realised the Ostrogoth attack was breaking.

CHAPTER SIXTY-SIX

GUNHILD HURRIED DOWN the slope, picking her way around the piles of equipment and supplies that cluttered the ground behind the battle lines of an army engaged in fighting.

Auxiliaries and servants scurried around, fetching new arrows, shields or other pieces of war gear to those who needed them. Exhausted warriors, rotated away from the front lines gulped water and took welcome rest. Their faces and arms were streaked with sweat, dirt and blood. They sat in silence, their eyes hollow from the horrors they had witnessed and committed, waiting until it was their turn to return to the slaughter.

Roman medics tended to the ever growing numbers of wounded, who waited to be treated beside ever higher piles of corpses. Next to them lay those who were in between: the casualties whose wounds were too severe and now waited to die. The battlefield itself was obscured by thick grey smoke drifting from the burning grass. When the wind changed it wafted through the rear where Gunhild was, stinging eyes and catching in the throat.

It was now late in the afternoon and Gunhild had found she could wait in the Burgundar camp no longer. She had sat with the other women, waiting, though no one had been happy with this Roman way of war. They all felt their place was beside the battlefield, screaming their encouragement to the menfolk, not sitting here behind the lines, waiting like children. The fact that Brynhild was actually out their fighting with the other women of the Valkyrjur made it even harder to bear.

They heard the roar and clash of the fighting which added to their vexation. Then as the day wore on, unsettling rumours began to drift back from the field of conflict: News that the Huns were winning, the Alans had run away and that at least one leader of the Alliance army had been killed in the fighting. When smoke began to drift through the camp from the now burning fields it made things more confusing. What on earth was going on?

Gunhild's meeting with Brynhild that morning still unsettled her as well. Her old friend had always been a little bit strange but that morning she had been unnerving. Gunhild preferred to tell herself that what Brynhild had said was not true, but if it was indeed fantasy it appeared to have had a profound effect on Brynhild. What would she do next? Were any of them safe from her madness?

In the end Gunhild had resolved to go and see what was actually happening for herself.

As she passed a gathering of the dying she spotted someone and stopped. The wounded lay scattered across the ground. Blood from their sometimes horrific wounds ran into the dry, dusty earth. Some were silent and Gunhild would have judged them already dead but for the faint flutter of their chests moving up and down. Others moaned in pain or fear as they hovered on the brink of eternal darkness. Their friends and the medics had done their best to make them comfortable with folded blankets under their heads and goatskins filled with watered-down wine within their grasp.

Among them Gunhild had spotted the blonde-haired Valkyrjur who Brynhild had seemed so attached to when they had visited her realm. Wondering if she might learn more about Brynhild, she approached. Two other badly wounded women horse warriors were beside the blonde woman, who lay on her back, eyes closed, a grimace of pain on her face. Both hands were clasped over a large, red wound in her stomach. Either it went right through her or she had already bled a lot, for her torso was surrounded by a dark pool of thickening blood. A cloud of flies hovered above her. As Gunhild approached, her shadow fell over the woman's face and she opened her eyes.

'I am Gunhild,' Gunhild said. 'You are Brynhild's... friend, aren't you?'

A look of momentary concern crossed the wounded woman's face.

'Is she with you?' she said. 'I'd rather she didn't see me like this. I want her to remember me the way I was.'

She tried to raise her head but only had the strength to lift it a little off the ground. Then she flopped back again and closed her eyes once more. It was clear she was near the end.

'She is not with me,' Gunhild said, crouching down beside the wounded woman. 'Do not worry.'

'Worry?' The woman, eyes still closed, made a wan smile. 'If she really was here it would be you who would be worried. She told me what has happened to her. My Brynhild is on her Hell Ride today. She rides for vengeance. Today she will redden her sword with the blood of Huns and all those who did her wrong. Including you. Your brother. Your husband, and the other betrayers.'

Gunhild started. The vague worry she had felt since that morning became a little more intense.

'I approach my death time,' the horse warrior said, her voice becoming a breathless whisper. 'I go to the land of the dead ruled over by Queen Hel. One day Brynhild will join me there but I hope it will not be for some time yet. But you all will be with me before the sun sets. Brynhild has vowed this. Brynhild has sworn an oath she will take her revenge and Brynhild never breaks her oaths. You, of all people, should know that.'

Then the woman let out a little sigh. A rattling sound came from her throat then she lay still as if she were carved from wood.

Gunhild glanced at the other two Valkyrjur in case she might be able to learn more from them but saw both were already too far gone towards death. She stood up, brushing dry grass and dust from her dress, then carried on her journey, now with a renewed sense of urgency.

After some time and plenty of asking, she managed to find Gunderic, Aetius and a few of the other commanders on horseback a short distance behind the ranks of Roman legionaries. The short distance of open ground between the fighting men and their leaders resembled the back of a hedgehog, so many Hun arrows were embedded in it.

'Sister!' Gunderic said, seeing Gunhild approach. Aetius frowned, no doubt disquieted by the sight of a woman near a battlefield.

'How goes it?' Gunhild said. 'With all this smoke I thought the world itself was burning.'

'Wodnas set fires to confuse the Hun cavalry,' Gunderic said. 'The Visigoths were getting pressed pretty hard.'

'Is it bad?' Gunhild said. She could read the concern in her brother's expression.

'They've been split apart from the rest of the army,' Gunderic said. 'And they lost their king. It's hard to say how long they will be able to hold out.'

Aetius's frown deepened.

'Really, Gunderic,' he said. 'It won't do to be repeating some of these things. The Alliance is fragile enough as it is. If word of Theodoric's death gets around the rest could give in and run.'

'Your husband has done well,' Gunderic said. 'He was personally responsible for repelling at least two attacks on our lines by the Gepids. He has kept the Burgundar shield wall and held his position, as ordered.'

'Even though he gives every impression that he would rather charge headlong into the enemy in search of personal glory,' Aetius said with a smirk.

'I have no worries about Sigurd,' Gunhild said. 'Nor should you, General Aetius. He is not the wild barbarian you seem to think he is. What of Hagan?'

'From what I heard, the fellow has done well so far,' Aetius said. He went on to relate the desertion of the Alans and the rest of the tale of the battle so far. 'Wodnas sent him up that ridge to try to take it before the Huns did. Your brother here was furious when he heard Hagan had been moved away from the front ranks. Anyone would think he wanted him dead.'

Gunderic and Gunhild exchanged looks.

'At Wodnas' request I've ordered cavalry up the ridge to help hold it,' Aetius went on. 'We can only pray they can manage that. Otherwise the Visigoths will be surrounded and wiped out. They make up half our army so if they are lost, all is lost.'

There was a moment of sombre silence. They all looked out at the drifting smoke and the clashing armies.

'Speaking of whom...' Aetius said at last.

They turned and saw Wodnas riding towards them along the rear of the Roman lines. He was accompanied by two of his Raven Warriors who rode behind him.

'What is the news from the field?' Aetius said as the newcomers joined them.

'General, I bring great news,' Wodnas said. He was out of breath and uncharacteristically excited. 'The Visigoth prince, Thorismund, has charged from the ridge. They took the Hun reserves by surprise and routed them. Then they attacked the Ostrogoths from the rear. It broke their attack on the Visigoths. The Visigoths are now advancing on the Huns and their allies attacking our lines. They will hit them from the flanks and rear.'

Aetius looked around at the others. His face lit up with delight.

'This is our chance!' he cried. 'The tide is turned against Attila. Sound the signal horns! Order all cavalry to attack. Throw everything we have at those bastards.'

CHAPTER SIXTY-SEVEN

H AGAN FOUND HIMSELF riding amid a great mass of charging warriors. Like him, they should have been on the edge of exhaustion but somehow were not. The Visigoths had been fighting all day through the heat and the dust. They had been on the brink of collapse, beset on all sides. They had lost many of their number including their own king.

Now, with the immediate threat lifted and seeing the men who had been oppressing them suddenly break and run, they surged forward, baying for blood, thirsty to pay back their enemies for everything they had put them through. The Ostrogoths had broken and run. Some had headed for the Hun camp, some had headed for the Roman lines where the rest of their army was attacking and some, confused by the smoke, just ran off across the battlefield. The Visigoths now charged after them but seemed equally divided as to which way to go. The cavalry wedge formation Hagan had been part of when they attacked the Ostrogoths had disintegrated in the chaos.

Hagan was unsure if he was charging amid the throng or if they were pushing his horse along with them. The smoke stung his eyes. He could hear horns blowing but for all the heed the warriors around him paid to them, the signallers may as well have saved their breath.

Hagan used the power of the horse to shove his way clear of the throng. When he got to a reasonably clear area he looked around. There were some other horsemen not far away and he saw they had white eagles on their shields so he made his way to join them. There was no sign of Brynhild however, nor any of her Valkyrjur.

'Lord Thorismund orders us to attack the rear of the Huns attacking the Romans,' one of the horsemen said.

'You've seen him?' Hagan said.

'Yes, he was here a moment ago,' the other man said, shouting to be heard over the racket around them. He coughed as he sucked in a mouthful of smoke. 'He's ridden off to try to rally as many of the men as he can.'

Hagan nodded. The young prince was certainly a leader. He would be a capable replacement for his father, the Visigoths had no need to worry about that. Perhaps it was just the effect of his presence on the battlefield before his men, but whatever Thorismund did it appeared to work. Before long the bulk of the Visigoths' horde was charging in the direction of the Roman lines, or at least the direction he assumed they were in, as at that moment they were hidden by drifting smoke.

As they moved forwards, Hagan and the other horse warriors continued to regroup with others from the scattered Visigoth cavalry until there was once more a formidable contingent of them. Charging was still impossible without mowing down some of the warriors on foot who surrounded them, but by the time the smoke cleared and the Roman lines became visible ahead, the whole mass of men had managed to coalesce into ordered ranks of marching men with two wings of cavalry on either side of them. Thorismund was in one of these and Hagan in the other. While he saw a few of the Burgundar Bear Warriors, there was still no sign of the women of the Valkyrjur.

The Huns and their allies, intent on attacking the lines of the Roman Alliance, were oblivious to the danger approaching from their rear.

When they were about forty paces behind the enemy, signal horns began blasting above the noise. Hagan did not know the Visigoth signals but their meaning became clear as the horsemen around him surged forwards. He kicked his heels and sped after them, joining the charge.

As they closed the gap the Huns finally noticed them. Their own horns began to sound, this time in warning. Horsemen and foot warriors at the rear of their ranks turned and saw the threat coming.

Hagan saw their panic as warriors on foot tried to realign and form a shield wall to their rear. The horsemen wheeled their mounts, several knocking their own foot soldiers over as they did so, and began to target their bows.

It was all too late however as Hagan and the others were already charging into them in two wedge formations that split the enemy ranks asunder. Hagan heard men screaming as they were trampled beneath the hooves of his mount and pounded into a bloody mess. He slashed down at a man on his right, his sword gouging deep into the flesh where his shoulder met his neck, almost decapitating him.

The world around him seemed to slow down and it felt as though he was aware of everything going on around him all at once. He kicked down at another warrior on his left while at the same time he saw a Hun on horseback not far away loose his bow. Hagan could not see the arrow but still he managed to duck sideways in his saddle. He felt the wind and heard the angry buzz it made as it shot by, a finger's breadth from his left eye.

Then with a great roar of anger the Visigoth foot warriors arrived, throwing themselves into the attack. The whole Hun line appeared to shudder at their impact. Almost at the same time the sound of more signal horns blaring rose above the shouting of men, the screaming of frightened or injured horses and the clash of weapons. This time Hagan recognised the distinct sounds of the Roman *bucinae*. It seemed impossible but the din of screamed war cries got even louder.

From the vantage point of his horseback Hagan was able to look beyond the men around him towards the Roman lines and saw their cavalry was now attacking. The legionaries too were surging forwards all along the line. So too were their allies from the Burgundars, Franks, Saxons and Armoricans as they took advantage of the reduction in pressure on their shield wall caused by the warriors at the rear of the Hun companies turning to face the Visigoth attack.

One of the Visigoth horse warriors who had waded deep into the Hun ranks was struck by an arrow. His horse was struck at the same time and reared up on its hind legs, then toppled over sideways, crushing several warriors on foot beneath it. Several of the warriors retreating backwards tripped on the bodies and fell over. Each man pulled another with him. With the Romans surging forwards at the same time, it caused a great swathe of men to lose their footing. A loud wail of dismay rose as men went sprawling to the ground.

Complete chaos ensued.

All forms of organisation dissolved. The battle lines fell apart, reforming into smaller groups fighting hand to hand. What had been formal shield walls, units and armies now resembled a massive brawl and it was impossible to tell which side held which area. Horsemen rode this way and that, striking whoever was within reach then riding on. The feet of thousands of men and horses kicked up clouds of dust that merged with the smoke from the grass fires to obscure the view and choke the throat.

Hagan did his best to stay with as many of the other mounted warriors as possible but in the swirling mass of fighting men, with all the smoke and dust it was nearly impossible. Once Hagan raised his sword to strike a warrior on foot. Just in time he saw the white sea eagle painted on the man's shield, realised he was a Visigoth and stayed his hand.

The chaotic, desperate fighting continued for some time as the dust and smoke got thicker. To Hagan's astonishment he realised the sun was sinking, bringing the gloom of evening with it to add to the confusion.

A large contingent of Hun horsemen came galloping forward. Unlike everyone else they seemed to have managed to have stuck together. They were some way away and riding hard in the direction of the lowering sun that glowed blood red through the smoke and dust. The Huns cut down anyone who was in their way, friend or foe alike. When Hagan thought about it he reasoned that they were riding west, and therefore these Huns were heading for their camp.

Hagan wondered why his attention had been drawn to this group amid all the others around him when he saw the white banner flying from a pole carried by one of the riders. On it was emblazoned the same stylised bird – the Turul – that was engraved on his mother's amulet. It was the personal war flag of Attila. As they rode by Hagan just caught a glimpse of the man riding at the very heart of the band of Huns, protected on all sides by his warriors. It was the man himself: King Attila.

'Attila is fleeing,' Hagan screamed at the top of his lungs.

At that moment Attila glanced around. It was impossible that he had heard Hagan's words but nevertheless Hagan felt that for a moment they locked eyes. Then his view of the king was blocked as the riders continued on their way.

Hagan looked around, desperate. He could not pursue them on his own – one man against perhaps fifty – but if he could round up enough other riders they could catch him. They could end this whole bloody nightmare right now.

CHAPTER SIXTY-EIGHT

Hagan spotted Thorismund amid a group of his horsemen a little way off through the throng. He battled his way over to him, using the bulk of his horse to shove men on foot out of his way. Whether they were friends or enemies he could not tell.

When he reached the Visigoth prince he shouted across to him what was happening. Thorismund glanced at the group of fleeing Huns. They were now almost obscured by the smoke and dust but Attila's banner was still plain to see.

Thorismund yelled orders to those around him. His signallers began blowing their horns. Moments later they had wheeled their horses and were galloping off after Attila and his men. Hagan followed.

As they pushed their way through the throng others, summoned by the blaring horns, joined them and soon there were perhaps a hundred or more horsemen all in pursuit of the Hun King.

As they moved clear from the whirling mass of fighting men they were able to pick up speed, reaching a gallop. The Huns reached full speed too and soon they were all racing across the plain, the Huns making for the relative safety of their camp, the semi-circle of Visigoth, Roman and allied cavalry charging to catch them before they got there.

The exhilaration Hagan had felt earlier when charging down the ridge returned as they pounded across the plain.

Attila was the greatest war leader in the world. He had never lost a battle and here Hagan was at the very moment when that was about to happen.

He knew his horse was flagging and he prayed to whoever was watching from above, be it Tiwass or Jehovah, that they would manage to catch Attila. If they did there would be no mercy. Attila had to die if there was ever to be peace in the world. The army of the Alliance may have defeated Attila's horde but now Hagan had the chance to be among the few men at the last who brought Attila down.

They were now about three-quarters of the way across the plain and gaining on the Huns. This fact was proved when some of the rearward riders turned and began to shoot arrows in the direction of the pursuers. Hagan and the others were beyond range and all the arrows hit the ground before their horses arrived, but the warning was clear: if they drew any closer they would be riding into bow range.

Undaunted, the pursuers unslung their shields and held them before themselves. The wind roared in their ears as the horses' hooves drummed across the ground. They were about fifty horse lengths behind Attila and his warriors. They shot another volley of arrows. A horse four along to Hagan's right cried out and went down, spilling its rider into the dust. They pushed their horses harder. They were drawing close to the line of wagons that marked the perimeter of the Hun camp.

Then two wagons drew aside, creating a gap. A line of horsemen rode out, shooting their bows to provide more cover for their fleeing leader. The arrows thudded down all around Hagan, causing him to swerve his horse and almost fall from the saddle.

Attila galloped full speed through the gap in the wagons with some of his men. The rest skidded to a halt and wheeled their horses to face back the way they had come, adding their own arrows to the hail falling on their pursuers.

The wagons closed back together. Hagan and the others

found themselves facing a line of Hun cavalry, all shooting their bows. More arrows and spears came flying from defenders behind the wagons inside the camp.

Hagan's heart sank. To continue the pursuit of Attila they would have to fight their way through the cavalry outside, who nearly matched them in number, then fight their way into the camp itself. It was impossible. Attila had escaped.

Thorismund's signallers were already blaring their horns and the Visigoth riders were turning back in response.

Spears and arrows raining down around him, Hagan reined his horse to a halt. With a curse and a spit, he wheeled his horse around and began galloping away with the Visigoths.

As they rode back across the plain, they began to run into remnants of the enemy army fleeing in the opposite direction. At first a few horsemen galloped past, riding hard for the Hun camp. Then it became a steady stream of men on foot or horseback, hurrying to get to relative safety.

The fight was over. The Hun army had been put to flight. None of them bothered with Hagan and the other Visigoth riders as they passed each other, going in opposite directions.

'That was a close-run thing,' Thorismund said.

Hagan turned and saw the Visigoth prince had ridden up beside him.

'But a great day nonetheless,' Thorismund said. 'We have won a famous victory.'

'Attila got away,' Hagan said.

'For now, yes,' Thorismund said. 'But he is trapped in that camp with his army. Aetius and I will regroup our army and advance across the plain to besiege him. In fact, I wonder why Aetius isn't already on the march. Then when Attila is surrounded in that camp the end won't take long. His own folk will probably kill him. That or the Ostrogoths will turn against him. Attila's power lay in his ability to deliver victory and the plunder it brought to those who followed him. We've shown today he can be beaten.'

539

Hagan nodded. Perhaps things were not so bleak as they seemed. Perhaps the mounds of corpses they now rode among were not the remains of men who had died for nothing.

A Roman messenger rider approached through the bodies and the drifting smoke. When he spotted Thorismund he rode over and made the Roman salute.

'King Thorismund, General Aetius has a message for you,' the messenger said.

Hagan saw Thorismund's chest swell and his back straighten at the use of the title, King.

'Your brother, Theodoric the younger,' the messenger said, 'when he heard about your royal father's death, left the battlefield, took horses and men and set off to the south. It is General Aetius's conclusion that he means to get back to your father's palace in Tolosa to declare himself the new king.'

'What? That treacherous bastard!' Thorismund was aghast. He turned to one of his men. 'Theoden: I must ride for Tolosa straight away. I will take some men with me but the rest of the army needs to rest. I will need them, so I leave you in command. Follow us with the men in the morning. Gather up my father's body with full honours and bring it with you.'

Theoden nodded and rode off into the gloom.

Thorismund turned to Hagan.

'Farewell,' he said, his face set in a grim expression. 'I am thankful to have fought alongside the famous Burgundars today. If only every folk was as honourable and trustworthy.'

Then he rode off, taking his men with him.

Hagan, finding himself alone once more, rode on as smoke and the gathering darkness rolled across the plains. Thousands of men and horses, dead or dying, littered the ground all around. The great tumult of battle had abated to the eerie moans of the wind and the dying, along with the crackle of fires burning.

Hagan's mood of despondency returned, driven by an overwhelming feeling of tiredness.

There would be no final victory now. Without the Visigoths

the Romans would not have enough men to finish off the Huns. Why had Aetius told Thorismund this news? He must have known the young man would leave and take his warriors with him. Did Aetius not want Attila vanquished?

Perhaps that was it. Perhaps this was all a grand stratagem by Aetius. Attila was defeated but not dead. Theodoric was dead and the Visigoths had lost many warriors. Perhaps they would now be drawn into a civil war as the brothers Thorismund and Theodoric the younger fought for the throne. Neither the Visigoths nor Attila now had the strength to threaten Rome, but they could still threaten *each other*, and while they were doing that they would leave Rome alone.

Hagan felt sick. Had all these men died for nothing? Just to keep the creaking, rotting Roman Empire, already tottering on its last legs, alive for a few more years before its final, inevitable collapse? It was unthinkable. How could someone be so evil?

A pall of smoke drifted by, catching in his dry throat and making him cough. Realising how thirsty he was, Hagan remembered the stream running by the bottom of the ridge and made for it. Perhaps, as the fighting had moved away from there and the dying around it had bled out, the water would be fresh once again.

Approaching the stream Hagan dismounted and walked towards it, already imagining the taste of the sweet, pure water as it coursed over his parched tongue.

Someone was ahead of him. At first in the gloom he thought it was a large dead body lying face down. Then Hagan saw whoever it was was drinking from the stream. He also recognised the armour the man wore. It was made up of countless little scales of metal all joined together like the hide of a dragon. The tunic was too small for the wearer and did not meet at the broadest part of his back.

Hagan slowed down. He was about to turn away when somehow Sigurd sensed his presence. He looked up. Hagan stopped. Sigurd clambered to his feet. The front of his armour was splattered all over with blood, some dried to maroon, some still quite fresh, none of it his own.

'Well look who it is,' Sigurd said. 'The little man with the big ideas.'

'Sigurd, it has been a very long day,' Hagan said, holding up his hands. 'I'm tired. I just want a drink of water.'

'It has been a long day for all of us,' Sigurd said. He looked around. 'I have killed many men today.'

He unsheathed his great war sword.

'One more won't be much more work,' he said.

CHAPTER SIXTY-NINE

'WHAT ARE YOU talking about?' Hagan said with a frown. 'Are you serious?'

'You and I have been on the path to this meeting from the moment we met,' Sigurd said, taking a step forward. 'When my wife spoke so highly of you. She loves me, you know. Adores me, in fact. And I can't have rivals in anything. If you don't realise this by now you will have to learn the hard way.'

'You love Gunhild?' Hagan said. 'You have a strange way of showing that. I've seen you dallying with other women. And Zerco says you like to swive both slaves and noble ladies.'

'They mean nothing to me,' Sigurd said, taking another step towards Hagan. 'Gunhild understands that. Besides, what's a man like me to do? I am the champion of the people. I have women literally throwing themselves at my feet. Am I to ignore that? Gunhild knows I can't do that. What sort of a man would people think I was?'

'An honourable one,' Hagan said.

He dropped his hand to his own sheathed sword.

Sigurd grunted derisively.

'A man like you wouldn't understand,' he said.

'My father was the champion of the people,' Hagan said. 'He did not behave as you do.'

'Ah, Godegisil, your father,' Sigurd said, swiping his sword left and right. The runes on its blade somehow glittered in the dim light. 'Or rather the man who said he was your father.

Gunhild has told me about that too. He wasn't your real father, was he? She knows who your real father is, and that is another problem. That is why you have to die. The Gods have presented you to me here, and now I must complete my part of the bargain.'

Hagan glanced around and realised that they were alone, apart from the mounds of dead and scattered, broken war gear. He was weary and thirsty. His sword arm ached and he did not relish the idea of trying to fight a man as huge as Sigurd.

'You don't have to do this,' he said.

'But I do,' Sigurd said. 'I explained this to you before. The Sword of Tiwass has a curse. Whenever it is drawn it must taste blood. And I have already drawn the blade. Now. Enough talk.'

He began to stomp towards Hagan. Hagan unslung his shield and readied himself. He placed his feet shoulder-width apart and readied himself. He felt a strange feeling of unreality, as if this were not really happening. He found it hard to believe after such a day he was now facing off against someone from his own folk. Was he really going to die?

Sigurd did not bother with his shield. Instead he gripped his sword in both hands. With surprising speed for such a big man, he skipped across the last few paces between them.

He swung the sword overhead in a great arc. Hagan raised his shield to counter the blow. The great blade smashed into the face of the shield with an impact that made Hagan's whole arm and shoulder shudder and his teeth rattle. There was an ominous crack and Hagan watched with dismay as his shield, already battered from the day's battle, shattered and fell into pieces.

Hagan acted on instinct. He knew Sigurd was in range of his own sword and lunged with it, driving the point of the blade into the big man's chest.

Hagan's sword did not pierce the big man's armour. Instead it poked into it, then with a rattle of metal on metal, scattered off sideways. Sigurd chuckled and drew his sword up to strike again.

Hagan twisted and staggered away from the big man, just making it far enough as Sigurd swung at him again. The blade just missed him.

Hagan attacked, not even looking where he was hitting. His arm checked with a painful wrench of his elbow as Sigurd blocked his attack with his own blade.

Hagan turned and struck again. He hit Sigurd with all his might, an overhead blow that landed on this other man's left shoulder. Hagan watched in dismay as the blade yet again failed to pierce Sigurd's scale mail and just skidded over the surface.

'You are wasting your time,' Sigurd said. 'This is Byzantine armour. I took it from the Eastern Roman dragon warriors we ambushed and slaughtered when they tried to steal the treasure of the Nibelungs. So far today it's proved impenetrable to Hun arrows, Ostrogoth swords and Gepid spears. Your puny sword stands no chance.'

'So it *was* you who took the treasure,' Hagan said. 'As they all guessed.'

'It was me who *saved* the treasure,' Sigurd said. 'For the people who it belonged to. Why should the Romans take it just because of a moment of weakness by Gunderic?'

'I don't see the ordinary Burgundar folk sharing in much of the treasure,' Hagan said.

He was really just trying to stall Sigurd while he thought about what he might be able to do. Sigurd was right, his sword could do nothing against the Byzantine armour. The big man was twice as strong as he was and he still seemed to be as fresh as he was first thing that morning. Hagan on the other hand was exhausted and if the massive blade of the Sword of the War God so much as touched him it could well take off an arm or a leg. It did not seem like he had many options.

'They benefit from it in many ways,' Sigurd said. 'It makes their war horde strong. They have a rich king who brings pride to the realm.'

Sigurd swept his sword in an arc aimed at taking off Hagan's head. Hagan used the last remnants of his strength to jump out of the way. He almost made it but the blade struck his left shoulder. It was a glancing blow but still split the iron rings of Hagan's mail shirt like it was linen. He felt a searing pain as the blade sliced through his flesh beneath.

Hagan staggered away; the world seemed to spin a little before him and countless black specks danced and swirled before his eyes. He could feel the warmth of his blood running from the wound to his shoulder.

'You think Gunderic will be content to continue to share the treasure?' he said, trying to keep Sigurd talking rather than attacking, though with the dawning realisation that he was only postponing the inevitable.

'It's of no consequence,' Sigurd said. 'I am named as his successor, remember? It is he who will have to be wary of me.'

With that he swung a great blow, bringing it down from above in a strike designed to slice Hagan's head in two from crown to chin. Hagan swiped his own sword above his head to block the attack. The two blades met in a tooth-jarring collision that sent sparks showering down onto Hagan's face.

The impact made Hagan stagger backwards. Now utterly drained of all energy, he lost his footing and fell flat on his back. At the same moment there was a resounding dull metal clang as the blade of Hagan's sword broke and fell in two.

Hagan gasped, the impact of his fall driving the breath from his lungs. Sigurd stepped forward and stood over him, one foot on either side of his chest. He reversed his sword so the point of the blade hovered over Hagan's heart.

Hagan realised it was over for him. He was so tired that for a moment he almost welcomed death. But then anger flared in his heart. He did not want to die and he definitely did not want to die at the hands of Sigurd.

It did not look like he would have any choice, however.

He closed his eyes.

Hagan felt rather than heard the beat of horses' hooves. He heard Sigurd cry out in either surprise or pain.

He opened his eyes again and saw a warrior on horseback riding past. Instead of stabbing Hagan, Sigurd swiped at the rider. He missed, then with a curse he hurled his sword after the galloping warrior. The blade struck, impaling the riding warrior who fell out of the saddle.

Sigurd stumbled sideways. Then he dropped to his knees with a rattle of his scale mail. For a moment Hagan saw Sigurd looking at him, a look of utter disbelief on his face, then the big man gasped and collapsed face forward onto the ground.

For the first time Hagan saw the broken shaft of the spear embedded in Sigurd's back, driven into the unprotected gap below his neck where his mail shirt did not meet.

Hagan sat up, confused as to what had just happened. He scrambled to his feet and saw the rider who had struck Sigurd lying on her side a little way away.

It was Brynhild. She was transfixed by Sigurd's sword. The point of it had burst from her stomach and glistened with her blood.

Hagan ran over and crouched beside her.

'Here we are again, Hagan,' Brynhild said, her breath coming in gasps because of the pain. 'Just like at Vorbetomagus all those years ago. Except this time I will not survive.'

Hagan felt helpless as he stared at her wound. It was fatal, there was no doubt about that.

'Pull it out, Hagan,' Brynhild said through gritted teeth. 'I want to lie back.'

'If I do that you will die,' Hagan said.

'I am going to die anyway,' Brynhild said. 'I may as well be comfortable. Please, Hagan... it's hard to breathe like this.'

Hagan took a deep breath then wrenched the sword free of Brynhild's body. Eyes screwed shut, she let out an agonised scream as a great torrent of bright blood gushed from her body.

Hagan tossed the sword away as far as he could. It clattered to the earth not far from Sigurd. Then he helped Brynhild lie back on the ground. For a moment he thought she was already dead, then her eyes sprung open, filled with fury and fixing his own with an unflinching gaze.

'I curse them all,' Brynhild said. 'I cursed you as well. Today was to be my day of vengeance and I killed many of the Huns. I killed Sigurd. I paid him back for his part in what happened to me. But he has killed me as well. Now it looks like my revenge is incomplete. Gunderic still lives. Gunhild still lives. *You* still live.'

'Brynhild, I am sorry for my part in deceiving you,' Hagan said. 'I never thought of the consequences. I just wanted to please everyone.'

'If you really mean that...' Brynhild said. She grimaced, blood staining her clenched teeth pink. 'Then you will complete my revenge for me.'

'Brynhild, I—' Hagan started to speak.

'Swear you will do it!' Brynhild said. She continued to glare at him and she gripped his forearms, her nails digging into his flesh.

The effort drained her last energy. Hagan saw the light fade from her eyes and the pupils became fixed. Her fingers relaxed and let go of his arms. Her last breath left her in a sigh as she fell onto her side.

Hagan flopped down on his backside, panting and staring in disbelief at the two corpses of Sigurd and Brynhild.

Then he heard a high wail.

Gunhild rose from behind a nearby pile of corpses. She staggered like someone drunk to where Sigurd lay and thew herself on top of him. She began to heave great sobs.

Hagan looked at her, unsure if he could believe his eyes. Had she been watching the whole thing?

'She killed him,' Gunhild said in a weak voice. 'She wasn't supposed to do that. I don't know where she came from.'

She sounded as if she was talking to herself.

'He was going to kill me,' Hagan said.

'He was supposed to kill you!!' Gunhild screamed.

Hagan was taken aback by the anger in her voice and the glare in her eyes. He had heard grief could do strange things to the mind, which if it was twisting Gunhild's then all Sigurd said must have been true. She really did love him. Or was there something else?

Either way he felt too exhausted to try to work it out.

'I came to find him on the battlefield,' Gunhild said through sobs. 'To warn him about Brynhild. She'd gone mad. Then he insisted on killing you. He was such a wonderful man. A hero. There will be no one like him again for a thousand years!'

'You must have seen a different side to him,' Hagan said. 'I only saw a bully and a thug.'

'What would you know?' Gunhild said with a sneer. 'What would any of you know? He was truly great. And now he's dead because of a stupid battle, the cowardice of my brother and the weakness of Brynhild.'

'It was hardly weakness...' Hagan did not press his point. Even at a distance he could see the hard glitter in Gunhild's eyes and knew there would be no reasoning with her.

Gunhild rose to her feet.

'We were supposed to rule together,' she said. 'If not through manipulating the weakness of my brother then in his stead. Gunderic had already agreed Sigurd as his successor. And I would have been queen. I was the *eldest* after all. It was my birthright. Then all of you – Wodnas, Aetius, Attila and *you*, Hagan – came along with your stupid schemes and now he's dead.'

She heaved a huge sob that spoke of thwarted hopes and endless sadness. Hagan wondered if her grief was due to the death of Sigurd or the end of her hopes. Perhaps they were both entwined.

'Well I'll show you,' Gunhild said, her lips turning to a snarl. 'I'll show you all! I will rule all of you.'

She staggered over to where Sigurd's great war sword lay and lifted it. For a moment she struggled under the weight of it. Hagan felt a brief moment of panic that she was going to attack him with it but instead she ran the sword into its jewelled sheath. With tender fingers she unclasped it from Sigurd's dead body and slung it over her shoulder by the strap.

'Attila wants a bride and he wants this sword,' Gunhild said. She was talking now as if to herself as she strode over to where Brynhild's horse, its saddle now empty, stood waiting for its owner who would never ride again. 'Well, I will give him both. I will offer him the sword as my dowry.'

Hagan began to struggle to his feet. He looked around. His own horse was nowhere to be seen.

'Wait, Gunhild,' he said. 'If Attila gets that sword he could grow strong again—'

'That is my fervent hope,' Gunhild said, swinging herself up into the saddle. She kicked her legs and trotted off a little way.

'One thing, please!' Hagan said, his voice pleading. She was already too far away for him to try to stop her. 'Sigurd said you know who my real father is.'

Gunhild reined her horse to a halt. She looked over her shoulder at him.

'Yes,' she said. 'I do.'

Then she kicked her heels against her horse and galloped off.

PART VI

THE WOLF'S LAIR

Hvat hyggr þú brúði bendu,
þá er hon okkr baug sendi,
varinn váðum heiðingja?

What is she trying to say, that she sends us a ring,
Woven with a wolf's hair? I think it's a warning.

Atlakviða, the Song of Attila (ninth-century Old Norse
poem)

CHAPTER SEVENTY

TWO YEARS LATER

Aquileia, North-West Italia

HAGAN SURVEYED THE devastation with a cold gaze. It was hard to believe that this was the same place he and Zerco had sailed into two years before. Then it had been a vibrant port city with wide squares, impressive sculptures and fountains, a cathedral, huge villas and the palaces of several former emperors.

Now it was just a smoking ruin.

Piles of blackened rubble lay heaped where buildings once stood. The noise and bustle had been replaced by the silence of the tomb. Even though it was weeks since Attila's army had destroyed the city, their fury had been such that it still smouldered in places. The wisps of grey smoke hovered over the shattered, pockmarked paving stones of the streets, mingling with the sickly smell of decay from corpses still buried in the ruins. Architecture that had stood for centuries, works of art and untold treasures, as well as countless human lives had all been swept away, utterly obliterated for the crime of daring to refuse to submit to the Huns.

Wodnas had been right. There would never be peace in the world while Attila still lived.

Hagan had heard the old man say it several times; the last time was as they withdrew after the battle on the plains two years ago. The Romans had laid siege to Attila's camp but with the Visigoths leaving to support their king, Thorismund, the army of the Alliance was no longer strong enough to assault the camp and finish the defeated Attila off. Instead they had just had to watch as Attila's army made an ordered withdrawal from the far side of their camp.

As the Romans had held the field Aetius had claimed victory, though it was a hollow one. Attila had been defeated, his power weakened and his reputation for invincibility cracked. Yet he was not dead, and someone like Attila could always recover. Despite Aetius's boasts, everyone knew Attila would go home, lick his wounds, rebuild his power and then come back and start the whole bloody saga once again.

And that was just what he did.

He had returned to his kingdom. The bloodletting continued there. Now he had lost a battle there were those among the Hun nobility who began to question if Attila should be king. He beheaded over a hundred nobles and their families, leaving everyone else in no doubt that he should.

Attila also now had further proof of his right to rule. Gunhild, it turned out, had fled to the Hun camp after Sigurd's death and delivered the Sword of the War God into his hands.

Now even more secure in power than ever, Attila had rebuilt his army and renewed his assault on the Western Roman Empire. He renewed his claim to half of the Empire on the grounds that Honoria, the Emperor's sister had proposed marriage to him. This time he rode over the mountains and attacked northern Italia. His first target was Aquileia, the ruins of which Hagan now looked at. After a short siege Attila had razed it to the ground.

There was no help from the Visigoths this time and Aetius did not have a big enough army to confront Attila's army and just had to do his best to harass him then run away again, all the while waiting for the inevitable killer blow from the Huns that would bring the final end to the Empire.

That blow never came, however. Attila ravaged further south then, his army struck by an outbreak of plague, packed up and went home again. The Romans could breathe once more.

After the battle of the Catalaunian plains, Hagan had remained with Aetius and the army. It was from no great love of Rome but rather a lack of other choices. Even with Sigurd dead Hagan did not feel safe returning to the Burgundar realm and the power of Gunderic. Aetius needed all the soldiers he could get and so Hagan had resumed his service in the exploratores.

Now with the Huns retreating, the Roman army were shadowing them as they retraced their bloody steps back to their homeland, like a nervous tavern owner making sure a drunken, violent client was firmly off the premises. So far they had reached as far as Aquileia, which is how Hagan came to be looking at its ruins that day.

He had entered what was left of Aquileia with a company of exploratores ahead of the main Roman army to check there was no enemies lurking in the rubble, waiting to launch an ambush to slow down any pursuit of Attila's horde.

The exploratores had split up shortly after entering the perimeter of what was left of the shattered city walls and Hagan was now alone, completing his search of his assigned section of the town. He had come to the conclusion that the town was empty apart from the dead. The heavy silence alone told him that. The Huns had passed through it weeks before and were now long gone.

As he walked across a blackened street in the devastated city Hagan wondered at how many other towns and cities like Aquileia had now died at the hands of Attila.

A fallen stone column lay shattered across the street and a large, well-fed cat jumped up on it. Hagan shivered at the thought of what that cat must be chewing on amid the ruins of the town to have got so big.

He frowned. There was something familiar about the cat. He had seen it before somewhere.

There were three figures standing in the street.

Hagan dropped to a crouch, spear ready. Where had they come from? He was sure the street was empty only a moment before.

The cat jumped off the broken column and scuttled across the street to the newcomers. Hagan now understood where he had seen it before.

The Lady Freya, lovely as ever, dipped and scooped the cat up into her arms. Wodnas stood beside her, dressed in his faded old blue robe, wide-brimmed hat on and spear walking staff in his right hand. His leather satchel was slung over his left shoulder. As usual he was barefoot. On the other side of the street was the diminutive figure of Zerco.

'I would like to say I am pleased to see you,' Hagan said. 'But I feel a foreboding at your presence.'

After the battle of the Catalaunian plains, Wodnas and the others had returned to Geneva with the rest of the Burgundars. He had not seen Zerco since before the battle.

Wodnas, impassive as ever, regarded Hagan with his one eye.

'It seems I was right about Attila,' he said.

'Of course you were,' Hagan said.

'It seems he has been stopped again, though, for now,' Wodnas said. 'The great creaking edifice of the Roman Empire will continue to stand for a few more years. At least while the luck of Aetius continues to hold.'

'Attila's retreat had nothing to do with Aetius,' Hagan said. 'The Pope claims credit for it. He says it was his prayers that made it happen. The arrival of the plague was divine intervention.'

'And perhaps it was,' Wodnas said, a faint smile flickering across his lips. 'Perhaps also someone made sure of it by secreting the corpses of men who had died of the plague into Attila's camp. Eh, Freya?'

'Are you saying you had a hand in Attila's retreat?' Hagan said, narrowing his eyes.

'I'm not saying anything,' Wodnas said. 'Though faced with a similar problem it's what I would have done.'

'What was it all for, though?' Hagan said. 'This is just a stay of execution. Attila will be back next year. He won't stop returning until he rules all the world.'

'Or he's dead,' Wodnas said.

'True,' Hagan said. 'But what are the chances of that?'

'That is why we are here,' Wodnas said. 'Gunhild did not just give Attila the Sword of Tiwass. She offered her hand in marriage.'

'What on earth is she up to?' Hagan said with a sardonic grunt. 'I can't get a woman to so much as look at me, yet Attila has the most beautiful and powerful women in the world throwing themselves at his feet. I wonder how he does it!'

'Now it looks like his plans of marrying Honoria will not be happening, at least this year anyway,' Wodnas said. 'He seems to have accepted Gunhild's offer. They are to be married.'

'So Gunhild has been living among the Huns for the last two years?' Hagan said.

'She has,' Wodnas said. 'And now she has sent you an invitation to her coming wedding. She has also explicitly asked that her brother too travel to Attila's palace in Hun Land to attend the ceremony.'

Hagan's jaw dropped open a little. He remembered her wild angry eyes and her howling at the death of Sigurd.

'She wants us both dead,' he said. 'This must be some kind of trap.'

'I would say it almost certainly is,' Wodnas said. 'But it is also an opportunity. What if we struck first? If the right man could get close enough to Attila he could perhaps kill him.'

'In his own house, at the heart of his own realm, surrounded by his most loyal warriors and all his people?' Hagan said. 'Such an attempt would be suicide.'

'When he believes he is most safe is sometimes when a king is most vulnerable. Who would expect an attack at such a time and place?' Wodnas said. 'There are ways it could be done and the attacker still escape. Perhaps there was a way to dribble an undetectable poison into Attila's drink. When he dies in his sleep later no one will be any the wiser. In the sorrow and hysteria the next morning the killer could slip away.'

'Do such poisons exist?' Hagan said.

Wodnas looked at Freya. The lady held up a little bottle made of blue glass. She shook it a little and Hagan saw it contained a liquid. Freya smiled.

'Such an act could finally rid the world of Attila,' Wodnas said. 'We would not have to continue to fight him every year.'

'There would finally be peace,' Hagan said. 'But is Gunderic going to accept this offer? He must know it's a trap too.'

'The king's temperament has got worse over the last two years, I'm sorry to say,' Wodnas said with a grimace. 'Now he is sole possessor of the gold it has taken over his mind. His suspicion knows no bounds. He thinks everyone is trying to steal his wealth away. The hangings and beheadings have become much more frequent. The folk have begun to whisper that he is a tyrant. I spend most of my time in my own hall in the mountains these days. Geneva has become a dark place. Gunhild says that once she is married she will relinquish her claim to her part of the treasure. He has not told me this but I believe that perhaps King Gunderic thinks by travelling to Hun Land he might have the chance to kill his sister, and remove the last other person who knows where the gold is hidden.'

'It sounds like he has gone mad,' Hagan said.

'Quite possibly, yes.'

'What about you, old man? Are you going to this wedding?' Hagan said. 'What's in it for you?'

'I just want my sword back,' Wodnas said.

'*Your* sword?' Hagan said. 'I thought it was the Sword of the War God?'

Wodnas remained impassive.

'What about you, Zerco?' Hagan said. 'You've been very

quiet. What happened to all that noble talk of forsaking the treasure?'

'I was invited too,' Zerco said. 'Except my invitation was from Attila himself. But I am going on the orders of General Aetius and I will be the excuse for you not being beaten to death for desertion if you join us. Besides, I had forgotten how cruel the world can be. If there is some way to get a little gold from this it would make life a bit more comfortable for me.'

'If you are looking for your "right man", Wodnas, I am not it, alright?' Hagan said. 'Gunhild must think I'm stupid if she believes I'd walk right into her trap like a simple, wide-eyed child. Why does she think I would accept this offer?'

'She says in her letter,' Wodnas said, 'that if you come to her wedding she will tell you the truth about your father.'

CHAPTER SEVENTY-ONE

A WEEK LATER, AND far into the journey to Hun Land, Hagan could still not quite believe he had agreed to come along.

One of his objections had been that it would make him a deserter. The punishments for desertion in the Roman Army were brutal and could, if his officer stuck to the letter of the law, result in Hagan being beaten to death by his fellow soldiers in front of the rest of his unit.

Zerco had explained that Hagan did not need to worry about that as they were travelling under the orders of the Magister Militum, General Aetius. Zerco was very popular with the Hun nobility, who thought he was hilarious, though Attila had always hated him. Attila had requested Zerco be returned to his court so he could be the entertainment at his wedding feast. Zerco was not happy with this but Aetius had agreed.

Why the Magister Militum would do that, Hagan could not work out, and said so.

'Aetius thinks it will appease Attila in some way,' Zerco had explained. 'He thinks that by accommodating Attila's demands then the Huns will leave Aetius alone long enough for Rome to rebuild sufficient strength to fight them off. What a fool the man is. If you feed a wolf scraps of meat it won't make it leave your sheep alone. And I am the scrap of meat in this instance.'

The little man looked so miserable Hagan could not help

feeling pity for him. He was returning to a life of pampering, yes, but at the price of constant ridicule and degradation. Nevertheless, Hagan wondered if that was Aetius's real reasoning. Did he know what Wodnas was planning? Was he in fact behind Wodnas' plan?

Needless to say, Wodnas kept tight-lipped. Regardless of his reasoning, Aetius knew of the journey, and so ostensibly Hagan was to go as an escort to ensure Zerco made it to the court of Attila.

The Lady Freya had not come with them, saying she was returning to Geneva to ensure her father Forsetti and the other Aesir were ready to leave quickly in case Wodnas' plan failed and Attila sought vengeance. Before they parted, however, she had handed her blue glass bottle to Wodnas, who placed it in one of the pack ponies' saddlebags.

Gunderic was travelling from Geneva separately and was to meet them at Attila's palace, which suited Hagan fine. That was one reunion Hagan was not looking forward to. Wodnas had assured him he would make sure of his safety but Hagan was still wary.

They had sailed across the Mare Hadriaticum, this time heading east. When they landed at Dyrrhachium they took the Via Egnatia through the dusty plains of Macedonia for two days then went north, leaving the relatively easy travelling of the Imperial road for dirt tracks and navigation by reckoning the sun. Here there were no mansiones or stabula, and they had to sleep out in the open in leather sleeping bags under whatever makeshift shelter they could build.

When they reached Naissus they began to see signs that they were travelling in the wake of Attila's army.

Hagan had never been there before, but it was clear Naissus was – or rather had been – a thriving city of considerable size.

'This was a major city at the edge of the Eastern Roman Empire, ruled from Constantinople,' Wodnas said. 'The last time I was here it was a teeming hive of commerce and life. Now look at it!'

The city was deserted. Its gates were broken, the houses, churches and shops ransacked. Eventually they came upon a church in the centre of the town where the sound of voices made them approach with caution. Peering in through the door they made out people lying on makeshift beds on the floor. Sweat glistened on their ghastly pale, gaunt faces. A couple of priests tended them.

Seeing the men at the door, one of the priests approached, then stopped.

'I won't come any closer,' he said. 'These people have an infectious sickness.'

Hagan and Wodnas exchanged glances.

'What happened to the city?' Wodnas said. 'Where is everyone?'

'The Huns attacked us,' the priest said. 'They destroyed everything. Those they didn't kill have run away. These sick people were the only survivors and they will not last much longer.'

'Let's leave this place,' Zerco said. 'The last thing we need is to catch plague.'

After resting for the night in a deserted building, they set off again in the morning. There was a meadow outside the city that led to the banks of a river. It was littered with the bones of maybe a thousand dead men and horses. They must have been killed in Attila's first assault, or perhaps even in previous raids by the Huns, for the bones were picked completely clean, dislocated and scattered all over the ground. Grass was growing around and through them.

There was, however, still a decent road running north from Naissus. It was a military road, built for soldiers to get quickly from Constantinople to the borders of the Eastern Empire. That border had now retreated considerably south. As evidence of this, the next day they came upon an outpost fort of the Eastern Empire.

Again it had been attacked and burned, but this time there was no sign of any bodies. The walls were crumbling and it looked like the place had been derelict for some time, perhaps many years.

The company proceeded north on the road but had to turn off it as it turned north-east and they went north-west. Both Zerco and Wodnas were familiar with the route. Zerco had travelled through this countryside many times, both with Aspar, the Magister Militum of the Eastern Empire, and when he was Bleda the Hun's jester. Wodnas explained that they were not far from where his former kingdom had been in southern Scythia, before it was overrun by the Huns.

They travelled down a wooded valley, following a winding, circuitous path. Sometimes the path was so twisting and the sides of the valley so high it seemed like they were heading the wrong way, as it appeared the sun was in the east rather than the west, but it turned out to be just an illusion caused by the wild, rugged terrain.

After another few days' travel they emerged overlooking a wide wooded plain. Before they descended to it they could see the wide blue waters of the Danube far ahead, weaving its way through the trees like a huge serpent.

It took most of the next day to get to the mighty river. Hagan had been wondering for most of the way how they might get across. From a distance there had been no sign of a bridge. However when they arrived he found he should not have worried.

Both banks were littered with hundreds of boats. Someone had cut down many of the surrounding trees, sawing the trunks in half lengthways and hollowing them out. There were huge heaps of wood shavings and stripped branches piled on the riverside. Countless feet and hooves had churned the ground to mud that was pocked with footprints still, perhaps weeks now since they had been made.

'This was how Attila got his army across the river,' Wodnas said. 'And how he got them back again.'

'They took their horses in these too?' Hagan said.

'The horses swam alongside,' Wodnas said. 'As will ours.'

They unburdened the pack ponies and loaded their saddlebags into one of the abandoned makeshift boats. Then, holding the reins of the horses as they waded then swam along behind, they rowed the boat to the other side of the wide, fast-flowing Danube.

When they grounded on the far bank, Wodnas stepped out and looked around.

'We are now in Hun Land,' he said.

'This was once your kingdom?' Hagan said, as he clambered out of the boat himself.

'Part of it was,' Wodnas said. 'My kingdom was over to the east, towards those mountains. It was once part of Roman Dacia before my people arrived. They called it Trans-Sylvania, the land beyond the forest.'

Hagan looked and saw a line of high, craggy mountains in the distance, visible because of the broad river and the trees that had been felled.

The woods and area seemed deserted, but the party reasoned that Attila's army had only recently passed through the area. Such a body of men could strip it of everything useful, from food to provisions, for their own ends, so it might be some time before the locals returned.

As they resumed their journey they did begin to come upon villages. Hagan noticed that the inhabitants seemed a strange mixture of peoples. Some looked like Greeks, others Goths, Scythians and Dacians. Their dress and language was also a strange mixture of different cultures. Both Wodnas and Zerco were able to converse in the local dialect, which meant the company was able to buy fresh provisions, a welcome relief from the dried food they had been living off for some time.

There were also Huns, of course, but they were fewer in number. They were the chiefs and governors of the villages, the judges and the warriors, and they always had the largest houses in the villages, usually protected behind a palisade or enclosure. They had conquered this land, and now they ruled it.

Everyone was welcoming enough to the travellers and they were not robbed or swindled, but Hagan could not help notice that soon after they left each village a horseman would come galloping out of it, overtaking them on the path they were on and riding on ahead.

'They are warning Attila of our presence,' Wodnas said. 'Or at least that there are strangers in the country.'

'Attila must command considerable respect,' Hagan commented.

'They fear him,' Wodnas said. 'No one wants to be the village head man who did not report the presence of foreigners when others did. It would bring suspicion – and punishment.'

The journey continued for seven more days. The company crossed three more large rivers, this time using ferries provided by the locals. The forests thinned out and they passed lakes and meadows. At night they camped and if they were lucky ate fish caught in a river or bread made from millet they had bought from the locals. The wine they had brought ran out and they had to make do with a local drink made from barley that tasted bitter and made the head swim a little. Wodnas, who until then Hagan had only ever seen drinking wine, found it particularly unpleasant.

At night they sat around the campfire, chatting and drinking the bitter barley wine. Wodnas entertained them with tales of his astonishing travels. There seemed very few places in the known world the old man had not been to.

After another day of travel, as evening drew on, the wide plain opened up and there was a large settlement on it beside a winding river.

'That's where Attila's palace is,' Wodnas said.

'Where is his army?' Hagan wondered. The surrounding fields were flattened and stripped of undergrowth, the grass dead or stripped to mud. There were all the signs that a large army had camped there.

'He will have sent them home,' Wodnas said. 'The plague made him retreat from Italia. To the plague, a large band of men all camped together is like a bowl for proving bread in, or a dry heath when a wildfire starts. If they are scattered there is less chance of them spreading it among themselves.'

'That's good, isn't it?' Zerco said.

'He'll still have plenty of warriors around him, don't worry about that,' Wodnas said.

'So what now?' Hagan said.

'Give me a moment,' Wodnas said. 'I need to think.'

He walked a little way off until he found a tree stump which he sat on. He turned his back to the others, though they could still see him take his satchel off, set it on his knees and unlatch it.

'You see what he's doing?' Zerco said in a low voice. 'He's talking to that bag he carries.'

'I've seen him do it a few times before,' Hagan said. 'He does it whenever he tries to make decisions.'

Zerco made a twirling gesture with his forefinger beside his temple.

'I just hope he hasn't lost his mind,' he said. 'He's leading us on this quest and I'd hate to think our destinies were in the hands of a madman.'

After a time the old man closed his bag, slung it over his shoulder and stood up. Then he returned to the others.

'Well?' Hagan said.

'We should go and announce our arrival,' Wodnas said. 'We

need to try to discern what Gunhild's real purpose is. Perhaps now feels she has made a mistake and this is a cry for help, a veiled plea to be rescued. She might be able to aid us in getting the poison into Attila's drink. Or perhaps she really is going to marry him, and during the revels after the ceremony the opportunity might arise to somehow get Freya's poison into his wine.'

'Or perhaps they will just have us put to death as soon as we arrive,' Hagan said.

'True,' Wodnas said. 'But we will never know if we stay here.'

CHAPTER SEVENTY-TWO

'**I** WOULD HAVE THOUGHT Attila would have lived somewhere grander,' Hagan said. 'In a big city perhaps.'

'Attila has many houses, many palaces, all over his realms,' Zerco said. 'This is just his favourite. His favourite son was born here and he believes it's a lucky place for him.'

They arrived at the gates of the village, which was surrounded by a circular rampart topped by a palisade of sharpened stakes. There were many Hun war horses in a pen outside and the gates were guarded.

'What do we do?' Hagan said from the corner of his mouth as they approached the five surly looking Huns in mail and helmets who barred the way into the settlement. At the sight of the three obvious foreigners approaching, the guards stiffened and grasped their spears.

'Tell them the truth,' Wodnas said. 'We're here for the wedding.'

They dismounted, then Wodnas spoke to the guards in their own tongue. They looked sceptical but one of them hurried off into the town while the others told Wodnas he would have to wait. After some time of standing, awkwardly regarding each other, the fifth Hun returned, this time accompanied by another man. Hagan recognised Ediko, the Hun emissary who had delivered Attila's message that night in Geneva years before. Then he was dressed in practical, simple riding clothes.

Now he wore much grander attire, including a white silk tunic and dark blue felt britches.

'Zerco!' Ediko said, breaking into a broad smile at the sight of the little man. He spoke in the Roman tongue for the sake of the foreigners. 'I'm glad you finally accepted the invitation to return. We shall have fine entertainment after the wedding feast now!'

Hagan noted the fixed smile on Zerco's face and imagined how he must feel, having escaped after years spent in forced humiliation, clowning for the amusement of drunken barbarians, only to now be faced with returning to that same torture.

Ediko spoke to the guards who nodded then pulled open the gate, allowing Hagan, Wodnas and Zerco to enter the settlement.

'This is excellent,' Ediko said as he led the way through the streets. 'The nobles had gathered here to witness the king's latest marriage, but no one is keen to stay together too long, not with the plague abroad. Now you are here the wedding can be held.'

The streets of the settlement were simple beaten earth tracks, mere pathways between the buildings, which were mostly wood and straw and almost all circular with conical roofs.

'The Huns spent centuries roaming the plains of the world from the east to here,' Zerco said. 'All that time they lived in tents. Now they are settling down they build their houses in the shape of their tents.'

There may not have been an army outside, but the interior of the settlement was packed with warriors. They lounged outside what looked like taverns, guarded the doors of large houses or strutted around in their mail and helmets. Hagan noticed they were all Huns. When it came to guarding the king and his closest noblemen, foreigners and allied warriors like the Gepids and Ostrogoths could only be trusted so far, it seemed.

Hagan began to get nervous. If something went wrong or they were discovered, they were outnumbered perhaps a hundred or more to one. They would not stand a chance.

In the centre of the settlement was a building that was larger than all the others. It too was circular and the exterior was clad in polished wooden boards that shone in the sunlight. It was taller than the other houses, having some sort of second storey to it, and the whole thing was surrounded by another wooden fence, an enclosure within an enclosure, that had four towers for guards to watch from at intervals along it.

From its grandeur compared to its surroundings, and because they were heading straight for it, Hagan concluded this was Attila's palace.

At the sight of Ediko the warriors guarding the gate to the fence at Attila's palace stood up straight and let them all enter.

Now inside the enclosure, Hagan spotted another building beside the main one that looked as out of place as a fish on the main street. It was built of white stones, its entrance was lined with carved Roman columns that held up a triangular marble portico. From its shape and what was clearly a furnace room built alongside it, Hagan recognised what it was, but could scarcely believe his eyes.

'Is that a bathhouse?' Hagan said.

'Yes,' Ediko said. 'Onegesius, who was king of the Scythians here, had it built many years ago. He was a great admirer of all things Roman. He even brought an architect from Dacia to oversee the construction and transported the stones for it from Pannonia.'

'Can we use it?' Hagan said, looking with longing at the entrance and imagining sinking his tired, aching body into the hot water inside.

'We have no use for Roman comforts,' Ediko said. 'No one knows how it is supposed to work any more. The king has found a new use for it though.'

He gave a little chuckle but did not say anything else.

'You are the last to arrive,' Ediko said as they walked towards a line of wooden steps that rose up to two huge, carved wooden doors that formed the entrance to the house. 'King Gunderic got here three days ago. He has been staying in the palace with his sister and the king. They are most eager to see you.'

Hagan saw a group of men standing not far away and recognised some familiar faces. They were Burgundar warriors: about twenty of the Berh Herjass, clad in their bear cloaks, and five of Wodnas' Raven Warriors, including Gunfjaun.

'Alright, lads?' Hagan said, unable to stop the grin spreading across his face.

The Burgundars turned and jogged over. They nodded their respect to Wodnas and all of them were genuinely pleased to see Hagan. They clapped him on the back, the Bear Warriors asking what he had been up to since the battle on the Catalaunian plains. Some gripped his arm and all said how good it was to see him again.

Hagan felt totally overwhelmed by emotion. His habitual loneliness dissolved in the warmth of the camaraderie the warriors displayed for him.

'What are you doing here?' Hagan said.

'We came with King Gunderic from Geneva,' one of the Burgundars said. 'We're here as part of his bodyguard.'

'If you please,' Ediko said, trying to usher Hagan and Wodnas away from the Burgundars. 'The king is expecting you.'

'You're having dinner with the nobles?' Gunfjaun said, smiling. 'It's well for some. We'll be having bread, meal and that awful barley beer in the warriors' quarters. Enjoy yourselves.'

'We shall catch up later,' Hagan said. 'Over a decent drink.'

Ediko led them to the steps. Just as they reached the bottom the great doors at the top swung open. Three figures emerged from the gloom beyond to stand at the top of the stairway. Hagan saw that it was Gunderic, Gunhild and, holding her hand, Attila, King of the Huns.

Gunhild's smile was warm and she waved her free hand. Hagan was stuck however by the contrast with the time she had greeted him in Geneva. Now there was no rushing down the hall and embracing. She looked as beautiful as ever, and the manic rage that had twisted her face the last time he saw her was gone.

Her brother however looked very different. He had lost a lot of weight and his tunic hung loose around his large frame. His skin was pale, as if he had not seen sunlight in a long time and there were dark rings under his eyes. He was trying to smile but it looked more like a sneer.

Both siblings wore their black cloaks with the eagle on the shoulder.

Attila was simply dressed in white linen. He stood at the top of the stairs, feet shoulder-width apart, his free hand on his hip. Under his left arm in a scabbard sheathed in red silk swung the Sword of the War God. He looked down at Hagan, Wodnas and Zerco and grinned.

It was the look of a wolf who spotted newborn lambs in a field.

He spoke some harsh-sounding words in his own tongue.

'The Mighty King bids you welcome to his palace,' Ediko translated for the Burgundars. 'While he is not pleased to see Master Zerco again, in fact the very sight of him disgusts the Great King, he understands that the little man will bring great pleasure to the king's loyal followers.'

Attila spoke again, this time his words were directed at Wodnas. He patted the hilt of the big sword at his side as he spoke.

'The Mighty King welcomes you at last to his home, King Wodnas,' Ediko said. 'He says you have long been rivals but he knew there would be a day when you came to his door. I am sure you recognise this weapon?'

Wodnas nodded.

'It was once yours, but now the War God has decided Attila is more worthy to bear it.'

Hagan felt uneasy. Attila's words were far from welcoming.

'Hagan! Wodnas!' Gunhild said. 'It's so good to see you once again. Hagan, I am sorry we parted with such harsh words. I was stricken by grief. Maybe you can understand?'

'It was a bad day for us all,' Hagan said. 'I hear you are to be married. Congratulations.'

'Yes,' Gunhild said. 'Now you are finally here we can hold the ceremony. The king and I will be married in the morning.'

'Hello, Hagan,' Gunderic said. His voice was cold and friendly as a tomb. There were no apologies from him. No attempt at any reconciliation.

'Come,' Ediko said, spreading his right hand up the steps. 'You are just in time for dinner.'

'Should we not get dressed?' Wodnas said. 'We have not unpacked.'

Hagan could see concern on the old man's face and wondered what was going on.

'There is no need,' Ediko said. 'Half the Hun nobility who are here rode in this afternoon. They see no need for these Roman virtues. We are a simple folk. Let us eat and you can unpack later.'

He ushered Wodnas, Hagan and Zerco up the steps while some servants led their horses and pack ponies away to the stables.

At the top of the steps they found themselves at the end of an entrance hall. Attila, Gunhild and Gunderic had proceeded into the palace ahead. Hagan wondered if this was the time when he would get to talk to them before the wedding. There was much to discuss, not least whatever Gunhild had to tell him about his father.

Several Hun warriors surrounded Hagan and Wodnas and searched them thoroughly, going through every inch of their clothing and taking away knives, the spear Wodnas used as a walking staff and any other sharp objects that might be used as a weapon.

Hagan's stomach lurched a little as he wondered if they would find the bottle of Freya's poison on Wodnas and ask what it was, or worse, ask them to taste it to see whether or not it was harmful. To his relief they did not find it.

The cup-bearers came forward and gave each of them a cup of wine.

'This is a Hun custom,' Zerco said. 'You are supposed to pray and take a drink before you sit down to eat.'

They took a sip. To Hagan's relief it was decent wine instead of the dreadful barley drink they had been forced to drink for the last week.

Ediko then led them into the main banqueting hall of the palace. It was long and narrow like Gunderic's feasting hall, except instead of a high seat at the far end there were two couches of the sort the Roman's reclined on when they ate. Attila lounged on one and Gunhild on the other.

The room was lit by burning torches. Unlike any other hall Hagan had been in there was a staircase behind Attila's couch that led up to what looked like a bedroom.

'If he drinks too much he doesn't have too far to go to bed,' Hagan said.

There were seats lining each wall, facing each other across a fire pit that ran up the centre of the floor. The seats on the wall to the right of Attila were all taken already by Hun noblemen.

'The seats to the right are for the most honoured guests,' Zerco explained, as Ediko ushered them to seats on the left of the king.

'Zerco will come with me,' he said. 'It's time to prepare for the entertainments.'

Zerco sighed. 'It is almost time for the show, I suppose,' he said over his shoulder as Ediko marched him off. They both left the hall by a side door.

Seated on Attila's left, Hagan and Wodnas found some men who looked like Gepid and Ostrogoth nobles, and Gunderic, who looked up at them. He nodded his head to Wodnas.

'How is life in the Roman Army, Hagan?' he said. It seemed a pointed question.

'I can't complain,' Hagan said.

They took their seats.

'It was good you hid Freya's bottle,' Hagan said out of the corner of his mouth to Wodnas. 'How did you keep it from them?'

'It's still in the saddlebag,' Wodnas said. 'That's why I was so keen to unpack before we came in here.'

Hagan rolled his eyes.

A cup-bearer came and handed Attila a wooden cup of wine. He took it, and saluted the Hun noble first on his right. The Hun stood up and bowed his head. He remained standing while Attila drank the wine then returned the cup to the bearer. The servant refilled the cup and gave it to the most honoured guest, who toasted Attila then drank. One by one everyone in the room toasted the king then sat down again.

After this, tables were brought in and set up before Attila and all the guests. Servants came in bearing dishes laden with meat, river fish and bread, which they laid on the tables.

Everyone ate though there was a tense atmosphere in the room as former enemies eyed each other across the room. More food and more wine helped to relax everyone a little, however, and soon even Hagan was starting to feel a little easier.

After all the food there were entertainments.

First, two Scythians came forward in front of Attila and sang songs that Wodnas explained celebrated the king's victories and deeds of valour. Four musicians accompanied them on flute, lyre, *cithara* and drum. It was clear that the songs were good as the Huns listened, rapt, to every word. Hagan even spotted one of them wiping a tear away.

When they finished, two warriors brought in a Scythian.

He was dressed in rags, his hair was filthy and he appeared to only have one tooth in his head. Hagan could see the man was clearly mad. The warriors shoved the Scythian into the centre of the floor where he stumbled around, wild-eyed and uttering outlandish, senseless words.

The Hun nobles found this very humorous and laughed. Hagan could not understand what they found so funny. The man was some unfortunate who deserved pity, not derision.

As the nobles began to grow tired of the madman's antics, the warriors dragged him out of the room again. As he left by the side door, Zerco entered. Recognising him, the Huns all stood up, cheering with delight and pointing at the little man. He had been dressed up in a girl's robe. As the musicians played he danced around the room, chanting snatches of poetry and song in different tongues, now Latin, then Hunnic, then Gothic.

If the Huns had found the madman funny they found Zerco unquenchably hilarious. They roared with laughter, pointing and holding their ribs, some with tears rolling down their cheeks.

Through it all Attila remained stony-faced, betraying not even the ghost of a smile.

Hagan found the humiliation of Zerco too hard to watch. He stood up and began to move towards the door, intending to claim he needed to relieve himself if anyone asked. At that moment the main doors opened and Ediko returned, now flanked by eight Hun warriors. They had their swords drawn.

Ediko moved quickly to the couch where Attila was reclining. He bent over and said a few words to him, then passed something to him.

Hagan saw it was Freya's blue glass bottle.

CHAPTER SEVENTY-THREE

H E STARTED TO move for the stairs but the Hun warriors had already spread out to block the exit. He turned around and saw Attila was on his feet, as was everyone else in the hall as well. The musicians stopped playing and Zerco stopped prancing around.

Attila pointed at Hagan then Wodnas. He shouted something in the Hun tongue.

To Hagan's surprise Gunderic did the same. Hagan could understand his words.

'Seize them!' Gunderic cried.

The eight Huns came charging down the stairs and grabbed Hagan. He started to struggle but they kicked and beat him with their sword blades. One blow struck him across the temple and countless coloured stars exploded in his vision. He fell to his knees and a moment later his arms were pinned behind him and a sword blade was held across his throat.

More Huns laid hands on Wodnas.

Moments later their wrists and ankles were bound by rope.

Attila barked an order.

'The king says take them to the bath,' Ediko said.

Hagan and Wodnas were dragged along the floor, warriors punching and kicking them as they went. They went through another side door and down another set of wooden steps. The doors slammed behind them.

Hagan was being half dragged, half carried face down.

Blood was dribbling from his nose and he could taste it in his mouth as well. Looking below him he saw the floor change from dirt to white stone. Then he was dumped without ceremony on the ground.

For a few moments he lay on his front, waiting for his head to clear. Then he looked up. Wodnas lay a little way away. They were both on a white stone floor inside what could only be the bathhouse he had seen earlier.

It was lit by torches held by some of the warriors who had dragged them in, as well as some set in brackets in the walls. The bathhouse had seen better days. The plaster of the walls was cracked, flaking and dirty. The mosaics on the floors were missing many tiles.

It looked like they were in what had once been the frigidarium. Hagan frowned, wondering if his eyes had been damaged by the beating he had just endured. Then he saw that Attila had indeed found a new use for this bathhouse.

Instead of cold water, the plunge pool was filled with snakes. They were of every size, width and colour. There were hundreds of them, curling and twisting, slithering over each other at the bottom of the pool like an obscene living liquid. The sheer sides of the pool stopped them crawling up and out.

'This pit is where King Attila throws traitors, those who have betrayed him or those who think they can usurp him,' Gunderic said. 'These snakes take care of such snakes and worms.'

Hagan and Wodnas clambered to their feet and turned around. Attila, Gunderic, Gunhild and Ediko stood behind them. The Hun warriors were lined up behind them. Gunhild carried two cups of wine, one in each hand.

Ediko held up the blue bottle.

'This is poison, isn't it?' he said. 'What did you intend to do with it?'

'Why do you think it's poison?' Hagan said. 'Perhaps you should drink it just to be sure.'

'This is treachery,' Ediko said. 'You planned to poison the Great King with this.'

'Let's stop this play-acting,' Wodnas said. 'This was all just a trap from the start, wasn't it, Gunhild?'

Gunhild smiled. It was not a warm expression but one as cold as ice.

'Of course, Wodnas,' she said. 'Though it does look like you've been very obliging by bringing this poison along with you. Which gives us an excuse to get rid of you. One of Freya's concoctions, is it?'

She turned to Attila.

'Great King,' she said. 'Considering what we are about to discuss, should we have extra ears in the room? We don't want others hearing where the treasure is hidden, do we?'

Ediko translated to the tongue of the Huns. Attila nodded. He replied to Ediko in his own tongue. Ediko looked dubious but Attila patted the hilt of the great war sword slung under his arm.

Ediko gestured to the warriors and to Hagan's surprise, they filed out of the room.

Still smiling, Gunhild passed a cup of wine to Attila and kept one herself. She held up her cup in a toast and took a drink. Attila did the same.

Hagan thought bitterly how it looked like they were toasting their victory.

'So what is there to discuss?' he said. 'It looks like you two have decided to join Attila. Does what happened at Vorbetomagus mean nothing to you any more?'

'The world changes,' Gunderic said. 'Attila has shown he is the greatest power in the world. It is only a matter of time before the Roman Empire falls. Honour and revenge are fine things, but what matters, what really matters, is power and who wields it. We can stand alone and be swept aside. We can stand with Rome and fall with it. Or we can join with the new greatest power in the world and thrive.'

'I can understand that,' Wodnas said. 'But what puzzles me is why someone as powerful as Attila would bother making an alliance with a kingdom as insignificant as yours. Gunhild, despite her growing age, is beautiful but Attila has the pick of any woman across his vast realms. How many wives have you now? Nine?'

Gunhild glared at Wodnas. The veins in her neck stood out from her skin. Hagan could see the blood pulsing within them.

'I have much to offer!' Gunderic spluttered. 'We are not insignificant!'

Attila noticed the obvious furore and looked at Ediko. Ediko did his best to translate what had been said.

Attila chuckled. Then he pointed at Wodnas, nodding. He held up his forefingers, rubbing them together in the air. Then he spoke a few words.

'The Great King says,' Ediko translated, 'old Wodnas is wise as ever. It will be a loss when we kill him. Why indeed would one so mighty as Attila benefit from such an alliance? The answer is: gold.'

'We have told Attila that we shall share the treasure of the Nibelungs with him in return for his favour,' Gunhild said.

She lifted her wine cup in another toast to Attila. Attila smiled and drank. Gunhild did the same. Attila, his cup now drained, passed it back to Gunhild.

'Share?' Wodnas said. 'Your father stole that treasure from the Huns. Do you really think Attila will share it with you? Do you realise who you are dealing with? He must not know where you've hidden it otherwise he'd already have taken it all.'

'Of course he doesn't,' Gunhild said, 'Do you think us stupid? The knowledge of where that vast treasure is hidden is the thing that makes us valuable to him. He knows he has to please Gunderic and me or he will never get his hands on the gold.'

'He will lose patience,' Wodnas said. 'I know Attila. I fought him and his kind for years. When he does he will torture that knowledge out of you.'

'Why are Wodnas and I here anyway?' Hagan said. 'What have we to do with all this?'

'You helped kill Sigurd!' Gunhild shouted. Her teeth were clenched now and eyes staring. All of a sudden she resembled the Gunhild Hagan had last seen on the battlefield of the Catalaunian plains. 'And for that you will die. We will cast you both into the pit of snakes and watch you writhe in agony as you die. That is the favour Attila has granted us in exchange for sharing our treasure with him.'

'If I helped kill Sigurd,' Hagan said, 'then your brother did too.'

Attila let out a sudden cough. He frowned. Then a look of consternation crossed his face. His right hand went to his throat.

Gunhild laid a hand on his arm, watching the Hun King's face with fascination.

Attila coughed again and this time a great gout of froth came out through his lips. It was tinged with pink. His eyes bulged and he reached out as if to try to grab Gunhild by the throat but she stepped back. A tide of blood gushed from both his nostrils and dribbled down his chin. Attila lurched forward after Gunhild then, with a strangled cry, he pitched forward and fell face first on the floor. He gave a brief snort, then lay still. A pool of strong-smelling urine began to form around him.

Gunhild let out a little laugh. She turned to Wodnas.

'The Lady Freya's potions are as potent as always, I see,' she said. 'I poured some of the contents of that blue bottle into the wine I gave Attila.'

Ediko gasped in horror, glaring down at his fallen king. An instant later Gunderic slammed his fist into Ediko's chin. The Hun's eyes rolled up into his head and he too fell to the floor.

Hagan felt sudden hope. Had this all been a ruse? Had Gunhild and Gunderic carried all this out just to get close enough to Attila so they could kill him?

581

The thought was quickly dispelled.

'You killed him,' Wodnas said in a tone of voice that suggested he could hardly believe his own eyes.

'It seems I have,' Gunhild said. She looked at her brother. 'Now we can rule the Burgundar kingdom unhindered, without the need to bow down to Attila or any other king who thinks he is our overlord. But I'm sorry, Hagan. You and Wodnas still have to die. Attila intended to throw you in the snake pit. We may as well fulfil his last wishes.'

Realising his hopes were forlorn, Hagan felt rage, anger, despair. 'Why?' he shouted. 'What has all this got to do with Wodnas? With me?'

Gunhild crouched down beside the prone body of Attila. She undid the leather thong on a purse that hung at his belt and rummaged inside. Withdrawing something, she stood up and held it aloft between her thumb and forefinger.

She stepped closer to Hagan and he saw that what she held was a golden medal, a bracteate used to decorate horse bridles. He recognised it. While it only had the image of the bird on it, the Turul, and no horse, it was identical in style to the one Hagan wore around his throat. The amulet he had taken from his mother's corpse.

'This is a piece from the great treasure hoard. We gave it to Attila to prove we had it,' Gunhild said. 'It is Hunnish in style. Recognisably so. You see the way the bird is engraved on it.'

Hagan tried to finger the amulet he wore around his throat but his bound wrists hindered him.

'There are countless ones like this in the hoard. They are real gold, by the way,' Gunhild said. 'But they have either an image of the bird or one of a horse, never both. My father, King Gundahar, gave me several over the years and he told me he had only ever seen one that had both horse and bird on it. So he wore that one himself.'

Hagan's jaw dropped open.

'I'm older than Gunderic so he won't remember,' Gunhild

went on. 'But I do. I remember my father wearing that amulet around his throat when I was young, very young. The amulet you wear, Hagan, is the same one. You said your mother took it from the man who raped her. Well, that man must have been my father. You are my half-brother.'

'We will not share the throne or my treasure, Hagan,' Gunderic said. 'Especially not with a bastard.'

Hagan's mind raced. The thought that his real father had been King Gundahar was unbelievable. But then it also made perfect sense: which one man in the kingdom had been more powerful than Godegisil, the Champion of the Burgundars? His mother had been right. Gundahar was the one man who could have had Godegisil put to death if he suspected any threat. That was why she had kept her attacker's identity a secret all those years.

'In fact, dear sister,' Gunderic went on, 'I have no desire to share the throne – or more importantly the treasure – with anyone.'

Hagan realised all of a sudden that while everyone was watching Gunhild, Gunderic had somehow unsheathed the Sword of the War God from where it lay in Attila's scabbard. He now held it in both hands.

'What are you doing, Gunderic?' Gunhild said. She had caught sight of the weapon in her brother's hands.

'Now I wield the Sword of the War God, Gunhild,' Gunderic said. 'I have the blessing of Tiwass. It is he who says I have the right to rule. Alone.'

Gunderic swung the sword. Gunhild dropped the golden bracteate as both her hands flew to her face. Gunderic dealt a great, sweeping blow aimed at Gunhild's waist. Before it landed, Hagan squeezed his eyes closed, not wanting to look on the carnage the great blade wrought. He heard the pings as the bracteate hit the floor and bounced twice before it lay flat and still. He opened his eyes again and frowned.

Gunhild still stood upright. There was a bemused smile on her face.

'It seems the great sword is not as sharp as folk think,' she said.

Gunhild bent forward to pick up the fallen amulet. Her fingers never reached it. As she did so, a red line opened up across her middle, then her torso fell forward, severed from her hips by Gunderic's blow. The top half of her body tumbled to the floor. Her legs toppled sideways, jetting blood as they fell, and landed in the opposite direction to her top half.

Hagan glared in horror, looking down at Gunhild's now lifeless eyes that stared ahead, as if still fixed on the gold amulet.

'Now I shall rule alone,' Gunderic said. 'And the treasure shall all be mine.'

He stalked over to where Hagan and Wodnas stood, bound on the edge of the snake pit.

'Which means no bastard brother who might have a rival claim,' he said to Hagan.

Gunderic turned to Wodnas.

'I'm afraid you will have to go as well,' he said. 'The ordinary folk have begun to hold you in higher regard than me, their rightful king. Your work is done now anyway. You have set my kingdom on the road to greatness. We will revere your memory. Perhaps in the future you will even be thought of as a god.'

The sword in his left hand, he raised his right hand to shove Hagan into the pool full of writhing snakes. Hagan, his ankles tied together, hopped sideways and tried to headbutt Gunderic. Gunderic jumped out of the way but looked wary of getting too close again. He raised the sword and levelled its point at Hagan's chest.

'Perhaps I should just do this the easy way,' he said.

At that moment the doors burst open. Zerco and the Burgundar Bear and Raven Warriors poured into the room.

They were armed and ready for war. They surveyed the carnage in the room for a moment then crowded round the three men on the edge of the snake pit.

'I thought you might need a hand,' Zerco said. 'So I fetched this lot from their quarters.'

Hagan felt a dismay that hurt worse than any of the punches or kicks he had suffered. Was Zerco really helping Gunderic by bringing his bodyguards?

'You've come at exactly the right time, lads,' Gunderic said. 'Throw Hagan in the snake pit.'

The Bear Warriors looked unsure what to do. Their king was ordering them to kill the man who had trained most of them and the man who had led them at the battle of the Catalaunian fields.

Gunfjaun and the four other Raven Warriors were less hesitant. They surged forward as one. Gunfjaun snatched the war sword from Gunderic's hand as the others shoved the Burgundar king backwards.

With a horrified scream, Gunderic toppled back, arms flailing, into the pool filled with snakes. The shock of his landing caused many of the creatures to sink their fangs into his body straight away.

Gunderic's back arched as their venom spread through his body. His teeth clenched and his mouth widened in a rictus grin. His cries ceased, strangled by his already constricted throat.

The Burgundar warriors freed Hagan and Wodnas from their bonds, then they all ran to the doors.

Zerco was shouting out into the main palace. His words were in Hunnish so Hagan could not work out what he said.

'What are you doing?' Hagan said.

'I shouted out that the Great King Attila is dead,' Zerco said. 'Then I shouted that Ediko was named his successor. I waited a moment then called that Attila had said Ernas was to succeed him. Then I said it was to be Ellec. A few more shouts and they were all either fighting each other, desperate to be the one to take Attila's crown, or running for their horses to get home before another rival tries to murder them.'

They all looked out through the door and saw the chaos in the main hall as warriors fought each other, turning over furniture and smashing the plates and cups.

'Good work, Zerco,' Wodnas said. 'Now let us set fires to add to the confusion. With any luck we can slip away under their cover.'

They grabbed torches from the walls and rushed back to the main dining hall, setting fire to rugs, cushions, whatever they could find. As Zerco had predicted, there were Huns there but they were too busy fighting each other.

Running to the main door of the palace, Hagan and the others saw that the streets of the settlement were just as chaotic as the interior of the palace. The streets had become a battleground as different Hun factions fought each other either for control of the palace and its enclosure or just survival.

'It is always this way when a tyrant falls,' Wodnas said. 'Unless there is a clear successor with a strong hand, every ambitious noble tries to seize the throne.'

'And I never met a nobleman who was not ambitious,' Zerco said.

Hagan wondered what would happen in Geneva when the news of Gunderic's death arrived there. The council of nobles had been quick to fall to rivalry even when Gunderic was alive. Would there be similar bloodletting there?

'We need our horses,' Wodnas said. 'There are plenty in a pen outside the ramparts, so we must fight our way out of here.'

'Perhaps you would like this?' Gunfjaun said, offering the great Sword of the War God to Hagan. 'We all have our own weapons.'

Hagan took it. Despite its great size and considerable weight, when held in a fighting grip it was so well balanced it felt light as a feather. For a few moments he gazed at the reflections of the fires that flickered up and down the blade. Then he readied himself for the fight.

Wodnas ordered them to form up in a wedge formation, with the biggest Bear Warrior at the tip. Once ready, they stormed out the doors and down the steps of the palace as smoke from its now burning interior began to billow out behind them.

For the most part the Hun factions were too busy fighting each other to pay attention to the Burgundars, but some did stand in their way. They were quickly cut down by the power and fury of the charging Burgundars.

The most determined resistance they faced was at the gates, where the five warriors had been reinforced. After a brief skirmish the Burgundars defeated the Huns, killing eight of them, wounding five and sending the rest running. Hagan felt almost like the great war sword had a life of its own in his hands, so easy was it to handle. It was as if it were thirsty for the blood it spilled so sought out the perfect point to strike the enemy all by itself.

They ran on to the pen filled with horses outside the settlement ramparts. Moments later they were riding off into the night.

CHAPTER SEVENTY-FOUR

THEY RODE UNTIL dawn, meaning to get as far away from Attila's palace as they could, just in case there was anyone with still enough reason to start searching for them. By day they built shelters of sticks and moss and took turns at watch while the others slept. So they carried on, travelling hard by night and living off the land for the rest of the journey to the border of the Hun realms. Once they crossed the Danube and into the devastated borderlands, they felt more comfortable about slackening the pace and reverting to riding by daylight.

As the days turned to weeks Hagan began to feel sadness creeping back into his heart. The band of friends who had grown up together was now well and truly gone. His entire clan was gone. Over the course of the journey he had enjoyed the camaraderie of being with the other warriors and even Zerco, however he knew that time too would come to an end soon.

When they got to the deserted city of Naissus with its haunting field of bones he knew that time had come. It was the last point on the journey where they could split. The Burgundars, heading for Geneva, would go west. He would go south to return to Ravenna.

They camped outside the city. The company of hardened warriors reasoned that there was a chance of contracting plague from the corpses of those sick people in the church inside the walls, though everyone knew it was actually the dread of what ghosts might haunt the creepy ruins of that sacked town that kept them outside.

After darkness fell they ate and sat around the campfire. As he was accustomed to do, Wodnas announced he had some thinking to do and wandered a little way off and sat down just beyond the ring of light from the fire.

After a time Hagan got up and walked over to where Wodnas sat. The old man sat cross-legged with his leather satchel on his lap, staring down into it. At the sight of Hagan approaching he pulled the top of the bag closed.

'I came to say goodbye,' Hagan said. 'Tomorrow we must part ways. Before we do however, I'd like to ask a question.'

'Go ahead,' Wodnas said.

'What's in the bag?' Hagan said, pointing to Wodnas' satchel.

The old man smiled his enigmatic smile.

'Do you really want to know?'

'Yes,' said Hagan.

Wodnas flipped the top of the satchel back open.

It was hard to see in the gloom and Hagan squinted but when he made out what was inside he stiffened and grimaced. It was a human head. The head was desiccated, its skin dark, wizened and tanned like leather. The black hair was dry like straw and tied in a knot. The eyelids were sewn shut with what looked like string. The mouth was slightly open, revealing a shrivelled tongue and small, yellow teeth.

'His name was Mimir,' Wodnas said. 'He was my older friend. One of the wisest men I ever met. He helped me rule my old kingdom long ago. We used to talk long into the night, discussing issues, making plans, arguing sometimes. I was king but I really used to enjoy our talks. He was the only person I ever felt I could talk to as an equal. He helped me make all my most important decisions. Once I wanted to take my kingdom to war with another people called the Vanir. They were great fighters and Mimir advised against it. But I insisted. The war was a stalemate. We couldn't beat them and they couldn't beat us. So we arranged a settlement. To keep the peace we exchanged hostages – that old fellow Kvasir you met in Geneva was the one the Vanir sent to us. We sent Mimir to the Vanir. The truce was breached, however. The Vanir suspected treachery on my part and they beheaded Mimir. They sent me his head in a bucket.'

'Were they right?' Hagan said. 'Were you going to break the truce?'

'I preserved the head with herbs and other techniques,' Wodnas said, ignoring the question. 'And I keep it with me. Whenever I need to think about something I talk to it. It helps me come to what is hopefully the right decision.'

'It doesn't really answer, does it?' Hagan said, frowning. 'You're really talking to yourself.'

'When you get to my age,' Wodnas said with a sardonic grunt, 'that can sometimes be the only way to get a decent conversation. So you have chosen not to return home? You are going back to Aetius?'

'Home?' Hagan said. 'Geneva is not really my home. My home was Vorbetomagus. That is where I grew up. It's gone now, along with all the folk I knew.'

'Vorbetomagus was not your mother's or father's home,' Wodnas said. 'The Burgundars have called many places home in their wanderings over the last couple of centuries since they left that cold island in the distant north that was their original home. Sometimes home is just wherever you feel most at home.'

'What about your home?' Hagan said. 'Is that Geneva now?'

'I am a wanderer, like you,' Wodnas said. 'I have called many places home. I think the time is approaching when I shall be moving on again. I feel drawn towards the northern realms of the world.'

Hagan thought for a moment. He realised the old man was just as alone in the world as he was.

'If you're going north you had better have this,' he said,

passing the Sword of the War God to Wodnas. 'You said all you wanted was to get your sword back.'

The old man looked up at him.

'I am not going north yet,' he said. 'I still have work to do in Geneva. As do you, which is why I am surprised that you say you are here now to say goodbye.'

'What do you mean?' Hagan said.

'The king of the Burgundars is dead. As is his sister. As is Sigurd, the man he named as successor,' Wodnas said. 'You heard what Gunhild said. You are the late king's half-brother. You are next in line to the throne.'

'Me?' Hagan started.

'Yes, you,' Wodnas said. 'Why not you? You have as much right as anyone to the Kin Helm.'

'The folk would never have me as their king,' Hagan said. 'I am still a stranger to them.'

'They will if I tell them I support you,' Wodnas said. He stood up and laid his free hand on Hagan's shoulder. He fixed him with the gaze of his one, mesmerising eye. 'Hagan, you saw the chaos and bloodshed that erupted when Attila died with no clear successor. Do you want that to happen to the Burgundars?'

Hagan shook his head.

'The one way to avoid that is for you to take over straight away,' Wodnas said. 'The Three Great Women who control our fates have woven you into this position here and now. You don't have to do it. We all have free will. But there was a reason they put you in this place and this time. Think about it.'

Hagan heaved a heavy sigh. He thought of Gunhild, Gunderic, Brynhild, his mother, his father – both Godegisil and Gundahar. Were their spirits watching him from above or had they just ceased to be, their lives snuffed out like a candle and their mortal remains now nothing more than cold meat for worms?

'Do you think there is an afterlife, Wodnas?' he said. 'Does anything survive of us after we die?'

The old man smiled and tapped the side of his nose.

'The answer is yes, Hagan,' he said. 'Everyone dies. You and I will die. All our friends and everyone we know will die. But there is one thing that lives on when we are gone: the reputation we leave behind us. It is the deeds we do and the choices we make in life that determine what people continue to say about us when we are gone. Will they still tell tales of us a thousand years after we are gone? That depends on what we do now.'

He began walking back to the campfire.

'Come on,' the old man said over his shoulder. 'We have an early start in the morning. And let me hear no more of goodbye.'

Hie hât daz mære ein ende: daz ist der Nibelunge liet

Here the story reaches the end: This was the song of the
Nibelungs

The Nibelungenlied (twelfth-century Middle High German
epic)

GLOSSARY OF PLACENAMES

This story is set amid real historical events in real places that still exist today. Over the years, however, the names of the locations have changed. Some of the fourth-century names were close enough to the modern ones that I used the current spelling without straying too far into modernity (e.g. Geneva). Others are very different. For that reason this glossary is provided so readers can orient themselves as to where events in the tale are set.

Ancient name	Location	Modern name
Aquae Sulis	Britannia	Bath, Somerset, England
Aquileia	North-east Italia	Aquileia, Italy
Arelate	Southern Gaul	Arles, France
Argantoratum	City in Roman province of Germania Inferior	Strasbourg, France
Armorica	North-west Gaul	Brittany and Normandy, France

Ancient name	Location	Modern name
Aurelianum	Gaul	Orléans, France
Bleda Vár	Bleda's fortress, Hun Land	Budapest, Hungary
Bonaven	Britannia	Unknown: childhood home of St Patrick, somewhere in northern Britain
Comum	Northern Italia	Como, Italy
Constantinople	Capital of the Eastern Roman Empire	Istanbul, Turkey
Dacia	Roman province	Transylvania, Oltenia and Banat in Romania
Divodurum	City in Roman province of Belgica	Metz, France
Dyrrhachium	Roman city	Durrës, Albania
Hispania	Roman province	The Iberian Peninsula
Lugdunum	Gaul	Lyon, France

Ancient name	Location	Modern name
Mare Hadriaticum	Sea north-east of Italia	The Adriatic Sea
Mare Nostrum	Sea	The Mediterranean Sea
Mauretania	Province in North Africa	Mid-Algeria and northern Morocco
Maxima Sequanorum	Roman Province	Burgundy, France and parts of Switzerland
Naissus	City in Roman Dacia	Niŝ, Serbia
Noviomagus	City in Germania Inferior	Nijmegen, the Netherlands
Pannonia	Province of the Roman Empire between the Danube and Dalmatia	Areas of western Hungary, western Slovakia, eastern Austria, northern Croatia, north-western Serbia, northern Slovenia, and northern Bosnia and Herzegovina
Ravenna	Capital city of the Western Roman Empire, Northern Italia	Ravenna, Italy

Ancient name	Location	Modern name
Remorum	City in Gaul	Reims, France
Santen	City in Germania Inferior	Xanten, Germany
Scythia	Kingdom extending from the Don in the east to the Danube in the west, and covering the territory north of the Black Sea's coastline	Lands extending from the Danube in the west to the Black Sea in the east
Sirmium	City in the Roman province of Pannonia	Sremska Mitrovica, Serbia
Tanais	River	The Don river in Ukraine/Russia
Tarvisium	City in northern Italia	Treviso, Italy
Tolosa	Visigoth capital	Toulouse, France
Tungrorum	Roman District in Belgica	Liège and Limburg, Belgium
Trans-Sylvania	Roman Dacia	Transylvania, Romania

Ancient name	Location	Modern name
Tricassium	City in Gaul	Troyes, France
Verona	City in northern Italia	Verona, Italy
Vicentia	City in northern Italia	Vicenza, Italy
Vorbetomagus	City in Germania Superior	Worms, Germany

AUTHOR'S NOTE

IT WAS A time of legends...
Of all the historical eras that could lay claim to that title, the first half of the fifth century AD – the time in which this novel is set – must be the one for which the sobriquet is the most appropriate. The Western Roman Empire fell, sending ripples in all directions, and from its ruins rose the tribes and powers that would dominate Europe for the next millennium. Whole peoples moved their homes from one end of the continent to another, kingdoms rose and fell, and some of the figures whose legends still entertain us today lived, achieved their fame and died.

In this tumultuous time a number of ostensibly Germanic tribes swept down from what is now Scandinavia and northern Europe to force their way inside the boundaries of the Empire. Goths, Vandals, Alemanni, Franks and Burgundars swept south, crossing the frozen Rhine and carving kingdoms of their own from lands that had been ruled by Rome. Like a line of dominoes, each newly arriving tribe pushed others out, resulting in more pressure on the already stretched Imperial Army.

In desperate need of soldiers to fight the barbarian menace, Rome withdrew its legions from Britannia. The Irish (at the time referred to as Scoti/Scots) were quick to see this opportunity and began raiding the coast of Britain, taking plunder and slaves wherever they landed. One of the slaves they carried back to Ireland, the son of an official called Calpurnius, took the Christian faith with him and is today known as St Patrick.

The Britons, used to the protection of Rome's Legions, began hiring Saxon mercenaries from Europe to help them defend themselves. Within a decade these mercenaries turned on their paymasters and began to take Britain for their own. The Britons fought back under the leadership of a warlord called Arthur (a name proposed to mean 'the Bear') and the legends of the ensuing adventures are still told and retold today.

The Huns came from the east. Like a jackal scenting the blood of a wounded lion, Attila spotted his chance and attacked, riding through Europe in a storm of blood and destruction. It looked as though Attila's would be the blow that would herald the final collapse of the whole crumbling edifice of the Empire.

Yet Rome did not go down without a fight. General Flavius Aetius, the man Edward Gibbon described as 'the last of the Romans', gathered together what he could of the Roman army, formed an unlikely coalition with some of Rome's deadliest enemies, and brought Attila to battle at the Catalaunian Plains, the conflict that forms the heart of this novel.

From this turmoil arose legends and myths that have echoed down through the ages, and are still told today, long after the historical events that inspired them have been forgotten. Attila, Arthur, the Geats, Sigurd the Dragon Slayer, the Rhine Gold and the fate of the Nibelungs have all been immortalised in Old Welsh poetry, Old English poetry, Old Norse sagas, and medieval epics such as the *Nibelungenlied*, which over time influenced Richard Wagner's *Ring* cycle and in turn helped inspire Tolkien to write *The Lord of the Rings*.

While the Franks would eventually become the French and the name of the Vandals would live on as a byword for wanton violence, what of the Burgundars, the small tribe this tale focuses on? Their kingdom lived on, and eventually morphed into the Duchy of Burgundy, an entity whose nobility and people played a central role in European politics for centuries to come.

Some readers will notice the similarity between a few of the characters and certain Norse Deities. In the early thirteenth century, Icelandic poet, politician and historian Snorri Sturluson who wrote his *Heimskringla*, a history of the world that began by explaining the people we now think of as the Norse gods were originally chieftains of two lands (Asaland and Vanaland) in the Don river basin in what is now Ukraine. Odin was the greatest of them, a king so wise and powerful that the remembrance of him after his death turned into worship of a god. Why did I name him Wodnas and not Odin? *Wodnas* is the form of his name recorded in what is believed to be the earliest reference to him, found on a gold pendant unearthed in Denmark in 2023 and reckoned to date from the early fifth century, the time when this novel is set. This seems accurate, especially when compared to the day of the week those Saxons who crossed the seas to Britain at that time named for him: Wednesday.

What the true nature of this individual was, I will leave up to the reader to decide.

Tim Hodkinson
January 2024

About the Author

TIM HODKINSON grew up in Northern Ireland where the rugged coast and call of the Atlantic ocean led to a lifelong fascination with Vikings and a degree in Medieval English and Old Norse Literature. Tim's more recent writing heroes include Benne, Giles Kristian, Bernard Cornwell, George R.R. Martin and Lee Child. After several years in the USA, Tim returned to Northern Ireland, where he lives with his wife and children.

Follow Tim on @TimHodkinson and
www.timhodkinson.blogspot.com